Praise
Path to Justice

"Nick Drummond…a droll, middle-aged jazz aficionado…works as a prosecutor for the California [A]ttorney [G]eneral [and is] head of a money-laundering task force…A literally explosive first chapter leads into a lengthy flashback that introduces much information and many characters well. Characterizations are intricately detailed and realistic, especially for Drummond, who, when the text begins, has already been tossed out of his home for being a workaholic…Background information on such diverse topics as Glacier National Park, criminal law, authentic Italian cooking, the Holocaust, police procedures, and Father Damien's Hawaiian leper colony is subtly woven into the text, adding an educational aspect…Brisk, jaunty dialogue adds another dimension to the book's relationships…**In this fast-paced and serious drama, just the right amount of humor is injected in just the right spots**…*Path to Justice* **follows a harrowing case from its beginnings to its conclusion in an absorbing way, providing a behind-the-scenes picture of the personalities who work diligently on the side of justice.**"

—*Clarion Review*

"'We'll take good care of you. You can only be safe when we get Luis and the other two heads of the cartel convicted.'

"Nick Drummond, a San Diego prosecutor who heads up a money-laundering task force, finds himself involved in establishing a case against leaders of an international drug cartel. The Baja Norte Familia is brought to Drummond's attention when a Montana firefighter becomes suspicious of off-road vehicles near the Canadian border, and surveillance of these vehicles reveals a nefarious San Diego accountant to be involved in this dubious activity. Nick and his task force begin building the case against these criminals, even getting an ex-girlfriend of a cartel lieutenant to agree to testify. This proves to be a dangerous proposition, however, as the cartel discovers the witness's safe house and destroys it, proving that everyone involved in prosecuting the crime family is in danger.

"**The author's debut crime novel can best be described as having an authentic narrative.** This is understandable, as the author is a retired prosecutor who worked in the Special Prosecutions Unit of the California Attorney General's Office in San Diego for twenty-four years. He tried major cases in federal court, and some of his murder trials have been featured on a variety of television programs. This author knows his subject matter, which is evident when reading the book. Fans of crime fiction will appreciate the detailed information about evidence building and the presentation of the case included in the narrative, mostly in dialogue. **Dutton creates fully rounded characters in this novel that is filled with the fast-paced action** of great thrillers. It is a fascinating read which reveals the real world of prose-cutorial law. Readers will eagerly be turning pages with this one."

—RECOMMENDED by the US Review of Books
book review by Kat Kennedy

"A San Diego prosecutor puts together a case against top leaders of a new but men-acing drug cartel in Dutton's debut legal thriller...**A hero who audaciously takes on bad guys, whether in court or out in the field.**"

—Kirkus Reviews

"No one is above the law in this jargon-heavy legal thriller from former California prosecutor Jim Dutton, who relies on his own experience for realism...**There's a solid action thriller here...**"

—blueink review

"Career prosecutor Jim Dutton investigated and tried complex international drug, money laundering and fraud cases in federal court. *Path to Justice* reveals, in a compelling fashion, how a case against an international drug cartel is prosecuted."

—Gary Schons,
former Chief of the Criminal section of the San Diego Office of the California Attorney General

"Career prosecutor Drummond and his task force follow a path to justice on their own terms, no matter the consequences. The action and insights into the crimi-nal justice system build throughout. A must read for true crime and legal thriller aficionados."

—Bill Salisbury,
former U.S. Navy SEAL commander,
former prosecutor, and co-author of *41 Seconds to Freedom: an Insider's Account of the Lima Hostage Crisis*

"*Path to Justice* combines scintillating action and well-developed characters in a riveting legal thriller that exposes the reader to the *real* criminal justice system."

—Gary Mitchell,
former prosecutor and criminal defense attorney

"I worked with Jim Dutton for several years. Many of the investigation and court-room incidents in *Path to Justice* are derived from his actual experiences. The inves-tigative techniques, case strategies, and courtroom portrayals are authentic."

—Barry Klein,
former career prosecutor

PATH TO JUSTICE

JIM DUTTON

PATH TO JUSTICE

Copyright © 2017 by Jim Dutton
Authorhouse edition published 2018

Printed in the United States of America.

ISBN 978-1-953150-14-1 (Paperback)
ISBN 978-1-953150-15-8 (Digital)

Lettra Press books may be ordered through booksellers or by contacting:

Lettra Press LLC
30 N Gould St. Suite 4753
Sheridan, WY 82801, USA
1 307-200-3414 | info@lettrapress.com
www.lettrapress.com

CHAPTER ONE

Pato had been busy the last ten days. He had an army surplus Humvee brought up to El Paso that the cartel kept in central Mexico. He arranged for a rocket launcher that the Baja Norte Familia had stored in their munitions warehouse in El Paso to be transported to the team he put together in Topeka. At the warehouse, they mounted a fifty caliber machine gun onto the center of the modified Humvee and covered the back with metal framed canvas. The cartel's weapons and munitions had come from different sources, mostly from arms dealers, but some from military base thefts. The operations team wasn't difficult to put together. Franco, one of the cartel's weapons experts, would be there to ensure the weapons performed without mishap. He wouldn't be part of the actual assault. The actual shooters were young, but experienced. They had been recruited at age 15 by another cartel and had been Familia soldiers for three years. They were paid well and killed without remorse. They knew how to operate a 50 caliber machine gun and a rocket launcher. Both had used them in the field against the cartel's enemies in Mexico. The driver was older. He'd been a Familia soldier, but had moved on to become the personal driver for the cartel heads. There was nothing he didn't know about driving vehicles in the most dangerous circumstances. Pato would also be there, to oversee the operation.

Pato flew to Topeka from San Diego on Saturday, using his attorney Lorenzo identification. He'd gotten the word late Friday that the prosecution planned to call their key witness, Felicia, the former girlfriend of defendant Luis Hernandez-Lopez, to the stand on Tuesday. After an 18-month investigation, it was the first week of trial against the three heads of the Familia drug cartel. It was lucky Pato had everything in place. His surveillance team had been following Felicia from her safe house to her dental hygienist school and back, every day. He had instructed them to let him know immediately if there was any sign of her preparing to leave. The only visitor Felicia had at her home was a young black woman, who drove a car that had to be government issue. It was a boring white sedan, two years old, nothing that the hip looking visitor would have bought on her own. Pato assumed the woman was Felicia's handler, most likely a Deputy U.S. Marshal. Pato knew that the team probably had until Sunday night to send their dramatic message. Pato believed the government would fly Felicia to San Diego on Monday. If she left in a car with a suitcase before Monday, the surveillance team was ordered to take her out in a standard car shooting. It would not be nearly as dramatic as what Luis had ordered, but Felicia had to be stopped from testifying at trial.

Deputy U.S. Marshal Lily Perkins got out of her white sedan in front of Felicia's home on Saturday afternoon. Felicia was in the backyard, enjoying the sunshine, on the warmer than usual January day. She was rocking herself to sleep on a hammock, reading a hygienist textbook. Lily let herself in with a duplicate key and gently shook Felicia awake. "I just made plane reservations for us. We leave early Monday morning on a direct flight to San Diego. ICE Special Agent Ana Schwartz from the Money Laundering Task Force will be arriving early evening on Sunday. She will fly with us to San Diego."

"Good, I like Ana. She understands how difficult this is for me. I trust her with my life. She saved it once."

"We'll take good care of you. You can only be safe when we get Luis and the other two heads of the cartel convicted. Then, you'll no longer be a threat to them."

"I understand that now. I'm willing to go to San Diego. But I don't know if I'll ever feel safe. I still wake up in a cold sweat, dreaming of bullets flying over me, face down on my aunt's concrete driveway. I wake up terrorized, just when I know the next spray of bullets will hit me."

"In time, the nightmares will recede. We'll get you psychiatric counseling after the trial to help put this behind you."

"Thanks Lily. Enough about me. Did your boyfriend pop the question?"

"He did. Look at my ring. Isn't it gorgeous? Who knew that an elementary teacher had an heirloom diamond in the family. I'm bringing Chinese take out for dinner tomorrow and we'll celebrate. Hopefully, Ana will arrive in time for dessert. I'm staying with you tomorrow night and I'll drive us to the airport on Monday morning."

Pato met with his team in his Best Western hotel room. Refugio and Raul, the two shooters, were fidgeting on the couch. Refugio was a big man, with a thick neck and broad shoulders. Raul was slender and looked like a hawk, with piercing eyes. Raul did the talking for both of them. Raul told Pato that Refugio would be shooting the rocket launcher and he'd handle the mounted 50 caliber machine gun. Felipe, the driver, sat quietly at a small desk, taking it all in. Pato asked his weapons' man, Franco, "What can the launcher do?"

"I've checked out both the launcher and the machine gun. They needed a bit of a tune up. Now, they're in excellent condition. I wouldn't want to be in that little three bedroom house."

"You don't have to be, Franco, unless you continue to not answer my direct question. Don't ever forget that this operation was ordered by Luis. He wants the traitorous bitch Felicia to die a fiery and dramatic death."

Franco knew Luis was a sociopath and did not want to cross him in any way. So, he said, "We've a Russian RPG-7V2 rocket propelled, reusable, shoulder rocket launcher. We're using PG 7V1, 93mm heat rocket warheads. The rockets are launched from the firing tube by a gunpowder booster charge. The rocket motor ignites 10 meters after it exits the launch tube and can hit a target at least 500 meters away. Three rockets will penetrate the 1,000 square foot home, completely destroy it, and leave it burned to the ground. Refugio will be wearing a fire retardant, padded vest and neck garment, which will protect him from the heat discharged from the weapon. Refugio will be located to the side and back of the mounted machine gun. Raul, to the front and side of Refugio, won't be injured by any recoil blast by the launcher."

"Thank you Franco, much better. Felipe, take me through the driving protocol and the switch out to the getaway car."

"I've arranged an exit vehicle, a nondescript, late model Camry, parked two blocks from the target site. It'll be across from the vacant lot where we'll dispose of the Humvee."

"Take me through it Felipe, step by step."

"Early evening, around 7:00, the Humvee will approach the target home. Surveillance has shown that the neighborhood is quiet around that time, especially on a Sunday night. People are watching television or having Sunday dinner. We strip back the canvas, and Raul starts firing his 50 caliber bullets though the front of the home. This will get Felicia's attention and the agent's attention, if she's there. These bullets are armor piercing and will easily go through the wooden front door and the stucco. If Felicia tries to escape, she'll be mowed down. After the initial machine gun burst, Refugio will shoot the first rocket into the middle of the house. That will ignite a portion of the house. He'll reload and fire two more rockets into the house. The house will be in flames and no one inside will be alive at that time. The whole operation should take about a minute. I drive the Humvee to the vacant lot, two blocks away, and we torch it, leaving the rocket launcher and machine gun inside. There'll be no trace evidence in the vehicle. Refugio will shed his flame retarded vest into the Humvee before it's torched. We will get into the Camry and drive slowly away."

"How long to torch the vehicle?"

"No more than 30 seconds. I douse it with gasoline from a can stored in the Camry, light it and we're gone."

"Should we be worried about police response time Felipe?"

"No Pato. The closest police station is three miles away. This is a quiet residential neighborhood that is seldom patrolled by the cops, especially on Sunday evenings. We should be driving away in the Camry within three minutes of Raul first firing the machine gun."

"Excellent. I'll be down the block from Felicia's home, in my rented Volvo. I wouldn't want to miss the fireworks."

After the team left, Pato had plenty of time to shower, and put on a silk suit, donning his Lorenzo personality for his dinner date with the waitress he had met on an earlier trip searching for Felicia. Pato hoped Mary Ellen had something more dressy than the cutoff jeans and gingham blouse she wore as a waitress at the barbecue joint. She seemed excited about going to the Blue Moose Bar and Grill. Pato always enjoyed mixing business and pleasure. The thought of razing Felicia's home excited him.

Mary Ellen did not disappoint. The butt-hugging, strapless red dress, was a promise to Pato of things to come. Her blond hair fell over her bare shoulders, the ends caressing the back of her scarlet dress. He escorted her into the restaurant and they were seated in a quiet corner as he had requested. They started with a pitcher of sangria. Pato expounded about his make-believe homeland—having tapas and cocktails off Madrid's main square, promenading with others around the cobblestone streets of the old part of the city before eating roast pork at Ernest Hemingway's favorite restaurant. Pato thought, *Americans love the Hemingway twist. A Farewell to Arms* seemed to be required reading at all the high schools. Pato graciously, in European custom, ordered for Mary Ellen, whom he was now calling Maria Elena. He ordered her lemon chicken saltimboca, a chicken breast stuffed with spinach and cheese and wrapped with prosciutto and sage. It gave him a chance to enthrall her with his favorite foreign city, Roma. He promised her he would take her to the Trevi Fountain one day. Just before dawn, they would walk through the narrow streets and turn the corner to the small Trevi square. No tourists would be there. It would just be the two of them and God, as they tossed coins in the fountain together to ensure their return to Roma. She would be Audrey Hepburn to his Gregory Peck in *Roman Holiday*. Pato had to explain to Maria Elena who they were. But she loved it when she heard Audrey Hepburn played a princess in the film. Pato could not believe how many American women fell for his bullshit. It made him smile inside.

Pato took Mary Ellen back to her apartment in the early morning hours after a delightful assignation in his hotel room. They had savored the champagne Pato had on ice, waiting for them in his room. He had never lacked confidence. All in all, it had been a very satisfying evening. Mary Ellen was eager and charmingly inexperienced in bed. It was an excellent portent for Sunday to be a memorable day.

Ana was trying to catch a couple of hours of sleep on her flight to Topeka. However, she found that her thoughts wouldn't slow down. She wondered, *If her gruff, but vulnerable lover, Nick Drummond, would divorce his estranged wife after the trial.* Ana had fought her attraction towards the lead prosecutor of the Money Laundering Task Force, but had succumbed to her feelings. Ana thought, *How difficult it was going to be to live up to our agreement to stop "seeing" each other during the trial to avoid the appearance of a conflict of interest because I'm a key witness to the murder conspiracy count.*

Ana's flight was scheduled to touch down at 6:05 p.m. She had reserved a rental car. She wanted to go directly to Felicia's home before she checked into her hotel. Deputy Perkins had spoken to her this morning, and had given her the good news that Felicia was mentally prepared to fly to San Diego and testify. Ana still wanted to see Felicia herself and talk with her. She didn't want any last minute surprises.

Lily knocked on Felicia's door with a suitcase in hand and a bag of Chinese take-out. Felicia greeted her with a smile. "Come in. The take-out smells good. I have a freshly baked apple pie for dessert. Hopefully, Ana likes apple pie."

"Everyone loves apple pie. Anything else would be un-American." They sat down and Felicia opened up the various boxes with the joy of a child opening Christmas presents.

"Pot stickers and Mu Shu pork. I love that," said Felicia.

"That's just for starters. We have for your eating pleasure, lemon chicken, shrimp chow mein, and the piece de resistance, duck. I don't get engaged every day."

"To you Lily," said Felicia as she raised a glass of wine. They touched glasses.

"And to you Felicia. I'm so proud of you being strong, willing to face Luis and the other heads of the cartel on the witness stand. To your future as the best dental hygienist in Kansas."

"Let me modify that a bit. To the best hygienist anywhere I end up in the United States."

Nick had a little down time on Sunday afternoon. The witnesses were prepped for Monday. Everything was ready. He sipped on his Jack Daniels and stared into his fish tank. The tough part of the case was over—the thousands of hours of investigation and preparation for trial by his team. Now, they just had to put on the witnesses. Things were looking good. His *Saints Go Marching In* ring tone awakened him from his reverie.

"Mr. Drummond, this is Lieutenant Granger from the San Diego Metropolitan Prison. Sorry to bother you sir, but earlier this afternoon we caught a trustee who was passing kites for Luis Hernandez-Lopez. The note, found under a washbasin in the public rest room, off the visitor reception area, spoke of wanting a full weather report on Kansas."

"Tell me exactly what the note says!" Nick demanded.

"It reads, *I can't wait for this evening's Kansas weather report.*"

"I want that trustee interrogated fully about the kite, and any other kites having to do with Lopez, immediately! Got that?!"

"Yes sir."

Nick hung up and dialed Ana's cell. "Pick up please, please pick up. Ana please pick up. Come on!" The phone continued to ring.

Ana heard her cellphone ring in her purse. She was just three blocks from Felicia's witness safe house. She had called ten minutes earlier and Lily and Felicia were warming the apple pie for dessert. Ana opened her purse to grab the phone when she heard the loud staccato of gun fire or fireworks ahead. She stepped on it.

Raul was raking the home with 50 caliber bullets. The woman agent was inside. Too bad for her. Refugio let go with the first rocket grenade. The heat from the blast scorched Refugio's face. The rocket slammed through the outer wall of the house and exploded into a burst of flame and debris. In rapid succession, Refugio rammed two more rockets into the launcher and fired. Flames enveloped the entire house. None of the front or interior walls were standing.

At the first sound of gunfire, Deputy Perkins knew they were high velocity rounds. Rounds slamming through the walls left no doubt. She pulled Felicia from her chair and ran to the pantry just off the dining area, in the back of the house. This neighborhood had been on the path of many tornados and had a storm cellar. Lily pulled open the latch of the cellar trap door in the floor and pushed Felicia down inside it. "Don't come out until its safe!" Lily closed the door hatch and turned low towards the front of the house just as the first rocket grenade burst through the front door. The blast of the explosion blew Lily through the back door into the yard.

Ana turned the corner and came upon a scene out of a war zone. It felt like Bagdad to her. A small home had burst into flames. A Humvee was in front of the house, 100 yards away from her, firing rocket grenades into the home and strafing what was left of the house with machine gun fire. Ana yelled, "You Bastards!" She pulled her Glock and started firing at the Humvee as she drove towards it with one hand on the wheel. The mounted machine gun pivoted, and pointed in her direction. Ana swerved, and felt the impact of rounds slam through the back of her car. Her car careened off the road and slammed into a telephone pole.

The Humvee sped off. In the opposite direction, a Volvo, driven by a Hispanic man, pulled away from the curb and drove past Ana's car. Pato saw the driver slumped over the wheel with blood running down her face.

Nick finally gave up after calling Ana over and over. He called ICE's National Dispatch Center and reported the situation to the dispatcher, asking for an immediate response by ICE agents to Felicia's address. He then called Topeka 9-1-1. Nick identified himself and requested a patrol car to immediately go to 131 Elm Street. The dispatcher replied, "For the last five minutes we've been receiving frantic calls about a military attack on that address. Neighbors say the house has been burned to the ground." "You have to patch me in immediately to the officer in charge at the scene. It's my agent and protected witness at that address!"

"I'm sorry sir. I can't do that. I will take your number and relay the message when the situation stabilizes."

"Damn it! I know the situation. Those are my people there. Connect me!"

"Give me your number—that's the best I can do for you." Nick gave her his number and made her promise to convey it to the officer in charge right away.

Nick called his lead agent and friend of 20 years, Pepe Santana. Nick filled him in with a rapid fire account. Pepe was used to Nick going verbal hyper-speed when he was excited. Pepe assured him that he would go down to the MCC right away and help the jail commander interview the trustee and investigate any of Luis' visitors at jail. Pepe tried to assuage Nick's anxiety. "Ana always lands on her feet. We don't know if she was even in the area. She just arrived at the airport an hour before. She probably checked into her hotel first and is taking a shower."

"You know Ana. It's the job first. I'm sure she went to Felicia's safe house straight from the airport. But just in case, please call Rona and find out the hotel where she's staying. Rona booked her room. Find out if Ana checked in."

"Will do."

"I have to get off the line. I'm waiting for a call back from Topeka P.D." Nick put his cellphone on his lap and hunched over it. He thought, *How could I have allowed this to happen—the safe house with his key witness inside, burnt to the ground, and Ana, who had put love back into my life, is probably dead in the house with Felicia. If I had known, I would never have followed up on Drury's and Zack's report 15 months ago.*

CHAPTER TWO

Drury leaned against a pine tree next to his camera in the north-ern Montana woods. After 20 minutes of daydreaming about a semi-hottie, new female clerk at the 7-Eleven in Libby, Drury thought maybe he wasn't going to get a photo of the elusive black bear and her two cubs. As he started to unscrew his camera from the tripod, he heard what sounded like motorized vehicles approach-ing from the south on the old logging road. Drury wondered, *Who in the hell could that be? It's dusk, too late for any fishermen or hunters.* He decided to stay in his tree blind and check it out.

A minute later, the first of two Polaris Ranger Crew off road vehicles came into view. They looked like golf carts on steroids, with seating for four, and a small, open back for hauling stuff. Depending on the size of the engine, can cost anywhere from $12,500 to $17,000 apiece. They appeared brand new and had camouflage paint jobs. No locals had that kind of money. Looking through his viewfinder, Drury saw that the first vehicle had two persons in the front seat, both Latino looking. He snapped off four quick shots. The back seat and luggage compartment were filled with duffle bags. The second Ranger Crew, traveling about 20 yards behind the first, had a Latino man driving and a Caucasian in the passenger seat. This one also had duffle bags in the back, but not as many. Drury took several photos of the second vehicle before it drove out of range.

Drury's gut reaction was to pack up his gear and follow the vehicles. On further reflection, he knew not to be a dumb shit. The road dead ends at a barrier at the Canadian border, Drury wasn't carrying any weapon, and they might be. Who travels down a little used track, three miles from the Canadian border at 7:00 at night in off-road vehicles, loaded with duffle bags? Probably not anybody on a Mormon mission. Drury decided to high-tail it back home, check out the photos on his computer, and call his photography buddy Zack, a retired cop from Bakersfield, in the morning.

Back at the house, Drury liberated a Pabst Blue Ribbon from the fridge and put his camera's storage chip into the computer to look at his photos of the evening riders. *Not bad*, he said to himself—one photo of each vehicle picked up the faces of the respective occupants. The two Latino guys in the front vehicle looked buff, in their late 20s, with light beards and longish hair. The Latino guy in the second vehicle appeared to be slender, in his 30s, with manicured hair and a thin mustache. Drury couldn't tell for sure, but it looked like he had a scar above his right eyebrow. The white guy, also in his 30s, looked plump, and bookish with his horn-rimmed glasses. Drury went into his photo enhancing software, cropped the picture to focus on the Latino with the possible scar, increased the contrast in the photo, and lightened the shadows. Presto! A thin scar above his right eye was clearly visible.

The next morning, Drury waited until a decent hour, 7:00 a.m., and called Zack, who answered, "Hello, who's the asshole calling me at this time in the morning?"

"Who do you think, American Clearinghouse to tell you that you won a million dollars?"

"No Drury, it could only be you who is rude enough to call this early. Besides, I thought you were tired of my ass, cramped up in my van for two weeks taking grizzly and wolf pictures in Yellowstone."

Drury responded, "I am, especially when you farted all night."

"Don't blame me Drury. You were the gourmet genius who suggested that we cook beans, hot dogs and Velveeta cheese together over the campfire."

"What are you complaining about Zack? That concoction slid down your gullet real easy."

"Yeah, but after that it wasn't pretty. Enough of the pleasantries Drury, why did you call?"

"Well, retired detective, I ran across something last evening that should get your juices flowing." Drury told Zack what happened.

"You may be right Drury, they're probably moving contraband across the border, or paying for some. Is there still a market in the U.S. for Cuban cigars being smuggled from Canada?"

"No Zack, relations are easing between the two countries. Cuban cigars are a lot easier to get. Obama probably even smokes them in the White House. Also, it looked like the contraband was going into Canada, not from it."

"Okay, so are we talking about 'run of the mill' drugs?" asked Zack. "I don't know how 'run of the mill' this is. There were a lot of duffle bags and those off-road vehicles looked brand new."

After a moment's pause, Zack asked, "So what do you want to do?" "I thought we could look into this, and if there is anything, we can report it to your former brethren."

"I gave up that shit a long time ago. That's why I got as far away from Bakersfield PD as possible and retired to this insulated enclave, where the deer outnumber the people, ten to one."

"Come on Zack you know you miss it. It would be fun to do some investigative work."

"Yeah, I miss it like my ex-wife, who soaked me for everything I had. She even took half my pension."

"What are you *bitchin* about Zack, you retired from the force at 50, after 30 years in, at 90% of your salary. No wonder California is going broke."

"I deserved every penny you asshole. I was the one who arrested zonked out dudes high on PCP—all those supermen who could take on three or four cops. My back has never been the same since it took five of us to tackle and restrain that 6 foot, 6 inch, boxer from the *Bake*, who used to be ranked in the top ten in the heavyweight division. He loved his horse tranquilizer—PCP made him feel immortal."

"Look Zack, you don't have to worry about any PCP, it's no longer the drug of choice for anybody. Why don't we give that real estate lady, Biker Sue, a call. She always has her nose in everyone's business. She must miss people, being a transplant from Southern California. She'll let us know if there have been any strangers poking around."

Zack relented, "Okay Drury, you give her a call. She has the hots for you, the heroic wildfire fighter."

"Alright, I'll exude some manly charm and offer to buy her lunch at her choice of Yaak's fine eating establishments, Yaak River Tavern, or my personal favorite, Dirty Shame Saloon. I love the sign on Dirty Shame's door, *Check your guns at the Bar*. I always wanted to be packin', just so I would have a gun to check."

"Okay cowboy, just call her and let me know."

Yaak has about 200 all season residents and is in the middle of nowhere, 20 miles from both the Canadian border and Montana's western border with Idaho. It is on the Yaak River, at the junction of two country roads, State Highways 92 and 508. Yaak is no teeming metropolis—it has a gas station, two restaurant-bars, a volunteer fire department and a one room schoolhouse for grades one through eight, with a total enrollment of 20 kids in a good year. High schoolers travel 35 miles to the nearest real town, Libby. October is pretty quiet. The summer tourists no longer wander through and the seasonal Yaak residents have already packed it in for the winter.

Towards 1:00 p.m., Drury and Zack were outside the Yaak River Tavern, waiting to hear the angry rumble of Sue's Harley. They had already secured drafts from the barkeep and were just biding their time when rolling thunder vibrated their eardrums. Zack yelled over to Drury, two feet away, "God, I wish she would get a proper muffler for that bike."

Drury responded, "Doesn't fit her image of a *badd* ass biker chick from L.A."

Zack retorted, "She is close to 60. It's time for her to tone it down."

Biker Sue came into view, her long wavy gray hair flowing in the wind, no helmet, jeans, black leather jacket, and her standard shade goggles and blue bandana.

"I wonder if she ever washes that bandana?" asked Zack.

Drury strode over to greet her, "Thanks for coming Sue. You and your bike are looking good."

"You got that right Dru. You always were the charmer, unlike your buddy, grumpy old Zack."

"Lighten up Sue, we're paying for lunch," said Zack.

They were sitting out back on the deck, overlooking the Yaak River. On either side of the river were large splashes of green grass, closely cropped, like goats had been let loose. On the far right side, past the grass, was a forest of pine trees. The river was extremely peaceful, no current detectable. Charlene brought them their second round of a Missoula brewed pale ale, Bottomfish. The drafts were served in 16 ounce glass jars with the name of the brewery on it. Zack mused, "We're getting more and more like California, may be time to move."

As they devoured their burgers and homemade fries, Drury asked Sue, "Has any stranger stood out, possibly asking about properties?"

"Now that you mention it, I did have a couple of guys come into my office a month or so ago, who didn't seem to fit. They asked about any large rental properties being available for a corporate retreat in the Yaak area. Who ever heard of corporate execs coming to Yaak?"

"What did they look like?" asked Zack.

"In their 30s. The white guy looked like a typical suit and talked like one. He was pudgy with glasses. The Mexican was slick and seemed to be the decision maker. They wanted to know all about the area around Yaak, what the corporate employees could do for team bonding, crap like that," said Sue. "They asked about off-roading, what sort of vehicles were available and how far away the Canadian border was. I remember my smart ass response, 'Why, do you want to defect? Obama too much for you?' The white guy responded, 'No, no, just want to fix my position.' 'Fix your position? Are you some sort of engineer?' I asked. 'Close enough, an accountant.'" Drury glanced over at Zack and gave him a look like this is getting interesting.

Zack asked, "Did they tell you their names or leave any cards?"

"Don't remember their names, they didn't leave cards, but the accountant type talked about being from San Diego. They were driving a fancy "gangsta" car, a black Escalade with tinted windows and 'look at me' rims."

Drury commented out loud, "This is coming together."

Sue demanded, "What's coming together? Why the interest in an accountant and a slick Mexican?"

Zack replied, "We're just looking into something. If anything develops we'll let you know."

"Hey, Mr. CIA man, I want to know now."

"Sorry Sue, we don't divulge our confidences that easily," said Zack.

Drury said, "It's better you don't know just yet. We'll fill you in when we can, over dinner. Our treat."

"I'll hold you to that. Dru, do you need a lift anywhere?"

"Thanks Sue, but I have my truck."

As she zoomed off, Zack said, "I told you she has the hots for you. The classy dames are attracted to you like coyotes to road kill."

No femme fatale had been able to tie Drury down yet. He had a close call some fifteen years back. He had lived with a mountain girl for a couple of years in the Mission Mountains, outside of Saint Ignatius. Their nearest neighbors were grizzly bears. The isolation and bears finally got to Drury's woman, and she ran off.

CHAPTER THREE

Zack was grilling brats, peppers, and some zucchini on his deck overlooking the Yaak River while Drury was making a salad in the kitchen. Just as the brats began to split and sizzle, Zack pulled them off the grill and yelled, "Ready, bring out that salad!"

"I can't find any Green Goddess dressing."

Zack shook his head in disgust, and yelled back, "I don't think they're making that green goo anymore. If you must have an artery stuffer, there's a bottle of ranch on the side of the fridge, upper shelf."

"Okay Detective, what is the game plan for this evening with our tenderfoot off-roaders?"

"Well Drury, how about just popping a few more PBRs, then going down to the Dirty Shame Saloon and listening to music. Let's just forget the whole thing, probably wasn't anything."

"Hey wuss, man up! You know they're up to something. We can check out the border and set up a few motion cameras."

"Alright, but I'm not getting paid anymore to get shot at. You better not do anything stupid, as you're known to do," retorted Zack.

"Finish your last bite of brat. Let's grab the motion cameras and head out. We should arrive at the border about an hour earlier than they were there last night," said Drury.

Forty-five minutes later they were at the border. They veered right around the road barrier on the U.S. side, weaving between the pine trees before coming to a rusted out sign that read, *Welcome to Canada*. Looking around, they saw multiple sets of footprints. A couple sets looked like hiking boots, and one set like cowboy boots. Several prints led along the footpath to the U.S. barrier about 10 yards away, and other prints led in the opposite direction, towards the Canadian barrier. "Document those prints, get the measuring tape and photograph," ordered Zack.

"I love it when you talk police to me."

"While you are doing that Drury, I will walk over to the Canadian barrier and see if there are any recent vehicle tracks." A couple of minutes later, Zack was at the Canadian barrier. He noticed wide tire tracks of a single vehicle, a vehicle that had taken up the entire width of the logging road. He took photos of the tire tracks, using a discarded Starbuck's cup as a measuring aid. He decided to keep the cup as it may have been used by one of the bad guys to suck down a latte. Zack wasn't a big fan of Starbucks. Pay twice as much for some fancy sounding coffee drink, and order snob-infused sizes, a "grande", a "venti"? This is America, where we still speak English—it's small, medium and large. Zack mused to himself, *What is wrong with the clerk at 7-Eleven? I don't need some Barista to serve me my coffee.*

After Zack had finished getting himself riled up over one of his many pet peeves, he walked over to Drury. Drury said, "We better hurry and set up the motion cameras, they could be coming along in a half hour or so." They found three suitable trees with branches to shield the camera bodies from the casual onlooker. They put some camouflage netting over each of them for improved concealment. The fixed, wide angle lens, would take digital photos of anything that moves in front of the lens. Wildlife photograph use the lens to capture reclusive predators like wolf, bear, and mountain lion.

They moved their quads back into the woods and set up with binoculars at about 200 yards from the border crossing. Each had different sight lines. They were silent for an hour, each standing in the same position. They were used to this, it was the standard dreary drill for wildlife photography. Drury broke first and walked over to Zack. "It's more than a half an hour from the time they were here last night. I don't think they're coming."

"It was your idea Drury, bringing me out here. We're here, let's give it another hour."

"Zack, you're an ornery cuss. You're making me pay for dragging your ass along on this adventure." Zack looked at Drury crosswise. "Okay Zack, another hour." The hour crept by, nothing. They left.

They decided they weren't going to go to the border every night in the hopes of seeing an exchange in person. A week later, Drury volunteered to exchange out the photo storage chips on the motion cameras to see what they had picked up. Later that afternoon, Drury put the first motion camera's chip into the adapter for the computer. He began to scroll through the 50 photos. After a deluge of deer pictures, the last four shots were of a group of four men, some distance away, just within the outside range of the camera's capacity to pick up movement. All four were Latino, one looked to have the same build as the slick Mexican, who had talked to Biker Sue at her real estate office. The first shot showed two of the men walking from the Canadian side, each carrying a duffle bag. The two who were standing with their backs to the U.S. side did not seem to be carrying anything. The time and date stamp on the photo showed it to be about the same time of the evening and exactly one week after Drury saw the two off road vehicles heading toward the border.

"What do you think Zack?"

"If the duffle bags you saw the first evening were drugs, then the two duffle bags from the Canada side could be payment for drugs delivered the week before. Down the line distributors often don't pay for the drugs upfront. Instead, they pay off the "up the chain" wholesaler as they sell the drugs."

Drury asked, "What happens if the drugs get ripped off before the distributor can pay his wholesaler the money?"

"He will find a way to pay or may lose his life. Only if there is a well-established relationship and the distributor is blameless for losing the drugs, will the cartel sometimes just write off the payments as a cost of doing business. Also, a pattern of timed exchanges isn't unusual. The instructors at the California Narcotics Officers Association conferences that I attended, said, 'Drug sales are a business, they're in it for the money. Scheduled, routine drugs for money exchanges are more efficient.'" Zack continued, "There's a good chance they'll have another meet at the same time next week."

Drury said, "The question is, do we want to be there for it?"

"Are you crazy? These guys aren't carrying granola bars in their pockets, try guns."

"Look Zack, we could set up a safe distance away, some 300 yards, and still get good photos with our A-game equipment. You could be on one side of the border and I could set up on the other."

"No Drury, it's time to go to the cops with this."

"Zack, Sheriff Terry is a good guy and writes a decent accident report, but you know ten times more about this stuff than he does."

"Do you understand what we may be getting into? What happens if one of those guys happens to run across one of us while they are passing contraband back and forth?"

"We'll just play the stupid, local hick card, out taking pictures of wildlife," said Drury.

"Well, it may be easy for you to play the stupid hick, because you are one. It's not so easy for me."

"Hey, I'll give you a lesson—we all live in trailers, have an outhouse in the back, drink PBR and never graduated from high school."

"Well, at least the PBR part is true," said Zack. "You're such an adrenaline junkie. Isn't parachuting out of planes to fight raging forest fires enough for you?"

"Remember Zack it's the off-season. I need my fix. Humor me."

"All right, why do I let you talk me into this? I hope your life insurance is paid up and I'm the primary beneficiary."

"If I had a life insurance policy, you'd be my primary beneficiary. Does that make you feel better Zack?"

"Yeah, a hell of a lot better."

The next week, they were at the border by 5:00 p.m., some two hours before they expected the weekly visitors. Drury and Zack parked their respective quads close to where each was going to set up, one on either side of the border. It took awhile for them to find locations a few hundred yards out that still had at least a partial sight line to the border crossing. Zack was on the Canadian side, lying prone with his lens resting on a flat rock. He was able to see the crossing area under low lying tree branches. Drury had to climb five feet up a tree on the U.S. side, which afforded him a clear view. He had his lens propped against a tree branch and the trunk of the tree.

They discussed contingency plans if one of them were discovered. Drury suggested, "First, the 'lucky" one will talk his way out of it, pretending to be alone, just taking photos of wildlife. If a gun comes out, start praying."

Zack grimaced and said, "What a weak contingency plan. We better be able to B.S. ourselves out of this if the shit hits the fan."

Drury replied, "Maybe we should have carried guns."

"And look even more suspicious? We'd be outgunned anyway. We better get back to our locations—if they're coming, it should be within 40 minutes."

"Okay Zack, don't worry, they won't see us."

"Famous last words," retorted Zack.

Thirty minutes later they heard the distant sounds of a vehicle approaching from the U.S. side. A minute later a similar sound could be heard from the Canadian side. Drury was first to see the vehicle on the U.S. side, the same Ranger off-road vehicle he had seen before. Just one this time, with two Hispanics inside and a couple of duffle bags. Neither one looked like the slick Mexican guy. Both were stocky with longish hair. Drury moved his camera in line with the expected meeting spot by the rusted out *Welcome to Canada* sign.

Zack was feeling an anxiety pit in his stomach, like an unwelcome old acquaintance. The Canadian vehicle was getting closer. Zack got a glimpse of it through the trees, an old, long bed pickup truck, with high clearance, probably had four wheel drive. Either a Chevy or a Ford. He lined his camera lens up with the expected meeting place.

Two men from the U.S. side came into Drury's viewfinder, each carrying a duffle bag. From the sound of the Ranger's idling motor, Drury believed they had just left it parked at the barrier that crossed the logging road. One of the men was talking on a cellphone.

Drury thought it must be a satellite phone because there's no cell-phone reception in and around Yaak. A couple of minutes later, two Hispanic men stepped into the clearing from the Canadian side, one of them carrying a duffle bag. Drury started clicking off photos, trying to catch the facial features of the men. He was able to get the two Canadians, who were facing his general direction, as well as one of the Hispanics from the U.S. side, who was looking around the area. They exchanged duffle bags, only meeting for a couple of minutes. It looked like words were exchanged, but Drury was too far away to hear what was said.

Zack was getting good shots of the faces of the two men from the U.S. side, but only saw the backs of the two from the Canadian side. He decided to risk calling out his Barn Owl hoot that he had learned for a bird calling contest in high school. Once you hoot like a barn owl, you never forget, it's like learning to ride a bike. Zack let out a few loud, low hoots. It had the desired effect, and the two Canadians turned in his direction. Zack got a couple of good facial shots. Drury heard the hoots as well. He thought, *What in the hell is a barn owl doing in this region? Their habitat doesn't extend into northern Montana and Canada.*

On the path back to their Ranger, the two Hispanics got within 150 yards of where Drury was set up. At the worst possible time, Drury let out a loud raspy cough. His lungs had been damaged by breathing in fire and he had a tendency to cough, especially when he tightened up from nerves. One of the men yelled out, "Who's there?" Drury didn't answer. For one of the first times in his life, he had nothing to say. The man approached Drury's location and called out, "Show yourself!"

Drury responded with an irritable growl, "Shut the fuck up, you're scaring the wildlife!" The Hispanic kept walking towards him. Drury got out of the tree, fumbled with his camera a bit, and started walking towards the man. "I'm coming out, your yelling scared away any animals." They met 50 feet from where Drury had set up. The Hispanic had his hand on a gun stuck in his waistband. "Hey, relax man, it's just ole Drury, trying to take some pictures of elk and bear."

"Why are you out here with that fancy camera taking pictures when it's almost dark?"

"That's when the animals come out."

"I thought you locals were all hunters, what are you doing with a camera?"

"What do you think I'm taking photos for? It's to check where they hang out for next hunting season. How do you like my camera?"

"How do you like my gun, gringo?" as he pulled a gun from his waistband and placed the long black barrel against Drury's forehead. "It's not so funny now, wise ass. I'd like to see the photos you've been taking." The Hispanic made the "request" as he continued to point the gun at Drury's head.

"What's with the gun, señor?" asked Drury in a deferential voice, "I'm just mindin' my own business, trying to get photos of bear."

"Shut up! I'm the one asking the questions."

"If you insist amigo, here is the playback button." The Hispanic took the camera, pushed the button and saw a picture of a wolf, then a couple of grizzly bears, and finally some pronghorn antelopes. Drury said, "I took those a couple of weeks ago in Lamar Valley, Yellowstone. Do you mind putting the gun back in your belt?"

The Hispanic took a long look at Drury and Drury smiled. The Hispanic relaxed, and put his gun back in his waistband. "Big mouth photographer, it's dangerous out in the woods at night. You never know what type of predator is roaming around." He walked away.

Drury took a quiet few moments for himself. Blood had left his face and Drury tried to control his shaking. He thought, *Maybe Zack was right, he might be too much of an adrenaline junkie for his age.* He waited another couple of minutes before he heard the Ranger start up and drive back towards Yaak. Drury then walked to the border and met up with Zack. Drury told him what happened.

Zack's only comment was, "You dumb shit. You have to do something about the cough."

The next morning over coffee at the Yaak River Tavern, Zack told Drury, "There's no next step to this self-initiated, reckless, civilian investigation. The fantasy is over. You're lucky you didn't end up with a few bullet holes in your carcass."

"We can't stop now."

"Yes, we can Drury. I'm going to call the Director of the California Narcotics Officers Association and see if he has any ideas about whom to call about this. The accountant type did say he was from San Diego. By the way Drury, the only smart thing you did in all of this, was to delete the border crossing photos from your camera when the Hispanic called out. If you hadn't, you would've been done."

"It was a tough thing for me to do, delete the photos on the off chance he might want to see them. But I had confidence in you buddy, that you had taken the necessary shots, and you did."

"Hello Jorge, this is Zack Reynolds, I used to be with Bakersfield PD. I attended a few of your CNOA conferences, four or five years back."

"I remember your name Zack. What are you up to now?"

"I retired a couple of years ago and took what was left of my pension, after my ex-wife got ahold of it, to Yaak, located in the far northwest corner of Montana. Around Yaak there used to be only a few unruly bears and a couple of dopers to worry about, but that has changed. It looks like there is a drug smuggling operation into Canada, run by Mexicans and a white accountant out of San Diego." Zack filled Jorge in on the entire story. Zack asked Jorge if he had any ideas about who to talk to about this.

"Well, do you remember Nick Drummond from the California Attorney General's Office? He was the guy who lectured on money laundering and financial investigations at a few of the conferences."

"Yeah, a big guy, in his early fifties, grumpy and sarcastic."

"That's him. He's heading up a joint local, state, and federal money laundering task force in San Diego."

Zack said, "I think I still have a copy of the *Money Laundering Manual* he passed out, with his phone number in it."

"He had this mantra, 'Follow the money,'" said Jorge.

"Good idea Jorge, I'll give him a call. Even though I would love to see you, don't bother to come to Yaak. We don't need anymore people up here. Good-bye."

CHAPTER FOUR

Nick Drummond sat at his government-issued, pressed sawdust desk, and looked over at the ugly set of metal file cabinets, brim full with cases and money laundering materials. Most of the other prosecutors, generally quite a bit younger, had their working files in electronic form, stored in their computers. Nick preferred to call himself a tech dinosaur, not a technophobe. He liked the feel of paper, going back and forth through materials the old-fashioned way, making comments on the side of pages. Also, he didn't have the patience to learn how to use the computer well. Fortunately, he had Rona Delphi, a fantastic paralegal, who handled computer document organization. Rona was worth her weight in gold, and was "the one who must be obeyed" as to case administration. Nick always told the brand new, often too-full of themselves prosecutors, "There's only one person you have to keep completely happy in this office, Rona."

Nick had scheduled a Money Laundering Task Force meeting in the conference room. Nick was no longer housed at the downtown San Diego AG's Office, but was now off-site with the rest of the Money Laundering Task Force in a nondescript warehouse in north-central San Diego. Nick had brought his security blankets with him, Rona and his longtime secretary, Abbie Chivas.

Nick had been chosen to lead the task force because of his many years of prosecuting complex crimes and heading up the California Attorney General's Money Laundering Program. Now, Nick was frustrated. The Money Laundering Task Force had been up and running for six months. There were some solid leads, but it was becoming apparent that it was extremely difficult to tie Mexican drug cartels to the flood of U.S. dollars going back and forth across the border. The meeting would update the status on the more promising, incipient investigations.

Everyone wandered into the conference room by 11:05. Several dragged along coffee cups with their investigation notebooks. A couple were affixed to their iPhones. Nick had thought about banning phones from the meetings. He decided against it when he had to admit it was useful when one of the techies checked on something, in an internet flash, during the meetings.

"Okay guys, let's go through the 'to do' list generated from the last meeting," Nick said in his command voice. "Pepe, let's start with you."

California Department of Justice Special Agent Pepe Cantana was a get-it-done type of guy. He had grown up on both sides of the border. He had a large family; some still lived in Mexico, while the others lived in the El Centro area of Imperial County, about a 100 mile drive from San Diego. Pepe started with the El Centro PD, then moved on to California DOJ where he was eventually assigned to the liaison division, working with Mexican officials on extradition and child abduction cases. He had numerous law enforcement contacts on both sides of the border.

Pepe reported, "As you know, we have been looking at Hector Morales and his two, so-called legitimate businesses, L&M Freight and Recycle Yard, for five months. The Bank Secrecy Act (BSA) currency reporting documents show three million dollars per month, in cash, being deposited in eight California-based bank accounts along the border with Mexico. These accounts are either in Hector's name, his wife's name, or one of the two companies. Different couriers are bringing in cash in backpacks, in amounts of $75k to $100k, for deposit in these accounts. The various banks are filling out the BSA required forms. We have compiled a spread sheet, showing each deposit, and the totals for each month."

Banks file Currency Transaction Reports (CTRs) for cash deposits or withdrawals over $10,000 with the Internal Revenue Service.

"Have you checked out his businesses?" asked Nick.

"They are incorporated in California and have fictitious business name statements filed with the county clerk. The corporate papers list Lester Sendow as their agent for service of process, with a San Diego address."

Detective Mario Cipriani of the San Diego County Sheriff's Office added, "We visually checked out the two business addresses and surveilled our buddy Hector a few times over the last week. There's no way that either business or both together are generating three million in cash a month. There are a couple of old trucks in the lot behind an empty warehouse that has a sign, *L&M Freight*. And the recycling business looks like a junkyard, with an old codger in a booth reading a newspaper. On two of the surveillances, Hector visited a few of the banks, and on the third day he went to his recycle business for an hour. He isn't burning the midnight oil working. He spends most of his time holed up in his five-acre spread in Rancho Santa Fe. He has big name golfers and entertainers as neighbors."

"Sounds promising Mario and Pepe, but we still need to tie all this cash flow to drug trafficking or another felony," said Nick.

"As if we don't know that Nick," retorted Pepe, "We're working on it."

"We can get federal tax returns on the two companies and individual returns on Hector and his wife from the IRS," offered Homeland Security Investigations Agent Jerry Slater.

"Good Jerry, let's do that. We're going to need a complete financial profile on Hector and his companies," replied Nick.

Pepe said, "There's also a business address for L&M Freight in Tijuana. I can use my contacts to get the Baja Norte State Police to check out the address. Depending on what the *policia de estado* tell us, I can follow up, and go across the border to sit in on any interviews conducted by the *policia*."

"*Bueno! Vaya con Dios, Pepe.*"

"Nick, I won't do anything if you keep using your mangled Spanish on me. Just because I was born in Mexico, it doesn't mean I have to be subject to your fifth grade Spanish."

"Pepe, give an ugly American gringo a break,"

"Ugly," retorted Pepe, "I can live with."

Immigration and Customs Enforcement Agent Ana Schwartz suggested, "We could put GPS trackers on the undercarriages of Hector's high rolling cars, his Benz and Range Rover."

Assistant U.S. Attorney Josh Sterling spoke up, "With the recent U.S. Supreme Court case, *U.S v. Jones*, we have to be careful about secreting a tracker on a car without a warrant. We can place a tracker on a vehicle at the border if we have reasonable suspicion of criminal activity."

"Let's wait until we establish more cause before we start slapping on trackers right and left." Nick continued, "Good work on the Morales case, keep digging! Next?"

Jerry responded, "There's the Sakia trade-based money laundering case. It's one of those we could be looking into for years and still not come up with enough proof to make a case."

Nick said, "We don't have years. The higher ups are looking for something to talk about as soon as possible. You know how the state AG likes favorable media coverage."

"Those politicians are all the same, they don't care about what's going on in the trenches, just how it makes them look on the six o'clock news," growled Jerry, with a disgusted look.

"You're preaching to the choir. But this task force depends on the 'benevolence' of those politicians," said Nick.

Jerry continued, "Mr. and Mrs. Sakia have an import-export food business, called Latin America Productos, which mainly imports beef and other foodstuffs from Mexico and Argentina. They were born in Argentina and still have family ties in Buenos Aires. They have an office in Chula Vista, located halfway between the border and downtown San Diego. The business has been filing income tax returns and everything looked on the 'up an up' until the fall of 2012 when the married couple and their agents started declaring large amounts of U.S. cash as they crossed into California from Tijuana."

In 2012, Mexico passed its Anti-Money Laundering Law (MAMLL), which severely restricts dollar cash deposits into Mexican financial institutions. Under MAMLL, drug cartels and others could no longer deposit U.S. cash into Mexican banks. They had to find other ways to get the cash dollars into the Mexican banking system.

Ana added, "We went through the international financial unit organization, EDMONT, and obtained export documents from Argentina and Mexico. We compared them with our U.S. Customs trade documents for the last ten years. Up until late 2012, the company appeared legitimate, importing foodstuffs into the Los Angeles Port of Entry and then brokering the food to other places in the the U.S. and Canada. The tax returns, both corporate and individual, lined up with expected income and expenses for a legitimate business. This all changed in late 2012, when all, but a few of the imports stopped, and huge amounts of cash began coming across the border."

Jerry said, "It's not unusual for legitimate trade businesses to become compromised by the drug cartels and allow their businesses to act as fronts for the laundering of drug dollars."

"Unfortunately," lamented AUSA Sterling, "Where there are corrupt businesses that were legitimate, and portions of their business are still legitimate, it's much more difficult to get a jury to buy off on money laundering."

"Exactly how are they moving the money?" asked Nick.

Ana answered, "The couple and their agents are declaring around $200,000 per northbound border crossing on Currency Monetary Instrument Reports(CMIRs). The forms state that the money originates from their business, World Food Imports, located on Avenida Revolucion, Tijuana. For the last few months, they have been transporting $2.5 million a month, and then depositing the same into 10 accounts in four banks, located just across the border. The cash is declared on CTR forms, and immediately wired to the same Mexican bank account."

It's not illegal, in itself, to bring $200K or any large amount of cash across the border as long as the cash is declared at the border on the CMIR form.

Jerry said, "We're also getting in Suspicious Activity Reports (SARs) from some of the banks."

SARs are required to be filed by U.S.-based financial institutions when a transaction, or series of transactions, deviate from the norm of legitimate financial practices to the extent it raises a suspicion of criminal activity. Banks are trained by the government as to what transactions constitute "suspicious activities". A section of the form allows an institution to specify exactly what aspects of the transactions are deemed suspicious.

Jerry continued, "One SAR sets forth Anthony Sakia's explanation as to why he was bringing so much cash from Mexico and then wire transferring it back to Mexico. He told the bank official, 'Our company trades food in Mexico, and the Mexican purchasers pay for the food in cash pesos, which we then exchange into U.S. Dollars at Mexican exchange houses (casas de cambio). We then have to bring the cash dollars across the border because Mexican regulations don't allow the deposit of cash dollars into Mexican banks. We then deposit the cash dollars into our accounts in California, and wire the dollars to our food suppliers. The suppliers want to be paid in U.S. dollars because of the historic fluctuations in the dollar-peso exchange rates.'"

"Wow!" exclaimed Pepe, "You have to have majored in economics to try to figure all that out."

"All right, this case could be an incredible resource drain where we end up with no prosecution," said Nick. "We need to do the following investigative steps, then re-evaluate. We must refute the Sakias' only defense, a legitimate import-export trade business. Go through all relevant federal databases, the internet, and state filings as to their business and to them as a married couple and as individuals. Also check on their key employees. Make sure to query the U. S. Customs TEC database for all border crossings by the couple, family members and key employees over the last ten years. This could show a pattern, or a contrast, in their border crossings over the years. Let's surveil the Sakias from when they wake up until they go to bed. Pepe, I want you to use your contacts in Mexico to check out the Sakias' business located on Avenida Revolucion. Finally, have the banks, under our supervision, segregate some of the future cash deposits and conceal the deposits in the vault. Then see if a drug sniffing dog can make positive alerts on the cash. Make sure the dog has the right credentials and that a positive alert signifies that the cash has come into recent contact with a controlled substance. The dog must be beyond 'reproach' because the courts are clamping down on allowing this type of evidence in trial. Once we get this information together, we can run it by an import business expert to see if the couple's business practices are within an acceptable norm. Of course, we have to find an expert first, but I have some ideas on that."

"Gee Nick, anything else? We should be able to get that done by the end of the day," the sarcasm dripping from Jerry's voice.

"I know it's a lot of work, but to make these cases, we have to do it. We need to know if we can get enough information to support search warrants on the couple's business office and their home."

"One more thing, back on the Morales case. We should also segregate some of their new cash deposits and run it by our sensory-enhanced canine friends."

"Nick, I knew I should have left the meeting after we finished talking about my case," said Pepe.

"That will teach you to wait around for the extra donut before leaving. That's why I bring them for you guys."

"Are we exhausted yet?" asked Nick. "Only one more thing to discuss. Ana, your Saladez investigation which has ties to the Sakia money laundering operation."

"In this one, we've a direct association with drug trafficking," said Ana. "Two couriers, each with close to $80,000 in cash, were arrested at the border for not declaring the cash over the $10,000 threshold. Upon being questioned, they told customs officials that they received the cash from Numero Uno, a casa de cambio in Calexico, Mexico. Numero Uno is owned by Jorge Saladez, who has a U.S. record for marijuana and cocaine distribution. The couriers had written instructions on them to deposit the cash in a U.S. border bank on behalf of Anthony Sakia and then obtain cashier's checks in the same amounts, payable to a Mexican bank account. The busts of the two couriers, eight months ago, must have inspired the Sakias to transport the cash in large amounts themselves, or through their own couriers. Also, we determined that the cashier's checks were going to be payable to a Mexican bank account with Banco Real. The Mexican account holder is a high ranking Mexican government official, Armando Ruiz Castillo."

Mario said, "I don't want to sound like a dumb shit, but if these cases are about Mexican drug cartels running drug dollars through U.S. banks, why cross into Mexico with all the drug dollars to just courier them back across? Wouldn't it make more sense to just deposit the cash in U.S. banks upon collecting the cash for drugs in the U.S., without bringing it back and forth across the border?"

Nick replied, "Good point. Nobody said drug dealers are the sharpest tools in the shed. This question has been kicked around and there are a couple of possible explanations. First, the cartel's drug distribution and cash collection networks are usually set up to bring the cash back into Mexico. Because Mexico now prohibits the deposit of significant amounts of cash dollars directly into Mexican financial institutions, but allows dollars to be wired to Mexican banks or deposited via checks, the cartels have to get the cash dollars into U.S. banks so they can be transferred by wire or checks to Mexican banks.

"Some people in law enforcement believe the drug lords like to see and 'feel' the drug money in their own greedy, little hands before they launder it. Often, it's only when the drug cash initially crosses the border into Mexico, that the money laundering side of the cartel kicks in. The money laundering operation is responsible for getting the money into Mexican banks. Once the cash dollars take their circuitous route back and forth across the border to reach their Mexican bank destination, the launderers can take additional steps to try to legitimize the money through off shore accounts or other front companies.

"Wake up, Pepe! That's all for today. We'll meet in two weeks, same place, same time."

CHAPTER FIVE

ater that day, Nick was packing up to go home when Mario asked him if he wanted to go with a few agents to their favorite watering hole, Days End. Visions of sawdust on floor, dart boards, and pong tables came to mind. "No thanks Mario, I have got a few things to do at home."

"C'mon Nick, it'll do you good, a couple of games of darts. Then you can go back to your dreary apartment.

"What do you mean dreary?" asked Nick in a feigned, hurt voice, "Don't you like IKEA, posters, and an orange shag rug? I haven't had time to hire a decorator since Judy kicked me out.

"You and Judy can work it out, she's prima."

Nick replied wistfully, "Too many long nights at work, mixed with a bit of alcohol, not a good concoction. See you Mario. Jack Daniels and some jazz awaits me."

Over the din of the music and twenty-somethings yelling at each other, Ana asked Mario, "Where's Nick?"

"He had a previous engagement with an old friend."

Josh came up with some ping pong balls, a pitcher and cups, saying, "The pong table is free. How about Ana and I against Mario and Jerry?"

Ana said, in a disapproving voice, "Josh isn't it time you put away childish things."

"Thanks for the advice Mom, but pong helps with one's eye-hand coordination, consider it training for you agent types."

"Remind me Junior, how do you play this asinine game?"

"It's easy. We set up six of the red cups at each end, in a pyramid shape, fill them half way with beer, then each side takes turns trying to get a ping pong ball in one of the other side's cups. If it happens, the side who has the ball in their cup drinks the beer and removes the cup from the playing surface. Whoever has the last cup standing, wins."

Jerry said, "I take my drinking seriously. This game makes no sense. The team that gets the ball into the cup is penalized, the other team gets to drink. Any rational player would just take a dive and let the opposing team get all the pong balls in their cups."

"Not all pong players are alcoholics. Most like the competition of throwing a ball into the other team's cups," explained Josh.

Beer pong was going well—they had gone through a pitcher and were working on a second. Josh and Ana were winning most of the games. Josh was sort of a ringer, having played basketball at Yale. It seems that shooting a basketball translates to throwing a ping pong ball into a two inch diameter, 16 oz. cup. Josh and Nick had met while playing in the San Diego Legal Basketball League a couple of years back. Although most of the pop had gone out of Nick's legs, one could say he was a wily veteran. He knew how to use his bulky body and how to push off with his elbow to create space for a shot. Josh, knowing Nick's reputation in the legal community as a great trial attorney for the State AG's Office, took it easy on him. However, on occasion, Josh couldn't resist, skying above Nick to grab a rebound over Nick's back. You could tell how much this pissed Nick off—to be in position, boxing someone out for the rebound, and have a young attorney go right over the top, like your feet were glued to the floor. Josh struck up a conversation with Nick after their first game and they became friends, with Nick, over the last couple of years, acting as a sounding board for Josh's legal questions. This relationship resulted in Nick asking Josh to be part of the Money Laundering Task Force. Josh, a prosecutor with the United States Attorney's Office, jumped at the opportunity to work with Nick.

Ana called the games off. "Enough beer and fun. Time for me to go home and feed my cat."

Pepe, who had been watching the pong games, drinking beer unfettered by whether a ping pong ball landed in someone's cup, told Ana, "Your cat will survive another hour without its kibbles." Ana ignored Pepe and kept walking towards the door of Days End, when a drunk, who had been leering at Ana all evening, grabbed her ass. Pepe jumped on him, twisted his arm behind his back in a lock, and smashed his forehead into the bar. The drunk grunted in pain, with a trickle of blood dripping down his face from a cut over his eye.

Ana said, "Thanks Pepe, but I can take care of myself," as she turned the drunk around and kneed him in the balls.

"Ooooh Baby!" exclaimed Pepe, "That's the kind of ball playing I can understand." The drunk, gasping for breath, looked up, glassy eyed, at Pepe. Pepe using his street voice for crooks, and a look like you better not mess with me, said, "Friend, I think you owe this lady an apology." The drunk looked around, and seeing no support, mumbled an apology and stumbled out of the bar. "Well," said Pepe, "The Days End didn't go so well for him."

"A drink at Days End neither guarantees happiness nor a good pun," laughed Ana, and followed the drunk out the door. As she climbed into her old Porsche, Ana thought, *She had to get a life— 36 years-old, divorced for three years, no children, and worrying about feeding Sneakers, her white pawed, grey cat.*

Ana grew up in Newark, New Jersey. She was one of the few Jews at her inner-city school. She put up with name-calling, having her lunch money taken, and being pushed around for years. It all ended one afternoon when Ana struck back during her geography class. Her main tormentor sat in front of her. When the girl made another religious slur, Ana responded by pulling the girl's hair back, and while standing over her, pummeled her as she struggled to get up from her desk. It was well worth the five day suspension. And, it didn't later jeopardize Ana's scholarship to Columbia University.

Pepe walked over to where the others were. Jerry asked, "What was that commotion over by the bar?"

"Nothing, just some drunk management."

From work, Nick stopped off at Trader Joe's, bought some frozen meatballs and mac 'n cheese, and drove to his one bedroom apartment in Pacific Beach. As soon as Nick unlocked the door, he went over to his tropical fish tank and liberally sprinkled the dry flake food on the surface of the water. The twenty or so Dalmatian Mollies went into a feeding frenzy. Nick had had tropical fish since college. He used to keep his tank filled with a variety of fish, but found it a lot easier to just have Mollies. They reproduced every three months or so, which resulted in a self-perpetuating fish ecosystem. Nick never had to go to the store to buy fish. They were the perfect pets. When you came home and walked back and forth in front of the tank, they followed you, almost like dogs. Unlike dogs, there was no clean up. And you could leave the fish for up to a couple of weeks by dropping long-lasting food cubes into the tank. Nick only worried about his sanity, when after a few glasses of Jack, he found himself talking to the fish.

God, he missed his kids and Judy. But at least here, Nick could eat mac 'n cheese, which was absolutely "verboten" in their family home. Judy ran a tight ship when it came to food, being both German and a nurse. Come to think of it, Judy ran a tight ship when it came to everything. The home was her domain. She had cast him out of her domain a few months ago. He was too tired and beaten down to fight it much. She was right, he was not home enough because of his work, and he drank too much. He was thinking of ways to get back into her good graces. He hadn't come up with much yet.

Nick felt it was a Boz Scaggs night. There was something for every mood he was feeling. He planned to start with, "Look What You've Done to Me" and We're All Alone", and move on to "Dinah Flo" and "Slow Dancer". Nick put a couple of Boz' CDs on the player, and turned up the volume. The stereo equipment was the only piece of property worth anything in the apartment. He did like the posters of his photographs that he had taken on his youthful world adventures. He had the Taj Mahal, in the early morning light—its beautiful ivory-colored dome shimmering in the reflection pools, with Buddhist monks walking beside the pools. Shots of a rainbow over

Machu Picchu, a woman working in a rice field in Bali, a hunched over old woman in black, walking in a snow storm in Kashmir, and an owl flying right towards the camera lens, also adorned the off-white walls of his living room. Nick settled down, trying to get comfortable in one of his IKEA chairs, and sipped Jack Daniels over ice. He thought about the task force cases, knowing they needed a breakthrough to tie the money to one or more Mexican cartels.

After his third glass of Jack, he fought off the urge to call his kids, Jake and Gabriella, who would be getting ready for bed. He knew they had soccer games coming up this weekend that he had promised to go to. Nick started to drift off in his chair. He roused himself, looked at his watch and realized he should turn in. He hadn't even cooked the turkey meatballs and mac 'n cheese. That feast would have to wait for another night. He went to the kitchen and got himself a bowl of cereal, afloat in nonfat milk. Nick had been trying to lose 20 pounds for 10 years. It hadn't happened yet. After gobbling up the cereal, he brushed his teeth, got undressed, and lowered himself to the mattress on the floor. Nick kept telling himself that he had to get a bed frame, if for no other reason than it was too tough to push himself up from his bed in the morning. Also, It was uncool for a 55 year-old man to be sleeping on the floor.

Nick let himself into his office about 8:30, feeling a little hung over, but not too bad. He avoided the common gathering room, full of bad coffee and idle chit-chat. Abbie C. buzzed Nick an hour later, saying there was a former Bakersfield PD detective on the line. Nick picked up the phone, "Nick Drummond here."

"Nick, this is Zack Reynolds. I retired from Bakersfield P.D. a few years back. I attended your CNOA money laundering class in San Francisco."

"I hope you weren't one of those in the back, sleeping."

"No, I was sitting to one side, trying to make time with a cute deputy sheriff from LA."

"Well, Zack, it seems like you were using your time wisely. What's going on?" Zack relayed what had happened in Yaak a couple of weeks before. "Do you and your buddy have pictures of the guys transferring duffle bags across the border?"

"Yes, I can send you the photos by email."

"Thank you, and the white guy who said he was an accountant from San Diego, anything more about him?" asked Nick.

"No, but we've a good frontal photo of him."

"Zack, hold onto everything, especially that Starbucks cup you found on the Canadian side of the border, and we'll send over a Homeland Security agent from Spokane this afternoon to pick up the evidence and make a direct transfer of the photos from yours and Drury's computers onto an USB-drive. At some point, if the case goes somewhere, you two will have to testify in court and lay a foundation for the photos."

"I know the drill Nick, no problem."

"We'll run the photos in our facial recognition database, and hopefully we'll get lucky. Thanks for calling Zack. The HSI agent should be at your home by two o'clock. We'll keep in touch. Before you go, how did it work out with the L.A. deputy?"

"Like it usually does, nothing."

"That's what an old married man likes to hear, but not a newly separated one."

Zack chuckled, and said, "Welcome to my world Nick."

Nick retorted, "I have to go now. I don't want your bad luck rubbing off on me."

Nick called Jerry into his office and told him about Zack's phone call. "We need an HSI agent from Spokane to go to Zack's house in Yaak by two this afternoon to interview him and his buddy, and to pick up evidence. I want to move on this, it could be the break we need."

Jerry responded, "It could take a Spokane agent until 2:00 to find Yaak on the map."

"You're one of those tech guys. Ever hear of Google Earth or Mapquest? No excuses, just get it done, please."

"You got it Nick."

A few minutes after Jerry left Nick's office, Nick heard the incoming email ping on his computer. It was from Zack, with a number of photos attached, several with four people standing by an old border crossing sign, with duffle bags, as well as photos of various tire tracks. Nick laughed when he saw that Zack had used the Starbucks cup as a measuring reference for the size of tire tracks. As he was studying the photos, another ping resonated throughout his office. Nick thought, the computer is calling me again. He opened the new email. It was from Zack's friend, Drury, with a number of new photos attached. A few of these photos showed a white male with glasses, sitting next to a Latino with slicked back hair, in a small off-road vehicle. Others, of poorer quality, showed four men talking at the border. *The last photos must be the ones taken from the motion camera*, thought Nick.

Nick called in Ana. "Can you run the photos of the people through facial recognition?"

"Sure Nick, who do you think we have?"

"Maybe persons associated with a drug cartel, and a dirty accountant. Also, enhance their faces, print the photos out, and show them to the guys at DEA who are working the Mexican cartel drug cases along the border. You, Jerry and I will meet in the conference room at four and see what we have."

Nick tapped his pencil on the conference room table as he waited for Ana and Jerry to report in. Ana and Jerry burst through the door with papers in their hands. "What have you got?"

Jerry replied, "An agent from the Spokane office was able to make it to Yaak by two o'clock. He's interviewing Zack and Drury separately and collecting evidence. He'll send the evidence by overnight Fed Ex and I'll book it into our evidence locker. The agent will draft his reports tomorrow and hopefully get his Special Agent in Charge (SAC) to sign off on the reports right away. As soon as he gets the reports signed off, he'll email them to us."

Ana said, "I ran the photos through the facial recognition database and got three hits. "The purported white accountant is in fact an accountant, Lester Sendow. He has a one-person office in Mira Mesa, a few miles from our task force. His license was suspended for a year over his misdemeanor plea to receiving stolen property. This was a favorable plea bargain for him because it avoided a revocation of his license and significant jail time. He'd originally been charged with felony embezzlement of a client's assets. That's how his photo ended up on the database. Mr. Sendow seems to be the same person who's the agent for service of process for L&M Freight and Recycle Yard, Hector Morales' front companies."

"Wow!" Nick exclaimed, "Now it seems like we have something to go on."

"Wait, there's more," interjected Ana. The slick Mexican who was riding with Sendow in Yaak has been identified as Luis Hernandez-Lopez, one of the two lieutenants of the Familia Baja Norte cartel. He's in charge of drug distribution and money collection. He's 37 years old, and was busted 15 years ago in the states for a drug distribution charge. The third ID is 26-year-old Sergio Bustamante, an enforcer for the Familia. He has a long rap sheet for drug and violent crimes. Nick, there is another cartel link. Saladez, the owner of Numero Uno in Calexico, who gave couriers $80,000 apiece for the Sakias, is a known associate of the Familia."

"Great!" exhorted Nick, "Two of our money laundering cases are connected to the Familia."

"I know that Baja Norte Familia is rather new on the scene. Can you give me more information about them?" asked Nick.

"Let's get Pepe in here, he knows more about them," responded Ana. "Pepe's not here. He's across the border checking out the Sakias' business in Tijuana. Ana, just tell me what you know."

"Okay Chief. They have only been around for a few years. They're moving in on the Tijuana cartel's and Sinaloa cartel's control of the drug and money flow across the border between San Diego and Imperial Counties, and the Mexican state, Baja California Norte. They saw their opening with the imprisonment and killings of many of their rival cartels' leaders. The Mexican authorities are now focusing on the Zetas, the most violent and brutal of the cartels, headquartered in Nuevo Laredo, just across the border from Laredo, Texas. With the two cartels in this area weaker, and Mexican authorities elsewhere, it gave the Familia the opportunity to jump into the mix."

Nick queried, "I'm sure they just didn't just appear out of nowhere?" "No, and that's what makes them scary. Their leader, Mateo Gomez-Encinas, was a high-ranking member of the Sinaloa cartel. He recruited valued assets from the other cartels, promising more money and a "high tech" operation. The Familia, though smaller than other major cartels, is doing well."

"It would be quite a coup to make a major dent into an up and coming cartel," said Nick, his voice resonating with conviction. "We've a lot to do. We need to focus on the Sakias and Morales cases, and we need to do a complete work up on the Familia. I will contact the Royal Canadian Mounties to set up a meeting to work out a joint surveillance of the Canadian border at Yaak. Get a good night's sleep while you can. At some point eight hours of sleep will feel like a vacation."

CHAPTER SIX

Pepe was getting bored. They had been surveilling the front of Sakias' World Food Imports warehouse on Revolucion for two hours. Pepe's old friend from the Baja Norte State Police, Nacho Gutierrez, had picked him up at the border in his government car. The car screamed u*ndercover police car*. Pepe sprung for lunch at El Potrero Carnes. Over chilaquiles (fried corn tortilla strips simmered in salsa) with eggs and beans on top, Nacho caught Pepe up on his three kids. Nacho wanted to retire from the state police, draw his small pension, and work in private security where it was safer.

It looked like a slow business day for World Food Imports. Only a few people had come in or out of the front door. "How about circling around to see what is going on in the back of the warehouse?"

"Sure Pepe. I can only give you 30 more minutes. I'm expected back." Nacho drove to the back and parked on a small street that was lined with empty, boarded-up businesses. They had a direct view through stacked pallets of the warehouse's loading dock. Pepe focused his camera on the back door, leaning over Nacho to take a photo. Suddenly, revved up motors and screeching tires filled the air. Pepe turned and saw two black S.U.V.s skidding to a stop on either side of their car, blocking them in. Pepe thought, *Fuck, I don't have a gun, I had to leave it at the border.* That was his last thought before his eyes were blinded and his ears assaulted by horrific bangs and flashes of light. Pepe automatically doubled over below the front dashboard. He felt confused, had no equilibrium, and felt piercing pain in his ears. Both doors opened. Pepe turned and saw a hooded figure swinging his arm at his head. Pepe moved his head slightly, just enough to avoid the full brunt of the blow from a gun's handle to the right side of his head. He went limp.

Pepe slowly came back to consciousness. He didn't know how long he had been out. His arms and legs were bound, a gag was in his mouth, and a hood was over his head. He had a crushing headache and his ears still ached. Pepe knew he was in a vehicle, lying under something. He was being jostled about. Pepe rolled around, trying to feel for Nacho. Nacho wasn't there.

The road was getting bumpier. Pepe could smell the dust in the air. For a few minutes there was a terrible stench in the air. He heard seagulls squawking. *Maybe a dump?*

Minutes passed and the vehicle stopped. Pepe was dragged out onto the ground. Strong hands grabbed him and he was dragged along a path. He heard a door open. He was pulled up steps onto some type of a floor. Another door opened and he was flung to the ground. The door closed.

For what seemed like hours and hours, Pepe laid in complete darkness under a hood. His head throbbed with pain. He thought, *I have to stay awake. I have to stay alive. I want to see my family again. I can get out of this somehow.* Pepe fought the doubt creeping in. Deep down he knew it was unlikely that he would survive this. He prayed for the first time in years. He thought about his years as an altar boy and the hours he spent praying on his knees on the cold stone floor of the village church.

A hooded man came into the room, removed Pepe's hood and gave him some water. Pepe was so parched he could barely speak. "Where, where is my friend Nacho?"

The man answered Pepe with a slap to his face. "Don't talk. It isn't your concern what happens to that pig."

"Chacal" (Jackal) felt good about himself as he watched television in the living room of the safe house above the Tijuana dump. He had led the team of six who had penned the cops in their car, blasted them with stun grenades, hogtied them, and brought them in separate cars to the safe house. His team had gotten rid of the two S.U.V.s they used in the kidnapping. There were two old pickups out front that could be used to haul produce, materials, or bodies around.

Chacal's source in the state police had told him that there was an all out manhunt for the two officers. The Norte-Americanos were exerting extreme pressure on Mexican law enforcement to find the California agent. Chacal waited for his boss' call.

Nick tried to reach Pepe on his cellphone in the afternoon. Nick had expected Pepe to be back in the office by 4:30. After working 20 years together, both knew that Pepe would check in if he was delayed. Pepe didn't answer Nick's multiple calls. Nick checked with the rest of the team—no one had heard from Pepe. Everyone thought it was strange.

Nick called his old friend, Bea Kowalski, the United States Attorney for the Southern District of California. "Bea, this is Nick. I have a missing agent, Pepe Cantana, who was surveilling a business this afternoon on Avenida Revolucion with Baja Norte state police officer Nacho Gutierrez. The business is World Food Imports, housed in a warehouse. We suspect it's a money laundering front for the Baja Norte Familia. He should have been back an hour ago, or at least checked in. I have worked with him for 20 years. Pepe is very dependable."

"Nick, it has only been a short time. I'm sure he is okay. He's probably having a cerveza with his Mexican colleague."

"Bea, I know my agent. He would have checked in. Something has happened. I can feel it."

"Okay, I know your feelings and how they have worked out in the past.

What do you want me to do?"

"I know the DEA has a few agents working with the state and federal police in Tijuana. Can you contact them and send them out to World Food Imports right away?

"Will do. I will let you know as soon as we hear anything."

"Thank you. I owe you one."

Nick was counting the minutes from the end of his conversation with Bea. Forty minutes later his cell rang. "Nick, bad news. The government car Pepe and Nacho were in was found on a back street behind the World Food Imports warehouse. Pepe's cellphone was on the center console. Four expended stun grenades were just outside the car. Federal, state, and city police have been instructed to do a complete sweep of the area."

"I want to go down there. I'll bring my agents."

"You can't Nick. We have to comply with our international treaties and agreements with Mexico. We can't have unauthorized law enforcement flooding into Tijuana. I was able to send a few more DEA agents to help with the search. Everything that can be done, is being done. They will find Pepe." "Please have the DEA agents keep me informed. I will be at my office."

Nick's head drooped. He began to nod off. A half dozen cups of coffee and updates every couple of hours weren't enough to keep his eyes open. Jerry gently shook Nick awake. "The sun is coming up Nick. It's 6:30. What do you want us to do?"

"Any word yet?"

"No. They have expanded the search. Every business and house within a mile radius of the kidnapping has been searched. They are canvassing known cartel body dumping spots from Tijuana to Tecate to Ensenada. It doesn't look good."

"I'm not giving up hope. We're going down there to help. I don't give a shit about international treaties."

El Toro's call came at two in the morning. "Chacal, I haven't seen law enforcement out like this. It must be because of the American cop you snatched."

"Yes sir. I heard from my state police contact that they have never been rousted in full force like this before. The gringos want their cop back real bad."

"They can make it tough on us if the American cop shows up dead. It's bad for business. The message still gets sent for the state policeman. We can't have them messing with our friends. Do away with him. Don't hurt the American. Send a more subtle message. Lay him next to his dead Mexican colleague with a message to stay on his side of the border. Drop the bodies at La Bufadora by 5:00 A.M. That should get their attention."

John and Gretchen Sparrow wanted to see the famous La Bufadora in Ensenada before the crowds. The ocean bursting through the hole in the rocks with each wave was supposed to be spectacular. It was the first time that John and Gretchen had traveled abroad from their farm in Iowa. They were used to getting up early in the morning to feed their livestock.

At 6:30, John pulled into the parking lot by the blowhole. They could see the spray erupting above the rocks from the parking lot. As they walked closer, they saw two dark shapes lying by the edge the blowhole. John crept closer and saw two bodies. Both were tied and gagged. One was lying in a pool of blood. His throat had been slit. The other man's eyes were dancing about, reflecting fear and determination. The man had I.D. credentials open on his stomach and handwritten words in dark red across the chest of his white shirt, *STAY ON YOUR SIDE OF THE BORDER.*

Gretchen came up. Her loud, high-pitched screams competed with the noise from La Bufadora. John removed the gag. Pepe gasped, "I'm an American police officer. Get the police!"

Nick and the team were loaded to leave when Nick's cell rang. "Nick, tourists found Pepe alive next to La Bufadora in Ensenada. His friend Nacho was beside him, dead. His throat had been slashed."

Tears came to Nick's eyes. He couldn't talk. Bea said, "Nick, are you still on the phone?"

A few seconds past. Nick got ahold of himself. "Yes, I want to go there."

"He won't be there by the time you arrive. A life flight helicopter is on its way to pick him up and bring him back to Scripps Hospital in La Jolla. Pepe should be there in 30 minutes."

"Thank you. Thank you so much. I will be there when he lands."

Nick and the task force members were at the rooftop helo pad when the helicopter landed. Pepe was on a stretcher. Nick went to him as the medics were lifting him out of the copter. Pepe was hooked up to an I.V. and had a blood pressure cuff around his arm. Pepe reached out and grabbed Nick's hand. "I'm alright Nick. I took a blow to the head, but the bleeding has stopped."

"Thank God. I always knew you were one tough son-of-a-bitch. There's no way you'd die on me."

"Die on you and miss your cheapskate team party at the end on the year? No way."

The medics intervened. "We have to take Mr. Cantana to the emergency room. Although his vitals are fine, he did suffer a blow to the head. He may have a concussion."

Nick said, "Thank you. Pepe, I'm sorry about Nacho. He was a good man."

"I know. He won't be forgotten."

"You and I have long memories, Pepe. One way or another the men who did this to Nacho and you will get their due."

CHAPTER SEVEN

Nick looked at his watch, only 11:30 p.m. What a way to spend a Friday night, on a red-eye to Ottawa to meet with the Royal Canadian Mounted Police about the Baja Norte Familia cartel bringing drugs through Yaak to British Columbia. He kept thinking of Pepe. *I'm so glad he is alright. Just a mild concussion and he is cleared to go back to work on Monday.*

With the three-hour time change, the plane should land at about 7:30 a.m., Canadian time. Nick's legs were crunched into the seat ahead of him. Nothing like flying coach across country when you are 6 feet, 4 inches. No food except pretzels. Flying was more like taking the Greyhound bus. Pack 'em in and move 'em out. But what really pissed him off was that Ana was flying business class with all that legroom and warm towels to cleanse her dainty fingers after enjoying veal scaloppini, a berry tart and champagne. At least that's what the menu showed that he had grabbed as he walked through the first class and business class sections. Nick was lucky to even get last minute approval. He didn't think the AG's Office would have signed off unless it had been a budget, red-eye flight. Ana, being with ICE, flush with federal funds, was flying business class because the agency allows the upgrade on any flights over five hours. Nick thought they must want to keep their agents fresh and at their best. Not so for the tag-along state attorney. He put aside his craven envy and realized at least one of them might get a decent night's sleep.

Ana was savoring her first bite of the veal, thinking about why Nick had chosen her over the other agents to accompany him to the meeting. She thought she was the logical choice, an agent with

Immigration and Customs Enforcement, and this being a border operation with Canada. She still wondered if there might be more to it. Although irascible, close to 20 years her senior, and losing the fight to a middle-age paunch, there was something attractive about Nick. He had this commanding personality, brokered no fools, and seemed comfortable in his own skin. She wondered if her attraction to Nick had anything to do with her father, who had been 20 years older than her mother. Ana had adored her father. He was a quiet, thoughtful man, who immigrated to the United States from Germany after World War II. Her father died when Ana was 15. She still spoke to her father when she couldn't sleep at night. She had better stop these mental meanderings. It'd be more fruitful to worry about whether her neighbor would stop by and feed Sneakers.

Nick was lightly shaken awake by the blond stewardess with a southern drawl, "Going to be landin' sir. Please fasten yo'r seat belt." Nick caught a glimpse of the western end of Lake Ottawa in the dawn's light as the plane began to descend. The skyscrapers along the lakefront looked like a steel wall keeping the water at bay from the rest of Ottawa's urban sprawl.

The 35-minute taxi ride into their small hotel in old town Ottawa was uneventful. He let Ana pay the cabdriver, ICE could afford it. So much for old-fashion male responsibilities. He liked the hotel. It was built in the 1700s, was four stories tall, and used to be a bank building. The rooms were small, but had decent size bathrooms, and most importantly the bed had a firm mattress. Abbie C. had sweet talked the hotel proprietor into allowing them to check in early without paying for an extra night. Ana had a room down the hall. Nick told her that he'd meet her in the lobby at noon, after he caught up on a few hours sleep.

Ana was sitting in the lobby when Nick appeared. He was wearing his Irish tweed sport jacket in honor of the British empire. It probably would irritate the police officials of the French-oriented province. Oh well, can't please everyone. Nick wasn't feeling on the top of his game, languishing through a sleep-deprived hangover. Some good French food and a glass of vin rouge for lunch would perk him up. Nick actually livened up a bit when he looked at Ana.

She was doing her Sandra Bullock federal agent imitation, professionally dressed, but still looking sexy as hell. Nick said, "Aren't those heels a bit high for walking on cobblestones?"

"These shoes have seen me through a lot rougher times than a few cobblestones."

"Suit yourself. I thought we could go to lunch at a little French restaurant around the block, Cafe St. Elena. It's known for its onion soup."

"Sounds fine to me Nick, lead on." It turned out that Ana could navigate the cobblestones just fine. In a few minutes, Nick ducked his head to get through the old wooden door that led to an intimate dining area. A dozen tables were scattered on the tongue-and-groove, wood flooring. One table was free by the window that allowed most of the light to filter into the darkened room. At the far end of living room-size area, behind a bar, stood a middle-age woman with bright red hair, tied in back. Her head popped out from under the hanging glasses.

Her voice boomed, "*Bonjour! Bienvenue!*" Nick smiled at her and took a seat across from Ana. Madame Redhead weaved her way over to their table and handed each a menu.

Nick said, "My apologies, we don't speak French, just English."

"*Quel Dommage!* You won't starve. The duck and spinach stuffed ravioli is good today."

Ana, quickly glancing at the menu, and seeing just a few words in French she understood, responded, "*Bon*, the ravioli for me".

Nick holding up two fingers said, "Make it two, and a half liter of *vin rouge de maison*. Plus, *deux potages de l'oignon, sil vous plait.*"

"*Merci, monsieur.*"

"Your French accent is worse than your Spanish accent. I hope *potage* means soup, I don't want to be eating a potato and onion dish," said Ana. "No worries Ana, a glass of fine red wine will relax you."

They each savored the red wine, smooth, not too heavy, perfect for lunch. Ana looked around the room and was delighted by the large, unfinished wood beams. There were three wood pillars placed between the tables, holding up the beams. It looked like they had been transported into a tavern from an old Robin Hood movie she had watched as a child. She didn't really feel like Lady Marion. And Nick was a far cry from Errol Flynn. But he might pass for King Richard. There were copper kitchen items dangling from the beams, and whimsical paintings somehow tacked to the grey brick walls. She felt she was no longer in North America.

The smells of onions, gruyere cheese, and French countryside herbs waffled up, the steaming soup immersed Ana in the moment. A layer of melted cheese and soaked slices of baguette hid the cooked onions in the broth beneath.

Nick broke her sensory spell, "I read that the chef starts to prepare the soup the day before, allowing the sliced onions to simmer overnight in a large cauldron."

"Whatever they do, it works. This is absolutely delicious. The flavors blend so well, everything just melts in my mouth."

"Glad you like it Ana. I didn't know it was going to be such a sensual experience for you."

"There's a lot you don't know about me Nick." Nick couldn't leave that alone and as he tasted the onion soup, his mild imitation of Meg Ryan's fake orgasm while sharing a meal with Billy Crystal in "When Harry Meets Sally" brought a smile to Ana's lips.

"Touché," laughed Ana.

Nick and Ana thought that the stuffed ravioli would be a disappointment after the soup. They were both surprised and lingered over the last few bites. "I never thought about moving to Canada before this meal," said Ana.

"Maybe if this case goes large, we can have a branch office here," joked Nick.

They were a few minutes late for their two o'clock meeting at RCMP. It was a modern complex, lots of glass interspaced with structural steel. Manicured grounds and a conglomeration of large metal statues, thrusting from the earth by the walkways, greeted them as they walked towards the entrance. RCMP had moved in a few years earlier, taking over the property from a high tech company. Nick thought how different this modern sprawl was from the old RCMP building in Toronto where he had coordinated with Canada's lead federal law enforcement agency on a drug trafficking case in the nineties. He remembered going to the bar in the basement after the meeting and being served Irish whiskey by a Royal Mountie. Nick thought having a bar in a police building would be the ultimate morale booster for the rank and file. He imagined the outcry in the United States if a police agency had a bar in its station.

Constable Edwards led them to a conference room on the third floor. It could comfortably seat 30 people and had state of the art audio and video equipment at one end. Nick and Ana were introduced to Inspector Cedric Harding, Sergeant Major Jeft Rosen, Corporal Sophie Beret and Criminal Intelligence Specialist Francois Prueur. Nick couldn't help thinking to himself that none of the gentlemen looked anything like the Royal Mountie cartoon character, Dudley Do-Right, of his youth. Nick and Ana politely declined the offer of a veggie smoothie from the building's fitness center. After the usual small talk and Nick reminiscing about the bar in the old Toronto headquarters, they got down to business.

Inspector Harding said, "Sergeant Major Rosen will be overseeing the Canadian side of the operation and Corporal Beret will be in charge on the ground."

Nick replied, "Most of the agents for ground surveillance will be supplied by Homeland Security and Immigration and Customs Enforcement. We'll also have air support on call, weather permitting."

"Excellent, we we plan to have an Aslak 350 helo on tap. It'll be able to fly out of the airport at Cranbrook, British Columbia. It's only about 30 miles from the Yaak border crossing," said Sergeant Major Rosen. Rosen continued, "We looked over the reports and photographs you emailed us. We're pretty much up to speed."

Nick inquired about whether RCMP had any positive hits on the photographs taken by Drury and Zack of the two persons who came twice from the Canadian side of the border for the duffle bag exchanges. Criminal Intelligence Officer Prueur replied, "Yes, it was the same two men both times. Low level thugs who came up from the States five years ago. One has a brother in the Mexican Mafia. The brother is currently housed in your federal lock-up in San Diego, awaiting trial on drug charges."

Nick nodded his head, "Impressive, you seem to know a lot about 'guests' in our facilities."

"We, like you, have our ways. All the information about the two Vancouver residents is contained on this USB-drive," handing it to Nick.

"Thanks Francois, I'll trade you. Here are satellite photos of the border crossing to use as a reference to plan the surveillance operation. After 9-11, we can get just about anything on short notice." *About the only good thing to come out of 9-11,* Nick thought.

They pored over the satellite photos that filled the 10-foot by 15-foot screen. The photos showed the small logging road extending from either side of the border from the Yaak crossing. They discussed logistics: how many surveillance personnel on each side, where to place them, what vehicles to use and how to coordinate the two sides' operations. It was decided that HSI would supply both international teams with the same radios that operated outside the frequency range of commercially sold equipment. Their transmissions would be scrambled and secure. It was agreed that RCMP wouldn't use a helicopter for air support because it would be more apt to scare off the smugglers than one of the single wing Cessnas in RCMP's fleet. They were also very cognizant of the need to get the surveillance up and running quickly. It was already the week before Thanksgiving, and the first snows often came by Christmas.

They set ten days from the meeting, the first Thursday of December, for the initial surveillance. Thursdays were the days that the smugglers had met at the border in the past. On that Thursday morning, all of the surveillance teams would meet in Cranbrook, B.C., the closest airport to the border, for a briefing. Teams from both sides of the border would've already inspected their respective sides of the border for exact surveillance locations.

They worked straight through for six hours, just stopping to gobble down pizza and salad delivered by a local Italian restaurant. The pizza was a thin-crust margherita, garnished with fresh basil. Nick made the acute observation between bites, "Not bad, they could franchise this pizza joint. All they'd need is Peyton Manning to pitch it."

53

Ana replied, "Your ugly American persona is showing."

"Someday Ana you will learn the difference between slightly veiled sarcasm and a heartfelt observation."

Cedric smiled, "I have tasted your Papa J's. I will stick to the family run restaurant around the corner."

Finally, Nick said, "I give up, I'm exhausted. How about calling it a day?" Everyone agreed. The taxi got them back to their hotel just before nine.

"Not to sound like a cliche, but do you want to come to my room for a quick nightcap?" asked Ana. "They have a well-stocked bar in the room."

"Good idea. I knew I liked you for some reason." Sitting next to Ana on the couch, working on his second Jack Daniels, Nick couldn't help but notice how attractive Ana was. Her brown hair falling to her shoulders, her large hazel eyes set off by high cheekbones and soft, olive-colored skin. And to be fair, he was also aware of the way her silk blouse clung to her breasts. The top two buttons were unbuttoned and it was driving Nick crazy.

Ana turned to Nick, staring into his eyes, not saying anything. Nick whispered, "I thought women always had something to say."

"Only when the time is right. Is the time right Nick?"

Nick stammered, showing his nervousness, "I, uh, it could be, um, what, what do you think?" Nick felt like a total idiot. Talk about a suave response. A hick from the hills could do better than that. Ana unbuttoned the next button of her blouse, revealing her firm breasts. How she looked, was no longer just a product of Nick's imagination. Nick reached to caress her before pulling his hand back, saying in a low, emotion-filled voice, "You are so beautiful, I want you so badly. But I can't do this, at least not yet." He could see the hurt in her eyes.

"I understand Nick, we shouldn't mix business with pleasure."

"It's not that. It's just too soon with me and Judy. I better go. Thanks for everything tonight."

Lying in bed, thinking about what happened in Ana's room, Nick was kicking himself. Ana was gorgeous, had a great body, was funny and intelligent, and could take care of herself. His last conversation with Judy was when he told her two nights ago that he couldn't make it to the kids soccer games because of the Ottawa trip. She blew up. "I was beginning to think you were changing, placing family where it belonged, on top of the priority list. No way! It was just you trying to put on a good show for a few weeks, coming to their games, calling them. It's always work first!" Judy hung up mid-explanation about how important the new case was.

Ana woke up that morning thinking what a fool she had been. That type of move could be a career stopper. She got carried away, letting the attraction and a foreign weekend go to her head. On the other hand, what the hell? What is wrong with a little sex on an exotic weekend get-a-away? They were consenting adults. Nick had been separated from Judy for months. It wasn't like she was asking him to make some type of commitment. Ana spent her time getting ready, ruminating about the relative merits of her actions in her head. While she was packing her suitcase, she heard a knock on the door, followed by "Concierge, Madam". Ana opened the door to a grey haired, slight man, holding a single red rose and a note. "*Pour vous, Madamoiselle.* Your beauty puts the petals of this perfectly formed rose to shame."

Reddening, Ana replied, "*Merci.*" She thought why couldn't she meet someone like him in the states, about twenty years younger and a foot taller? She opened the card. *Thank you for the wondrous evening in your boudoir. Sometimes a man turns away from what he passionately desires. Nick.* Ana couldn't help feeling touched and warm. She thought, *He sure knows how to send mixed messages.*

CHAPTER EIGHT

"Who would believe we would be at this one-strip, Cranbrook airport at eight in the morning? That puddle jumper from Vancouver dropped us straight out of the sky. Any plane that only has one seat on each side of the aisle and propellers makes me nervous," said Pepe.

"You can relax now, we're here. The agents from the Spokane office will be by any minute to take us to meet the RCMP. The Spokane agents are the ones that had to get up by 4 a.m. to cross the border and drive over here."

"Jerry, you'll never hear me complain about overtime. Mas dinero, mas fun."

HSI Assistant Supervising Agent-in-Charge, Jeft Springer, and HSI agent, Jena Saunders, sat with Jerry and Pepe, across the table from RCMP Master Sergeant Rosen, Corporal Beret, and Constables Emilie Rousseau and Paul Roberts. They were in a nondescript, grey building that had two signs out front, *No solicitors* and *Bering Consultants*. Each RCMP employee had a card key and the password for the numeric pad to gain entrance.

ASAC Springer explained, "We've been setting up on our side of the Yaak border crossing for the last three days. In a line with the actual border, two agents will be behind camouflage blinds, 250 yards out. Each has a scope, with 70 times magnification, and an 800mm lens on a camera that brings up the subject by 25 times. Within 80 feet of the border exchange location, we have placed a highly sensitive, multi-directional mike, which looks like a pinecone. There are also hidden remote control video cameras, no larger than cigarette lighters. The video cameras feed the images to our electronics van a half mile away. We have seven, two person, vehicle surveillance teams. One is set up north of the lumber road entry on State Highway 92, in case they head northwest after the exchange. One each, south of Yaak, on the two access roads leading to State Highway 2. Two more vehicles are set up in opposite directions at the intersection at State Highway 2, where the two different roads from Yaak come in."

"Sounds like you have all access roads covered," said Rosen. "Any sense what route they'll take?"

"My best guess is they will go southwest from Yaak onto Highway 2, follow it west into Idaho where they will head straight south to Coeur d'Alene and on to Spokane. We believe the Baja Norte Familia cartel is a west coast operation and probably has stash houses in Seattle. How are you set up on the Canadian side?"

Rosen sipped his coffee and waited for Constable Roberts to put the Canadian map on the projection screen before answering. He cleared his throat and remarked, "Our side of the border isn't quite as complicated. We have five, two-person surveillance teams. Two at the location where the old lumber road intersects with Canadian 95, just a mile south of the Canadian town of Yahk. It's similar to your Yaak version, except where your Montana town features two saloons, our Yahk has a gas station and a community center. We're placing another vehicle southwest of Yahk, where Canadian 95 intersects with westbound Canadian Highway 3. Traveling north on Canadian 95 leads to Cranbrook, then on to the Trans-Canadian Highway. At that intersection, two more teams—one to cover eastbound to Calgary, the other westbound to Vancouver. Most of the drug trade in western Canada goes through Vancouver. We expect the Canadian smugglers to head in that direction. A control center for this operation has been set up at the community center in Yahk."

Springer said, "Does everyone on each international team have the HSI-issued satellite radios?"

Corporal Beret and HSI Saunders replied, "Yes". Corporal Beret added, "I understand that HSI gave us the radios. Thank you."

"All in the spirit of international cooperation. We appreciate how fast RCMP moved on this," said Springer.

Sgt. Rosen said, "I just want to make sure we're all on the same page about the strategic aspects of this joint investigation. On this first surveillance, we'll just let the suspects' vehicles, on either side of the border, drive to their respective destinations without any pretense traffic stops. Each side of the border will put together search warrants to allow the fixture of a GPS monitoring device on the undercarriage of each of the suspect's vehicles for 30 days. From information obtained on this evening's surveillance, we hope to affix the GPS devices during the second planned surveillance, a week from tonight. On the second surveillance, we again let the vehicles go through without stopping the vehicles, but will document all events. On the third surveillance, the U.S. side will arrange a traffic stop before the suspects reach the border exchange point. You will bring in a drug-sniffing dog, the dog alerts and you seize the drugs. The Canadian side monitors the Canadian suspects who will be going home without their weekly drug supply. Both sides will evaluate the case at that time and make further surveillance and seizure decisions."

"Exactly right," boomed Springer. "We are looking at this case for the long term. We want to establish as many connections on both sides of the border without scaring the cartel off. When the time is right, both sides will execute simultaneous search and arrest warrants to take everyone down and seize all the assets and drugs. We all know how important it is for the crooks to not make the surveillance. I even had HSI dig up a few old pickup trucks so we could fit in up here."

Corporal Beret smiled, "I hope the pickup trucks have gun racks to meld in with your authentic western frontier. For us, we have a mixture of Priuses and old Fords, fits the Canadian gestalt better."

"Well, I'll leave you Canadians to your aperitifs and Cuban cigars. We Americans like to suck down an Old Milwaukee brew and work on a wad of chew," replied Springer with a sardonic grin.

"What do you think Sergeant Major, both sides set up on the border by 3:30 p.m.?" asked Springer.

"Fine by us, the sun sets at 5:02 tonight. It should give us plenty of time before the smugglers show. Don't they always go to the border for the exchange at dusk?"

"Yes," replied Jerry and Pepe together.

"We will be on channel 12 and have a radio check-in at 3:30. Talk to you then," Springer said as he stood up and shook hands with Sergeant Major Rosen and the rest of the Canadian team.

At 5:30, the Yaak surveillance team closest to the turn off onto the lumber road reported that a Dodge Ram pickup, towing a Ranger off-road vehicle, had just pulled into a side clearing by the lumber road access. A young white male backed the Ranger down wooden boards from the trailer to the side of the road while the Hispanic unloaded two bags from the back of the cab and put them into the Ranger.

Ten minutes later, teams from both sides of the border heard single vehicles coming towards them. In their respective command posts, ASAC Springer and Sergeant Major Rosen were getting direct audio and video feeds on the four suspects at the border. The two Canadian-based men carried one duffle bag between them while the American suspects each had a duffle. The white male handed his bag over, saying, "Hey partner, sweet Mary Jane, all buds, along with south of the border brown sugar."

One of the Canadians replied, "Hey, Gringo, I'm not your partner and this isn't for a frat party, college boy."

"Hey, relax, be cool, just a little chatter."

"Chatter gets you in trouble." Without another word said, the bags were exchanged and the two groups walked back to their vehicles.

The surveillance team south of Yaak, on the road that led southwest, reported they had picked up the Ram truck and were following it about 200 yards back. There was no traffic and no reason to risk following more closely. Pepe swore to himself when he heard this, no action for him and Jerry tonight. It seemed like the perps were heading towards Spokane and then probably on to Seattle as expected. Jerry and Pepe had drawn the surveillance southeast at Libby, on State Highway 2. One half hour later, Jerry's and Pepe's luck turned. Surveillance team #4 reported that the truck had taken a left on to eastbound 2 towards Libby, 28 miles away. Pepe poked Jerry in the ribs, "Get ready, hot shot, they're coming our way."

"You spilled my coffee. Settle that Latin fire down Pepe."

Fifteen minutes later an excited call came over the radio from team #4, "They just took a right onto a small paved road. A sign says

Noxon. I'm afraid to continue surveillance because I had to stay fairly close to the truck through a series of curves just a few miles back. Please tell me what you want me to do!"

Springer instantly answered, "Stay put, I'm checking options." After what seemed to be an indeterminable wait, but was only about 20 seconds, Springer came back on. "Terminate surveillance #4. Jerry and Pepe, get your asses moving, head southeast on Highway 2 for 30 miles to a sharp left curve in the road. At that curve, take a right onto a gravel National Forest road which runs directly south for 20 miles and then intersects with Highway 200, just above the town of Trout Creek. We think the suspects may go to the intersection of Highway 200 and turn left on 200 to go east towards Trout Creek. Highway 200 eventually leads to Missoula, where the University of Montana is located. This fits with the college boy crack made by one of the Canadians. The gravel road is windy and goes over a 5,000 foot pass. Have either of you driven gravel mountain roads?"

"You bet boss. I've been driving up and down a 25-mile long, windy mountain road to Mineral King, east of Visalia, for ten years on camping vacations. Couldn't afford to take the kids to Hawaii," said Jerry.

"Stop bitchin' about your pay grade, just go. By the way, the local sheriff says the only traffic you'll see on the road are four-legged friends. Be careful, I don't like road kill venison," said Springer.

Pepe said, "I agree with you on the venison, but a moose steak isn't too bad."

"Be careful what you wish for agent," retorted Springer, clicking off.

Springer spoke to his air support at the small airport serving the resort town of Sandpoint, Idaho. The feedback wasn't good. It was dark and a plane flying back and forth at night over a small paved road would be suspicious, no matter how thick-headed the perps are. Springer told the Sandpoint aerial support team to stand down.

Jerry was scaring the shit out of Pepe. The U.S. Forest road was only a lane and one-half wide. It followed a river ravine on one side, with a steep drop-off. The road was deeply rutted and had its fair share of potholes. Jerry, except on the sharpest corners, was driving the V-6 Toyota Tacoma at 50 mph, at least double the safe speed for the road conditions at night. Somehow, they got to the top of the pass without spinning out to their death. Pepe breathed a sign of relief, thinking, *We may get through this.*

Jerry broke his revelry, "Now for the tough part, going downhill on gravel. There's always a chance a vehicle's tires will lose traction and just slide off the road on a curve."

"Thanks Jerry. That's making me feel a lot better." Halfway down the pass, Jerry misjudged the sharpness of a curve and Pepe felt the tires slip into a four wheel slide. Jerry was lightly applying the brakes and turning into the skid. Luckily the outside of the curve didn't end in a 1,000 foot drop to the river below, but instead ended in a carved out cliff, rapidly approaching. The brakes finally gripped and the Tacoma slowed and rammed into the side of the cliff at 10 mph.

The truck bounced back into the middle of the road and Jerry stepped on the accelerator, laughing and yelling, "Just like bumper cars, heh Pepe!" Pepe didn't say anything for a long moment, then screamed at Jerry, "You crazy son-of-a-bitch, slow down! This job isn't worth it."

"Fine, I'll take it down a notch."

Pepe finally unclenched his fists when the road straightened out on the floor of the valley.

Pepe could barely make out the marshy grassland on his right when he screamed, "Look out for the elephant!"

"It's a big bull moose, just out for his evening graze. You're the one who said he liked moose steaks."

Pepe swore, "I'm going vegan. Except maybe carne asada, now and again, on family occasions."

They pulled up on a side road outside Trout Creek and called in to Springer. "We're in position outside of Trout Creek."

"If you have beaten the perps to Trout Creek, filet mignon dinners for you, on me."

Jerry responded, "Just buy the two steaks for me, Pepe has just sworn off meat." Two minutes later, Jerry called in again and told Springer, "You owe me two steak dinners."

The perps' pickup was driving along at the speed limit, heading southeast on Highway 200 towards Missoula. Jerry let a car pass between him and the perps before he pulled out to follow. An hour into the surveillance, the perps turned into Mountain Burger, located in the one-block-town of Dixon. The neon sign advertised buffalo burgers and huckleberry milk shakes.

Pepe's stomach was growling. He bitched, "Here we are with a stale bag of potato chips, while the scumbags are munching on juicy burgers and fries, all washed down with huckleberry shakes. And they say crime doesn't pay."

"Stop whining Pepe. I'm sure we can dig up a Mexican restaurant for you in Missoula after we put the perps to bed."

From the food stop, it was only another 45 minutes before the pickup truck left the main east-west interstate, Highway 90, at the University of Montana exit in Missoula. Jerry followed them down several tree-lined residential streets near the University to a large brick house with an unkempt front yard. The perps pulled up in front, taking the duffle bag inside. Jerry and Pepe documented the address and physical description of the residence for a future search warrant. They reported into Springer and were told to get some sleep and to be back at the residence at seven in the morning to renew surveillance. By 10:00 a.m., Springer would arrange for another surveillance team to relieve them.

At seven o'clock sharp the next morning, Pepe and Jerry were sitting on the residence, munching on Egg McMuffins and hash browns. Jerry wondered aloud, "With all this fine dining we enjoy on surveillances, can I get workman's compensation for my anticipated clogged arteries heart attack?" ASAC Springer's call put an end to the fruitless conversation. He briefed them about the Canadian surveillance. The Canadian suspects had traveled north on Highway 95 to the TransCanadian Highway and then on to Vancouver. They dropped the two duffle bags at a small warehouse, which had a sign near the door, *World Food Imports*. The suspects were then followed to an apartment complex in North Vancouver.

At 9:15, the same two U.S. perps exited the brick house, the white guy with a book under his arm, walking towards campus, while the Hispanic, with a duffle bag, got into the pickup.

He drove to eastern Missoula and pulled into an industrial complex. There, the Hispanic parked behind a warehouse, which had a sign in front, *World Food Imports*. Fifteen minutes later the pickup came from around the back, minus the trailer with the off-road Ranger. Jerry called for a team to check out the warehouse and followed the suspect back to the brick house. At the house, Jerry and Pepe were relieved, a new surveillance team took over.

Pepe and Jerry took the next flight out to Salt Lake City. They flew into Lindbergh Field as the sun was setting over the ocean. Pepe commented, "It's nice to be at sea level with no windy, gravel mountain roads in sight."

CHAPTER NINE

I t was the Tuesday after the first successful joint surveillance of La Familia at the Canadian border with RCMP. Nick assembled his team in the conference room. The room looked almost as tired as the people in it. There were scattered files, laptop computers, an empty pizza box, as well as a half dozen, brown-stained coffee cups. The team had been working 16-hour days since the joint surveillance, gathering information and writing up a search warrant to authorize GPS trackers on the target vehicles. Their RCMP counterparts were equally spent, and also putting a case together to obtain an authorization to place a GPS tracker on the Canadian vehicle.

Nick thanked everyone for the extra hours and hard work. Nick looked at Ana and asked, "Where are we with tying Familia's drug smuggling operation into Canada with the two money laundering operations, Morales and the Sakias?"

"San Diego-based accountant Lester Sendow, who was at Yaak for the original drug distribution, may be involved in both money laundering operations. He's the agent for service of process for Morales' front companies, L&M Freight and Recycle Yard, and is the accountant who prepared the individual and corporate returns for the Sakias. Last week, IRS sent over Sakia-related tax returns for the past five years."

San Diego Detective Cipriani said, "The Sakia tax returns also list a Subchapter S corporation, *World Food Imports*, which was the name on the Missoula and Vancouver warehouses as well as the Tijuana warehouse where Pepe was kidnapped. We have an expert lined up who has 30 years of experience importing food from Mexico and Latin America for distribution in the United States and Canada. He's reviewing the Sakia tax returns and other documents pertaining to their import businesses, Latin America Productos, and World Food Imports."

Ana added, "We're confident we can establish these are front businesses that can't begin to support the millions of dollars each month they are bringing into California from Mexico."

AUSA Josh Sterling said, "Visitor logs for the Canadian suspect's brother in San Diego lock-up show three visits in September with Sergio Bustamente, a Familia enforcer, who was also with Lopez and Sendow delivering drugs in Yaak."

Nick added, "Follow up with the prison to get copies of the tape recordings of those meetings."

"Already requested."

"Pepe, do you have any more on the Familia's drug operation?"

"Sure do Nick. The cartel is mainly dealing in Mexican black tar heroin and a finer grade of marijuana than what usually comes across the border. First the marijuana. The Familia is getting greenhouse grown marijuana from the state of Sinaloa. According to my contacts with DEA, the growers are using grow lamps to improve their productivity and quality. The Familia is trying to carve out a market niche between the standard Mexican commercial grow, aptly called Mexican 'crud', that goes for around $500 a pound, and our domestic and Canadian grown marijuana, the high tech 'prima bud', which can sell for as much as $5,000 a pound. The Familia is undercutting the domestic high tech grow with their own high quality version. Informants say they're selling it wholesale for around $2,500 a pound."

Nick said, "It's like Walmart coming in and undercutting the local retail stores."

Pepe replied, "Nick, I know you do most of your shopping at Walmart and Target, but it's more like Nordstrom coming in and undercutting boutique clothing stores." Pepe continued, "The real profit for Familia is in the tar heroin. The poppies grow well in the coastal mountains of Sinaloa. Over the last few years the black tar trade has really taken off along with a major increase in heroin overdoses suffered by teenagers and people in their twenties because they turned to black tar heroin as a cheaper alternative to opioid-based painkillers. The kids start by lifting a pill here and there from their parents' prescription bottles. Then they start buying pills on the black market. It's about $80 a pop for OxyContin. That gets way too expensive, so many try heroin where you can get high for as little as $10. Add these market forces to the fact that they reconfigured OxyContin a couple of years ago to make it more difficult to inject and snort. The combined effect—a heroin epidemic among our youth."

Ana said, "This is very serious, over 8,000 fatal heroin overdoses last year, almost triple the number a few years ago. Many law enforcement agencies rank heroin right up there with methamphetamine as the greatest drug threat currently facing Americans. With the increased supply of heroin coming from Mexico, other Latin American countries, and Southeast Asia, the purity is up when it hits the street, even after being cut with lactose, flour, or whatever. This increases the risk of overdoses, especially among users just out of rehab, who relapse. Their bodies can't tolerate the higher doses they were taking before rehab."

Nick replied, "I get it Ana. Even more reason to bust these *sons-of-bitches*. How much is the Familia selling a kilo of tar for, Pepe?"

"Between $20,000 to $30,000, depending on the supply route used, and how far the cartel has to transport the product in the States before distribution."

Nick said, "You can't get much farther 'in country' than Yaak, Montana."

"Mario and Josh, I want you to work off of the tracker warrant and see if you can get a federal wire tap on the accountant and the college boy drug mule, Jim Mitchell. I want the taps up on their phones before we seize the drugs on a vehicle stop, a week from Thursday. 18 U.S.C. section 2516 allows a wiretap based on drug sales and federal money laundering. I know there are a lot of hoops to jump through to secure a judicial order, but it'll be worth it. We can use California DOJ's wire room to monitor the calls."

"Nick, you're really infringing on my social life."

"A few long hours won't hurt you Josh. You'll bounce back with your lady friends. Remember, when one is away, the heart grows fonder."

Jerry said, "Biker Sue in Yaak talked about Lopez and the accountant driving a tricked-out black Escalade with tinted windows. A black Escalade matching that description was found parked behind the Missoula warehouse. Agents from Spokane tracked down Biker Sue and showed her photos of the Escalade. She told me it looked like the same car."

Nick said, "I bet there can't be more than one tricked out black Escalade in Montana."

"We don't even need to rely on your off-the-cuff opinion on Montanans car purchasing habits. The Escalade is in the name of L&M Freight, one of the companies owned by suspected money launderer Hector Morales," said Pepe.

"How would I look driving around in a tricked-out Escalade, smoking a cigar, after we seize it?"

"Nick, you've already turned into an out-of-shape, old white guy. I suggest that if we seize a bicycle in this case, you ride that."

"Pepe you're only saying that because you want the Escalade so you can put hydraulic lifts in, and bounce up and down as you drive it to a *fiesta de quinceanera*."

Ana broke in, "Now boys, let's stay focused."

"Ana is right. By the way, Josh and Mario, how are the search warrants progressing for placing the trackers on the target vehicles?"

Josh responded, "Great, we have a draft and have sufficient cause for five vehicles—the Escalade, the pickup truck surveilled from Yaak to Missoula, the Corvette and Range Rover in the driveway of the Missoula house, and accountant Sendow's car, a BMW 633i convertible. I can get them signed by a judge tomorrow morning."

"Excellent," replied Nick, "That will give us time to get the trackers placed for Thursday's border surveillance. Jerry and Pepe, I want you to go back to Montana for the surveillance and placement of the trackers on the vehicles. Let the surveillance team watching college boy's house put the trackers on the Corvette and Range Rover. I want you to put it on the pickup and Escalade personally."

"Okay, Boss Man. We'll take a flight out to Missoula tomorrow afternoon," said Jerry.

On the flight from Salt Lake City to Missoula, Jerry and Pepe decided they would go by the Missoula warehouse early in the morning and hope the Escalade was still parked in back. They had no trouble placing the tracker in the center of the undercarriage of the Escalade at about 6:00 a.m. Nobody was around, no guard dogs, and no surveillance cameras.

They argued about how best to place the tracker on the perps' pickup truck in a safe and timely manner. They figured young male drug dealers were always hungry and creatures of habit. They gambled on the perps stopping at Mountain Burgers again in Dixon on the way to Yaak. In any event, Jerry wanted to try a buffalo burger and Pepe was eager for a taste of a huckleberry shake.

They arrived at Mountain Burger just before noon to taste the local fare and wait for the pickup to appear. They parked at the side of the parking lot beside a beat up old truck with a flat tire that blocked them from casual observation. However, they still had a good sight line into the burger restaurant and to the main parking stalls in front. Sleet began to fall. "Oh, shit!" said Jerry and Pepe together. They knew what that meant. Crawling under a truck, with sleet, mud, and whatever else, was no picnic. Neither wanted to do the honors. They resolved the conflict in the civilized manner in which they always resolved their conflicts—rock, paper, scissors—sudden death. Each had a distinct strategy. Paper came to Jerry's mind, maybe he was thinking it could give him some protection from the sleet. Pepe figured that Jerry was due to pick scissors because he had only done so twice out of the last ten times. When Pepe flipped a closed fist for rock on the count of three, he was astounded, Jerry's paper hand enclosed his fist like a glove. Jerry said, "I have told you not to overthink things with that calculator brain of yours. Just go with the flow." "I'll be going with the flow alright, I'll be immersed in sleet, mud and water."

The perps didn't disappoint. The same two from last week parked the pickup in one of the front stalls. They ran through the sleet to enter the restaurant. They watched the perps at the counter, ordering food. Jerry nudged Pepe, "Show time." Pepe hopped out of their vehicle, walked towards the perps' truck, and pretended to stumble, dropping his wallet under the truck.

Pepe was under the perps' truck, beginning to place the tracker device when Jerry spoke in his earpiece, "Lay perfectly still, the white guy has exited the restaurant and is heading for the truck." Pepe laid perfectly still, face down, breathing in mud.

After about 20 seconds, hearing nothing, Pepe whispered, "Jerry, what's going on? I don't hear anything."

"Oh, false alarm, it wasn't the perp after all."

"You son-of-a-bitch Jerry, I promise you'll get yours."

"Lighten up Pepe. Put on the tracker and let's get out of here." Pepe was fuming all the way to the local gas station where he changed out of his clothes.

The next morning, Jerry and Pepe received a telephone briefing from ASAC Springer letting them know that the drug transaction went down just as it had the week before, two duffels from the Montana side for one duffle from the Canadian side. All the same players and everything was on video and audio. The audio picked up a gem. Once again, it was the big mouth college kid. He said, "Can you handle 50 kilos of tar? I've been lugging a bag half that weight for over a month. Another 25 kilo bag would balance me on my border stroll."

One of the Canadians responded, "Shut the fuck up. That's not for us to decide."

"Cool your jets, just a little Yankee initiative."

Jerry called in to Nick. Nick said, "Write your reports on the plane ride back to San Diego, have a good weekend and get your asses in here at 8:00 a.m. sharp on Monday morning so we can plan how to seize the drugs on a traffic stop this coming Thursday. Also,

Jerry, it was funnier than hell to have Pepe swallowing mud on a false alarm while placing the tracker, but it wasn't a good idea to compromise the mission for even 30 seconds for a good laugh."

"Hey, how did you find out about that?"

"Just remember, Uncle Nick knows all."

CHAPTER TEN

S tarting just before eight on Monday morning, the team began to filter into the conference room. The ones with a semblance of taste, Ana and Mario, were gripping their Starbuck lattes, while the more marginal types, Nick, Pepe, and Jerry, were drinking the house brew from dirty coffee cups. The new age refined one, Josh, was sipping on some exotic tea blend. Rona was also present to keep everyone focused and let them know about the document protocol.

Nick, with a fire up the troops exuberance, said, "All is going great. We're ready to take down some drugs. We need to go over how we're going to execute the vehicle stop on college boy Mitchell when he's on route to the next delivery on Thursday."

Josh said, "I've been looking at the vehicle stop, detention cases. I know the overall plan is to stop the pickup on a traffic violation and then have a drug sniffing canine circle the truck to alert on the drugs inside. We have to be careful how we do it to avoid running afoul of the Fourth Amendment. We have the violation lined up—past surveillances of the pickup show that the right rear brake light is out. We can get the Montana Highway Patrol to pull the pickup over as soon as they get on Interstate 90, outside of Missoula. Working in tandem with the Highway Patrol, will be a separate canine unit."

"Why the two car protocol?" asked Ana.

"We want to make the stop without revealing in the reports the background information we have on their drug distribution network. We don't want to scare the cartel off. The fact that we are really stopping the pickup because we know drugs are in there—making a "pretense" stop based on a traffic violation, is fine with the Fourth

Amendment because it's objectively reasonable for law enforcement to make a traffic stop, irrespective of their true subjective intent for stopping the vehicle. It's set out in the 1996 U.S. Supreme Court case, *Whren v. United States.*"

"Okay law school professor, enough with the case law," said Jerry.

"Let Josh finish, this is important. Josh and I will be fighting all their suppression motions in court. We need to get this right," said Nick.

"So the stop isn't a problem. Where it gets tricky is bringing in a drug sniffing dog for a routine traffic stop. There's a case before the U.S. Supreme Court, out of the Eighth Circuit, that challenges the admissibility of drugs found in a car where the driver was detained for an extra eight minutes after the traffic violation was written for a canine to perform a drug sniff around the car. The driver contends it was unreasonable under the Fourth Amendment to extend the traffic stop beyond the time it took to write the citation. That's why it's imperative that the canine unit pull up right after the stop in order for the dog to circle the pickup to make a positive alert for drugs while the traffic officer is still writing a ticket and checking I.D. The United States Supreme Court in *Illinois v. Caballos* upheld a positive alert which occurred simultaneously with the traffic stop."

"Excellent Josh. Also, make sure we arrange for a top of the line drug sniffing dog. We want impeccable credentials as to its training and field performance. The defense at trial will be attacking everything, even Fido. It's also a good idea to pull over the pickup when it gets on the Interstate. This can add some cause for the belief that drugs are in the truck because interstate freeways are known to be drug transportation corridors. Additionally, the fact that the registration of the truck is in the name of L&M Freight out of Imperial County, and not in college boy's name, will add to the probable cause," said Nick.

"The title to the truck to Hector Morales' money laundering business is a real sweet tie in," said Mario.

By the way Mario, have we run dogs by the cash deposited by the Morales or the Sakia organizations?" asked Nick.

"Sure have. Over the last two weeks, agents have monitored the segregation of three separate cash deposits into three Morales accounts in three separate banks along the border. Each time the cash was hidden among other cash in the vault. Jack, a shepherd, who was only trained on alerts to controlled substance stashes, not on currency, alerted each time."

"Why does it matter that Jack wasn't trained on currency?" asked Ana.

"Where a dog is trained on currency, he'll hit on currency that has minute amounts of drug residue on it. In certain areas of the country, like Los Angeles, well over one-half of the currency in circulation has some residue on it. So, the argument is that a dog alert on currency doesn't mean anything because most of the currency has drug residue. Where a dog is trained just on narcotic stashes, he'll only hit on currency where the controlled substance has come in recent contact with the currency."

Mario continued, "We did the same thing at three separate border banks with the currency deposited by the Sakia couriers. Same results, same dog."

"Mario, you're on a roll. How is the wiretap application going?" asked Nick.

"We'll have the order by Thursday for the accountant's cellphone and landline phone and college boy Mitchell's landline. We aren't even bothering with Mitchell's cell because that will be seized at the time of the bust. Mitchell's indiscreet comment at the last delivery, about lugging a 25 kilo bag of tar heroin to the Canadian border for the last month, really helped."

"I want you and Josh to catch a flight out on Wednesday to oversee the take down operation in Missoula."

"Before I let you go, the most important member of our team, Rona, has something to say."

"Thanks Nick. We're gearing up. We're generating a lot of paperwork and there'll be much more to come. Everything goes to me first. Once we scan the documents into the computer, our Bates stamp program will number each page of each document electronically. I keep the originals, and index the same for easy access. You can

73

work off the copies that I'll provide. That way nothing slips through the cracks and every page will be accounted for when we turn discovery over to the defense. If you have any questions, or just want to pick up some candy corn, come on by my office."

Nick added, "I just started working on my annotated exhibit list. I'll refine it for use at trial or any pre-trial hearing. As I go through the documents and other evidence, I'll list the tentative exhibits in categories and give each category a group of numbers, like records from a particular bank will be pre-marked one to twenty. The first line of the description for each exhibit will later be used for the exhibit list for court and the defense. In my annotated list, I'll continue to describe the important aspects of the exhibit and how it may relate to other exhibits. This expanded description, of course, isn't given to the court or the defense. It acts like my short hand "Bible" at trial. Rona will make copies for you."

Josh had some time to kill on Wednesday night. He was sitting on his bed at the Holiday Inn watching Sports Center, and thinking there had to be something better to do on his first ever evening in Montana. He heard that Missoula was a town of micro-breweries. Checking on his laptop, he found Kettle House Brewery nearby, close to the University of Montana campus. It featured Bongwater Hemp Ale and Double Haul I.P.A. The name of the beers fit the theme of the trip. It was meant to be.

Josh walked through the brewery door around 8:00, hoping he wasn't too early for the local beer drinking crowd. He wasn't. The brewery was jammed. He found an empty seat next to an ever so sweet looking cowgirl, sporting jeans, cowboy boots and a plaid shirt. Her clothes and her auburn hair, pulled back in a ponytail, couldn't mask her beauty. Josh said to her, "I didn't expect this place to be so crowded at this time on a Wednesday night."

She looked him up and down before answering with a smirk on her face, "City slicker you'd better drink up. This drinking establishment closes at nine. We get up early around these parts. We have things to do."

Josh looked down at what he was wearing, suede loafers, pleated slacks, and a light jacket over a polo shirt, and responded, "You're right. My outfit doesn't fit in, but my pickup truck with a gun rack is parked in back."

"I bet you don't even own a gun, let alone know how to shoot one."

"You got me there beautiful blue eyes, but I was a terror in water gun fights in my youth. As for my pickup, it morphs into a Ford Escort rental car at closing time."

She laughed with a smile that draws you all the way in. "What are you doing here?"

"I work for the U.S. Attorney's Office in San Diego and I'm going to be here for awhile on a case."

"Is it criminal or civil? I'm curious. I'm getting my masters in criminal justice at the University."

"Welcome to the club. It's a criminal investigation."

"Can you tell me about it?"

"Maybe... after a few beers. No, really, I can't, even if you ply me with alcohol. But it does involve a student at your school."

"Come on, I'm part of the law enforcement fraternity. My dad was the captain of a small police force for a town called St. Ignatius. It's only 30 miles north of here, east of Dixon."

Dixon sounded familiar to Josh. He thought about it. It was the town that the crooks had stopped for a burger on route to the drug deal. "What was it like growing up in a small town?"

"St. Ignatius wasn't your typical small town. It's on the Flathead Indian Reservation. Three groups share the town, the Indians, an Amish settlement, and other Montanans. The Amish drive their horse-drawn carriages to the stores. The entire Amish community turns out for barn or house building. They sometimes get a structure up in a few days. I grew up with the rodeo crowd. No barrel riding for me, I roped calves."

Josh grinned, "Remind me never to ask you to tie me up." "Fat chance greenhorn."

For the next hour they swapped stories. Josh felt a connection between them. He said, "I don't even know your name."

"It's Juliet."

"I'm Josh, but you can call me Romeo."

Juliet said, "What a tired joke. Never heard that one before and I was just beginning to like you."

Josh, pretending chagrin, said, "That's what all the beautiful ladies tell me. You're going to have to excuse me while I polish up on my joke repertoire. Here's my card if you ever want to give me a second chance."

"I believe in second chances. It's your lucky night. I'm writing down my cell. Don't abuse it. If you ever need any help on your hush-hush investigation, like talking to the student, let me know. I could use some real life experience for my masters."

"You don't know what you might be letting yourself in for. It's a rough crowd."

"I can take care of myself. I'm a calf roper remember. I grew up around a rough crowd. Hunted with them. Drank with them. And cussed with them."

"Fair enough," said Josh, "I know I never want to make you mad."

"I will hold you to that Romeo, see you around." Josh had the privilege of watching her gently sway back and forth as she walked out of the bar.

At 10 the next morning, Josh and Mario were at the command post with ASAC Springer and other law enforcement. Josh and Mario briefed the interdiction team—not giving them any background on the case, except that the occupants could be armed and dangerous and might be transporting contraband. The traffic stop vehicle would have a two man team as would the canine vehicle. There'd also be two back-up vehicles, following the two primary vehicles. They were to take every safety precaution and pat down the occupants for weapons when they exited the vehicle for the canine sniff.

Josh and Mario monitored the surveillance and traffic stop from the command center. Mitchell and Jorge Ramos left the brick house at 1:30 p.m. in the same pickup truck they had used in prior deliveries. They went down Orange Avenue to the Interstate 90 entrance ramp. The Montana Highway Patrol car picked them up once they entered the freeway, waiting for braking to show the faulty rear light. Before the Highway 93 exit that led to Dixon, the pickup had to brake for a car that cut in front of them. The pickup was red lighted by the Highway Patrol, and pulled over on the shoulder. The officer informed Mitchell of the brake light violation which seemed to ease quite a bit of tension among the occupants. As the officer was asking them about the title to the car being in the name of L&M Freight out of Imperial County, California, the canine unit pulled up with German Shepherd, "Klink", and two officers. Mitchell and Ramos were informed they had to exit the car while Klink circled it. Mitchell and Ramos looking anxious. Mitchell said, "You've no right to do this."

"That's for the lawyers and a judge to decide," replied the ticket writing officer. Mitchell and Ramos were patted down for weapons. Ramos had a 22 caliber handgun in his coat pocket. Klink alerted to the compartment in back of the cab where there were two large duffle bags. At this point, Mitchell and Ramos were cuffed and put in the back of the patrol car.

Inside one duffel were multiple, vacuum sealed packages of marijuana buds. The other bag contained larger size, vacuum sealed bags of a black, tar-like substance.

A back-up team was called to transport the contraband to the state police evidence room. Another team waited for a truck to tow the pickup to the police yard for a complete inventory of the truck's contents. It was all over by 2:30.

Josh and Jerry flew out a couple of hours later. They landed at Lindbergh Field, dead tired, but looking forward to the early morning team meeting.

Nick opened the team meeting on a congratulatory note, "Well done. It went like clockwork. I just got a call from ASAC Springer. One duffel contained 60, one pound bags of high quality marijuana buds, while the other duffel had 25 kilos of black tar heroin. Value of the buds about $150,000 and roughly $750,000 for the tar."

"The cartel should feel that a bit," said Pepe. "We're up on the accountant's phones and hopefully we'll record some 'fall out' chatter about the bust."

CHAPTER ELEVEN

The Familia investigation was going well after the drug bust two weeks before. The team had reason to celebrate the year's accomplishments. However, Josh wasn't interested in staying too long at their end of the year team party at Days End. Only the best for their task force. Cheap draft beer and Nick was springing for h'ors d'oeuvres. Nothing like buffalo wings and poppers, washed down by a pitcher of Milwaukee's finest. Josh was eager to move on to his date with a hot court reporter from the federal district court. He had met her at a recent motion on another case. Josh had arrived at the courtroom early and was greeted with a big smile from Dawn. They chatted for a few minutes and met for coffee later. It turned out that they were both country western fans. For their first date, they were going to see Ramblin On at a small venue in Hillcrest. After that, Josh was hoping to get lucky.

Josh was thinking about how the evening would go with Dawn, when his reverie was abruptly interrupted by Nick's booming voice, "I'm not satisfied about how far along we are on the Baja Norte Familia case. The bad guys have resumed the drug distribution, although they now seem to be keeping the drugs at the warehouse in Missoula, instead of college boy's house. College boy has been sprung from jail by a pricey San Diego drug defense lawyer. He's on bail. We need more evidence tying the upper echelon of the Familia to the overall drug-money laundering operation. We also need to know more about how they move the drugs across the border into California."

"On the plus side, the document part of the case is going well. We have boxes of records from the border banks and our forensic accountant is putting together transaction spread sheets."

Ana replied, "Nick, I thought this was a work free conversation zone. The idea was to relax, down a few beers, and look forward to the New Year."

"You're right. It's just that I'm frustrated and impatient. I want this case to move along as fast as possible."

"I hope you don't have that same philosophy in bed," said Ana, smiling.

Pepe remarked, "Boss, either you're blushing, or you just went under a tanning lamp to redden your pasty skin."

"Enough out of you wise ass. Pour me another beer."

Josh suggested, "Let's take our mind off Nick's sudden color change by playing a game of beer pong."

Mario said, "You got me and Jerry to play last time, never again."

"Ditto that!" exclaimed Jerry.

Ana said, "I don't know what is worse, the thought of playing beer pong again, or listening to a Rush Limbaugh inspired phrase, 'Mr. Dittohead.'" Jerry replied, "Get off Rush's back. He has a big influence on Republican candidates."

Ana, with a satisfied smirk, "I rest my case."

Nick intervened, "If I can't talk shop, you can't talk politics. As for gamer Josh, one drinking game. Anybody with *huevos*, girl included, will fill up their pint glasses for a winner takes all chugging contest. Just one time, and no sloppy spills of suds down the chin."

"Because I don't have *huevos*, and never wanted them, I'll referee for you boys," said Ana, filling up each of their mugs to the top. She added, "On my count to three, go at it, and once drained, slam the mug back on the table, without breaking the mug."

On the count of three, Josh was the first to get the mug to his lips. More beer seemed to be pouring down Jerry's face than his gullet. Josh was slowing as he reached the halfway mark. Pepe, Mario, and Nick were neck and neck. Nick then stretched out his neck, tilted his head further back and vacuumed the last eight ounces down. He slammed the mug down just before Mario, not spilling a drop. Nick let out a throaty roar, "Yeah, the old dog still has it. How does it feel to get whupped? It's like riding a bike, you never forget how to chug. I was unbeaten in the fraternity circle at U.C. Davis."

Ana looked at Nick askance and said, "That's incredibly impressive. Some people can talk about academic achievement or excelling in college sports, or making a significant positive impact on the college community. But who ever heard a grown man bragging that he was a frat boy, beer chugging champ?"

"Okay, Ms. Politically Correct. I get it."

Josh said, "No matter what Ana says, I'm impressed. You beat me fair and square. I'm going home to lick my wounds."

Pepe said, "You may want your wounds licked, but only by the court reporter you're taking out tonight. Good luck with that. *Adios amigo.*"

"Later guys," called out Josh as he walked towards the door.

Jerry said, "I guess I have to bail too. I have to give my eldest boy the standard speech, to not drink or do anything stupid on his date tonight. I hope he keeps listening to me. He's only 16, but is bigger and stronger than me."

Mario replied, "You don't have to worry about that. You can still kick his ass—just fight dirty."

"Thanks Mario for the words of encouragement, but I wasn't thinking along those lines. Your kids are only five and seven. You're still in that non-worry, bliss stage, where everything you say to them is golden."

"You're right partner. I'll walk you out."

Pepe said, "Wait up guys, I have to get going too. To think I fought to stay alive in Tijuana for this year-end party. Nick, I thought you would have least upped your game to pitchers of Dos Equis in my honor."

Nick smiled at Pepe. "Old Milwaukee is a tradition. Just one of the fine traditions of this task force. However, I can't tell you happy I am that you are here."

"Okay Boss, don't get sentimental on me.

Nick turned to Ana. "Well the beer chugging certainly cleared the room. I'm glad you didn't take part or I'd be by myself. How about upgrading our drinking establishments? I know a nice restaurant in Del Mar, with a view of ocean that serves food at the bar."

"I was wondering when you would ask."

"I'll meet you there. The restaurant is called Jake's, off of 15th Street."

"I know it Nick. I live in Solana Beach."

"Fancy digs for a government employee."

"No, just a one bedroom condo. But it does overlook Fletcher's Cove."

"Wow! You and your cat are living the good life. Where did I go wrong?"

"Probably stems from your childhood Nick. Too late to do anything about it."

"I'll mull over your sage observation while I'm waiting for you at Jake's, sipping on a rum and tonic."

Twenty minutes later, Nick, out of breath, with sweat dripping down his face, saw Ana, cool as the far side of a pillow, sipping on a gimlet. "How did you beat me to my one and only upscale drinking establishment?"

"Two things Nick—I drive a Porsche and you're too cheap to pay for valet parking."

"Hey, they wanted five bucks. For five bucks I can jog two blocks."

"Tell me something I don't already know. Nick, once in a great while, a guy has to spring a fiver to impress a gal. Not that it doesn't impress me that you're dripping with sweat and look like you're ready to have a heart attack."

"Time to change the subject. Rico, get me a double rum and tonic. Make it with Myers and put a slice of lime in it. Thanks."

"Coming up Nick. Do you want the bar menu?"

As Nick nodded yes, Ana commented, "On a first name basis with the bartender—I don't know if that is a good thing or a bad thing."

They finished off a few appetizers in short order. The ceviche was great and the chipotle chicken quesadilla went down real easy. So did the drinks. They were on their third. Ana had moved her bar stool closer to Nick for some privacy from the other patrons. A sixties guitarist was playing soft rock. He had a good voice. The music and the third rum and tonic lifted Nick's spirits. He began to relax and stop thinking about all the things that needed to be done in the investigation. This night he promised he would just let it all wash away. "Dreamer boy, come back to earth," said Ana.

"I was just thinking of having Scotty beam me up to the USS Enterprise. *Star Trek*, the best television show ever made. Did you know it ran for only five years?"

"It was before my time. I was never a Trekkie."

"You're never too young or too old to be a Trekkie," said Nick, flashing her the Spock, Vulcan peace and prosperity sign.

Ana laughed, "You can't even get that right. There is supposed to be a large gap between your ring finger and middle finger, not a space that you can barely get a piece of paper between."

"I was just testing you. I knew you really were a Trekkie."

"Well, maybe our ages are not so far apart."

"Right Ana, what's almost 20 years between friends."

"Is that all we are Nick, just friends?"

Nick paused for a long moment. He looked directly in Ana's eyes. A smile crept over his face, tension went out of it. It was as if a few years had slipped away, just for that moment. "I have been fighting it. But no, Ana, we aren't just friends. You're so beautiful, intelligent, and incredibly sexy. I've been attracted to you for a long time."

Ana was completely taken back. She knew that Nick was attracted to her. But for him to come out and tell her was a shock. She beamed and gave her best Lauren Bacall imitation, "Nick, you really know how to chat up a dame."

"Ana, I keep asking myself how could such a knockout possibly be interested in an old warhorse like me?"

"Well, Nick, even though you can be commanding, demanding, and a real pain in the ass, you are vulnerable and sensitive. Whether I like it all the time or not, you do have quite a presence. Most importantly, you make me laugh in your sarcastic and sometimes self-deprecating way."

"Thanks for sugar coating it. What you mean is, I'm usually an asshole, but I occasionally have my moments."

"That's one way to put it Nick, but those are your words not mine."

Silence. Both were searching for the right words. Nick felt intimidated. He never felt intimated at work or in trial. Ana could make him lose his composure with one coy look, or any look for that matter. Ana began to smile, enjoying Nick's discomfort. She knew that in this arena she was in charge. Ana took his head in her long, graceful fingers and said, 'Let's let life move on. Come on over to my condo for an aperitif or a Jack Daniels. I know Jack is your favorite late night drink."

"Okay, you seem to know all my secrets," whispered Nick.

Nick left his car on the street a couple of blocks away and they went in Ana's Porshe to her condo on the cliff. The sheer cliff rose a couple of hundred feet above the sea. Ana had a 180 degree ocean view from her upstairs bedroom, her living room and her patio. Nick spent the first five minutes on the patio, gazing, letting the cool onshore breeze caress his face. "This feels so good," murmured Nick.

"Here's an aged port for my aged prosecutor. It should be very smooth, with a pleasant after taste."

"How many more sensations do you have in store for me, Ana?"

"Wait and see. Let's start with some Miles Davis drifting in from the living room and a fire in the pit. The gas heats up the volcanic rocks in no time." They sipped the port and told each other a few chapters of their lives.

"Before you get too comfortable Nick, I have a final exam for you. Do you see the steps over there which cascade down to the beach? We're going to take those steps, strip down and jump into the ocean. Then, after our leisurely swim, we will race back here and relax in the hot tub."

"I knew you were crazy when I checked you out for the team, but not this crazy. The water temperature can't be more than 55 degrees, it's a public beach, and there's a real question about whether my knees can get me back up those stairs before morning."

"No risk, no reward old man." Ana took off for the stairs, starting down, without looking back. Nick knew this was a defining moment. There really wasn't any choice. He had to follow her. When he got to the beach, Ana was slipping out of her underwear and brushing her hair over her ears. It was almost more than Nick could stand.

Ana didn't hear Nick shout, "Wait up," because she was diving into a breaking wave. Nick shed his clothes in record time and jumped in. His whole body contracted. He gasped for breath. The only thing he could think was, *What would they say in the papers?—Naked Prosecutor Found Strewn on the Beach, Dead from an Apparent Heart Attack.* Luckily, the thought washed away when Ana rose from the sea, facing him, water dripping between her taut breasts. He scrambled to her, falling into her, grasping her to him as they plunged underwater. They came up together. Nick found her lips and they melded into one.

Separating at last, Ana whispered, "I always wondered what would win out, cold water or hormones. To your hormones," nibbling on Nick's ear.

"I love this first act, but as you said at the bar, 'Let's let life move on'. Time for the race up the steps to your condo. And we can skip the hot tub, just a very quick warm shower and bed."

"That's the command presence I know and love. See you at the top." Ana only had to wait for him at the top of the stairs for 30 seconds. When there is sufficient incentive, and numbed knees, Nick does surprisingly well. The shower was brief. Nick didn't even look at the gorgeous ocean view from the bed. He could've been anywhere as long as Ana was intertwined with him.

CHAPTER TWELVE

A few weeks later, Nick was sitting at his desk, staring outside at a cement walkway, a narrow strip of grass and the adjacent wall of a warehouse. Nick was deep in thought. For once, it wasn't about the case. He allowed his mind to go back to the night with Ana. Plunging together into the frigid waters, racing up the steps, his skin coming alive again under the warm shower, and finally a full night with Ana in her bed overlooking the ocean. He hadn't felt that relaxed and good about himself for years, if not decades. A smile came unbidden to his face. The smile was brief. A wave of guilt flooded in. He thought about the years he and Judy had together, and their two kids. Nick believed his marriage was worth saving. He just had to convince Judy of it. But they had been separated for over six months and Judy hadn't shown any signs of wanting him back.

She kept saying, "I need personal space to know what I really want."

The last time she said that, Nick made a cardinal mistake—he spoke his mind. "This isn't the sixties Judy. We're middle-aged people with adult responsibilities. Everything can't be just as you want it. It takes compromise and tolerance." For that he got a door slammed in his face. He had to admit the compromise and tolerance statement was a bit holier than thou. Compromise and tolerance hadn't been strong points for Nick in their marriage. He expected the family to adapt to his job pressures. He still needed to work on that. Nick pushed all these thoughts out of his mind. He was good at that. If his job taught him nothing else, it was how to compartmentalize. He had learned to shut off most of his emotions and just do the job at hand. That was the only way he could handle child molest prosecutions or interview family members of murder victims. Years before, when a five-year-old girl told him all the awful things her stepfather did to her, he didn't want to hear it. He just wanted to throttle the perpetrator. Instead, he had to have her repeat what happened, and if the case went to trial, she would have to tell a jury about the most private and painful events imaginable.

Nick knew he had to leave the sexual assault/child molestation unit years ago when he felt impatient with a 12-year-old victim who was crying on the stand. He just wanted her to get through it so he could go to lunch with his fellow prosecutors. He had become so numb to the horrific things that the child victims had gone through, that he was no longer connecting, shutting everything out.

Just as he had cleared his head, Nick heard a knock on the door, and Ana's voice, "Can I come in?" as she opened the door and walked in.

"Sure, oh…, you're already here."

"I'm not that easy to get rid of," she retorted, with a hint of anger in her voice.

Nick thought, *Oh shit, we're going to have to talk about what happened that night sooner, rather than later.* He had been putting it off, pretending at work with Ana that the best night he had spent in years somehow had never occurred. Nick chose to ignore the underlying tension, and asked, "What have you got for me?"

"Personally or work wise?" responded Ana.

"Last time I checked we were at work."

Nick's snarky comment was aptly rewarded by Ana's curt response, "I happen to have good news on the case which I'm still going to let you know about, even if you are an asshole."

"I thought it was already established that I'm an asshole. Go ahead Ana."

"Last week I went to the San Ysidro and Tecate border ports of entry and talked to the officers of the day for U.S. Customs and Border Protection(CBP). I gave them the names of the targets and their vehicle licenses. They put the information into the computer data base. Anytime one of the vehicles comes northbound to the checkpoints at the border, it's flagged. Once flagged, the border agent will have the discretion to send the vehicle to secondary for further investigation. CBP also briefed their border interdiction teams about our case. I just got a call from an agent at the San Ysidro port. A Toyota, owned by Luis Hernandez-Lopez, was sent to secondary. A Felicia Esperanza-Salas was driving, date of birth, 2/15/1992. A dog alerted on the car and the dog handler seized a few ounces of a white, powdery substance in the glove compartment. It appeared to be cocaine. She looked like she had been beat up. Her make up tried to cover up a black eye and a bruised cheek. When the drugs were found, she started sobbing and started talking about Lopez. She was his girlfriend and was afraid for her life."

"Christmas came late this year!" exclaimed Nick. "This could be the break we've been hoping for. You and Pepe go right to the border and bring her back here to the conference room. Also, get the substance over to the lab right away with a priority designation. I want confirmation that it's cocaine. A few ounces is enough for possession for sale. It can be the leverage we need to turn her. Meanwhile, I'll do some checking into the witness protection program. We have to move fast. I don't want her name in any arrest records yet. We can't have the arrest leaked back to the cartel. Great work Ana!"

Nick phoned the Chief of the State Attorney Criminal Division to let her know what was going on. She gave Nick advance approval to tap into California's Witness Relocation and Assistance Program for reimbursement for any hotel and living expenses for Felicia while they worked on turning her and getting her into the federal Witness Security Program, known as WITSEC. Nick pulled the state witness protection agreement from a secure law enforcement website in case Felicia agreed to cooperate. Nick then called his old friend, Ted Simpson, now a successful criminal defense attorney. Ted had been a career San Diego Deputy District Attorney until he changed sides a few years back. Ted was doing very well in private practice, competent and trusted by his former prosecutor colleagues. "Ted, this is Nick Drummond. I'm working on a complex money laundering case involving the Baja Norte Familia. We may have a person who will turn state's evidence. We'll know within a couple of days. The person may need representation to work out a cooperating informant agreement. Are you available the next couple of days?"

"You sly codger, you won't even say if it's a female or male. I'm around, just let me know."

"Thanks Ted, my paranoia has become a routine practice. You'll know if it's a female or male when the time comes."

Nick's next call was to Mario. He filled Mario in about Felicia and asked him to do a background check on her and have the information on his desk in 30 minutes. Thirty-five minutes later, Mario rushed in and dropped a small pile of papers on Nick's desk.

"She has some criminal contacts, nothing too serious. A finding as a juvenile for receiving stolen property, the successful completion of a drug diversion program for possession of cocaine when she was 19, and she's still on probation for a driving under the influence conviction. Her criminal records and DMV records show that she lived at a residence in Chula Vista until two years ago. The residence is owned by a Rosa Salas. Up until six months ago, she lived in an apartment in Chula Vista. There's no new address. She graduated from Southwest Junior College while she was living in Chula Vista."

"Thanks Mario. It looks like Felicia had something going for her, some stability, before she took up with her cartel abuser boyfriend. We can probably use that."

Right after Mario left Nick's office, Pepe came in. "No problems picking her up Nick. Ana developed a rapport with her. They're in the conference room."

Nick filled in Pepe about Felicia's background. "This is how we'll play it Pepe. Go back in there and have Ana read Felicia her rights. Here's a written waiver of her rights for her to initial and sign. Once that is done, let me know, and I'll come in. I will lean on her some. You two get to be the good cops. Just follow my lead. If she is willing to cooperate, we will put her up in a hotel. We'll have a female agent with her 24-7. We can debrief her fully over the next couple of days."

Pepe left and Nick amused himself by shooting a nerf ball into a small basketball hoop attached to his waste basket. He kept backing up each time he made a basket. He was just at his office's three point line when Pepe came back in, gave him the waiver, and said, "Signed, sealed and delivered Boss man."

As Nick entered the conference room, he took in Felicia, who was sitting at the table facing the door. She was attractive, with long brown hair, too much make-up that was smeared by tears, and a tight fitting blouse. Nick sat across from her. Nick opened the file he had brought with him and pretended to study the papers inside. He let a couple of minutes go by and said, staring into her eyes, "You're in quite a bit of trouble young lady." Felicia started to cry. Nick let her cry awhile before saying, "It's not just the cocaine we found in your car that exposes you to possession for sale charges, but also you're hanging out with a crowd where there's a good chance you'll end up dead. We can help you and protect you. You can get your life back."

"How?" sniffed Felicia.

Nick responded, his voice softening some, "If we charge you in state court, you're looking at a four year maximum term—in federal court it could be up to 10 years. If you fully cooperate and tell us the entire truth about your boyfriend and the cartel, we can put you in a witness protection program and you can start a new life."

"You're loco. He will kill me. You don't know what he's like. He, at the very least, will beat me badly for leaving him and crossing the border."

Nick replied, "I don't doubt for a moment that he will beat you. It looks like he already has knocked you around. Do you want to keep living like that?"

"No, but I can't get away from him and his cartel. My life is over."

"No, it's not Felicia," soothed Nick. "The federal witness program can give you a new identity. We can move you out of state. I know you're smart. You graduated from Southwest College. You have a future. You just need the courage to grab it and hold on to it."

"He'll follow me anywhere I go. He looks at me as his personal property. He even made me tattoo his name on my breast. See!" said Felicia. She pulled down the left side of her blouse, revealing the name *Luis*, with a small heart and arrow through it on her left breast, above her nipple. "Luis told me that if I ever leave him, that arrow will go through my real heart."

"Luis is a bastard and a bully. You don't have to worry about him anymore, if you just cooperate with us," said Nick.

Ana said, after brushing Felicia's hair off of her face, and drying her tears with a tissue, "We have used the witness protection program many times before. You'll be safe."

Felicia was quiet for a minute. "All right. What do you want me to tell you?"

"Just the truth. Let's start with how you met Luis and when you started living with him," replied Nick.

"We met at Opening Day of the Del Mar races, last July. I was wearing a new dress, and a fabulous black, broad brim straw hat, with red and orange bougainvillea interwoven on top. Luis came up to me in this perfectly tailored silk suit and thousand dollar shoes, and told me that bougainvillea was his favorite flower. It reminded him of where he grew up in Cuernavaca. He told me the buildings around the town square were shrouded in bougainvillea. He invited me to the turf club for a few drinks. Later we went back to his condo on Coronado Cay that had a view of South Bay and the Coronado Bridge. He literally swept me off my feet. We were living together two weeks later."

"Where was that?" asked Pepe.

"In a compound just north of Rosarito Beach, in the hills. It's about a 30 minute drive to the border. Luis has a seven bedroom, eight bath house, with a movie projection room in the basement. There are a couple of cottages on the grounds where his bodyguards stay."

"Tell us about the security at the compound," said Nick.

"The compound is surrounded by an eight-foot wall, with jagged glass cemented to the top. There's a guardhouse at the front entrance with a gate that only opens by a card key or by the guard. At all times there are four armed guards on the premises. There are motion detectors throughout the grounds and surveillance cameras outside all doors and large windows. I first thought it was cool, like a movie. As time went on and after I had to stay in the compound day after day, it felt more like a fancy prison."

"Did people come over? Were there dinner parties?" asked Ana.

I saw a number of guys over and over, all young Hispanics, except a few times I saw a white guy. I also saw two older Hispanic men, one, who even Luis deferred to. I was surprised, I thought that Luis was the cock of the walk."

"Let me show you some pictures of people. Tell me if you recognize anyone," requested Pepe. Pepe started with Sergio Bustamente, a cartel enforcer who was seen with Luis in Yaak, Montana, at the border.

"Yeah, I know him. That's Sergio. He's one of the guys who was at the compound many times."

"What about this guy?" Pepe said, showing her a picture of Rael Trujillo-Sanchez, the lieutenant in charge of enforcement for the cartel.

"He was one of the older guys I saw several times. Sergio escorted him. I'll never forget that ugly scar that ran down the right side of his face." Next, Pepe showed her a photo of Mateo Gomez-Encinas, a silver haired gentleman, who looked like he came right out of a high priced tequila ad. Encinas was the head of the cartel, and looked like the last person who would run a ruthless drug smuggling and human trafficking cartel. "I saw him a few times. He was the older gentleman who even Luis deferred to. He attended a dinner party that Luis and I gave at the compound. Luis spared no expense. Jumbo fresh shrimp, caviar, rib-eye steaks, spinach soufflé, and the most delicious flan I've ever tasted. The men after dinner went into the study for cigars and liquor."

"Who else was at that dinner?" interjected Nick.

"The older guy with the scar, a white guy who looked bookish, another Hispanic man who said he lived in Rancho Santa Fe, and a man with a different last name. I couldn't figure out his ethnic background."

The case was flying through Nick's mind. He took Pepe aside and told him to show her photos of Anthony Sakia, as well as Hector Morales, who owned L&M Freight and Recycle Yard, and accountant Lester Sendow. Pepe showed Felicia a photo of each in turn, and she identified each one as being at that dinner party.

"When was that dinner party?" asked Nick.

"It was on October 28th. I remember that because it was my aunt's birthday who raised me."

"Is that Aunt Rosa who lives in Chula Vista?"

"How do you know that Mr. Drummond?"

"We're thorough, we check everything out. Just like we'll check out everything you say to make sure you're telling the truth."

"It sounds like you spent most of your time at the compound. Did you ever get to go out?" asked Ana.

"I'd go shopping with bodyguard escorts in Ensenada and Rosarito Beach. A few times we went to Luis' condo in the Coronado Cays, and once we went to a warehouse on a ranch in Otay Mesa. Luis showed me a few classic cars he had stored there."

"Was there anything else in the warehouse?" asked Nick.

"I don't know. The section with the classic cars was closed off from the rest of the warehouse, which seemed quite a bit bigger. A couple of guards were there."

"Do you think you could show us where the warehouse is Felicia?" asked Pepe.

"Maybe. It was in Otay Mesa, off Highway 90. If we drove around, I might be able to find it. It was isolated, on the crest of a hill."

"What about the condo in Coronado Cays? Could you show us where that is?" asked Nick.

"That's no problem. I was there four or five times. It was at the end of a street, by a small park."

"Great. You can show Ana and Pepe the condo and warehouse tomorrow. It's getting late. We'll set you up in a hotel and have a female agent stay with you. I'll see you again tomorrow afternoon after you've had a chance to drive around."

CHAPTER THIRTEEN

ick saw his daughter's play-off soccer game in the morning. Gabriella played well, but the team lost, 3-2, on a late goal. It was a corner kick that their star player headed into the goal. There was a team lunch after the game. Nick sat next to Judy and they actually got along. No arguments. No, "Where were you?" No, "You should've done this." Nick chalked the lunch up as progress with his estranged wife. Nick even dared a kiss on her cheek when he left. Judy smiled when he gave her the soft peck. Nick drove to the office in good humor.

Just after Nick arrived, Pepe came in and told him about the morning drive with Felicia. There was no problem finding Luis' condo in Coronado Cay. A black BMW was parked in the driveway. The team would run the plate and check real property records for the title to the condo.

Finding the warehouse in the Otay Mesa area had been much more difficult. They drove around in an old pickup truck that had been seized as part of a drug bust. They had needed a vehicle that wouldn't shout, "standard government issue". They drove east on Highway 905 to Alta Road, then to Otay Mesa Road. The side streets off Otay Mesa Road didn't pan out. Pepe got to the end of Otay Mesa Road, near where the Donovan Correctional Facility was located, when they saw a small oil tanker truck head north towards the prison. Pepe thought this was strange, so he followed it on a hunch. It drove past the prison to McGuire Canyon Road and took a left. A few ranches were along that road, but Pepe couldn't see any warehouses. It was remote, virtually no through traffic. Pepe hung back and watched the tanker truck turn onto a gravel road. It was marked private. At the top of the road, at the crest of the hill, you could see a large oak tree and the front of a metal siding building.

Felicia said, "That's it. I remember the oak tree. Once you go up the gravel road, you'll be able to see a small ranch house to the back right of the property and the rest of the warehouse."

Pepe told Nick he decided to walk up the gravel road and pretend he was hiking in the area. He had Ana drive the pickup a mile or so back down the road to the last crossroads. He didn't want to arouse any suspicion if someone drove down the private road and saw a truck parked where it intersected with McGuire Canyon Road. Luckily, Pepe was wearing his standard weekend office attire, jeans, a t-shirt and tennis shoes. He grabbed a walking stick and started up the gravel road. He stopped half-way up the road, studying the layout at the top of the hill. He could see the small ranch house and got a better view of the warehouse building. Pepe heard an engine fire up behind the warehouse. He was stuck in plain view as a Range Rover rushed down the hill. Pepe figured the best defense was a good offense and waved for the car to stop. The car pulled right in front of Pepe, cutting him off. Three Hispanics were in the car. The driver shouted to him, "What in the hell are you doing here?"

Pepe replied, "I'm glad you stopped. I'm trying to find the Otay River. I looked at a map before I started hiking and I thought it..."

The driver angrily interjected, "I don't give a shit what you think, you're on private property! Can't you read English? There are *no trespass* and *private property* signs at the bottom of the gravel road."

"I'm sorry. I was cutting across country and just hit on the gravel road about 100 yards below. I didn't see any signs."

"Turn around now. Get your ass out of here."

"Will do, sir." Pepe turned and started jogging down the road, but not before he had memorized the license plate and the three faces. Once at McGuire Road and out of any possible eyesight of the ranch, he called Ana and told her to stay put, he'd walk back to the crossroads.

"Good work Pepe. But watch the cowboy stuff—walking up that gravel road with no back-up. Also, you could have tipped them off," said Nick.

"You know me boss, I can talk my way out of anything."

"You keep pulling it off until you don't."

Nick continued, "I'm going to phone a buddy at DoD and call in a favor. See if they have a satellite in the area to take photos of the warehouse. Might catch a break and capture them unloading the oil truck. This has to be a main way that the cartel is moving their product. Go on line and get the coordinates of the warehouse. I'll email you my buddy's contact information. This has to get done ASAP."

Nick made the call and his buddy told him, "You're in luck, we have a satellite going over that area in 15 minutes. Send me the coordinates. Remember the time you got me out of a bind in college? We're now more than even. You've been holding it over me for 35 years."

"You were pretty drunk, and streaking a sorority wouldn't have looked good on your resume. You're fortunate there were no cell phones and Facebook back then."

"Okay Nick, that's the last I want to hear about it."

"Mums the word. Thanks for the satellite help." After emailing Pepe, Nick went to the conference room where Felicia and Ana were waiting.

Nick and Ana spent a few hours going back over everything with Felicia, probing for more information. It turned out Felicia had seen several other things of interest at the Rosarito Beach compound. Twice a Mexican company oil truck had been parked by the garage. Additionally, once when Felicia was looking around the garage for a stray cat, she saw a large bullet beside a couple of crates stacked up at the far end of the garage. She described the bullet as being about six inches long, mostly gold in color, except the top third was copper with a black tip.

Ana asked, "How could you remember it so well?"

"It was by far the biggest bullet I had ever seen. I picked it up and looked at it carefully. I even asked Luis about it. He said, 'It must be some old bullet from the prior owners.'" Felicia told Nick and Ana, "It didn't look old to me, it was shiny and clean. The next day the crates were gone." She had gone back into the garage to see what was inside the crates, even though Luis had reminded her that she was never to go inside the garage.

Ana whispered into Nick's ear, "That bullet, with the black tip, matches the description of an armor piercing, 50 caliber round."

"I know Ana. Heaven help us if the Familia starts shooting those bullets around. A 50 caliber bullet has five times the muzzle energy of a standard bullet shot from a hunter's rifle."

The last gem they gleaned out of Felicia was about a late evening conversation she had with Luis at the compound. Luis was at the computer looking at tidal charts for the coast, north of San Diego. He asked her, "Have you ever been to any beaches in the Encinitas area, about 20 miles north of San Diego?"

She replied, "Just once. My college friends had a late night kegger and bonfire." Luis got very interested, wondering what time it was that they were there and if there were any other people on the beach. Felicia told him, "No, it was just us. It was after midnight and in winter time, nobody was around."

Nick took Ana aside, "The Familia could be moving drugs across the border at night by small boats. We need to check with the Coast Guard."

After a few hours of friendly grilling, Felicia seemed tired and began to lose focus. "Felicia, there's one more thing we need to talk about before you get dinner and go back to the hotel. You've been very helpful. We need to move on to the next step, your protection. I'll call in a defense attorney tomorrow and we'll work out an agreement for you to continue to cooperate, and to testify if needed. I checked with the federal authorities about getting you into the federal witness protection program. This will allow us to move you out of state, far away from La Familia. You'll get a brand new identity, a new social security card, help with employment or school, and living expenses. It's completely voluntary. You can leave the program at anytime. However, it's not advisable to leave until the targets are convicted and locked up."

"How long will that be?"

"It could be up to two years, maybe more. It's rough, but at least you'll be safe and have a future. Also, while you're in the program, you can't have any personal or electronic contact with friends and family members. There can be nothing to connect you to your new identity and where you are living."

"You expect me to cut off all my friends and family, especially my aunt, who raised me like a mother?"

"That's the way it has to be Felicia. We can be present when you make a call to your aunt and tell her you're safe, that you just need to get away. Also, you should think about what part of the country you want to resettle in. We have some ideas, but we want your input."

Ana put Felicia's hand in hers and softly spoke, "It's so hard Felicia, but you're not alone in this. We'll be in touch and the U.S. Marshal's Office will always be there. I know a couple of years feels like forever. But after that you have all your life ahead of you, 50 to 60 years, a husband, kids, grandkids. You need to be strong."

A female agent came in to take Felicia to dinner and back to the hotel. Ana and Nick went to his office. Once the door was closed, Ana said, "I hope you didn't get too turned on when Felicia flashed her breast tattoo yesterday."

"What's that? I must have missed it."

"Missed it Nick? I saw your eyes glued to the target."

"Well, Ana, as you know, I pride myself in being able to keep my focus, even under the most trying conditions."

"Trying conditions? You should have to give back some salary for that extra benefit."

"Ana, I only have eyes for you."

"Is that why you've treated me like an ordinary colleague the last few weeks?"

"I'm sorry, I've been thinking about you a lot. This is all new to me. It's difficult for me to sort it all out. I didn't take that night lightly. Part of me wants to spend every night with you and part of me hasn't given up on my marriage with Judy. Let's go out for drinks next week and talk about it. Now is not a good time."

"So Nick, will it ever be a good time? Are you just kicking the can down the road?"

"No, I just want to talk about it in a more relaxed environment? Can we get back to the case for now?"

"Ana, we need to get out a state and federal law enforcement bulletin that the Baja Norte Familia cartel appears to have 50 caliber weapons and ammunition. Please have Pepe talk to his Chief in Sacramento for his approval to transmit it in electronic form under California Department of Justice letterhead. I want to review the wording of the bulletin before it goes out. We want to make sure it doesn't shed any suspicion onto Felicia."

Ana replied, "I just hope that none of the Familia weapons are traced back to the ATF operation a few years back."

ATF ran an undercover operation, Fast and Furious, out of their Phoenix Office, where undercover agents sold guns to legal purchasers who were suspected of being "straw buyers" for criminals on both sides of the border. The operation was intended to ferret out criminal conspiracies to purchase guns by authorized buyers who turned around and sold them illegally to criminals. Many of these guns were trafficked south of the border to the Mexican drug cartels. Some of the guns used in this sting operation were later recovered in Mexico at scenes of cartel assaults. It was reported that even a couple of 50 caliber machine guns were sold. It was a public relations nightmare.

"I remember a local U. S. Representative who had a field day questioning ATF representatives at a congressional hearing," said Nick.

"Not a red-letter day for the good guys," replied Ana.

"I'm going to check to see if any satellite photos came through of the warehouse in Otay Mesa. This could take a few minutes, I have to navigate a series of Department of Defense passwords on my computer. It goes through the highest level of security. My computer is the only one which is set up for this protocol in the building."

"You don't have to worry about me memorizing your digit typing sequence from across the room. I'll get us some coffee. Still take it black like the color of your heart?"

"Play nice." After Nick spent a few minutes cursing the computer and the various passwords, he was able to pull up a series of 20 shots, taken over several seconds. The photos matched up with the Google Earth photos of the property. They showed two men unloading large bags from the back of an oil tanker. In at least one photo,

Nick could make out the identification number of the truck. Nick whooped and hollered.

Ana rushed in, "What did I miss?"

"Look at these photos, we got them!"

Ana replied, "It's amazing how close the satellite photos can bring things up from hundreds of miles above the earth."

"It's not for me to question how miracles occur, just reap the benefits of our good fortune."

"Okay old man Moses, what now?"

Nick replied, "Contact your DEA buddies in Mexico and see if they have anyone they can trust to discretely get us copies of the transportation logs for the past year of the Mexican company oil truck in the photos. I don't want to go through the Mutual Legal Assistance Treaty(MLAT) process. It's too slow and I don't trust the system, too many opportunities for leaks.

"A MLAT request will have to go out of main justice in Washington D.C., then go to their counterpart in the Attorney General's Office in Mexico and be overseen by the Mexican courts. No thanks.

"While you get that rolling Ana, I'll talk to the U.S. Attorney for the Southern District of California for approval to get Felicia into the federal WITSEC Program. I want to see how fast they can get the U.S. Marshal's Office up to speed."

The federal witness protection program has done an incredible job protecting at risk witnesses since it was started in 1971 at the initiative of a United States Department of Justice attorney in the Organized Crime and Racketeering Section.

Nick continued, "I also want to get Ted Simpson over here tomorrow afternoon to go over a cooperation agreement for Felicia. Ted and I have worked on a few of these in the past. It shouldn't be a problem."

"Anything else you want me to do, Nick?"

"No, Ana, except could you come in tomorrow at about three to finalize things with Felicia? I know it's a Sunday, but you have a great rapport with her."

"No problem Nick. The only living thing that I'll be missing time with is my cat."

"Thanks Ana. At least a cat purrs. Tropical fish don't say a damn thing."

The next day Nick filled Ted in about the case. Nick told Ted that Felicia was basically a good kid. As long as she fully cooperated and told the truth at all times, he wouldn't charge her with possession of cocaine for sale, or anything else. But she had to agree that the statute of limitations for charging any crime against her would be tolled until she completed the terms of the cooperation agreement. He also told Ted that Felicia had been tentatively accepted into the federal witness protection program. She could be moved out of state by the end of next week with new identification papers. Nick knew she was interested in a dental hygiene program. Rona, his paralegal, had found a good program in Charlotte, North Carolina. This would seem to be a good spot for Felicia, temperate weather and not located in a border state with Mexico.

Ted spent an hour going over everything with Felicia. Ted entered Nick's office with a grim smile. He said, "She isn't too happy about it, but she's so scared of Luis and the cartel that she will go along with it. It's no surprise that she wants to be as far away from the cartel's reach as possible. In her mind, that is Topeka, Kansas, which also has a good dental hygienist school."

Nick replied, "Topeka it is." Nick clicking his coffee cup with Ted's, and said, "To barbecue and the Kansas City Royals."

Nick prepared the cooperation agreement from one that he had used the year before. Nick and Ted went back into the conference room, and Felicia, Nick and Ted signed off on the agreement. After Ted left, Nick said, "Felicia, it's a good time to call your aunt and tell her you're safe and want to leave for awhile. You can tell her that living in Mexico was not a good idea, that you need a new start, that you have some money saved, that she shouldn't worry about you, that you can't talk to her for quite some time, but you'll send her a letter now and then. Felicia, any of your letters have to go through the Marshal's Office to ensure you're not giving out any clues as to your location and new life."

Nick called in Pepe and told him the ground rules of the conversation between Felicia and her aunt. He was to help monitor it if she spoke Spanish and to not let her say anything about the witness protection program or where she was going.

The conversation started with Felicia saying, "*Tia, soy yo.*" It ended in tears, but nothing was divulged that would jeopardize Felicia's safety.

During the phone call, Pepe turned to Ana and said, "Felicia's aunt keeps on saying, 'Where are you going? I need to see you. I will go with you.'"

After Felicia hung up the phone, she looked at Pepe, sobbing, "*No dije nada.* It was the toughest thing I have ever had to do."

Ana took her hand and said, "You couldn't say anything about where you're going. I know it's so very hard."

CHAPTER FOURTEEN

Ken Hamilton was elected Attorney General of California two years ago. Nick wasn't a big fan. Hamilton came from outside of the office as had all his recent predecessors. What made him different is that he took politics to new, sickening heights. Everything seemed politically driven. No real substance, all spin. The AG floor in San Francisco was jam-packed with dewy-eyed, twenty-somethings, who jumped at General Hamilton's beck and call. They worshipped him and spent tireless days behind their computers to further Hamilton's political career—like what openings and events to attend instead of tackling substantive office issues.

Hamilton would wait until the last minute to make decisions on whether the office would file petitions for review before the California Supreme Court concerning important legal issues that the office had argued and lost in the courts of appeal. This meant that the appellate deputies had to prepare lengthy petitions in every case because Hamilton might not approve the filing until the day before a petition was due, instead of giving deputies two or three weeks preparation lead time by pre-approving a filing. Every completed petition that was rejected by General Hamilton was a complete waste of office resources.

Nick should have known the office was in for a long four years under Hamilton when Hamilton first visited the various AG office locations. Instead of having an open-ended, sit-down talk with deputies about his vision for the office and gathering input from career deputies as prior AGs had done, General Hamilton held a receiving line where he greeted each deputy and shook his or her hand. It was like a cotillion greeting line to introduce young ladies to society, not how to best run a thousand-attorney office. Many of the deputies asked the AG to come back soon to discuss issues with them. He never did.

It was early in February and even in San Diego it was cold. It dropped to the high thirties at night and was in the low fifties during the day. The cold front fit Nick's mood. He had just flown back from San Francisco after an urgent meeting with the Attorney General. Nick almost got fired at the meeting. The AG had heard about the case and wanted to put in his two cents worth. It was fine for the AG to be informed, but the strategies in putting a case of this magnitude together were way over his head. The AG's last trial was some 15 years earlier, a domestic violence case he had when he was a deputy district attorney. When the AG started to tell him what he should say in closing argument at a potential trial, Nick lost his patience.

Nick said, "With all due respect, if this case gets to trial, how the final argument will be handled will be primarily dictated by how the evidence came in. I'll be trying the case and I'll be making the decisions about the closing argument."

The AG replied tersely, "You forget who's in charge and whose name is on the letterhead. You work for me."

"That's true and I'm very much aware that you are the AG. But if you insist on making trial strategy decisions, I'll no longer be working for you. I don't think that's a good idea. I know this case and I'm experienced in trying complex cases. If we are successful and obtain convictions against high level members of the Baja Norte Familia, it'll bode very well for your political career. If you want to fire me after the case, go ahead."

The AG took a long, hard look at Nick. He was barely keeping his composure. "We'll see how the trial goes Nick. I might just hold you to your offer. You can go now."

As Nick was ushered out of the AG's office suite, he muttered to himself, "That certainly went well. Who needs job security?"

The fiasco meeting with the AG put another layer of pressure on Nick. He sent out an email to the team members to go though the entire case at a meeting two days later. Everybody was there at the case review meeting, including paralegal Rona. Nick laid down the ground rules for the meeting. "We will go through the different areas of evidence, discuss the major things we need to do to get the case ready for indictment, discuss whether we bring this case in state or federal court, and finally what major charges we expect to bring."

"Josh, let's start with you. What's the status of the case in Montana?"

"Charges have been filed against the college boy and his Hispanic cohort. They were arraigned in state court and bailed out. The state prosecutors are playing ball with us and aren't pushing the case, letting it sit until we're ready to take it over. We've arranged for periodic surveillance of the border drug exchanges. Two weeks after the arrests, the Familia renewed the cross-border drug distributions. It's well documented. They appear to be using the same warehouse in Missoula as a holding location for the drugs. We've probable cause for search warrants on the warehouse and college boy's residence."

"Thanks. We need a tracker on the vehicle that transports the drugs to Missoula. That way we can trace the vehicle back to any other storage locations and know its route," said Nick.

"Can do. Nick, I've got an idea— just thinking outside the box. What if we use the criminal justice major I met at the brewery in Missoula to cozy up to college boy. She might get some interesting information out of him."

"Josh, we aren't in the pimping business and such an operation is fraught with legal minefields. College boy has been charged with drug distribution arising from the vehicle stop. I am concerned about the U.S. Supreme Court case, *Massiah v. United States*, and its progeny."

Under *Massiah* and other Sixth Amendment right to counsel cases, law enforcement can't intentionally create circumstances that would lead a charged defendant to make incriminating statements about an offense. Josh replied, "I'm aware of the cases, but if she acts as a 'listening post' and doesn't ask any questions, it should be all right."

Nick retorted, "That would be playing with fire. We would be instructing her to make contact with college boy, and our intent would be to elicit incriminating information. Also, if the trial court found a *Massiah* violation, any information obtained from him or derived from what he told her, would be excluded at trial. I know lover boy that you'd like to make another trip to Missoula to renew acquaintances with your criminal justice cowgirl. But no can do. You're restricted to the San Diego dating pool."

"Mario, how's the case coming together on the money flow across the border?" asked Nick.

Mario replied, "Quite well. Remember, one of the Sakias' companies owns the Missoula and Vancouver warehouses. They're still moving over two million in cash each month across the border to banks on the California side. We've recently found out that cashier's checks, in similar amounts to the cash deposits, are being made out to a bank in Mexico— Banco Real, for deposit into a specific account. This is where it really gets good. We obtained records from a U.S. Bank, based in Texas, that acts as a correspondent bank between the California-based banks and Banco Real to facilitate the international transactions. The Mexican account is in the name of Armando Ruiz Castillo. Señor Castillo is high up in the Mexican government and has diplomatic immunity. That's not all. Similar amounts of cash are being deposited in the Morales money laundering operation. Most of the banks are located in Calexico, the California border city that is adjacent to the Mexican city, Mexicali. In the Morales operation, instead of using cashier's checks, the money is being wired back to Señor Castillo's account with Banco Real."

The regulations under Mexican law, which restrict cash dollar deposits into Mexican financial institutions, don't apply to dollars deposited by check or wire transfer. These are huge exceptions that allow the drug cartels to get around the Mexico's dollar cash deposit restrictions.

Nick said, "Pepe, check with your contacts in Mexican law enforcement and find out whatever you can about Señor Castillo. Ana, get a photograph of Castillo and have the Marshal's Office show it to Felicia in Kansas. She has been there for close to a month and should be settled in by now. I want to see if the politico Señor attended any soirees at Felicia's former boyfriend's compound."

Jerry spoke up, "We need to focus on accountant Sendow. He's the main bridge between the money and the dope. Remember, we got the wire up on Sendow's phones at the time that the Montana drug bust went down. Sendow was a busy man on the phone during the few days after the bust. He spoke to Hector Morales and to Anthony Sakia. They were talking in code. Kind of corny. Something about a hunter bringing down a bird flying north and the migrating birds flying south were going to be late due to unexpected weather. There was also a call to him from a untraceable burner phone the morning after the bust. This caller was much more careful in his language. The caller was male and spoke in commands. He told Sendow to meet him right away at the regular place—something had come up."

"Thanks Jerry. We need to get a copy of the tape of that last call to the U.S. Marshal and see if Felicia can recognize the voice. It may be her ex. Also, Jerry, please run the TECS database for any vehicles crossing the border which are associated with her former boyfriend Luis, accountant Sendow, and the Mexican oil tanker seen at the Otay Lakes ranch."

The TECS database is operated by United States and Customs Border Protection (CBP). A TECS print out for a vehicle license will show the port of entry, the date, and exact time of each northbound entry into the southwest border states from Mexico. Information about northbound vehicle border crossings are readily accessible for the last twenty years.

Pepe added, "As far as connecting the drugs with the money, we have positive alerts by drug sniffing dogs on cash deposited by the two money laundering operations at each border bank."

"How about the drugs Ana?" asked Nick.

"We have the black tar heroin and the marijuana seized in the vehicle stop outside of Missoula. We have the connections between the money side and the drug side mentioned earlier. Also, remember, it was Sendow and Luis who were asking Biker Sue about real estate in Yaak and who were photographed at the first border exchange by our wildfire fighter, Drury. We have Luis and some of his underlings sufficiently tied into the drug operation, but we need more on the head of the Familia cartel, silver-haired Mateo Encinas, and chief enforcer, scar-faced Rael Sanchez. Felicia places them all together at Luis' compound for a dinner or two, but we can't directly tie them to the drug-money laundering operation."

"You're right Ana. We should think about turning Sendow. He was at that dinner. What do you guys think?" asked Nick.

Jerry said, "It's a good idea, but we shouldn't try to turn him until after we execute the search warrants. We don't want the case to go south, excuse the intended pun, by approaching Sendow too soon and have him not cooperate. It'll cause the rats to scurry back into their holes, dragging their 'cheese' with them."

Mario agreed, "Jerry is right. We shouldn't approach Sendow until everything is lined up and he has no choice but to cooperate."

"Guys, I knew there was some reason we had you on the team other than I can beat you in a beer chugging contest. Good analysis," said Nick. Nick continued, "What major investigative steps do we need to undertake before we execute search warrants on all the warehouses, offices and residences?"

Ana replied, "We need to further explore whether the cartel is using small boats to smuggle drugs to north county San Diego beaches at night. I spoke to the Coast Guard. A number of small bales of marijuana, wrapped in waterproof plastic, washed up on an Encinitas beach a couple of months ago. Also, Encinitas P.D. busted a couple of guys driving along a beach access road at two in the morning, three weeks ago. They had fifty kilos of marijuana and twenty kilos of black tar heroin, wrapped in waterproof packaging, in the back of their S.U.V."

Nick, with excitement in his voice, went to command mode, "I want all the reports on the heroin-marijuana bust and the washed up marijuana. Cross-check the dates of the bust and when the marijuana washed ashore, with tide tables and moon cycles. Who knows? There may be a pattern. The cartel may like to make their ocean runs on full moon nights or with no moonlight, during low tide or high tide. If we can determine a pattern, we can be waiting for them. What else?"

It was Pepe's turn to risk additional work falling on his shoulders. "We have to get on that tracking warrant right away for the vehicle that is delivering the drugs to the Montana warehouse. It could lead to additional distribution warehouses between the Mexican border and Montana. I'm sure the Familia isn't just distributing the drugs through the Montana/Canada connection. We can take down any additional warehouses we discover with all the rest."

"Make it a priority Pepe."

"Sure Nick, I'm here to obey and serve."

"I don't know about that. I can't remember the last time you obeyed me. And the only time I remember you serving me was when you brought me a beer from a bartender, along with yours. Which, if I remember correctly, I paid for."

Nick continued, "Once those investigative steps are completed, we execute simultaneous search warrants. After the execution, and reviewing the documents seized from Sendow, we approach him to cooperate with us. Then we seek a grand jury indictment. Any thoughts on whether we should take this case state or federal?"

Josh immediately responded, "It has to go federal. It would be a procedural nightmare to file it in state court. A number of our witnesses are out of state. We'd have to use the Interstate Witness Act to try to compel witnesses to come to California to testify."

"I have used the Interstate Act before and it took me six weeks to get an order from the out-of-state court to compel the witness to come to California to testify," said Nick.

Josh added, "Also, in a state grand jury we have to bring in all the witnesses to testify as compared to the federal process which allows an agent to recount their statements."

"I agree with Josh. It'd be a lot easier to bring this case in federal court. I tried to to get legislation passed in California which would have aligned California law with the federal process for grand juries—a qualified agent can testify to witness statements. I pretty much struck out except for getting Assembly Bill 976 passed in 1999 which allows an experienced law enforcement officer to testify about hearsay for the foundation of documents. Also, there is more bang for your buck in terms of imprisonment for the charges we bring in federal court. For a transaction or transportation money laundering offense under 18 USC section 1956, a defendant can receive up to 20 years in federal prison, while under the primary state statute, he is only looking at up to three years in state prison for each money laundering violation."

Josh said, "We also can bring a Continuing Criminal Enterprise count under federal law. Under 21 U.S.C., section 848, a conviction brings a minimum, mandatory sentence of 20 years, and a defendant could get life. A fine of up to two million dollars for an individual defendant is thrown in for good measure."

Nick looked around the room. He was proud of his team; however, he was worried about all the work that still needed to be done and the legal pitfalls lurking. He didn't let any of his anxiety show. "Great job guys! Federal court it is. I'll arrange a meeting with Josh, myself and the U.S. Attorney to get her blessing."

Josh was the last to leave the meeting. "Nick, I didn't know you worked on state legislation."

"Yeah, I ran the gauntlet a few times. You start with a comprehensive bill which makes sense and then the legislative committees chip away. One time in the nineties, I was trying to expand the qualifying transactions for California's primary money laundering statute. I wanted to add personal checks as qualifying monetary instruments under the statute, instead of just cash, traveler's checks, cashier's checks, and money orders. That immediately got shot down in committee. I always thought they were worried about personal checks from campaign donors. They didn't seem to understand that for a violation of state money laundering, a prosecutor must prove that the person receiving the check had to know it was derived from criminal proceeds, or had to know that it was going to be used to promote criminal activity. Receiving a campaign check, without that knowledge, isn't a violation.

"The legislative process is often likened to a sausage factory. I was responsible for the 'Drummond sausage'. The California money laundering statute allows you to aggregate, otherwise qualifying transactions over seven days, to meet the transaction amount threshold of $5,000. I drafted legislation that expanded the aggregation period to 30 days. While I was testifying in front of the committee, a legislative aide actually elbowed me in the ribs and whispered, 'Nick, they're not going for the 30 days, come up with something else.' So without missing a beat, I suggested a 30 day aggregation period to reach an alternative, higher threshold amount of $25,000. The second alternative became law, and to this day, one can either aggregate for a seven-day period to reach a $5,000 transaction threshold, or for a 30 day period to reach a $25,000 threshold. It wasn't until a year later that a fellow prosecutor brought it to my attention that there had to be at least one, five thousand dollar count in every $25,000, 30 day aggregation. The second alternative was thus mere surplusage—the 30-day aggregation alternative added absolutely nothing. Sorry, I know that's more than you ever wanted to know."

"No, Nick. You never know when it might come up in trivia. Have a good evening."

CHAPTER FIFTEEN

"**N**ick, I made contact with the U.S. Marshal's Office in Topeka and spoke to the Deputy Marshal who is Felicia's handler. I wanted the deputy to show Felicia the photo of Banco Real account holder Castillo and for Felicia to listen to one of Sendow's taped conversations. Deputy Lily Perkins couldn't find her. Felicia wasn't at her safe house and wasn't at her dental hygienist classes. The last anyone saw her was the day before yesterday."

"She may have skipped, Ana. Have the marshals stake out her bungalow and her classes. She shouldn't have much money. If she's coming back to San Diego, it's probably by bus. Have them go to the major bus companies and see if anyone remembers Felicia or if she shows up on any surveillance tapes over the last two days."

"Nick, this may not be a good time, but I want to let you know what I think about our relationship talk awhile back. I know you said that we should stop seeing each other on a personal level until you get things worked out with your wife. You know better than I do, it can take months and months for your divorce. Nobody knows what's going to happen in our jobs or our lives. I don't want to wait an indefinite period for you to get your act together. Either we continue to see each other or we're through."

"Ana, I don't need the extra pressure right now. There's too much on my plate. Can't we wait a few months or so for things to sort out?"

"No, we can't. I'll get moving on your Topeka demands, Mr. Drummond."

"C'mon Ana, don't be that way." Ana didn't hear Nick's plea. She had already slammed his door on the way out. Nick could only think he was glad he understood investigations and prosecutions better than he understood women.

Jerry was the next one in Nick's office. "After the meeting last week, I took over for Ana in checking out the two north coast drug cases. I summarized the two cases for you in this memo, and found a possible third case. Three months ago, Oceanside PD was busting a late night beach party when they saw a boat, powered by an outboard, with no running lights, heading for the beach. Oceanside PD shined their searchlight on the boat and saw two men with large plastic trash bags in the boat. The boat immediately swerved away from the beach, almost capsizing when a wave broadsided the boat. The PD wrote a field report on it."

"Good work Jerry, ferreting out the Oceanside incident."

"Thanks Nick, but that's not all. I followed up on your suggestion and charted the three drug incidents with the tide tables and lunar cycles. All three events corresponded to a very low, middle of the night tide, and no moon or just a sliver of a moon. The next time the moon cycle and the low tide are in a similar juxtaposition is seven to ten days from now."

"Fantastic! Line up the local PDs and the United States Coast Guard to work with us for night surveillances at likely beaches for the three night time slot."

The final agent through Nick's door that day was Pepe. "I have some news for you on the tracker for the van that makes weekly trips to the Missoula warehouse. It's a commercial van with no windows behind the driver and front passenger's seat. The van has already been tracked to a warehouse in Salt Lake City—about a nine-hour drive from Missoula."

"That makes sense Pepe. Salt Lake City is about halfway between Missoula and San Diego, off the same north-south interstate, I-15. Also, the east-west interstate, I-80, intersects there. I-80 goes from San Francisco to Salt Lake, and on through Nebraska and Iowa, to Chicago. Chicago could be part of a distribution route for the Baja Norte Familia."

"Should I put out feelers to DEA in Des Moines and Chicago as to the cartel?"

"Go ahead Pepe and let's get some help from Salt Lake law enforcement for surveillance of the Utah warehouse."

Nick went to his apartment that night, poured a Jack Daniel's and thought about his family and Ana. He must really be putting out a bad vibe. His tropical fish didn't even follow him back and forth in the tank anymore while they were waiting to be fed. He was completely torn. Judy had meant everything to him at one time. They were raising two wonderful children. Nick was no longer as much of a part of his children's lives. He didn't get to hear what happened on the schoolyard or how they thought they did on the latest test. Nick used to tell the kids make-up stories at bedtimes. How he enjoyed and missed that. No matter how it worked out between Judy and himself, he promised himself that he would be a big part of his children's lives. Ana was the X factor. Nick was so attracted to her. She was clever, provocative, and ever so sexy. Nick somehow had to get through the lust and determine if Ana and he could make a relationship work. It was better to put it out of his mind. Nick had a case to worry about. He poured another nightcap. Then dozed off in the recliner that he purchased at a used furniture store—listening to the smooth and soothing tenor sax of John Coltrane.

The next morning, Ana glided into Nick's office and said, "Nick, I have an update on Felicia." Nick thought, *A good start to the day, Ana is at least calling him Nick again.*

Nick responded, "Don't keep me in suspense, what's going on?"

"We found out from surveillance videos and records at the main bus terminal in Topeka that Felicia got on a bus two days ago, headed for Las Vegas. A surveillance camera has her getting off the bus in Vegas at 10:15 last night. We don't have video of her getting on any other bus. Maybe she knows someone in Vegas or someone is meeting her. Earlier this morning I went to Felicia's aunt's house and pretended that I was from the apartment complex where Felicia used to rent from. I don't know if the aunt bought it, but I told her I had a five hundred dollar security deposit check to return to her."

Nick commented, "Kind of weak, but I can understand there wasn't anything better you could come up with. Did her aunt give you any information about her whereabouts?"

"No, but I got the strong feeling they have been in contact recently. The aunt was very nervous. She insisted vehemently that she hadn't any contact with Felicia—protesting too much."

"Ana, you and Pepe better get over there and surveil the aunt's home. We don't know of any other place she would go. We'll have some other agents take over the surveillance by late afternoon. If she shows up, bring her in with as little fanfare as possible. I'll fill in her attorney."

"Thanks Nick. I need to get off early, I have a date tonight. Don't look so downcast, it's with my cat. We're going to share a bowl of ice cream. I eat the ice cream trying to get over you, the cat licks the bowl and spoon."

"Ana, keep your eyes open out there. Be careful."

"Oh Nick, I didn't know you cared."

Pepe wasn't too thrilled pulling surveillance duty when he had so much other work to do. When Ana filled him in about talking to Felicia's aunt earlier that day and believing that the aunt had recently spoken to Felicia, Pepe said, "We have to assume Felicia told her aunt she was coming back to San Diego. If the aunt knows, who else may know? We better play this smart.

"How do you look in a bullet proof vest?"

"Well, it doesn't do anything for my curves, but you can still tell that I'm female."

Pepe looked her up and down, "I don't think that will ever be a problem."

"At least someone around here notices that."

Pepe responded, "Is there something I don't know?"

"There's a lot you don't know Pepe and will continue to not know."

Felicia's aunt lived on a one block street between two busy thoroughfares in Chula Vista. Pepe and Ana were in an unmarked Camaro, parked a few houses down and across the street from the aunt's house. Pepe told Ana, "Call me paranoid, but I don't like this.

We're too exposed with busy streets on either end of this block. Maybe we should call in two back-up units, to sit on the thoroughfares."

"You're too paranoid. If anybody, only the aunt knows." A couple of monotonous hours passed. They went through their favorite movies, songs, and whether the Padres would ever go to the World Series again. They had just agreed it would never happen in their lifetimes when Pepe saw a woman with a scarf over her head, get off of a local bus at the corner of the thoroughfare in front of them.

Pepe asked, "Hey, check out the bus, could that be her?"

"Hard to tell with the scarf over her head, but she's walking this way."

"Yeah," responded Pepe, "and she's not walking like any old lady. I have a feeling it's Felicia. Let her walk closer to the house and then we'll get out real casual-like, to not scare her off. I don't enjoy foot races anymore."

They got out of the Camaro when the woman was two houses away from the aunt's house. Pepe was closer to the woman as they approached. From behind them they heard the high rev of a motorcycle coming toward them. They both turned in unison and saw two men on a motorcycle, with the man in back holding a submachine gun. Pepe yelled, "I'll grab her" and ran towards Felicia, knocking her down as he heard the staccato of bullets whiz over their heads. Pepe heard Ana's Glock firing rounds. The machine gun was now directed towards Ana. Pepe's body was covering Felicia. He heard the motorcycle continue down the street. He lifted his head up just in time to see the motorcycle scream around the corner onto the thoroughfare down the street.

Pepe ran over to Ana, who was lying face up, half on the sidewalk. She was conscious and blood was streaming out of her left arm and right leg. Pepe yelled for Felicia to call 911 and tell the dispatcher that an officer is down, shot, and give the address.

Felicia jumped up and ran into her aunt's house. Pepe got Ana onto the sidewalk and applied pressure to both of the bullet holes. The blood seemed to be stopping. He was worried about Ana going into shock. She looked clammy and ashen. Her breathing was rapid. Pepe spoke calmly to her, telling her she was going to be all right, that an ambulance was coming. Pepe needed to raise her legs slightly above the rest of her body to make sure sufficient blood was getting to her vital organs. He put his jacket under her legs. A neighbor came out—an elderly man, who said he was a war veteran and was familiar with trauma. The neighbor kept pressure on Ana's wounds while Pepe loosened her bullet proof vest. Pepe gave a silent prayer of thanks when he saw three bullet indentations in the front of her vest. He said to Ana, "You may not like how you look in a vest, but it saved your bacon. You're going to have some deep purple highlights. I bet Nick will even give you a few days off."

A slight smile came to her lips. "What a girl has to do for a few days off." Pepe kept talking to Ana. He heard the sirens in the distance. The paramedics rushed over. They placed temporary patches on Ana's wounds and gently rolled her onto a stretcher.

Pepe held Ana's hand tightly as she was lifted into the ambulance. He kept whispering in her ear, "We won't let anything happen to you. You're going to get through this." Pepe watched as the medics hooked up an IV and placed an oxygen mask over her face.

Police cordoned off the scene and kept the neighbors at bay. Pepe was on his phone as he hurried towards the aunt's house. He told Nick that Ana had been shot and was being taken to South Central General's ER. Ana had lost a lot of blood, but was still conscious. Felicia was inside her aunt's house, unhurt. Nick said, "Stay with Felicia. I'll send Jerry over to pick Felicia up. I want you to remain at the scene. I'm going to South Central to check on Ana. I'm counting on you to find out why the shit hit the fan."

Inside the house, Felicia and her aunt were hugging on the couch.

Felicia was sobbing and saying, "I didn't know this would happen. They tried to kill me!"

Pepe went right up to her, his face just two feet from hers. "You have to tell me who you told that you were coming back to San Diego."

"My Tia. Only my Tia."

"When did you tell her?"

"Two days ago when I left. I said I was coming by bus."

Pepe turned his head slightly to the right, to look Felicia's aunt directly in her eyes. "Who did you tell Tia?

117

"*Nadie*, I, I, I told nobody."

"Are you sure Tia? Why did a guy on the back of a motorcycle spray bullets at your niece and shoot my partner."

"Well, I was so excited that Fellcia was coming home, I told my nephew Alan."

"Where is Alan?"

"He's a senior at Sycamore High. He and his mom, my sister, live a few blocks from here in an apartment."

"I need his address and his and his mother's telephone numbers. What kind of boy is he? Has he gotten into any trouble? Does he hang out with any gang members?"

"He's a good boy. He does have a receiving stolen property conviction as a juvenile, but he said he really didn't know the stereo equipment was stolen. The family always tell him to stay away from gangs. Gangs are all over."

"I need to make a phone call Tia. Write down Alan's full name, his address and all the telephone numbers right now."

Pepe got on the phone with Mario and filled him in. Tia came over with the written information. Pepe read it off to Mario and asked him to go pick up Alan and find out whom he had spoken to. Pepe added, "If he is still on probation for the stolen property, see if you can round up his probation officer and bring the officer along. That should add some leverage and pucker the kid up." Pepe went back to talking to Felicia about what happened until Jerry came to pick her up and take her back to the office.

Nick was going 90 miles per hour in his beat-up pickup on Highway 805, hell bent for the hospital. He heard the siren before he saw the red flashing light of the California Highway Patrol. Nick slowed, but kept going, and pulled out his badge from his wallet, placing it to the driver's window. The CHP pulled along his driver's side, both vehicles now going about 65. Nick mouthed the words, "Emergency, partner shot." The CHP officer mouthed back, "Slow down, no more tragedies." Nick continued on.

Nick pulled up by an ambulance at the emergency room doors and ran in. "The woman, Ana Schwartz, who was just shot! Where is she?"

The nurse replied, "You can't see her. She's in surgery. She has lost a lot of blood." Nick told the nurse who he was and showed his badge. "I'm sorry, you'll have to wait. I'll ask the Doctor to speak with you when he comes out of surgery." Nick turned away and sat down. He put his head in his hands and bent over. He berated himself for sending Ana and Pepe on the surveillance. First Pepe gets kidnapped in Tijuana and now this. If Ana comes out of this, he'd make it up to her.

CHAPTER SIXTEEN

Nick spent a couple of hours in the waiting room, ruminating about what he could have done differently so that Ana wouldn't have been shot. He felt he had been naive and too cavalier about how dangerous Baja Norte Familia was. Nick had thought that violence wouldn't land at the team's doorstep. He had believed that they just investigated violent acts against others and dealt with anguished victims, not their own. He hadn't thought it could happen to his task force, to his friends, to someone he cared so deeply about. These cases were about men with money, power and unrestrained ego, which he now knew could strike out at anyone, any time. Nick wouldn't underestimate them again.

Pepe walked into the waiting room. He saw Nick sitting in the far corner, with his head in his hands. It tore Pepe up. He owed this distraught man his career. Almost twenty years ago, when Pepe was a rookie cop, Nick supervised him on a task force raid of a meth lab. The cookers were known to be armed and dangerous. Pepe was assigned to clear the back, right bedroom. He burst through the door with his gun drawn. Pepe saw movement and a glint of metal out of the side of his left eye. He fired off a shot. A baby cried. The movement had come from the wind coming through an open window, rocking a metal cradle. The bullet missed the baby by inches, lodging in the window sill. Pepe, stunned, was still able to yell, "Clear."

Nick told the other agents to stay at their assigned areas. Nick came in the bedroom and Pepe handed him his gun. "The cradle moved by the wind—I almost shot the baby."

Nick liked the rookie officer—he was smart and eager to learn. Nick went to the window and opened it wide enough for a man to climb through. He then moved the cradle to the other side of the room. He handed the gun back to Pepe, saying, "You're going to make a good cop. I won't let your career be ruined by a rash act. An armed man was climbing out the window as you came through the door. He had a gun. You fired a shot. You then had to check on the baby. The man got away." The report was written that way and signed off by Nick.

Pepe, his mind back in the waiting room, interrupted Nick's thoughts, "How is she?"

"Ana's been in surgery for over two hours and they haven't told me anything except she has lost a lot of blood."

"We should all be proud of her. She got off her full mag of 15 at the attackers. I believe she hit one; there was a blood trail down the middle of the street."

"Pepe, have all the hospitals and clinics checked in this county and Imperial County. I want to get these assholes more than anything."

"I already sent out the requests."

"Thanks Pepe. You always come through."

Pepe added, "I believe we recovered the gun. Two blocks along the thoroughfare that the motorcycle turned onto after the shooting, Chula Vista P.D. found a semi-automatic rifle in the bushes. It's an Israeli Taur Carbine. It looks like a small submachine gun. It just went on the civilian market a year back. Well-heeled gang-bangers like it because the gun is just 26 inches long and weighs only eight pounds. Easy for the scum to hide it under their jackets. It's also very reliable—doesn't jam. Unless modified, it shoots 15 rounds from a detachable magazine. We don't know if the shooter got off one or two magazines. I think two, but it happened so quickly. I remember a pause before the shooter redirected the bullets at Ana."

"They're all bastards Pepe. The ones that fire those human murder weapons, the gun brokers who sell a killing machine like that with no background check on the purchaser, and the lawmakers who won't ban them because they're in the pocket of the NRA. The only use for these type of guns is to kill as many people as quickly as possible."

"Nick, even though I'm career law enforcement, you're preaching to the choir. It makes my skin crawl knowing that at any time out on the street we can be outgunned by a psychopath with a machine gun."

They heard heavy steps running down the hall. Mario emerged, out of breath, gasping, "How's Ana?" They told him the little they knew. "I came as soon as I could after interviewing Felicia's cousin, that idiot Alan. I corralled his probation officer and we caught Alan still at school. We started with Felicia almost being shot by a passenger on a motorcycle outside his aunt's house. The kid went white and said, 'Oh no!' It turned out that yesterday afternoon, Alan ran into a couple of older gang-bangers at the mall who were from his neighborhood. They're part of a local Hispanic gang that has ties to the Familia. He told us the chance meeting seemed innocent enough to him. They just asked, 'Where is that hot cousin of yours, Felicia?' They made some snide remark about getting into her pants. Alan told them that she was coming home tomorrow but they didn't have a chance in hell of getting into her pants. They could dream on. They all laughed and the two gang-bangers walked away."

"Did you believe him Mario?" asked Nick.

"Yeah, he was pretty shook up. According to the PO, he is not a gang-banger, or a wannabe, but knows gang members and has a few gang member friends."

Pepe said, "That could describe half the teenage, Hispanic males in Chula Vista."

"Did Alan say if either of them owned a motorcycle?"

"He didn't know if they did Pepe," replied Mario.

Pepe continued, "A motorcycle enthusiast, living eight houses down from the aunt's house, saw the cycle turn onto the aunt's street just before the shooting. He told me it looked like a Ducati Streetfighter. Generates 130 horsepower on a 400 pound bike. It retails for a cool $13,000. The bike is red hot for the young racing crowd."

Nick added, "Throw in the $2,000 Israeli machine gun, and you have someone with a lot of money or access to a lot of money. Fits the Baja Norte cartel. Mario, can you follow up on the two gang-bangers?"

"Will do Nick, I'll get right on it." As he turned to go, Mario said, "Let me know when Ana gets out of surgery."

Pepe stayed with Nick. "Nick how are you doing?"

"Not so good. I feel responsible."

"Nick, you understand what we all knowingly take on with this job.

Is there something more than that? You feel something special for Ana, El Jefe?"

"No, I feel the same way about all you guys."

"Don't bullshit a bullshitter Nick. I've worked with you for 20 years. I know something is going on between you and Ana. Maybe nothing physical yet, but I see the way you look at her when you don't think anyone is noticing."

"You always could read me like a the book. She is special to me. That's all you're going to get out of me."

Nick was saved from more of Pepe's probing by the doctor. "Who's Nick Drummond?"

"I am. How is she?"

"She had lost so much blood, I thought she might not make it. But she's strong. We got her stabilized and performed bypass surgery where the bullet tore through her posterior tibial artery. I grafted a part of one of her lesser arteries from her left leg to the damaged artery. Essentially, I made a bypass from the two intact ends of her tibial artery with the transplanted one stripped from her other leg. That's what took so long. She's in recovery and is still sedated."

"When can we see her?"

"Well, she'll be in recovery for another hour and than we have to make sure she's doing all right. Maybe in a few hours, if she's awake. I can have the nurse page you when she can have visitors."

"I'm staying right here until I can see her. Will there be any permanent damage?" added Nick, with tears welling up in his eyes.

"She needs to go through physical therapy. She may walk with a slight limp because of the muscle loss and the overall trauma. But beyond that, she'll be fine. The wound in the left arm just went through the flesh. She'll recover completely from that."

"Thank you so much Doctor. Can you have a nurse give us any important updates?"

"Sure can. Remember when you see her that she's just starting the healing process from a life threatening trauma. She'll tire easily."

Pepe, sensing that Nick would want to see Ana alone, said, "Let me know as soon as you have seen her, so I can come over and pay my respects to one gallant, tough lady."

"Thanks Pepe, I'll let you know."

Nick got tired of staring into space and at the light green walls of the waiting room. His thoughts turned to the NRA, *The NRA used to support major federal gun control legislation—the National Firearms Act of 1934 and the Gun Control Act of 1968. It was founded after the Civil War to improve American training and marksmanship. It wasn't until the mid-seventies that they began to focus on opposing gun control, and created a Political Action Committee for that purpose. Now, it has devolved to being an obstructionist organization, with the primary focus to defeat any gun control legislation, no matter how sensible and whether or not the public supported it.* Just thinking about what the NRA had become pissed Nick off. Nick needed to get up and move around.

Nick told the admissions nurse he was going to the cafeteria and would be back in 15 minutes. The cafeteria didn't cheer him up. At 8:00 p.m., hot dinners weren't available. There were a few plastic wrapped sandwiches, apples, and candy bars. Nick went with the turkey and cheese; it had the farthest out expiration date—the next day. He indulged himself and got a Coke and a Snickers bar. Nothing like sugar to perk someone up for awhile. Nick was back in the waiting room and tried to finish his sandwich. He couldn't remember the last time he had eaten white bread—probably when he was a kid. Time slowly marched on. Nick dozed off.

Nick was gently shaken awake and heard a female voice say, "Sir, she's doing well, is awake, and wants to see you."

The nurse ushered Nick into a private room on the intensive care ward. Ana was lying on the bed with an IV in her arm and a drainage tube extending from her right leg. Her eyes were closed and her skin was so pale that Nick couldn't detect a blush of life. Nick took her hand and held it to his heart. "Ana, I'm so sorry. I'll never forgive myself. Waiting to hear about your surgery was the longest period of my life."

Ana slowly opened her eyes. It took a few seconds for her to focus on Nick. In a voice so soft that Nick had to lean close to her to hear, she murmured, "Sometimes a lady will do about anything to get her man to come to her bed."

"Trust me, it didn't have to be something this drastic. A sore pinky would've been enough. I've been thinking about nothing but us." Nick put his head softly on the crook of Ana's neck. She began to doze off. Nick sat by her side the rest of the night. When she woke in the morning, a hint of color had returned to her skin.

The nurse came in and asked Nick to leave because they were going to do a number of tests. Nick got a chance to talk to the doctor after the tests. "She's doing remarkably well. She can go home in a few days if everything progresses as we expect. She'll be on crutches for a week or two and will be able to get back to more normal activities in about a month. She won't be running a marathon anytime soon."

"I wouldn't bet against it—her running a marathon."

CHAPTER SEVENTEEN

Jerry came into Nick's office and said, "I know we've all been worried about Ana the last few days, but we need to implement the interdiction plan for the Familia's drug smuggling by sea. In a few days, it'll be the beginning of the three night window where there's virtually no moon and low, middle of the night, tides along the north coast of San Diego. The Coast Guard is willing to allocate a high speed cutter for the first two nights. Local law enforcement will assist. We need to narrow down the most likely landing locations for the smugglers and coordinate surveillance and interdiction."

"Okay, right Jerry. I've been distracted the last few days. But Ana is doing well and went home yesterday afternoon. Her mother flew in and is taking care of her. It's time to for me to get back on track with this case. Let's have a meeting at two this afternoon with a Coast Guard representative—you, me, and young AUSA surfer, Josh. He has surfed all of the north county beaches. He may be able to provide some inside information as to likely landing sites."

"Thank you for coming on such short notice Commander Ritter. I'm Nick Drummond, the head of a task force investigating the Baja Norte Familia. I understand that Jerry has filled you in on our investigation. Let me emphasize, we're dealing with a very violent, sophisticated outfit. It's also personal. We believe that one of our agents was shot by a cartel member while she was about to meet a protected witness in our case, the former girlfriend of one of the cartel's lieutenants."

"We are happy to assist Nick. With our resource limitations, we can only give you two nights of our Marine Protector Patrol Boat. From Jerry, it sounds like the cartel uses top of the line armaments and transportation toys, like the Ducati Streetfighter. We don't want to be outrun by any of the cartel's boats, so I've also arranged for the use of our Defender Class Response Boat. It's powered by two, 225 horsepower engines and has a top speed of 53 miles per hour."

"Fantastic Commander! Can you tell me more about the operational capabilities of your boats?"

"Sure Nick, but how about some coffee first? I haven't had any rot gut, government issue coffee since this morning."

"Coming right up Commander, we specialize in that," said Jerry.

After Commander Ritter settled in with his coffee, and a not too stale donut from the morning bakery run, he told the rest about his boats. "I'll be in charge of the 87 foot Marine Protector. It has a top speed of 30 mph and two 50 caliber Browning machine guns mounted on the starboard and port foredecks. It's capable of launching a rigid hull inflatable boat—RHIB—from its aft launching ramp, a 23 foot, Short Range Prosecutor, with a top speed of 35 mph when manned by 2 persons. The RHIB can be launched quickly while the Marine Protector is at speed. The rear ramp needs to be lowered to a 13 degree launch angle, and the front mooring hook disengaged. The RHIB slides into the water. It's powered by water jets so there are no engine parts extending from underneath the boat to impede a launch or a beach landing. The secondary boat, the 28 foot Defender, can be manned by up to 10 people. Both the Marine Protector and the Defender have powerful, blinding searchlights, mounted on their bows.

"Commander, it's great to have you nautical types with your impressive support craft aboard. With our state budget, we fight over how many paper clips are allotted each year," said Nick.

Jerry said, "Commander, Josh, and I went over north county coastal maps and believe there are three likely beaches the Familia may use."

Nick said, "Excuse me Commander, I didn't formally introduce you to Josh Sterling, but I see you've met. He's an Assistant United States Attorney. But his true value at this point in time is his surfing. He maintains that he surfs for the love of the ocean and the challenge of the waves. I think he surfs every chance he gets to pick up on the wahinis. My prognosis is backed up by the fact that whenever he's not surfing, he's walking some puppy down the beach that attracts the local beauties better than bees to honey."

Enough old man," said Josh with a grin. "I'm the Rodney Dangerfield of prosecutors. I get no respect. Just because on occasion there may be a comely young lady on my arm, it doesn't mean I forego academic and manly pursuits."

"Ah," said Commander Ritter. "To be young and confident, with healthy knees and a strong back. I used to surf a bit. My favorite north county beach was Swamis."

Nick added, "You're an officer and a gentleman, describing Josh as confident, instead of being flush with youthful arrogance—ignorance is bliss. Sorry gentlemen, I digress, what did you come up with as far as the likely landing sites?"

Josh responded, "I believe there are three likely sites. Each one offers different, distinct advantages and disadvantages. The closest to Mexico, is Black's Beach. It's below the Torrey Pines Glider Park, between La Jolla and Del Mar. Black's Beach is a nudist beach by day because of its remoteness, but could be the perfect drug drop from a beach landing craft at night. There are no houses or roads overlooking Black's Beach. Access is down a narrow path from the top of a 200 foot cliff where the glider port sits. There is a big expanse for parking at the glider port. The only possible people who could be around there in the middle of the night might be some love-stricken college kids. The University of California at San Diego is only about a half a mile away. I've been up and down that trail a few times. It's tough enough to lug a surfboard along the trail. Carrying 50 pound bags of dope on a moonless night would be quite a feat."

Josh continued, "The second site is geographically opposite from the glider port site in that there's a small access road down to Moonlight Beach in Encinitas. There are only a few residences on the cliffs overlooking the beach. About a quarter of a mile south of the access road, a residential street dead ends at stair access down the cliff to the beach. Smugglers could use either access."

Commander Ritter asked, "How much traffic would one expect on the beach in the middle of the night?"

Josh replied, "Not much. There are no roads that parallel the beach there. If anybody, it would be young people galavanting around." Nick said to himself, *Or a lust-filled, older guy, with a younger woman, regaining his youth with a midnight skinny dip.*

"Finally, another few miles up the coast in Carlsbad, south of the Batiquitos lagoon river mouth, is South Ponto Beach with easy parking access and low surf. The downside is that the coastal Highway 101 runs right along it. But considering that cars are driving by at 50 mph, a beach landing by a boat with no lights would probably not be noticed during the middle of a moonless night."

They all studied the coastal map. Ritter said, "We could have the Marine Protector idling about a mile offshore from Moonlight Beach, which is between the other two beaches. The Defender Response boat would also be in the vicinity. We have surface radar capability on the Marine Protector and may be able to pick up a likely candidate for drug smuggling before it reaches land. The land surveillance teams can alert us of any suspicious land activity at the sites."

Nick said, "Commander, it sounds like you've done this before. I like the plan. We'll coordinate with the land surveillance-interdiction teams to make sure we have the three sites adequately covered and set up a communication protocol with the Coast Guard."

"I've done it a few times. I was stationed in Florida. There was quite a bit of drug running in the Florida Keys."

Nick said, "As you know Commander, we've three target nights. Any way you could stretch it to provide coverage for all three nights?"

"I wish I could Nick, but on the third night we're scheduled to do sea exercises with my sister station in Long Beach."

"Okay, the first two nights it is. That will be this Monday and Tuesday. We'll iron out the details and be in touch with you over the next couple of days. Thank you again Commander. I can't tell you how much we appreciate your help."

On Monday night, at midnight, Nick found himself holed up in the glider port building, scanning the parking lot for any activity. There were four SWAT team members hidden two hundred feet below, on Black's Beach, and another four men on the cliffs. The Commander of the Sheriff's SWAT teams was beside him. All SWAT team members were using the same radio frequency. The frequency was also being used by the two other teams at the other beaches and the two Coast Guard boats. Everyone had been instructed to keep radio traffic to the essentials. The Glider Port team had to preface each conversation with Alpha, the Moonlight Beach team with Beta, the Carlsbad team with Cain, and the Coast Guard with Delta. Delta One was the 87 foot Protector and Delta Two was for the 28 foot Defender. The plan was to allow the Familia's boat to land and begin to unload before the SWAT team moved in. The Protector, using its radar, would hopefully pick up the approach of the drug boat while it was still at sea. The Protector and the faster Defender would trail behind. Once the drug boat landed, the Protector would launch its RHIB to help with the interdiction.

As the hours passed, Nick only had his cold coffee to sip. Each hour every team reported in. Nothing was happening. It was a clear night, with the stars affording some light in the moonless sky. The teams had agreed to close down the operation at 5:00 a.m., figuring the Familia would want to make the drop and get back to Mexico in darkness. Nick looked at his watch, 4:30. Just a half hour to go. Maybe this wasn't the best idea. So many different beaches, so many possible nights. A few minutes later Delta One came on line. Nick recognized Commander Ritter's voice. "Our surface radar has picked up a 12 foot boat, close to the shore, moving northbound. It's slow moving. I don't think it is our smugglers, but we're moving in closer and launching the RHIB to check it out. Over."

Two minutes later, Commander Ritter was back on the radio, saying that the RHIB had launched and intersect was expected in three minutes. Three minutes later the RHIB checked in. "False alarm. Some early morning exercise freak is paddling his ocean kayak for all he's worth. Besides the paddler, there may be room for a pack of cigarettes in the kayak. He isn't carrying any product. Over."

At 5:00, Nick got on the radio. "That's it guys. Tonight, wasn't our lucky night. Hopefully, tomorrow night will be. We'll set up at the same time this evening. We want to be in place by 11:00 p.m. Thank you for tonight's duty. Hope you'll get some sleep. If not, at least drink some hot coffee."

Nick fared better than the rest of the team that night. At least he'd been inside, out of the cold wind. Jerry had been on the Protector with Commander Ritter and Josh had been wearing a bullet proof vest under a life jacket aboard the rapid response boat, Defender. Mario had been on the beach at the Moonlight Beach location and Pepe had been at South Ponto Beach, Carlsbad. Nick walked the 300 yards to his car, which he'd parked along the roadway that led to the UC campus. He drove home and got four hours sleep before going back to the office.

When Nick got to the office, Deputy U.S. Marshal Lily Perkins was waiting for him. "I'm Felicia's handler in Topeka. We're flying back to Topeka this afternoon. I don't believe her new identity nor her location has been compromised. I've spoken with Felicia a number of times since I arrived two days ago. She never told her aunt where she was living and the name she was using. I had one of the shooting investigating officers interview Felicia's aunt and her cousin Alan. Neither knew where she'd been, or if she was using a different name."

"Okay. Have you spoken to my agent, Pepe Cantana, who was at the shooting and spoke to the aunt?"

"Yes Mr. Drummond. He agrees that it's safe for her to go back. There's no question in my mind that Felicia now fully understands the importance of obeying the rules."

"I hope so, because if she doesn't, next time the Familia will make it a moot point."

Deputy Marshal Perkins added, "Felicia recognized the voice on the taped telephone call to Sendow. It was her ex-boyfriend, Luis. She didn't recognize the photo of the Banco Real account holder, Señor Castillo."

"Thanks Lily, that helps a lot. We now have Luis, the day after the Montana drug bust, telling accountant Sendow, on a burner phone, that they have to meet—something important has just come up."

"Mr. Drummond, we'll be checking in on Felicia each day she's in Topeka."

"Thank you, have a safe trip."

Nick had used his "El Jefe" status to switch locations for the night. He would be at the Carlsbad beach and Pepe would monitor the glider port location. Nick had the feeling that the cartel wouldn't be overly concerned that Highway 101 ran along the beach. There were no residences or commercial buildings there, and the lagoon took up most of the eastern side of 101. Anybody driving that stretch of the road in the middle of the night would be focused on getting home, not on what might be happening on the beach. In any event, on a moonless night, a driver couldn't see people and a boat on the beach. This beach would be in keeping with the Familia's macho, in your face attitude. Further, the surf is less at the lagoon mouth and readily accessible parking is just down the beach. The more Nick thought about it, the more confident he became that South Ponto would be the beach.

Nick stopped at Ana's condo on the way. Her mother greeted him at the door. A spry woman in her mid-sixties, she had the same large hazel eyes which locked on to you. When her husband died, she took over his furrier business. She struggled the first few years, but made it work. She was the strong nudge behind Ana's academic success—always pushing her to do better. Mother Alina was disappointed that Ana didn't pursue pre-law or pre-med at Columbia. She didn't understand Ana's passion for criminal justice. Alina's parents had been raised in Romania and had instilled in Alina that there was no such thing as government-directed justice. Alina didn't realize that the years of abuse that Ana suffered in the hands of her classmates motivated her to seek solutions in the criminal justice system. Alina also didn't approve of Ana's first husband—an FBI agent. Even Ana realized it had been a big mistake—she said one time, "You can't have two hard asses living under the same roof."

Alina not so subtly interrogated Nick about his life. Nick's responses seemed to satisfy her. She gave Nick a kiss on the cheek and went to bed. Nick felt like he had just undergone a brutal cross-examination. He turned to look at Ana. She smiled and raised her eyebrow as if to say, *Oh well. That's my mother.*

Nick filled Ana in on the night's operation and his hunch. Ana said, "You seem to have a nose for trouble, yours and others. You may be right. How about an extra hand at South Ponto?"

"Yeah, maybe you could swat the bad guys with your cane. Ana, you already gave at the office. You're under wraps for now. A precious asset to be held in reserve for when we need you the most."

"Well, I would prefer you called me a precious piece of ass."

Nick grinned. "You're that too." Nick gave Ana a long hug, grabbed her precious ass, and kissed her good-bye. "Wish me luck Ana."

Four SWAT team members plus Nick were in desert camouflage in the bushes nestled against the sand dunes that led to the beach. Nick had strict orders from the SWAT team that he was just there to observe. He was to remain where he was, keep his head down, and stay out of the way.

It was beginning to turn into a rerun of the night before. No activity. The hourly check-ins by each interdiction group were standard. Nick was planning the upcoming search warrants in his mind when the radio stirred him from his reverie. "Delta One. Surface radar has detected two boats traveling north, close to the coast. They're traveling at about 25 knots." Nick quickly translated this in his head to about 30 mph. Delta One continued, "The 15 foot boat has a small vertical profile, consistent with a hard rubber platoon boat. The larger boat is trailing the first boat and has a higher vertical radar profile, consistent with a deep V hull, power boat. They have both just passed our Moonlight Beach check point and are heading towards the Cain checkpoint. Delta one and Delta Two are following, at speed, with Delta Two hanging back some in case anything develops at the other two sites. Over."

Nick then heard the leader of his interdiction team come on the air. "Cain, we hear you. Nothing to report yet. We'll be on the lookout for any activity at the beach parking lot, 200 yards south of our location. From your report Delta One, can we expect the boats to arrive here in about six minutes? Over."

"Delta One, correct. Over."

Nick felt the adrenaline flooding his body. He was wide awake, fully alert. He was hearing sounds in the night that he hadn't heard or paid any attention to before Delta One's call. A large pickup with a camper shell on its bed pulled slowly into the beach parking lot. "Cain, pickup truck with camper shell just pulled into the parking lot. Beta team, be ready to move to our location for back-up. Over."

"Beta, we'll be ready. Over."

At a time when there was no traffic on 101, two large men got out of the pickup carrying bags. They rushed over the edge of the parking lot and down to the beach. They were running along the shoreline towards the southern edge of the lagoon's mouth where the breakers were the smallest.

"Delta One, the two suspect boats are closing in on Cain team location. The larger suspect boat is hanging back. We're a half mile off shore, without running lights to avoid detection. Delta Two is about a mile behind us. Over"

"Cain, I hear an outboard motor approaching from the south. The two suspects on the beach have two duffle bags apiece and backpacks. One is removing a flashlight from his backpack. Over." Nick was thankful for their infrared googles which allowed them to make out the details.

"Cain. Suspect is shining flashlight out to sea. Other man seems to have a cellphone to his ear. Keep channel open. I'll report when I see the boat." Ten seconds passed, which seemed like 10 minutes.

"Cain, the perp's flashlight gave me a glimpse of a rubber platoon boat, heading straight for shore, just outside of the breakers. Time for Beta backup. Over."

"Beta, gear packed, leaving now, should be there within four minutes. Over."

"Delta One, launching RHIB off rear ramp. Running the water jets on silent mode. RHIB should intersect beach in two minutes. Over."

Nick could see the suspect's boat crash through the last breaker and the man steering the outboard motor lift it up as the boat reached the beach. Both men jumped out and pulled the boat onto the beach. The two from the pickup were hastily removing plastic bundles from the boat and putting them into their duffle bags. The two from the boat were pushing the boat back into the water when the SWAT leader said, "Now!" The four men rose from the dunes, specters in the night, pointing machine guns.

"Police! Get on the ground now!" One of the SWAT members shined a powerful beam directly in the eyes of the suspects. The two with the duffle bags dropped to the ground. The two others kept trying to push their boat back into the water. Delta One's RHIB could be seen powering towards the chaos, just outside the breakers. Rapid shots were heard from out in the water, way past the RHIB. Nick was taking this all in from his higher vantage point and his night goggles.

"Cain, this is Nick. RHIB, heads down! Shots being fired towards you from power boat. Delta One, need immediate support. Over."

"Delta One. We're coming full speed in support. Fifty caliber guns ready. Over." Nick soon saw tracer fire from two guns farther out in the ocean. They were going right over the top of the power boat. The power boat swerved to the right. A roar of its engine filled the air. The tracer bullets followed in its direction.

"Cain, Nick here. Thanks for the help, the power boat has sped back down the coast. Over." Nick saw the four occupants of the RHIB pop up over the hard rubber, with guns pointing at the suspects' platoon boat.

"Hands up! Any suspicious movement and you're dead!"

"Delta One. Delta Two, intercept power boat. Boat traveling south at 60 knots. Extremely dangerous, automatic weapons. Over."

Josh was thinking he was getting a hell of a lot more than he bargained for. He just wanted to come out of this alive. The Defender Response boat, with its crew of seven, counting Josh, was heading at top speed, 50 mph, with no lights, towards the intercept point with the power boat.

The squad leader shouted, "Contact in 20 seconds. Guns ready!" Josh could hear the power boat. It was to their front and to the right. A man was standing, crouched in the passenger seat, bracing himself, firing a machine gun at them. Bullets thudded against the side of their boat. Several whizzed right over Josh's head. Josh was ducking down as far as he could go. The Defender returned fire, raking the side of the power boat as it sped by. There was a splash as the man firing the machine gun dropped into the water.

"Delta Two, man on board power boat in water. Retrieve man or follow power boat? Over."

"Delta One. Get the man. You're overmatched by 20 mph. Radar has the power boat going 70 mph. You'll never catch him. Over."

The Defender came to an abrupt stop. Two of the Coast Guard team had stripped off their bullet proof vests and boots, re-donned their life jackets and jumped into the water by the body. They hauled him into the boat by the rear platform. The body showed no signs of movement. The medic for the Defender team checked vital signs. Nothing. They all saw the numerous bullet holes in his torso. "Delta Two. Have recovered body.

Dead. Multiple gunshots wounds. Should I bring body back to base or rendezvous with RHIB to bring body to shore? Over."

"Delta One. Hold on. Cain report. Is it safe to bring the body ashore? Over."

"Cain. It is. Beta back-up has arrived. Everything is under control. Ambulance is on its way. One of the perps was shot in the arm. Probably from the power boat. Four suspects in custody. Drugs seized. Looks like Mexican black tar heroin. Will send RHIB outside the breakers to pick up the body for transport to hospital. Over."

"Delta One. Delta Two will be on its way to meet RHIB. Over."

Nick saw the crew of the RHIB unload the dead body onto the beach. He went over to look at him. Nick had seen him before—the narrow face, the nose and jaw that jutted out. He looked like his nickname, Jackal or *Chacal* in Spanish. It was Sergio Bustamante. The enforcer that Felicia had seen many times at Luis' compound and who was with Luis in Yaak, Montana, for the first known border delivery. Nick smiled to himself. He was too tired to yell out. The adrenaline rush had left him exhausted. All he could think, *We've got you Luis, you son-of-a-bitch!*

CHAPTER EIGHTEEN

"Ana, it's great having you back with us," said Jerry.

"You don't know how great it is for me to be back. I was going stir crazy and about ready to strangle my physical therapist. It seems like four months from the shooting, not four weeks."

"You're getting around pretty well. I hardly notice a limp."

"Swimming each morning really helps. It loosens my leg up and strengthens it at the same time."

Rona came up to them. "I like having some feminine energy around. Too much free range testosterone around here when you were gone. Speaking of testosterone, Nick wants you both in his office. He wants to update Ana about the case."

"Ana, an official welcome back. Jerry has been working long hours trying to tie your shooter and the Carlsbad beach drug smuggling to the Familia. Tell her what you've got Jerry."

"The two gang-bangers that Alan told about Felicia coming home have been a dead end. We talked to them. They admit to having a conversation with Alan about Felicia, but nothing more. Just so-called friendly joking around with someone in the neighborhood. I don't believe them for a second, but we don't have any leverage on them. However, we've made some progress on the Ducati motorcycle. Deputy Marshal Perkins spoke to Felicia about whether she had ever seen a red Ducati around Luis' compound. She had—it was one of Luis' many high speed toys. She even went riding with him one time. Scared her to death—taking fast corners and leaning way over. Other people in the compound used to drive it. Luis was surprisingly generous with his play things. We don't think Luis was the driver for the shooting. He wouldn't be that stupid to get so directly involved and the general description of the driver is of a younger man. But you never know, Luis is a classic adrenalin junky."

Nick said, "Tell her about the power boat that exchanged fire with the Coast Guard."

"The Defender Response boat that exchanged fire with the suspects' power boat had a night camera on its bow. It showed the boat to be a 22 foot Donzi Classic. The Donzi has an open cockpit, with an engine that generates over 400 horsepower. It has a deep V hull for crashing through waves and a top speed of 75 miles per hour. We also asked Felicia about the boat. She remembers the Donzi well. It was Luis' pride and joy. She went out with him a number of times. She described where he kept it at Rosarito Beach. It was moored in a locked, covered dock. Pepe called in a couple of favors. He went along as an observer with a Baja Norte State Police Officer he trusts and has worked with in the past. They went on a 'safety inspection' of the portion of Rosarito Beach dock that has Luis' enclosed boat shed. They entered the secured premises and took photos. The boat has bullet holes which are consistent with the ammunition fired by the U.S. Coast Guard. The Donzi was otherwise spotless. It looked like it had been thoroughly cleaned. Felicia recognized a photo of the boat as the one Luis has. When she was riding around in it, the Donzi didn't have any bullet holes."

"Tell her about the black tar heroin."

"Hold your horses Nick, I was saving the best for last. The drug lab has been doing fantastic work on the black tar heroin. Forty kilos of black tar heroin were seized that night on Ponto Beach. The mineral make-up of the Carlsbad heroin was compared to the mineral make-up of the heroin seized in Montana and the twenty kilos of heroin seized by Encinitas PD seven weeks ago. The Encinitas seizure was just a few miles south of the Carlsbad seizure. For you wine connoisseurs, I'm sure you know that a wine can be analyzed for its exact nutrient and mineral composition. A wine's composition can be traced to a particular region where the grape vines are grown. The land of each region has a unique nutrient and mineral composition, which gives the wine a specific flavor. It's the same for poppies, the source plant for heroin. The three seizures had the same nutrient and mineral composition. The poppies for the heroin came from a region of the coastal mountains of the state of Sinaloa. It's about a 10 mile stretch of land, controlled by the Baja Norte Familia. I've spoken to a DEA expert who has worked with Mexican authorities in a joint interdiction, poppy destruction crusade in that area. He can testify to the Familia's control of that area."

Nick added, "Ana, we're in pretty good shape with tying the drugs to the cartel. Now, we need to work on the simultaneous execution of search warrants. Early next week, we'll have a video conference call to brief the warrant teams in Salt Lake City, Vancouver, and Missoula. We have to serve the warrants at the same time so that one part of the organization won't have advance warning and tip off the rest of the organization. There are eight locations—warehouses in Vancouver, Missoula, and Salt Lake City, college boy's residence in Missoula, accountant Sendow's residence and office in the San Diego area, Luis' condo in Coronado, and the ranch-warehouse in Otay Mesa that Felicia identified. Mario and Pepe have been working on getting the affidavits in support of the warrants together. They're almost finished. I'll let you know the exact time for the briefing. The entire team will be there." Ana and Jerry took that as a hint to leave and left Nick alone with his thoughts.

The search warrants briefing went well. It was decided that each team would be staffed by a combination of local, state and federal law enforcement. Law enforcement would wear bullet proof vests and helmets. The warrants would be executed at 7:00 a.m., Pacific Standard Time. Each team would have a satellite phone connection with the overall command center in San Diego.

The Royal Mounties would follow the same protocol for the Vancouver warehouse and have a corresponding satellite phone. It was agreed that only persons who are in possession, or in constructive possession, of drugs would be arrested. Suspects at the residential or office locations, like accountant Sendow, would not be arrested. In

Sendow's case, the task force was hoping to turn him after the execution of the search warrants. The morning for the execution of the search warrants, three days from the briefing, was chosen because surveillance and southwest border vehicle crossing records show that drug shipments would likely arrive at the Missoula and Otay Mesa warehouses the evening before.

The various judges in Montana, Utah and San Diego would sign off on the warrants the day before the planned execution. Nick wasn't worried that a judge would refuse to sign a warrant—the affidavits in support overflowed with probable cause.

The affidavits would be ordered sealed by the signing judges until formal charges can be filed. The order would be based on the fact that the continuing investigation would be jeopardized if the information in the affidavits could be accessed by the public. Felicia wasn't named in the affidavits—she was described as "Confidential Informant One". When court proceedings heat up, it would be expected that the defense would bring a motion to disclose the identity of the confidential informant.

Nick stayed at the command center during the execution of the warrants and helped coordinate the seizures. He responded to any questions about what to seize, or not to seize, at the various locations. The face of the individual warrant set out the items, or category of items, to be seized at each location. But occasionally, one of the agents would inquire as to whether a particular item could be seized under the warrant. Nick told the officers at Luis' condo in Coronado to seize brochures about Donzi Classic boats and Ducati Streetfighter motorcycles. The brochures were considered evidence of crimes because they tied Luis to the ownership of the type of boat and motorcycle used in criminal activities.

The search of accountant Sendow's residence, in an upscale neighborhood in San Diego, afforded his shocked neighbors with some entertainment. Sendow was roused out of his bed at 7:00 a.m. and he promptly rushed outside in his boxers where he protested the seizure of his beloved BMW. Sendow's pasty belly hanging over his boxers wasn't a pretty sight for his proper neighbors. Sendow's dignity was further assaulted by two officers restraining him and dragging him, limp limbed, back into his house. A file cabinet of documents attributed to the cartel was seized from Sendow's office.

Unfortunately, Luis's condo was fairly clean of incriminating evidence. Not so, for the four warehouses. Marijuana and black tar heroin were found at each location. The biggest haul was at the Otay Mesa warehouse and ranch. Five hundred pounds of marijuana and 100 kilos of heroin were found in an underground storage area, accessed by a trapdoor under a carpet in the warehouse's office.

Documents in a safe at the Salt Lake City warehouse included an apparent log of shipments to Missoula and two locations east of Salt Lake, an address outside of Chicago, and an address in Kansas City. This information was passed on to law enforcement in each area. College boy's checkbook showed monthly deposits of $15,000. Pretty good money for a starving college student.

After the search warrant teams in Missoula and Salt Lake City inventoried and sealed the non-drug evidence, it was sent to the San Diego's Task Force offices by overnight express. The seized drugs were logged in at the respective law enforcement offices. The out-of-state labs would perform their own drug analysis for later use at trial. Small samples of the tar heroin found at each location were collected by a DEA transport vehicle and delivered to the San Diego lab for a more detailed profile of their nutrient and mineral content.

That evening the team went to their favorite watering hole, the Days End, to celebrate the successful execution of the warrants. The highlight of their conversation, over pitchers of beer, was a recounting of what Sendow looked like in his boxers, with his bony legs, running around like a chicken with his head chopped off, on the cold pavement in front of his house. If nothing else, his pasty pouch kept him warm in the chill of the early morning hour.

Nick related his beer influenced thoughts to the others, "Sendow should be ripe for the picking. We will let him stew for a few days and then approach him about saving his hide. Otherwise, his goose, or in Sendow's case, his chicken is cooked."

Pepe said, "With that profound observation and torture of a trite metaphor, it's time to go home."

CHAPTER NINETEEN

The team continued to surveil Sendow. After exposing his skinny legs at the search warrant and losing his precious BMW, Sendow came up with a beat-up Ford Escort to drive around. On workdays, he would get breakfast at a diner near his office in Mira Mesa. The team had frequented the diner when they wanted strong coffee and heaps of hearty food. Nick knew Maggie, the owner of the place. She was in her sixties, widowed, and had lost none of her Irish flare. He had helped her son get out of a misunderstanding—a bar fight on St. Patrick's Day where her son's drunken antagonist disparaged leprechauns. Nick dropped in and showed Maggie a picture of Sendow. Maggie instantly commented, "I know that guy. He comes in most work days, and orders three eggs over easy, bacon, and hash browns. He keeps to himself, doesn't even talk to Sallie, our one, eye-catching waitress."

"Maggie dear, can you do an old Paddy drinker a good turn?"

"Nick, I didn't know you were a connoisseur of our finest Irish whisky. That's music to my ears. What do you want?"

"Tomorrow morning when Sendow comes in, have him sit over there in the corner, away from everyone else. One of my agents and I will unexpectedly be joining him for breakfast."

"Honey, I can do that for you and I know not to ask why."

"Only thing I can say, Sendow is one of those snakes that our blessed St. Patrick drove out of Ireland."

Nick and Mario parked across from the diner, and saw Sendow walk into the diner just after 8:00 a.m. "Mario, are you hungry?"

"You know better than to ask an Italian that question, I'm always ready for a good meal."

"I can't promise you a good meal, but there'll be a lot of it. Let's go."

Nick winked at Maggie when they entered. Sendow was sitting in the corner table with his back to Nick and Mario. Sallie was leaning over Sendow, pouring his coffee, angling for a good tip as her left breast pressed against his shoulder. Nick and Mario pulled up chairs on either side of Sendow and quickly sat down. Before he could say anything, Nick greeted him, "Hi Lester. I didn't know you appreciated such fine dining. I'm the prosecutor who arranged for the search warrants executed on your residence and office a few days back. I've been getting some complaints from your neighbors about having to see you in your boxers at the crack of dawn. Tough on their constitutions so early in the morning. Here's my identification. Say hello to Detective Mario Cipriani. He's a member of our Money Laundering Task Force."

Sendow blanched and began to sweat. Nick thought he might have a heart attack right there. He wanted Sendow to wait until at least they'd eaten breakfast. Nick, in a calm, soft voice, said, "Lester, relax, we're here to help you. If we wanted to arrest you, you'd already be in handcuffs. Let's have breakfast, I'll order." Nick called Sallie over. "Sallie, biscuits and gravy for me, with a side of pork links. For Mario, a stack of blueberry pancakes and for my friend here, three eggs over easy, bacon, and a side of hash browns."

"How did-did-did you know what I like to order?" stammered Sendow.

"We know a lot about you Lester. We know about your stolen property conviction that was bargained down from embezzlement of your client's funds. It saved your license. I think you got lucky. If the Accountancy Board knew all the facts, they would've yanked your CPA license. For your sake, we hope they don't find out. We also know about your drug usage as a juvenile and your successful completion of adult drug diversion before you got your CPA license. We know you still have a drug problem. A real big drug problem." Mario slid a photograph of Lester with Luis in the Polaris Ranger, driving towards the Canadian border with duffle bags in the back.

Sendow gasped, "Oh shit, oh shit, oh shit. What am I going to do? I'm ruined."

Nick leaned close to Lester. "You're right, you're in deep shit. But you don't have to be ruined. We have you tied to the Familia, both on the drug side and the money side. Our forensic auditors are going through your boxes of records and your business computer as we wait for our breakfast. Have you ever looked up the penalties for being part of a Continuing Criminal Enterprise? Up to life imprisonment. All the money laundering and standard drug distribution counts will be gravy.

"So, Lester, it's your lucky day. We're going to give you the opportunity to work with us in this case. We'll have your back. We'll fully debrief you and we want you to wear a wire for certain meetings. If you tell us the truth and fully cooperate, the heavy lifting felonies are off the table. We'd want you to plead to a money laundering count and a drug distribution count. When the time comes, if you live up to the deal, we'll tell your sentencing judge of your cooperation and positive impact on the case. You shouldn't have much prison exposure. And, it sure beats a life sentence."

"If I'm alive to enjoy all this future time among the free. You've no idea how violent and cruel these men are. They don't value life. It's not that they randomly go around shooting people. But if they kill people, it's just business to them! Nobody ever loses any sleep."

Mario replied, "We do have a good idea what the cartel is about. That's why it's so important to get the top leaders and shut them down. You'll be fully and discretely supported on any undercover work you do. Once the indictment comes down, you'll be whisked away to the federal witness protection program. You'll have to testify at trial. After the cartel members are sentenced, you'll be sentenced. Your CPA license will be gone, but you'll still have your life. You can start over. If you don't work with us, your life with the cartel will end in one of two ways—death by the cartel or life imprisonment."

Nick added, "In case you're thinking about telling the Familia about this conversation, that would just sign your own death warrant.

If they know we've approached you, they'll think you have turned no matter what. You said you know them. Cruel and violent, it's just business. Your death would just be tying up a loose end." Lester stared straight ahead. His eyes were miles away.

After a couple of minutes of silence, Lester said, "I need some time to think about it."

Nick responded, "Sure, we can wait until you finish breakfast." It was the longest breakfast that Nick and Mario ever had to endure. Lester savored every bite and followed the age old mother's axiom of chewing twenty times before swallowing.

As Nick watched Lester's last bite, he told him, "I don't care if working with you is a win-win for both of us. If you ever put me through an eating marathon again, you'll get life in prison."

"All right Mr. Drummond, I'll cooperate, but you have to convince me I'll be safe."

"We will. Tomorrow morning at nine Detective Cipriani will pick you up here and take you to our offices. You'll tell us all you know and we'll go over your safety concerns. Don't worry about the bill. We'll see you tomorrow. Remember, if you have any thoughts about going to the cartel about this, just imagine what Luis will do to you to ensure your silence."

They were waiting for Ana in the conference room to begin the debriefing of Lester. Ana limped in, a few minutes late, holding a grande cafe latte. She knew Nick hated to be kept waiting. He detested lines and took it as a personal affront when there was a long line in front of him to order lunch. Patience certainly wasn't one of his virtues. Ana felt the urge to explain her tardiness to try to forestall Nick's angry, you screwed up look. "I'm sorry I'm late. It was one of those mornings. I was dropping off dry cleaning when a guy zipped up in his Mercedes, parked in the red zone in front of the cleaners and beat me to the counter with an armload of clothes. Of course, he then had to explain each stain on each item of clothing and asked how the cleaners were going to handle his special situation. Boss, I almost arrested him right there for obstruction of justice. Then, at the other end of the parking lot, I drove over to the Starbucks drive-through on automatic pilot and it didn't register that there were 10 cars ahead of me. Before I could back out, another soccer Mom had pulled up behind me after dropping Junior off at the local elementary school. It was a child friendly van that I couldn't get around."

Nick studied Ana for a moment. "I think I know the Starbucks you're talking about; the one just off the freeway and Del Mar Heights Road."

"Yes".

"Why would you ever go to the drive-through when at the other end of the parking lot, at Von's, there's a Starbucks where you never have to wait."

Ana responded, "Hey Mr. Starbucks hater, how do you know so much about Starbucks locations? Are you a closet partaker?"

"No, Judy used to drag me along when the kids would play soccer games at the nearby grammar school." Nick thought, *Shit, probably shouldn't have brought that up.*

Mario said, "To answer your question Nick, I have done a study of women waiting in line at Starbucks drive-throughs. They enjoy the time sitting in their cars. They can listen to Public Radio, or Google something on their phone, check out Facebook, talk on their phones, or better yet, if another woman is in the car with them, they can have quality chat time. So, don't think they're just too lazy to get out of their car to go to a Starbucks at Von's, even if it saves them ten minutes."

Nick heaved a sigh of relief, "Mario, I'm glad you set us straight with scientific research. If it came out of my mouth, some people around here might think I was being sexist."

Ana smirked, "You sexist, never."

Nick replied, "I know this is probably a fascinating topic of conversation for Lester, but let's move on.

"Lester, we need to know how you met Luis and how you became the cartel's accountant."

"I like to bet on the ponies and I was getting behind with my bookie. He knew I was a CPA and told me about Luis and that he was looking for an accountant. I went over to Luis' condo in Coronado in late April of last year. We hit it off. Luis was really into horse racing. He told me he went to Del Mar each year. I told him I had some free time because tax season was over. He told me that he knew about my horse racing debt and my previous trouble with the law. He also told me he would pay well, but I shouldn't ask too many questions. He offered me a $50,000 retainer. It happened to be the amount of my gambling debt. I accepted."

Mario asked, "Did you know he wanted you to facilitate an illegal enterprise?"

"Not exactly. He said he was in a cash business as a wholesaler of agricultural products grown in Mexico. A couple of businesses, owned by others, were helping him move cash back and forth across the border. He wanted my help on moving the money and keeping track of it."

"Did you ask him what the agricultural products were? questioned Mario.

"No, I didn't really want to know."

Nick said, "So, you stuck your head in the sand and just followed instructions."

"You could say that."

Ana asked, "These companies which move cash back and forth, how is it done?"

"When I started to look at Luis' operation, it was a mess. He told me that one of the companies that was helping him was an import business that purchased food from Latin America and sold the products in Mexico and the United States. The company is called Latin American Productos and is owned by Anthony and Rachel Sakia. Luis' company was also dealing with L&M Freight, which is a cross-border, trucking business. That business is controlled by Hector Morales. Luis told me that his company had too many cash dollars. The Mexican purchasers of his food products were paying in U.S. dollars, instead of pesos, because the dollar was more stable. The Mexican peso was being devalued every few years which translated into losses for the companies that dealt in pesos. So, Luis had a huge surplus of cash dollars in Mexico that he couldn't deposit directly into Mexican banks because of Mexico's restrictions on cash dollar deposits. He was also going through a chain of Mexican exchange houses, called Numero Uno, which moved the dollars across the border for deposit into U.S. banks for a fee of three percent of the gross. The cash dollars were deposited in L&M Freight and Latin American Productos accounts for later transfer back to Mexico."

"Did you buy that?" asked Nick.

"Then, I didn't know enough about cross-border business, payment in pesos or dollars, and the Mexican currency regulations. So, although it sounded weird, I didn't think it was necessarily illegal. Luis said that a couple of cash couriers of Numero Uno got busted by the feds for not declaring the $80,000 in cash that they were carrying in backpacks into the U.S. I looked into it and told him, if he needs large amounts of cash transported into the U.S., just fill out the forms at the border and declare it. Nothing illegal about bringing large amounts of cash over if it's declared on the IRS Customs form. We set up a process to skip the middle man, Numero Uno, and just have Morales and the Sakias, or their employees, bring large amounts of cash over the border to be placed into their U.S. accounts. We didn't want to raise the suspicion of the U.S. bankers, so we spread the cash deposits into numerous accounts. Because of loopholes in the Mexican currency restrictions, once we had the cash in U.S. banks, the money could be wired directly into Mexican bank accounts, either in pesos or U.S. dollars. The Mexican restrictions don't apply to funds wired into Mexican accounts."

"Pretty damn complicated," commented Nick.

"Not really, once it got up and rolling. Luis also didn't want his cash sitting for any length of time in U.S. banks. I told him that in addition to wiring the dollars back to Mexico, the couriers could immediately obtain cashier's checks for the amounts deposited and transport those across the border to Mexico for deposit in a Mexican bank. The Mexican cash dollar deposit restrictions don't apply to cashier's checks."

Nick said, his voice heavy with sarcasm, "I wonder why Luis didn't want the money sitting in U.S. banks? It couldn't be that Luis was worried that U.S law enforcement would seize and forfeit the money?"

"It was things like that, along with Luis' highflying lifestyle, that made me seriously question what was going on. I looked into the standard business practices of businesses which operate on both sides of the border—how they are paid; whether in dollars or pesos; are they moving large amounts of cash dollars into the U.S. and then wiring it back?"

"What did you come up with?" asked Ana.

"If one is selling legitimate products in Mexico, it's generally paid for in pesos, not cash dollars. If legitimate products are sold in the U.S., they are generally paid for by check or credit card, hardly ever cash. So I questioned Luis about it."

"What did he tell you?" asked Mario.

"He just gave me a long line of bullshit. It didn't ring true. He acted real nice and invited me to take a trip up to Montana with him. We were supposed to combine fishing with opening up Canada as a market for his products. I went up there. We met up with a Harley-riding real estate agent about property and did some trout fishing. We also met with two Canadian guys who scowled a lot, grunted, and said there was a market for Luis' products in Vancouver. A few weeks later we went back and met a couple of lowlifes who were part of Luis' entourage. That's when we made the run to the Canadian border and traded duffle bags of drugs for bags of cash."

"So you finally figured out that something was amiss? That your $50,000 retainer was not just for balancing the books? That just maybe, Luis and his henchmen were exactly what they seemed, cartel drug dealers, with so much illicit cash on their hands that they didn't know what to do with it all?" Nick asked.

"I may be a bit slow on the uptake, but not entirely oblivious. It confirmed my fears; it was drug dealing. Luis, even told me after we made the Canadian border delivery, 'If you're thinking about getting out of this, it's too late. You're part of it. You're looking at 20 years if you are caught. If you think about going to the authorities, you're looking at life, not as in prison, but as in dead.'"

Mario asked, "Have you been to his compound in the hills above Rosarito Beach?"

"Yeah, a few times. I met with a couple of other bigwigs in his organization. Luis had an American Latina that we had dinner with, I think Felicia was her name."

"Oh, yeah? Tell us about her," said Ana.

"Not much to tell. When he said jump, she said how high. She was attractive, young. He met her at the track in Del Mar. Luis and at least one of his bigwig buddies are really into horse racing. I didn't see Felicia the last time I was down there, a couple of weeks ago. I asked Luis where she was. He told me we wouldn't be seeing that "bitch" anymore. She was being taken care of. I knew not to ask more questions about her."

"How did Luis seem the last time you saw him at the compound?" asked Nick.

"Nothing much different. Just a bit more pissed off than usual. His right arm was in a sling. I asked him what happened. He just said, 'Nothing, twisted my shoulder a bit.' I didn't ask him the follow up question, *If it is just a twisted shoulder, why is blood seeping through the sling?*"

Nick said, "You must be getting tired. We'll let you go in a bit. But before we do, we want to tell you about what you need to do for us. First, you're to keep us informed of what's going on. Mario will work with you on a protocol to report in. We're also going to want you to wear a wire a few times. We want you to meet with the Sakias and Hector Morales to pin down what they know about the illicit nature of the money they are laundering for Luis and the cartel."

"Wait a minute. Wearing a wire, I'm not going for that. If they suspect something, pat me down, it's all over."

"Relax Lester," said Mario. "First of all, the money laundering operators aren't heavy hitters. They were legitimate businessmen that have been turned by the lure of the all mighty American dollar and a bad economy a couple of years back. They won't be checking you for wires. Have they checked you in the past?"

"No, but the squeeze is on. The search warrants you just did made them uneasy, even if no search warrants were executed on their businesses or residences."

"Look Lester. It's not like in the movies. A radio size transmitter isn't taped to your body. We know you like to scuba dive. We saw your gear at your home. We'll provide you with a button size microphone and transmitter, hidden in a diver's watch. It transmits on 150 to 174 megahertz, higher than normal frequencies. Our receiver recorder will be hundreds of yards away. The watch is battery operated and has a two hour life. We'll discretely monitor the location. We'll have a pole camera set up outside the meeting places by our installation team. They look like your local utility company, fixing some wiring. You couldn't be safer."

"I still don't like it. But it sounds like I don't have much of a choice."

"Now you're getting the idea," said Nick. "We'll iron out the details tomorrow."

After Mario left with Lester, Ana and Nick stayed in the conference room. Nick seemed lost in space. "Earth to Nick, wake up!"

"I was just thinking. Luis had his right arm in a sling. That would've been just after the Coast Guard shot up the Donzi off of Carlsbad. The blood seeping through his sling, probably a bullet hole. It would've been the Donzi driver's right arm that would have been struck by a bullet as the Donzi crossed the Coast Guard's path. It seems that Luis likes to take risks. He delivered the first load of dope to Canada and he just drove the back-up boat for a coastal drug delivery. If nothing else, he has *huevos*."

CHAPTER TWENTY

Nick and Mario were in Nick's office, bullshitting about the Padres chances this year. "You know the Pads Nick, start out slow, get revved up after the All Star break, and then barely miss the playoffs. It'd tear your heart out if it didn't happen every year."

"Hope springs eternal at the start of every season. They got a couple of new ballplayers. Their starting pitching is pretty good, and they have a great bullpen."

"Yeah Nick, that just means a lot of 2 to 1 or 3 to 2 losses. Boring. I never knew you to be the optimist."

"Usually I'm not. Certainly, not about the scumbags we deal with. But with baseball, you have to let yourself go, dream a bit. All teams start even. Hell, even with a rotten season, a team is often not eliminated from the playoffs until September. But enough of that. We have a grand jury scheduled in three weeks. Give me a recap on how Sendow did with his meetings with the heads of the money laundering organizations."

"He did well. We had video cameras set up outside of each location on utility poles. Each had an excellent view of the front door of each office. For two weeks before the meetings, we tracked the comings and goings of the Sakias and Hector Morales, and others, into and out of their respective offices. Sendow met with Morales at his L&M Freight office in Calexico. We set up in a van a couple of blocks away, receiving the audio transmissions from Sendow's diver's watch."

"What were the reasons Sendow used to set up the meeting?"

"He said with the recent search warrants and the seized vehicle in L&M's name, as well as the fact that the feds seized some compromising records from his own offices, that they needed to talk. We have Sendow and Morales on tape talking about Morales' company being on the title of one of the drug transport vehicles in Missoula. We also have Morales expressing his concern that he got involved in laundering drug proceeds. He was really worried about what the feds would do next—execute search warrants on his home and business locations, or worse, arrest him."

"Smart guy," said Nick. "We'll get to him soon enough when we close down the investigation."

"They also discussed the need to upgrade the method they use to launder money. Sendow told them it was time step up the game to trade-based money laundering. Morales was familiar with the idea. He knew some people in L.A.'s garment district involved in that type of scheme. He gave Sendow some names that I'll pass on to the L.A. Money Laundering Task Force. Morales told Sendow that he has an auto parts business that could be used for trade-based laundering. He was fine with the idea that his car parts company would receive drug derived cash from the Familia for the purchase of auto parts. Morales would then use the cash, minus his small percentage, to buy the auto parts wholesale for resale to a legitimate Mexican auto parts dealer. That Mexican auto dealer would pay a Mexican casa de cambio for the auto parts he received from Morales' company. The casa de cambio would then turn around, minus its small percentage, and pay Luis the money in pesos. Morales said he would use the casa de cambio they had used to facilitate past laundering, Numero Uno. Morales agreed that even though this would be a more complicated method to launder the money, it'd be a safer method to avoid detection from law enforcement."

"This was all on tape Mario?"

"Every bit of it. We're getting it transcribed and pulling out the highlights to present to the grand jury."

"What happened with Mr. and Mrs. Sakia?"

"Basically the same thing. Sendow used the same reasons for the meet, the recent search warrants and need to upgrade the money laundering operation. The Sakias, through their food import business, are already operating a trade-based scheme. They discussed the need to insulate the Sakias more. They won't bring U.S. cash dollars across the border to put in their accounts in U.S. banks, but instead will receive the cash dollars directly from the drug distributors at their wholesale food offices in Chula Vista. They'll use the cash dollars to purchase wholesale food from Latin America and then sell the food to North American buyers. The Sakias agreed that this will create a paper trail that the feds won't be able to pierce. The Sakias told Sendow that it would take time for them to reconnect with their wholesale food suppliers in Latin America. All is on tape and is being transcribed. We'll have the important excerpts to give to the grand jury."

"Well done. Can you send in Jerry and Pepe? I need to talk to them about the witness list for the grand jury."

"Here's the updated witness list," said Pepe as he barged into Nick's office, followed by Jerry. Nick looked through it. It only had two civilian witnesses, the rest were law enforcement. That's the great thing about a federal grand jury. A prosecutor can present all the evidence in support of an indictment to a grand jury through law enforcement agents. Unlike a trial, where an attorney normally has to put on the witness who saw or heard something, an agent can tell a grand jury what an eyewitness told him he saw or heard—the agent testifies to hearsay.

Further, it's just the 19 grand jurors in the room with the witness and the prosecutor. There's no defense attorney. And, it only takes 12 of the 19 grand jurors to approve the indictment proposed by the prosecutor. Finally, the standard of proof to return the indictment is just probable cause to believe the suspect committed the crime. The prosecutor doesn't have to prove beyond a reasonable doubt that the person did it, like you have to at trial. Because of these lower standards, former New York Appellate Chief Justice Sol Wachtler, in a 1985 interview, told reporters that "by and large" a prosecutor "could indict a ham sandwich." A lesser known fact is that Judge Wachtler had the opportunity at a later time to reflect upon the grand jury process from a defendant's perspective. He was indicted by a federal grand jury and was sentenced to fifteen months in federal prison after pleading guilty to threatening his former lover and her daughter.

After looking through the list, Nick asked, "Have the two civilian witnesses been served?"

Jerry replied, "Felicia isn't a problem. We went through the Deputy U.S. Marshall in Topeka who is handling the witness protection. But we haven't been able to serve the Montana fire fighter, Drury Betts. He's off on another pre-fire season photo trip with his bud, Zack Reynolds. Neighbors think they're holed up in Glacier National Park. There's no cellphone service in the park. Glacier hasn't even opened yet because there's still quite a bit of snow on the ground. They're in Zack's old Chevy van."

"We need Drury for the grand jury. I want this case to come alive for the grand jury. It's about real people, not just law enforcement telling the jurors what witnesses told them. There are a couple of counts that are a little thin, like the conspiracy to murder Felicia and the aggravated assault on Ana. Drury is how we originally tied this investigation to the Baja Norte Family. He can identify Luis as making the first Yaak drug delivery and Drury was later held at gunpoint by one of Luis' minions. The jurors will relive the danger the cartel poses through Drury's eyes."

"I get it Nick, but Drury is off the grid, gone mountain man on us," Pepe said, exasperated.

With a slightly raised eyebrow, and a glint in his eye, Nick replied, "I hope you have winter clothes and snowshoes because you're going to Glacier National Park. Contact the law enforcement jurisdictions around the park and see if they can locate the van. You can fly into Great Falls and rent a four-wheel drive. Great Falls is only about two to three hours east of Glacier, depending on what part of the park you end up going to. If you have time, don't forget to send Rona a postcard. She likes to hear from us when we're out and about."

"Nick, you forget I'm a warm-blooded boy. I'm used to the desert. I'm Mexican. I think there must be a Civil Rights, Fair Employment Act, which requires you to make an accommodation and not send me into the cold."

"I'll make you an accommodation Pepe. You can take a bottle of tequila with you to keep warm. On your way out, send Josh in, we need to discuss the way we're going to approach the grand jury."

"Hello Nick. I guess I'm next. Where are you going to send me? Missoula maybe?"

"No such luck Josh. Your Montana cowgirl is just going to have to wait awhile longer for your charms. We need to make sure we're on the same page on how we're going to present evidence to the grand jury."

"What do you mean? We just put on the agents, present the favorable evidence, and presto!, we get our indictment."

"No Josh. We aren't playing it that way. This is too important of a case. We're not going to ram something down the grand jury's throats. We'll give them a fair view of the evidence. If there's some exonerating evidence that points to innocence, we put that on as well."

"Nick, you know we don't have to do that in federal court. As long as the prosecutor doesn't commit misconduct that prejudices the case, like misleading the grand jury, the indictment will be upheld if any evidence supports it. The evidence doesn't have to be substantial. The reviewing court doesn't look at the sufficiency of the evidence in support of the charges in the indictment."

"I'm aware of that. But we're going to handle this grand jury like it was before a California grand jury, subject to California law— we have to tell the grand jury about exonerating evidence and if they want to have that type of evidence presented, then we put it on. I also don't want any double hearsay. I don't want an agent to get on the stand and testify that another agent told him that an eyewitness said this or that. We need to put on the agent who talked directly with the eyewitness.

"We'll be splitting up the law enforcement witnesses. You'll take the ones who testify about the money laundering operations and the search warrants. I'll handle the two civilian witnesses and the agents who will testify about the drug smuggling operation. Are you good with that Josh?"

"Fine. It should make us better prepared for trial."

"Great, can you send Rona in?"

A few minutes later, there were three taps on Nick's door.

"Come in Rona."

"How did you know it was me Nick?"

"C'mon, after twenty years of working together, you don't think I know your door tap? The good news is that I reminded Pepe and Jerry to send you a postcard from their travels in the northern wilds. Any bad news for me about document preparation for the grand jury?"

"Not really. All the documents and evidence seized from the search warrants are numbered and indexed into the computer. You have separate hard copies of all the documents."

"Yeah, I've gone through most of them, and made a tentative exhibit list which identifies the documents I want to present by the Bates numbers. I've annotated the exhibit list to describe each document and how it fits into the case. I'll email you a copy of the list."

"Thanks. I know the drill. Abbie C. and I will pull the exhibits, number them and put them in separate folders, ready for the grand jury. You, Josh, and the witnesses will have separate exhibit books for use before the grand jury. Also, most of the blow-ups you requested are finished. We have photos of some of the Canadian border distributions by cartel members, the satellite photos of the Otay Mesa Ranch, maps of pertinent areas in Montana and southern California, and key phrases blown up and highlighted from the various transcripts of taped conversations."

"Rona, I don't know what I'd do without you?"

"Not much. Without me and your dedicated secretary, Abbie, taking care of you, you'd be even more of a mess. I see that Abbie cleaned off your desk and even washed your coffee cups. Nick, you have to wake up to the 21st century, just a little. Secretaries don't clean out their bosses' coffee cups anymore."

"Hell, I know that. Secretaries aren't supposed to even get you coffee. I have faithfully gone to my political correctness training. But Abbie C. is old school. I don't ask her to clean my desk or wash out my coffee cups. She just does it once in awhile. Maybe she can't stand the clutter, even from afar."

"It's probably the mold in your cups she can't stand. You don't know how good you have it."

"I know Rona, and I am eternally grateful to you and Abbie."

CHAPTER TWENTY-ONE

The offshore breeze gently brushed Ana's bangs from her forehead. Her eyes were half-closed, with a dreamy look. She was breathing slowly and deeply. "I just want to soak it into each one of my cells, the salt air and the beauty, Nick." Ana's gaze rested on the ocean and Coronado Islands from the top of Point Loma. She swirled around in the wind to face Nick. His normally furrowed brow seemed to have fewer lines, his eyes seemed softer, and the ends of his mouth were upturned. The San Diego harbor and skyline were spread out behind him.

To Ana's left was the old Point Loma lighthouse, built in 1855. At 400 feet above sea level, it was the highest lighthouse in elevation in the United States until it was decommissioned in 1891 for the new Point Loma lighthouse, located at a lower elevation, close to the water. The old lighthouse was now a museum at the Cabrillo National Monument, chock full of stories. It was said that on certain nights, the keeper would have to fire off a shotgun to ward off ships because fog and low lying clouds would obstruct a ship's view of the light.

"Nick, I'm so glad you suggested we hike along the cliffs. This is the first Saturday we've had off in months."

"I love being outside in the fresh air with you. I figured the whole team could use the weekend off. Even Pepe and Jerry are "vacationing" in Montana. Almost all the preparation is done for the grand jury. Time to relax before another stretch of long hours. Enough of that. Check out these binoculars. About half way to the horizon, straight out into the ocean, there are gray whales spouting water. Look, just where I'm pointing. See, there's a waterspout."

"No, I don't see it."

"Keep looking, every 10 seconds or so there'll be another spout."

"Oh, Nick, I see one. I can even see the top gray line of the whale's back. There it goes again. She's heading north."

"Yeah. The whale is part of the gray whale migration back to the northern seas from the birthing bays in Baja California. There's one near the town of Guerrero Negro, Scammon's Lagoon, but my favorite in Baja is Bahia Magdalena, southwest of Laredo. It isn't developed there. A long time back I drove close to 800 miles, rented a ponga, and motored around the bay. I saw so many whales. Some I felt I could reach out and touch. They were 30 feet longer than my 15 foot ponga, but I felt no fear. I wanted to jump in with them. I even had my wet suit and snorkel, but chickened out at the last minute."

"You mean to tell me you were actually going to jump in with those behemoths?"

"I seriously thought about it. It was in my younger days. Being one with nature. Nothing could hurt me. It's a male adrenalin-adventure gene. Why do you think young males are sky surfing out of planes and doing double flips off of ramps on their motorcycles? Turn on the X games sometime."

"Well, there's being stupid and there's being really stupid. I always had you in the stupid category, but not in the really stupid category."

"I didn't jump in. I belong in the plain stupid category. Enough about my lack of mental prowess. I brought some lunch and have a blanket in my knapsack."

Nick laid out the blanket for them to sit on. The knapsack revealed fresh sourdough bread, two varieties of cheese, grapes and slices of melon. With a flourish, Nick withdrew a thermos, "For you milady, chilled sauvignon blanc and two plastic wine glasses to allow us to properly imbibe."

As they were finishing the last of the cheese and bread, with the afternoon San Diego sun caressing their faces, Ana had a guilt-ridden thought. "I can't help thinking about Pepe and Jerry in the wilds of Montana, trying to track down our firefighter witness. All sorts of things could happen to them."

"Don't worry about them. Pepe told me late this morning that local law enforcement had found Zack's van parked where the road to Many Glacier hotel is blocked by snow. There are cross country ski tracks leading from the van along the snow-covered road to the hotel and the campground. They're probably camping and taking pictures. Pepe told me that they're going to try to hitch a ride with a search and rescue helicopter to find them. Right now, they're probably having a great helicopter ride, seeing the sights."

"Aren't there grizzly bears and other assorted wild things up there?" "Maybe a few. Nothing to worry about."

Mid-afternoon on the same Saturday, Zack and Drury were lying on the snow by their cameras, which were screwed into tripods. They had been taking pictures, trying to capture the essence of Iceberg Lake. Zack was looking at the lake below them and the looming backdrop of the cirque of snow-laden peaks. Drury was snoozing. The lake was covered in large chunks of ice. Between the chunks, the glacier-infused aquamarine water peaked through. It was so clear that the rounded rocks on the bottom of the lake looked wet and open to the sky. Zack, looking more closely, could see the cliffs of the far side of the lake reflected in every detail on the lake's surface.

Earlier that day, after snowshoeing the five miles from their camp at the end of the road by Swiftcurrent Lake, they had digitally captured a red fox hunting for gophers in the snow. The fox was so intent on catching lunch that he didn't pay any attention to the two human statues, 50 yards away, behind their cameras on tripods. The photos were incredible—sun glistening off the fire orange-red fur of the fox as he sprung several feet in the air to dive head first into the snow. Another photo showed the fox's head completely buried in the snow with his body sticking straight up. On the fox's third try, his head came up from the snow with a gopher in his mouth. The ugly dark grey gopher, with small beady eyes, a rat's tail, and long curved claws, didn't move in the fox's jaws. The grey stood out against the white band of fur along the fox's muzzle. The fox was completely alert as he trotted off with his prize, his two-foot long tail with a white bob at the end, trailing behind him.

Zack tried to nudge Drury awake. Zack thought, *That son of a bitch can sleep anywhere. It must be all those wildfires he has fought, catching a nap in the middle of burning infernos when he could.* Enough with politeness. Zack cracked Drury in the ribs, "Time to wake up sleeping beauty, we have to pack up and get down to camp before it gets dark."

"Let me rest a little longer. It's just us and this beautiful, untouched spot. This is why we came here, for moments like this."

"Drury, you've had plenty of moments like this, hours like this, days like this. I like the solitude as much as you do, but it's time to get your ass up and get going. Wait a sec. What in the hell am I hearing?"

"Shut up Zack, let me listen. It sounds like a helicopter coming up the valley towards us." They waited, listened and scanned the sky. The noise got louder. A helicopter popped over the ridge from Swiftcurrent Lake.

"Drury, what the fuck! What's the copter doing here? Violating our peace and quiet. We haven't seen anybody else around. There isn't anyone to rescue, and nobody to see but us." The helicopter hovered two hundred feet above them. Two lines were thrown out of the side bay of the copter. "Drury, two men are being lowered down on slings! This is either some hell of a training exercise or Al Queda has got their wires crossed. No terrorist targets down here unless they're after moose, bear, or bighorn sheep."

"I got my binocs on them. Not holding any weapons. Do have packs. We better go greet our new friends. Who knows, maybe it's a couple of my firefighting buddies dropping in to say hello."

Earlier that day, Pepe and Jerry had driven hell-bent, in their rented Range Rover, towards Glacier National Park from Great Falls, Montana. The Sheriff's Office closest to the Many Glacier entrance to the park had reported that Zack's van was located within the park, three miles from the Many Glacier hotel where the snow had blocked the road. Glacier National Park wouldn't even open until late May and the famous old railroad hotel wouldn't open until early June. The 200 room, wooden masterpiece, overlooking Swiftcurrent Lake and the glacier carved mountains around it, had been built in 1920 as an enticement for tourists to take the transcontinental Canadian railroad to an exotic location.

Hotel guests would leisurely sip cocktails on the balcony overlooking the lake, watching grizzly bears feeding on grubs on the mountainsides. In the morning, guests would often be treated to a moose swimming across the lake. A jagged peak towered over the lake, directly across from the hotel. The lake continued in two directions beyond either side of the peak, to the left along a submerged glacial valley that led to Josephine Lake and a hike to Grinnell Glacier, and past the peak to the right, which led to the end of the road and the campground below more majestic peaks. From the campground, various trails led to the high country, one being the 1100-foot vertical ascent over five miles to Iceberg Lake.

Pepe was bitching as usual on the ride. "I saw those so-called "Great Falls" as we flew in. Nothing great about them. A couple of falls in a row, 15 or 20 feet high."

"You'd think it was a big thing if you were part of the Lewis and Clark expedition coming up the Missouri River and had to carry your boats and supplies around the falls."

"Okay gringo. When the Lewis and Clark expedition happened, California, Arizona, and Texas were still part of Mexico. We California Mexicans were worried about Mexican history back then."

Jerry and Pepe pulled into Browning on Highway 89. Browning was part of the Blackfoot Reservation, about 40 miles from the Many Glacier entrance. The Sheriff's Office had a substation there. "Just in time for our meeting with Lieutenant Keme Mingan," said Jerry.

Jerry and Pepe were impressed by the Lieutenant. He was a Blackfoot and a Persian War vet. Keme meant thunder. He looked like thunder, tall and stern with a low, gravelly voice. Keme listened to their story. "This is the best I can do for you. I can justify the use of a search and rescue helicopter for one trip only. A short trip at that. We can fly you around the Many Glacier area and see if we can spot them. You can either come back and try to meet them by foot or we can rappel you down to meet them. We can lend you back country supplies—a pack, snow shoes, satellite radio, sleeping bag, heavy jacket, and some food."

Pepe's eyes went wide and he blanched, "What do you mean rappel down from a helicopter?"

"Well, maybe, I overstated it. We winch you down in a sling. It's perfectly safe unless high winds kick up. Once you meet with your guys, you snowshoe out. You'll have maps and a GPS. Probably those two guys you're looking for will come out with you. Montanans do not leave tenderfeet alone in the mountains unless the tenderfeet are obnoxious. If something really goes wrong, you have your satellite phone and we can rescue you for real and charge it to your department. This quick flight is a professional courtesy."

"Hey Lieutenant, you're getting compensated. I told you I'd share that fine bottle of tequila I brought along."

"Ugh Pepe. Firewater not good for Indians. But it'd be shameful not to accept your hospitality."

A belly laugh came out of Pepe. "Here I thought you were the inscrutable Indian type. You're my type of guy. Maybe us Mexicans and Indians should get together and kick the gringos out."

Keme replied, "Too late for that, I already have my Lexus and an iPhone. We'll get your stuff together. You drive to where Zack's van is and the helicopter will pick you up there in an hour. There's a large turnout that the snowplows have carved out."

Pepe and Jerry drove north along Highway 89, which paralleled the park. They could see the peaks to their left and the wind-blown trees on the side of the mountains. They passed along lower Saint Mary Lake, slender, long and blue, before arriving at Babb, population unknown, with a restaurant, a store, a church, and a gas station. Fortunately, Babb lacked the accouterments of most entry towns outside of National Parks—no strip of cheap motels, nor any, even cheaper souvenir shops, and no fast food restaurants. They turned left onto the road to the Many Glacier entrance, drove along Swiftcurrent Creek and most of Lake Shelbourne until they reached Zack's van at the end of the snow blocked road. They didn't pay sufficient attention to their beautiful environs—a crystal blue lake to their left, snowcapped peaks beyond the lake, and craggy peaks in front of them. Thousands of years ago, glacier movement had carved out the valleys extending into the mountains. In the upper glacial lakes, the glaciers had left a residue in the water, which when struck by the sun, reflects an impossibly beautiful, aquamarine color.

Pepe didn't have the peace of mind to ponder nature's beauty. He was wondering what the hell he was getting himself into. He had never been in a helicopter, much less being lowered down into a white abyss from one. With Jerry's special forces background, he was much more comfortable with the idea. Pepe didn't want to do it, but Jerry urged him on. Every part of his body was telling him no, but he wasn't raised to back down. Loss of face was not an option. Pepe finally told Jerry as they waited for the helicopter, "If Keme says it's safe to lower us down when we find them, then I'm in."

Right on time, a few minutes later, the helicopter landed at the cleared turn around. Jerry and Pepe crouched down behind their Rover to protect themselves against the gusts of wind piercing out from the rotor as the copter landed. Keme jumped out of the helicopter bay with two packs in his hands. He showed them each pack's sleeping bag, food packets, space blanket, snow shoes and other essential items.

Pepe and Jerry strapped into two pull down seats in the small cargo bay while Keme sat next to the pilot. Keme handed Jerry a satellite phone and passed out earplugs. They were up in the air before Pepe could get used to the idea. The copter was dancing around in the wind. Pepe could only think about the small sheath of metal between him and the air below. They headed past the Many Glacier hotel. It looked like a huge, wooden sentinel in a mountainous ice world. The helicopter flew past the hotel to the summer campground area at the far western portion of Swiftcurrent Lake. They didn't see any signs of humans until they spotted two low-lying tents, stretched out under the trees at the farthest campground. Keme shouted, "That must be their camp, they can't be too far from here. We'll first fly over two upper glacier lakes, Josephine and Grinnell. On a sunny day like this, the lakes will be shining like liquid aquamarines. Great photo ops."

They flew up the valley leading up to Grinnell Glacier, past the lakes. No sign of them. Above Grinnell Lake, they were face to face with Grinnell Glacier and the smaller Salamander Glacier above it. One hundred years ago both glaciers were one and the mass of ice extended 1,000 feet high, enclosing what is now ice-free Grinnell Lake. The remnants of this massive glacier are just ghosts of its former self, maybe 10 percent of its former mass. In another 20 years there may be no Grinnell or Salamander Glaciers to gaze at.

"The other place they could be, is up the glacier valley to Iceberg lake, nestled beneath a cirque of peaks," Keme yelled back at Jerry and Pepe. "If they're not there, we'll have to turn back because we're getting short of fuel." Pepe couldn't help thinking, *I hope they're not there. I'm ready for dry land, a nice warm bed and a steak dinner.*

As Pepe's luck would have it, as soon as the copter came over the last ridge to Iceberg Lake, they saw the two figures below, looking up at them. Moment of truth. "You boys ready?"

"Sure we are Keme," answered Jerry before Pepe had a chance to voice any objections.

"Time to hook you two up. We can wench both of you down at the same time. The winds are not up so the lines shouldn't tangle. Put on your packs and we'll hook you onto the slings. It'll be like being cradled in your mother's arms."

Pepe found his voice. "I don't know about your mother's arms Keme, but whenever my mother held me as a baby, she almost smothered me in her large bosom."

Speaking through a wide grin, Keme replied, "Okay, just think of the sling as being in the arms of your favorite supermodel."

Stepping off the side of the helicopter was a giant mental leap for Pepe, even with a metal cable attached to the sling. The copter's blades buffeted them for the first 20 feet. When that settled down, Pepe managed to enjoy it. Sort of like a vertical zip line. Instead of whizzing along the top of a jungle in Costa Rica, this was a slow motion, swinging panoramic ride. The two were grabbed by Zack and Drury below, and unhitched. Drury gave a couple of yanks on the slings and the slings were pulled back up. Zack looked at the two.

"You certainly don't look like terrorists, but you seem lost. Who are you guys?"

Jerry replied, with a note of sarcasm in his voice, "We're your friendly process servers. We go to any lengths to find our witnesses. My colleague, the one looking a bit green, is Cal DOJ Special Agent Pepe Cantana, and I'm Jerry Slater, Homeland Security Investigator, at your service. Remember the drug smuggling ring in Yaak that you reported to our task force leader, Nick Drummond, a number of months back? No good turn goes unrewarded. Drury, because you were the one who first viewed the crooks, and got a gun stuck in your face, you win an expense free trip to San Diego to testify before a federal grand jury in two weeks."

"What about me?" asked Zack. "I was there."

"You were there Zack. But you aren't as prone to violent encounters as your buddy. Uncle Sam doesn't have an unlimited budget, notwithstanding our dramatic helicopter appearance."

Pepe said, "Sorry to drop in on you guys without notice and I don't mean to be rude, but I'd like to get down the mountain as soon as we can. Twenty degree weather with snow everywhere in the middle of this glacier wonderland doesn't thrill me."

Zack replied, "We should get going. We were just packing up to head back to our tents at the Swiftcurrent Lake campground. We should tell you boys that we did see grizzly tracks coming up here. It might be the same female grizzly with her cub that we saw down by the lake at a bighorn sheep kill. They had both been munching on a thawed out carcass. Mama and the cub had blood saturated throughout their muzzles and claws. I got a couple of great shots of them from about 100 yards away. Here, let me show you on my camera." Zack flipped through the images until he found the ones that he wanted to show to Pepe and Jerry. A huge grizzly, with a red painted face, stared at them. Her four paws were resting on layers of rocks. The long curved claws were also red-hued, grasping onto the shale. Zack went to the next photo. A cub was walking towards them, with the same red face and curved claws, a miniature version of his mother.

Drury added, "Don't mean to freak you fellas out. But the one thing to worry about is a Mama grizzly protecting her cub. If you see a cub near the trail, back away slowly and hope that you're not between Mama and her baby. If a female or male grizzly starts paying close attention to you, don't turn around and run. They will chase you down. They have bursts up to 35 miles per hour. Face them and make yourself look big. Even when they begin to charge, stand your ground. They often perform mock charges and turn off. If it looks for real, curl up in a ball, with your back to them, and your head tucked in underneath you. Play dead, even if the grizzly swipes at you and starts gnawing on you. It shouldn't come to that. I have a 30 ought 6 that will stop a grizzly if my aim is true, and Zack is carrying some capsicum red pepper spray in a holster that does a number on their eyes and lungs. But the spray is only effective from within 15 feet. When one brings out the spray, it's close encounter time."

"Thanks guys for filling me in. That makes me feel a lot better. Can we go now and get out of this too natural wilderness?" asked Pepe.

They strapped into their aluminum snowshoes. Each pair had about an eight inch extension at the back end to disburse their weight over a larger area when they walked. The increased distribution kept their snowshoes from sinking as far into the snow. Zack led the way down the side of the mountain, following the summer trail. They walked past frozen creeks which were coming down the valley from the cirque of peaks. Ice formed on the surface of the creeks and along overhanging plants and rocks where water dripped. The water beneath the ice-surfaced creeks, still flowed.

Pepe called out to Zack ahead, "I thought bears hibernated when there's snow on the ground."

"For the most part, they do. Bears go into their dens after the first heavy fall snowstorm, but will come out in late spring while there's still snow on the ground. Females with their cubs, come out a little later than the males. I have to take a quick piss. I'll catch up with you."

Pepe passed Zack and became the leader. He walked slowly, finding his way down the trail that was mainly covered by snow. He was singing some of his favorite pop songs, having read somewhere that you should make noise to let bears know you're coming so as to not surprise them. Pepe's out of tune medley was interrupted by a squealing ball of brown fur that came rolling down the mountain, onto the trail just below him. "Oh shit," breathed out Pepe. He started backing up slowly, breathing rapid, shallow breaths as he looked around for Mama grizzly. The cub was still squealing as Pepe backed around a small curve in the trail. He began to breathe more normally, the sweat coming down his face lessened. He was thinking, *Whew! That was so close,* when he heard the loudest, deepest growl in his too short life. Pepe looked up to his left, in the general direction that the cub had come tumbling down, and saw Mama on her hind legs, seven feet tall and all of 500 pounds, staring at him. Her small, rounded ears were back, and throaty growls were emanating from her mouth. Pepe froze. His senses went on highest alert. He could count the teeth in her mouth from 20 yards away. He heard two pair of footsteps, quietly, but hurriedly, come towards him down the trail. Zack's soft, but firm voice, echoed in his head, "Don't move, don't say anything. I have spray. Drury is coming up with the rifle."

Zack's soothing commands rocketed out of Pepe's brain when 500 pounds of flesh got down off her hind legs, and rushed towards him. A yell in his ear, "Get down, protect your organs!" Pepe reacted immediately, dropped down and curled in a ball, his back facing the bear. The bear took a swipe at Pepe's form with her right paw, slicing his parka and drawing blood from his upper right arm before the claw ripped through the pack. The grizzly lowered her head to nuzzle the blood coming from Pepe's arm. He could feel hot globs of saliva dripping on him. Pepe's silent mantra of *please God* was shunned aside by Zack's guttural, primal shout behind him. The grizzly raised up to a full discharge of capsicum spray in her eyes and mouth from eight feet away. Zack's arm, outstretched towards the bear, never wavered. The grizzly had to close her eyes and her lungs were burning. Mama grizzly heard the squeals of her cub behind her. She snorted, turned and went to her cub.

Zack looked at Drury who had his rifle still raised in the direction of the bear. "Why didn't you pull the trigger?"

"Initially, I couldn't get a clear shot with the bear slobbering all over Pepe. Then, it seemed like you had everything under control. Also, who needs all the paperwork over a dead grizzly. I'd much rather take pictures of them than shoot them."

Jerry went to help Pepe up. Pepe was shaking uncontrollably. "Steady Pepe, the bear and her cub have gone down the hillside. It's safe to go on.

Pepe didn't say anything other than murmuring a thanks to Zack. They walked back to the camp in silence.

At camp, Drury got out the medicine kit he carries when he's fighting wildfires. "Pepe, we have to look at your claw wound and see if it needs patching." Drury washed out the slash. Blood was still oozing slowly from the wound. It was two inches long and about a half inch deep. "Looks like you're gonna need a few stitches. I've got a needle and some catgut."

"Catgut? What are you talking about?" asked Pepe, with a skeptical look.

"Not to worry, it's really strands of bovine intestines. I like it for its tensile strength when you are going to engage in physical activity. Just promise me, once I stitch you up with bovine intestines, you won't stop on the walk out to graze."

"I can promise you no grazing, but I'm stopping if I see a taco food truck."

Zack raised his cup, "I'll drink to that," gulping down his vodka, Tang, and ice cube snow concoction. Zack handed Pepe a tin cup of the same. "Have a few swallows before Doctor Drury works his magic." Drury went to work. A few minutes later, Pepe had four stitches on his upper right arm.

Pepe looked at his arm, surprised by how quickly and professionally Drury had stitched him up. "It looks like you've done this before. Have you had medical training?"

"Not really. A couple of first aid courses and stitching up about 100 or so of my fellow fire fighters over the years. My handiwork is usually rewarded with a free drink once we return to civilization."

"You can count on at least one more," said Pepe, with appreciation in his voice.

The sun was setting. Drury told Pepe and Jerry that he was sorry, but they needed to camp here for the night. It wasn't safe to hike out the four miles to their vehicles in the dark.

Zack started a fire. He told them, "You city folk just relax. We'll cook you up our specialty dinner. Those rations that Keme gave you, I wouldn't even feed to the bear that tried to eat you."

After their day of whale watching, strolling along the ocean cliffs, and savoring their picnic lunch, Nick and Ana went back to Nick's apartment to pick up a bottle of wine. Nick wanted to surprise Ana by taking her to a Romanian restaurant, Cafe Bucharest, located downtown, in a basement in the Gaslamp Quarter. The restaurant allowed its patrons to bring their own wine for a reasonable corkage fee. He had just the wine. The family of an old high school friend had an upper end boutique winery, off the Russian River, north of San Francisco, near the coast. Their pinot noir had a national reputation, and could only be bought by getting on the winery's mailing list. It was not sold in stores, and only a few restaurants had it for twice the retail price. The pinot, only a few years old, had a Robert Parker Jr. review of 98 out of 100. It was touted as a profound, modern classic, with floral notes and hint of sweet raspberries. The pinot was the most valuable item in Nick's apartment, next to his stereo system. This night with Ana was *vale la pena* (worth the pain) of opening up his cherished bottle.

Nick knew from looking at Ana's background check that her mother's side of the family had emigrated from Romania. He hoped that having her full of comfort food laced with family memories might ease the recriminations to come from what he had to talk to her about. Nick had called ahead and had reserved a small table in the far corner of the restaurant, with chairs on either side of a corner of the table, facing out.

Nick gently pushed in her chair. "I love this Nick. The low lights, the fire in the stone fireplace, and photos of my mother's Romania on the walls."

"It is very intimate. I like that there are only a dozen tables and no television hanging over the small bar. They each ordered a bowl of sour meatball soup and shared a stuffed cabbage appetizer. Ana went with a chicken kebab entree and Nick chose potato goulash with smoked sausage. They lingered over each bite, heads close together, sipping the pinot as they ate. After the second glass, Nick even imagined that he tasted the "hint of raspberries". But no matter how hard he concentrated, he couldn't make out the "floral notes". So much for being a wine snob. The bottle of wine was almost finished when the violinist came over to their table and asked what they wanted to hear. Nick usually shied away from restaurant minstrels, realizing a healthy tip would be liberated from his wallet. Not this time. The violinist was excellent, already having entranced other diners. Nick requested the theme from Dr. Zhivago. Ana reminded him of Lara, with dark hair, instead of blond. Beautiful, sensuous eyes as deep as darkened pools, and a fiercely independent woman. The violinist didn't let them down. Nick graciously separated a ten spot from his wallet. They looked over the menu for dessert.

Jerry and Pepe pulled up stumps to sit close to the fire. The temperature had dropped to 10 degrees above zero. Zack handed them metal plates, icy cold to the touch. Jerry's fingers stuck to the sides of the plate. He had to pull them off before some of his skin was permanently melded into the metal. Drury scooped out a brimming ladle full of the concoction percolating in the pot over the fire. Jerry's penlight gave him a good look at what he was about to eat. Beans, cut up hot dogs, and melted cheese. Drury proudly exclaimed, "Yep, this is our staple; cut up Oscar Weiner dogs and barbecue beans, mixed in with melted Velveeta cheese. If you like, there's some catsup over there. A splash of that and it's high gourmet."

"Isn't Velveeta cheese that processed cheese that comes in a rectangular brick? asked Jerry, hesitantly.

"Sure is. Tastes great and you don't have to worry about refrigeration," replied Zack.

Pepe murmured under his breath so only Jerry good hear, "You really need to worry about refrigeration around here. We probably won't have any long term effects from eating this. We we won't live long enough to experience them."

It actually tasted good. About anything would taste good in the cold and after what had happened, Pepe asked for more. "I gotta tell my Mamacita about this recipe. It might take over for homemade tamales during the holidays. Hell of a lot easier to make."

Zack added, "You haven't seen anything yet. Wait for dessert. We have ice cream for you. Not real ice cream, but the dehydrated kind. It's lightweight. It's the dessert astronauts eat in space."

Pepe tried to beg off. "Sorry guys, I only eat my ice cream with chocolate syrup and nuts on top."

"You got to try this. Part of the mountain experience. Top off a fun-filled day of rappelling out of an helicopter, snowshoeing, being attacked by a grizzly, and eating the finest dinner one can have anywhere."

"Okay Zack, you talked me into it. I forgot what a fine day I had." Drury broke up an ice cream sandwich size rectangle into four pieces. Pepe took a long look at it. It looked like styrofoam with a chocolate cracker crust. He could barely feel the weight in his hand. It was as dry as a bone. No ice, no cream. He took a tentative bite. It did taste like ice cream. Amazing. The mountain air must be playing tricks on him.

After dinner, no one felt like talking much. Each was immersed in his own thoughts about what had happened that day. They all turned in just after 8:00—Pepe and Jerry looking ahead to 10 hours of fitful sleep in a cold sleeping bag, wrapped in a space blanket, on the hard ground, counting off the minutes before first light when they could get up and go.

The candle was burning down. It still gave them enough light to eat their desserts. Ana had the raspberry cheesecake while Nick tried not to gobble down a delicious apple tarte tatin with a scoop of vanilla bean ice cream on top.

Nick couldn't postpone his conversation with Ana any longer. "Ana, we need to talk about seeing each other after the indictment. It's only a few weeks away."

"What do you mean? What does that have to do with our relationship?"

"We can't see each other like this until after the trial. I'll be asking the grand jury to indict the cartel members with conspiracy to murder Felicia, and an aggravated assault against you, for the motorcycle shooting. If they indict, we can't have the defense poking into our relationship. It could be the basis for recusing me from prosecuting this case. If they find out about our relationship, they're going to argue to the judge that I have to be kicked off the case because I can't "fairly" prosecute the case."

"That's bullshit. Anyone who knows you, realizes that you fairly prosecute cases no matter what. Even if your mother was on trial."

"I wouldn't go quite that far. But a judge can remove a prosecutor if it appears that he can't prosecute the case in a manner that provides a defendant with a fair trial.

"Is this what the romantic picnic and dinner were about? Pulling at my heart strings, just to cut them off."

Nick grasped her hands. His voice quavered as he looked her directly in the eyes, inches away, "I wanted the perfect day for us to last six months until this is over."

"Ana's eyes glistened with tears from anger and sadness. "It was the perfect day. It may last until we're all through, maybe right now." Nick didn't say anything. He continued to look her in the eyes and with his right hand, gently stroked her shoulder. Minutes passed. A smile gradually spread across Ana's face. "Well, if this is going to be the last day for a while, we may as well end it on a high note. You're coming to my condo tonight."

"How I love a woman who knows what she wants."

Nick was on his knees over Ana. She was lying naked on her back in her bed. His hands were slowly circling over her stomach, a fraction of an inch from touching her. Ana's skin reached up, seeking to touch his rotating hands. She could feel the energy between them. He moved his hands over her breasts, still barely not touching her. She yearned for his touch. He moved down her body, each hand traveling along the perimeter of her pelvis. Ana's legs were spread, with her knees slightly bent. His hands caressed, now gently touching her inner thighs before moving down to her calves, focusing on the scar where she had been shot. They lingered there. Nick leaned over and softly kissed her scar, from one end to the other. He moved up her legs, kissing her inner thighs, just up to and around where she was dying to be touched. "Stop teasing me. I want you, I need you now inside me."

"I always obey your desires, but not quite yet." Nick moved to her breasts, softly biting one nipple, then the next. Ana arched her back, her pelvis rhythmically moving back and forth to Nick's caresses."

"Now, damn it!"

"Yes, now." Nick plunged inside her. Both were lost to each other. Both were lost to the outside world.

CHAPTER TWENTY-TWO

"Pepe, I'm sorry about your misadventure in the wilds. You really shouldn't go one on one with a grizzly protecting her cub. Grizzly bear wrestling isn't your thing. Stick to something closer to home. Bullfighting maybe?"

"Thanks for the advice Nick. But because of my wound, Drury told me to lay off bullfighting for awhile. My only sporting activity in the near future will be going to Chargers games. Remember, you owe me. I braved frigid weather, fierce animals, and processed cheese and beans to serve your damn subpoena."

"He'll be well worth it. Drury will be my first witness before the grand jury next Monday. He will set the tone. A courageous, self-sufficient man, fighting wildfires to keep our rural communities safe. A man who, without regard to personal safety, exposed an international drug distribution cartel. A man who stared down a gun barrel in his face to do his civic responsibility."

"Hallelujah! Nick. Are you practicing your final argument for the jury trial? Remember, this is just the grand jury next week."

"You're right Pepe. I'm just trying to get in advocacy mode. I'll tone it down for the grand jury. If your arm is all right, I want you to be my investigator, outside the grand jury, to help coordinate witnesses and troubleshoot."

"No problem. The doctor said Drury did a good job stitching me up.

He'll take out the stitches in a week or two."

"Can you send in Josh. We need to finalize our preparations for the grand jury."

While Nick waited for Josh to come in, his thoughts turned to Ana.

He wondered if he could really refrain from being with her until after the trial. Six months was a long, long time. It helped and hurt to see her at the office, talking with her. Putting on the professional facade, keeping her at arm's distance, was hard. Josh walked in.

They went over the order of presentation of the evidence to the grand jury. They'll start with the Montana drug smuggling. The next category of evidence will be the San Diego coast drug smuggling, followed by the evidence seized from the search warrants executed at the various cartel warehouses. Then there'll be a series of witnesses about the Baja Norte Familia cartel. These include Mario recounting what accountant Sendow told him about the cartel and Luis' compound in the hills near Rosarito Beach. Also, experts will testify about how the cartel operates, where they grow their poppies and process their heroin, and the hierarchy of the cartel. One of the forensic laboratory chemists will tie in all the heroin seized to the region of Mexico where the cartel grows its poppies. The next to last category of witnesses will be about the money laundering operations that facilitate the cartel in moving hoards of cash into the banking system. This portion of the grand jury presentation will be document intensive and rely heavily on summary charts prepared by the task force's forensic auditor.

Finally, they'll put on evidence as to the conspiracy to murder Felicia and the shooting of Ana in the motorcycle drive-by. For these counts, it'll be difficult to prove a sufficient connection to the cartel leaders. Felicia, Pepe and Ana will testify. To bolster the tenuous tie to the cartel, Josh and Nick decided they would also call Felicia's cousin, Alan, who had told gang-bangers that his cousin was coming into town the next day.

Before presenting any evidence to the grand jury, Josh and Nick agreed that Nick would read them the proposed indictment. Their proposed indictment includes enough detail about the cartel's activities to operate as a roadmap for the grand jurors. Nick also planned to read several key jury instructions before any witnesses testified to help the jurors assess the evidence. The instructions included the considerations for evaluating a witness's credibility, the standard of proof to return a count of an indictment, and the difference between direct and circumstantial evidence. At the end of the evidence presentation, Nick would read the opening instructions again, and the instructions as to the elements of each count charged in the proposed indictment. Just before the grand jurors would commence their deliberations, Nick would review the evidence presented and how it related to each count of the indictment.

Monday morning, at 8:00, Nick met with Drury in the hallway outside the grand jury room. "Drury, did you find a good place for dinner last night?"

"I wasn't comfortable at all those fancy places in the Gaslamp. I headed to the outskirts. I 'figgered' I could find a place more to my liking and my price range. I'm trying to make a few dollars on the per diem you're giving me. On 10th Avenue, a place caught my eye. It was called 'Basic Pizza'. Big high ceilings and unfinished walls of brick and pipe. There was a big TV set at one end and draft beer. They only sell pizza and salads. Kept the choices down. I had a Hawaiian pizza and a couple of drafts of a local I.P.A. Good beer, good thin crust pizza. I was a happy camper."

"Great. Do you remember what we went over yesterday in my office? Just tell the truth. If you don't understand a question, ask me to repeat it. Don't guess at something. If you don't know the answer to a question, it's fine to say, 'I don't know.' This isn't a quiz show where you have to give an answer. I'm going to meet with the grand jury for about an hour, get to know them and explain some of the law to them. Then I'll call you in. Grab a coffee or something. Just make sure you're back in an hour. Pepe will be here by then as well."

"How is that grizzly fighting Mexican doing? I liked his spunk. Even more, I liked his bottle of tequila that we swigged back at their Range Rover."

"Pepe is doing well. His doctor is a big fan of yours. Said you did a fine job on the stitches. I was surprised that you could get a needle through that thick hide of his. See you in an hour."

As he walked into the room, Nick smiled at the 19 grand jurors. They seemed like a good group. Mostly middle-aged to elderly. Mainly white, with two Latinos, an Asian, and an African-American. Pretty much the composition one would expect in San Diego for a grand jury. The younger people don't have the availability to serve an on-call, one year time commitment. Nick bet there were probably five or six retired military people, which was always a good thing for a prosecutor. San Diego still had the veneer of being a military town. There were several military bases in the county and many former military come back for a second career or retirement.

"I'm Nick Drummond. I'm a prosecutor from the State Attorney General's Office and am cross-designated as a Special Assistant U.S. Attorney to prosecute cases in federal court. However, I don't know how 'special' I am. I'll be presenting evidence to you about a drug smuggling cartel and a money laundering operation. You will hear testimony from a few civilian eyewitnesses and quite a number of law enforcement agents who will tell you what they saw or what other witnesses to incidents told them. We will sprinkle in a few experts to help you tie it all together."

"I'm not going to go into a lot of detail about what I believe the evidence will be in this case. The drug smuggling part of the investigation started last October in Yaak, Montana, a few miles from the Canadian border. You'll hear about heroin and marijuana being smuggled into Canada. Also, you'll hear about drugs coming up the coast from Mexico to be off-loaded on San Diego beaches as well as drugs seized at various warehouses in the United States and Canada. You'll hear about the Baja Norte Familia cartel, which smuggles the drugs, and the millions of dollars from the drug sales that are laundered for the cartel through different money laundering operators. You'll also hear about a machine gun assault directed towards a former girlfriend of one of the leaders of the cartel. A federal agent was seriously wounded by a couple of bullets when she successfully protected the former girlfriend."

"I'll read the proposed indictment. In the indictment, there are three separate conspiracies—one for the overall drug distribution, one for the money laundering, and one for conspiracy to murder the former girlfriend. Each conspiracy tells you a summary story about what happened. Each conspiracy count sets forth the object of the conspiracy, the means to carry it out, and the individual overt acts performed by conspiracy members to implement the conspiracy. There are also individual drug distribution counts, money laundering counts, and a Continuing Criminal Enterprise(CCE) count. Elements of a CCE count are repeated drug distribution violations directed by a defendant in charge, who makes substantial money from the enterprise."

"I know this sounds like a lot to take in and it is. I'll read instructions as to how to evaluate the evidence before I present it to you. While the witnesses are testifying, there'll be photographs and summary charts to help you absorb the evidence. If you, at any time, aren't following my questions and a witness' answers, let me know and I'll rephrase the questions to the witness. Also, if you have any question for an individual witness, write it down on a piece of paper and give it to me. If I can ask it under the rules of evidence, I will."

After some more introductory remarks and give and take with the jurors as to scheduling for the week, Nick read them the 30-page indictment. He also instructed them on the quantum of proof necessary to return a count on the indictment for further prosecution at the trial court level. The standard is probable cause, a legal term which defies an exact, quantitative description. It is an abstract concept—if there is sufficient reason, based on facts to believe a crime has been committed and the defendant committed it, then a juror votes that the count may be returned to the court for trial. Nick also went over direct versus circumstantial evidence. Direct evidence is a relevant fact the witness saw or heard, while circumstantial evidence is proof of one or more facts that can infer the truth of a relevant fact to the issues. For example, an empty cookie jar and crumbs leading to 10-year-old Tommy's bedroom are circumstantial facts to the relevant issue of who took the cookies. Tommy's mother seeing him take the cookies is direct evidence. The law doesn't assign more weight to one type of evidence or the other, it's for each individual juror to weigh the evidence.

Nick finished and gave the jury a 15 minute break. He went outside. Pepe had some coffee for him and Nick briefly went over Drury's testimony with him. Walking back inside the jury room, Nick greeted the jurors, with a twinkle in his eye. "Are we ready to go? The first witness is Drury Betts." Nick opened the door to the hall and had Drury come in and sit in the witness chair where he was given the oath. Nick established that Drury was a career wildfire fighter and lived in the small town of Yaak, Montana. Nick brought a map of Montana up on the projector and had Drury point out where Yaak was in relation to the Canadian border, less than 20 miles away.

Drury told the jury about the evening in October when he was looking to photograph a bear near an old logging road that ran to the border, and how he saw two off-road vehicles with duffle bags. He told them about taking photos of the men in the vehicles from a hidden position off the road. Nick showed Drury a large picture board, with a number of persons on it, all but two being Hispanic. It looked like a family tree, with lines between the photos. The names of the persons were covered up. Drury identified the photo of Luis Hernandez-Lopez as one of the men he saw in the off-road vehicle, and one of the photos of a Caucasian on the board as the person who was riding with him. The white guy was accountant Lester Sendow.

Drury spoke about his meeting with Biker Sue at the Yaak River Tavern and his "brilliant" idea to follow up with surveillances of the border with his best friend, retired Bakersfield police detective, Zack Reynolds. Drury told them about taking photos of a subsequent duffle bag exchange from both sides of the border.

Nick asked, "After you took the border photos and they were walking back to their vehicles, what happened?"

"I have this irritating cough from inhaling so much smoke from fighting fires over the years. At the worst possible time, I couldn't help it, a raspy cough erupted from me. Loud enough to scare any deer around there. It certainly was loud enough to attract the border boys attention. One yelled at me to show myself. He came to where I was with his hand on a big old 44 caliber revolver. My eyes went wide and I puckered a bit. I told him I was just trying to take some photos of wildlife. I tried to remain calm and friendly. I showed him the camera and asked him how he liked it."

"How did he respond?"

"He drew out his big, black gun, placed its long barrel right on my forehead, and asked me, 'How did I like his gun?' We exchanged a few more "pleasantries" as he was pointing his gun at me, demanding to see my photos on the camera playback screen. I thanked God that right after I coughed, I deleted the photos I had taken of them, thinking one of them might want to see my recent photos. Luckily, my buddy Zack had photos of them. I showed the gun toting smuggler the photos of wildlife I had taken on a recent trip with Zack to the Lamar Valley in Yellowstone."

A juror raised her hand to pass to Nick a written question for Drury. Nick read the note to himself. *Were you scared? Did you think he was going to shoot you?* Nick read the first question to Drury and told the juror that he couldn't ask him the second question because it called for speculation as to what Drury thought the man with the gun would do. Drury answered the first question. "I have faced death many times fighting fires. I had a job to do and I couldn't allow myself to be overcome with fear. I put it aside. Here, in the woods, alone with a stranger who was pointing a gun at my face, capable of blowing my brains out— excuse my French, I was scared shitless. I felt lucky that I didn't have to buy new underwear."

"What happened after he saw the wildlife photos?"

"He gave me a sly smile and said, 'It's dangerous out in the woods at night. You never know what type of predator is roaming around.' Then he turned and walked away."

Nick asked Drury more follow up questions and had him identify the rest of the men he saw the two times at, or near the border. Next, Nick called a series of law enforcement witnesses who described the seizure of the drugs from the college boy outside of Missoula, the various drug smuggling incidents off the coast of north county San Diego, and the seizure of the heroin and marijuana from the various warehouses. That ended the first day. The jurors seemed exhausted and Nick knew he was. He had been mentally sharp for seven hours of testimony.

Nick and Pepe grabbed sandwiches to eat at the office for dinner. They walked into controlled chaos. Deputy U.S. Marshal Perkins had called an hour ago and described how Felicia was freaking out about coming to San Diego to testify in front of the grand jury. She was uncontrollable, sobbing, saying that Luis would kill her. Felicia was scheduled to fly in from Topeka around noon on Wednesday, testify in the afternoon, and be back on a flight east at 5:00. The task force was concerned about exposing her to possible recriminations by Luis and the cartel. Nick said in an exaggerated calm voice, "Settle down everybody. Ana and I'll talk to Deputy Perkins and Felicia on the phone and straighten this out."

Before the phone call, the team discussed strategy on how to handle Felicia. It was decided that Nick and Ana would push Felicia to come and testify. But if it seemed that she would be a complete mess, they could give her a pass on the promise she would testify at the trial. Before trial, one of the team members, probably Ana, would go to Topeka and work on her to make sure she came to San Diego to testify. Felicia couldn't say anything for the first few minutes of the conversation. Deep sobs and gasps of breath were interspaced with sniffling. Deputy Perkins was attempting to sooth her in a kind and soft tone. It seemed to help and Felicia calmed down.

Nick in his voice that he used to read bedtime stories to his young children, told Felicia, "I understand your concern. It's so frightening for you after what happened a couple of months ago. It takes so much courage to stand up to Luis and the cartel. You need to do it for yourself, and all the others he and the cartel will terrorize if he and the members aren't put away. You went out on your own when the shooting happened. Even then we were able to protect you. You know what lengths Agent Schwartz went to—returning fire and taking a couple of bullets. That type of thing won't happen again. The grand jury process is completely secret. The cartel doesn't even know that the grand jury has been convened in this case."

"I can't do it Mr. Drummond. It's too soon. Every night, the same horrific dream—the shooting and I'm getting shot. I wake up in cold sweats. I hide under the covers. I can't live this way."

"The only way you can live normally again, Felicia, is if we put Luis and his thugs away. Then you can get your life back."

"If I stay in Topeka, at least I'll stay alive. I'm so afraid to go back to San Diego. Luis has connections everywhere. When he sets his mind to something, nothing stops him. He's like an enraged bull, with bloody banderillas sticking out of his shoulders. He looks at me like I'm one of those sharpened stakes sticking out of his shoulder. He'll do anything to get rid of me." Nick and the team could hear sobs and moaning.

Deputy Perkins interjected over the wailing, "Her whole body is shaking. I don't think she can even handle talking on the phone right now."

Nick replied, "Okay, we'll give her a few minutes and work this out." In a few minutes, the sobs subsided. Nick continued, "Felicia, maybe it's too soon. But you have to testify at trial. It will be another six months until the trial. Do you promise me in the name of everything that's sacred to you, that you'll testify at trial? I can assure you that Luis and the others will be in custody at that time and can't get at you."

"Yes…Yes….Yes, I promise in the name of the Virgin Mary that I'll testify at trial. Thank you Mr. Drummond for not making me come to San Diego now."

"Just remember your promise and that we'll protect you. Good-bye."

Nick looked around the room at the disappointed faces. "Cheer up. We don't really need her for the grand jury. All her testimony can come in through agents. It'd have been nice for impact, but Ana's and Pepe's testimony about the shooting will perk the jurors up. We need to go over the drug experts' testimony and the beginning of the money laundering testimony for tomorrow."

The testimony over the next two days went well. All the preparation time and the use of charts and photos paid off. The jury became educated about the cartel, how it operated, and where it grew its poppies. The hundreds of kilos of seized Mexican black tar heroin were traced back to the region of the cartel's poppy fields. The jury also seemed to understand the Morales and Sakia money laundering operations for the cartel. Charts summarized the millions of dollars in cash each month that the cartel brought back into the United States to be placed into the U.S banking system for immediate transfer of dollars or pesos to a Mexican bank. After a few questions by the jurors, it finally sank in that the process of bringing the drug cash back into the U.S. to be placed in U.S. banks was necessitated by the Mexican banking regulations that severely limited the deposit of U.S. cash dollars directly into Mexican banks. They also understood that Mexican banks could accept wire transfers and cashier's checks in dollars, but not the cash itself.

Selected transcripts of the wiretap on accountant Sendow's phone and transcripts of his covert taped conversations with the Sakias and Hector Morales made an indelible impression on the jurors. Testimony from the agents concerning what Sendow and Felicia told them about the meetings in Luis' compound above Rosarito Beach and the entire operation, helped show the jurors how the the drug smuggling was intertwined with the money laundering. Drury's earlier testimony, and photos of Sendow side by side with Luis in the off-road vehicle near Yaak, cemented the connection between the drugs and the money. The jury heard about Luis and Sendow meeting with Biker Sue, the Yaak real estate lady, as well as Drury's more graphic description of her. Nick saw in the jurors' expressions that they were glad Biker Sue had moved from southern California to Yaak, Montana.

The presentation to the grand jury was going faster than Nick and Josh had estimated, partially because Felicia didn't testify. The team was hoping to wrap it up on Thursday. The morning would begin by tying up a few loose ends on the money laundering operations. But most of the morning would be spent on the shooting of Felicia and Ana, and trying to connect it to the leaders of the cartel. Nick wanted that murder conspiracy count bad. The afternoon would be spent going over jury instructions and Nick explaining how the evidence supported each count of the indictment.

The morning testimony went well. Ana's testimony about the shooting was compelling and horrifying. Nick saw grimaces and brows knotted in anger on the jurors faces. Some tears were shed when Ana described her injuries and how close she came to bleeding out. The shooter's motorcycle was described in detail as was the fact that Luis had the same model and color of motorcycle.

Sendow's statement to law enforcement about what Luis said about Felicia after the shooting was recounted word for word to the jury. "I didn't see her the last time I was down there a couple of weeks ago. I asked Luis where she was. He told me we wouldn't be seeing that bitch anymore. She was being taken care of. I knew not to ask any more questions about her." A DEA expert testified about what drug cartels do to people who they think have betrayed them. "The lucky ones are just killed. The not so lucky ones have their tongues cut out and stuffed in their mouths before they are killed."

Nick decided his final witness would be Alan, Felicia's first cousin. Nick wanted a civilian to testify last to bring it home to the jurors that this case was about real people, not just law enforcement. Alan was very nervous. He wouldn't look Nick in the eye when he questioned him. He couldn't sit still, jumping around in his seat. Nick tried to calm him down. Nick asked innocuous background questions about the family and how close he was to Felicia. Alan seemed to settle down a bit. He was able to give straightforward testimony about running into a couple of gang-bangers at the mall the day before Felicia was supposed to arrive in town and telling them she was expected the next day. Nick brought out that the gang-bangers were several years older than Alan and he knew them from the neighborhood. The next series of questions were sensitive and Nick had to draw Alan out about the connection of the two to the Baja Norte Familia cartel.

"Alan, are there quite a few people in your neighborhood who belong to gangs?"

"Yes."

"In your neighborhood, is it important to know who's who, and who you can trust? Who you need to stay away from?

"Yes."

"Are you a smart kid?

"Yes. I got all As an Bs on my last report card."

"Good for you. You must know what's happening in your neighborhood. That's just being smart."

"Yeah, I do."

"The two guys you told us about at the mall. Who are they affiliated with?"

"Uh, Uh, I'm not really sure."

"C'mon Alan, you're no dummy. Who?"

"They're wannabes with the Familia."

"What are wannabes?"

"Guys who aren't full-fledged members. Guys who hang around the members, do things for them."

"How do you know about these guys?"

"Everyone knows. I've seen them numerous times with Familia members."

"How do you know they were Familia members?"

"If you're in the neighborhood, you know. For one thing they have the Familia tat—an outline of Baja Norte with *Familia* written inside in red." Nick paused, looked around at the jurors. They were locked in on Alan's testimony. A thought came to Nick. He hadn't thought about it when he talked to Alan last evening. *Did Alan have any encounters with the two sometime after the shooting? After all, they were from the neighborhood.*

"Alan, since the shooting, have you talked to either of them?"

Alan's eyes bulged out. He looked like a deer in headlights. He jumped out of the witness chair, mumbling, "I have to go," and bolted out of the jury room.

Nick shouted to the grand jury as he ran after Alan, "Take a 10 minute recess, I'll be back."

Pepe said, as Nick came rushing out, "What in the hell is going on? Alan just ran down the hall."

"He took a flyer, follow me, we have to bring him back." Nick thought as he ran down the escalator to the first floor after Alan, *I am too old for this.* Pepe and Nick burst out of the front doors of the federal courthouse at the same time and saw Alan running across the street. Pepe pulled ahead of Nick. Both were shouting for Alan to stop. At Broadway, the main thoroughfare for downtown San Diego, vehicle traffic blocked Alan from running across the street. Pepe managed to grab his collar and pull him around. By that time, Nick came puffing up. "Son, you're gonna give me a heart attack. You wouldn't want that on your conscience. What's going on? Why did you bolt?"

"I did see them a couple of weeks later. They threatened me and told me the Familia never misses twice."

"You have to come back and testify. These people tried to kill Felicia." He reluctantly agreed.

When they returned to the courtroom, the grand jury was reconvened and Alan took the stand. He looked shaken and his body shrunk down into the chair. Nick resumed questioning, "Did you see the two after the shooting?"

In a soft, timid voice, barely audible to the jurors, Alan replied, "Yes, two weeks later at the same mall."

"What did they say to you?"

"'Felicia got lucky. The Familia never misses twice. You tell us the next time she comes into town or it'll be you dodging bullets.'"

"Did you tell anyone about this?"

"No, I was afraid. What could anybody do?"

Anger dominated the faces of most of the jurors. Several looked stunned. Nick helped Alan off the witness stand and walked him to the door.

After the lunch break, Nick told the jurors about the deliberation process. Copies of the proposed indictment were passed out to each of the 19 jurors. Nick reminded them that 12 out of the 19 had to agree to a count for it to be returned to the court for trial prosecution. He read instructions as to each element of the crimes charged. Nick spent the next two hours going over the evidence and how the evidence supported each count. He avoided any inflammatory language about the cartel, he just stuck to the facts.

The jury began their deliberations just after 4:00 p.m. Nick told them to carefully go over the evidence and not to allow bias or any prejudice to influence their individual decisions. They could go home at five, and resume deliberations at 8:30 in the morning. He reminded them that unless ordered by a judge, they could never discuss the case with anyone outside the jury room. It would be a violation of federal law.

Just before lunch on Friday, the jury foreperson told Nick that they had reached decisions on all the counts. They unanimously agreed to return all the counts except two; they voted 15 to 4 to return the murder conspiracy count and Ana's assault count. Nick felt a great sense of relief. The team had made it through the first major hurdle. Nick took the indictment over to the presiding judge along with an application and order to have the indictment sealed until the defendants were in custody, or further judicial order. The judge signed the order that kept the indictment confidential. Nick looked forward to a good night's sleep.

CHAPTER TWENTY-THREE

Nick sauntered into the conference room on Monday. He was still feeling pretty good about the return of all the counts in the indictment. He looked around the smiling faces of his friends and colleagues. The pressure was off for a while. He knew as the trial drew nearer, the pressure would ratchet up, higher and higher. He threw down the bagels, cream cheese, and sliced tomatoes and onions on the table. Gasps of feigned surprise from around the table. The boss actually springing for bagels instead of the usual dozen glazed doughnuts he normally brought in. Pepe stammered, pretending to be speechless, "Boss Boss, I-I-I-I didn't know you you you cared so much. Ba Ba Bagels cost real moooney."

"I get it wise guy. I'm a cheap bastard. But I'm a proud bastard of how you all came together so we could get the indictment. You all deserve to feel good about yourselves. But while we're feeling so good about ourselves, we have to figure out how to entice Luis, as well as chief enforcer Rael Sanchez, and the top cartel dog himself, Mateo Encinas, to come across the border so we can arrest them. There's no way we can wait around and hope the extradition process works with Mexico. I only had one case where there was an extradition from Mexico. It was an American gringo on a drug case who the Mexicans were holding in "prison" in Cabo San Lucas. They would take him out deep sea fishing each day. When his money finally ran out, five years after the indictment, the authorities gave us a call to pick him up." Nick continued, "We have to get the main players over here in sunny southern California. I don't want to wait five years this time."

Jerry said, "Remember Sendow spoke about meeting Luis through horse racing, that Luis and Encinas are both into horses and come up for Opening Day at Del Mar. We can work with Sendow to see how all three can be encouraged to make an appearance for Opening Day."

Mario exclaimed, "I like it. I've been known to bet on the ponies a time or two. I volunteer to go undercover as a gambler, all my losing bets can be underwritten by Uncle Sam as a necessary expense of a covert operation."

"Dream on Mario," responded Nick. "Other than Mario's twist, I like it also. Opening Day is coming up in about six weeks, mid-July. That'll give us time to organize the case for trial and discovery. It'll also give us time to work out a plan for taking them down at the track, with 40,000 spectators milling about. They'll be coming with armed bodyguards. There are no metal detectors or other security screens for fans coming to the track. High roller Mario, you're in charge of working with Sendow on how to get them to Del Mar. Once we know about their plans, we can figure out how to take them down without endangering the crowd."

"Thanks Lester for coming by to talk with me."

"Did I have any choice Detective Cipriani?

"No, not really, but I'm still glad to see you. We need to get Luis, Sanchez, and Encinas across the border together. We're thinking Opening Day at Del Mar could be a good draw."

"Shouldn't be a problem with Luis and Encinas, they wouldn't miss Opening Day. But the enforcer is a different manner. He isn't into horse racing. He just likes his women and fine wine."

"We could arrange for a few beautiful escorts for them for the day and evening. There's always a VIP party after Opening Day at the Hotel Mar Elixir near the track. I'm sure they serve the finest wine and tequila. You could also plant the seed that the books for one of the laundering operations don't add up. You could tell Sanchez that it looks like one of the operators is getting greedy, taking more than the agreed upon cut. It'd give Señor Enforcer a business reason to come across the border."

"I already know that a friend of Luis and Encinas owns a horse he's planning to run on Opening Day. The owner has lined up a top jockey to race his horse, Puma Sorpreza. I'll give it some thought about how best to get Sanchez across the border. It sounds to me that you want to get them all together to arrest them. What's going to happen to me?"

"Don't worry. We'll take you away separately and you can start your witness protection program the very same day. Come in next Wednesday and we can work out the details."

"Ana, I don't want you volunteering for the escort undercover. It's too dangerous. You have already paid your dues. Taking a couple of bullets was more than enough for this case."

"I have news for you Nick. What I volunteer for as an agent is not your concern. We both have our careers. I have my own sense of duty. After being shot, I want a piece of flesh back. This is personal. I'll keep a cool head. But no way are you going to stop me from taking these jackals down. In fact, I'm going to put in for Luis' escort. It'd be extra sweet to put the cuffs on him. I can stand an ass grab or two for a knee in the balls and dropping him to the ground."

"I don't blame you for wanting payback, but I couldn't take seeing you hurt in any way. I also don't like the idea of Luis or any of the scum touching you."

"Have you already forgotten our conversation a few weeks back. About us not even being able to see each other outside of work until the trial is over. Remember, conflict of interest. You don't have a personal claim on me. Maybe some year you will. If you ever do, we'll have a claim on each other."

"Okay. You should've been a lawyer. You argue too well for an agent."

A smile returned, and a sparkle to her eye. "You're lucky I didn't go to law school. I would've been an ass kicker with no conscience. Now I'm just an ass kicker, sweetheart."

"It's okay to kick me when I'm down. I put myself in that position. But go easy on my profession; there are a few of us with ethics." Ana looked at him with a furrowed brow and downturned lips. Utter disbelief registered on her face. "Well, Ana, we at least like to think we have ethics."

"That's better."

"Detective Cipriani, you didn't tell me that I rated Mr. Drummond and others for our next meeting."

"I wanted to surprise you. What are your thoughts about getting the big three over here for Opening Day?"

"Luis and Encinas are coming. They plan to bet on their friend's horse. Luis views himself, as in all things, an expert in horseflesh. He bragged he was going to inspect Puma Sorpresa before the race while she's in the paddocks. If he likes what he sees, he's going to lay a large, off-site bet on the big filly. I'm working on getting Sanchez to come along through my conversations with Luis. I let it drop to Luis that the Morales laundering operation may be skimming some extra cash off the top and it would be a good idea for Sanchez to pay Morales a personal visit to ensure compliance."

Lester continued, "Luis liked the escort idea and getting into the Mar Elixir VIP party after the races. By the way, Luis likes young, saucy Hispanic women like Felicia, El Jefe Encinas likes *rubios*— a tall, striking blonde will do, and the enforcer likes attractive, well-formed brunette *gringas*, like agent Schwartz over there."

Ana was quick to reply. "I guess I'll take that as a compliment. But there's no need to be delicate. He likes big tits, right?"

"Yep."

Nick spoke through a scowl, "I'm glad we settled the semantics of the scumbags' personal tastes. Let's move on to more pertinent things. How are they planning to get here? How many bodyguards will they have?"

"They'll come in a limo with bullet-proof glass. I don't know their exact route to the track. They'll be dropped off at the VIP gate with their bodyguards. I'm to meet them with the girls at the Turf Club. I'd think a total of two bodyguards, maybe three."

Nick was lost in thought. No one said anything. Nick rubbed his temples. He looked over the group. The seconds ticked by. Lester began to move around in his seat. Nick stared straight into the eyes of Lester, across the table from him. "I don't have to remind you Lester how much we all have riding on this. You're committed, no turning back. If we even get a whiff of you screwing us on this, you'll start collecting social security while you're still in prison, or maybe we'll let you out with a snitch jacket. How long will you last out there? Do we understand each other?"

Lester's pupils widened. He was clammy and taking small, shallow breaths. His voice cracked as he tried to speak. In a low, timid voice, he whispered, "I understand."

"Good, now take a few deep breaths and relax. I spoke to your attorney and we have your witness protection program set up. We know you like the ocean and the warm weather. Your going to the leper colony on the north side of Molokai. Mostly native Hawaiians live on Molokai, population 7,500. A limited number of tourists visit the colony, mostly by taking mules down the only mountain trail to the isolated peninsula. Switchbacks wind their way down 2,000 foot cliffs that seal off the colony from the rest of the island. There are still nine people with leprosy who live there. It's a national monument. We've arranged for you to live there and work as a bookkeeper."

"Mr. Drummond, what are you talking about? You're shipping me off to a leper colony?"

"No worries. It's just until the end of the trial. Then we can re-evaluate your situation. You can bring your snorkel gear. It's stunningly beautiful. I vacationed in Molokai a few years ago and hiked down the switchbacks to visit for a day. The colony has a store, a small bar, and medical facilities. There's no reason for concern, they're all cured. They found a cure in the forties."

"This is a lot to take in."

"Just remember the agreement you signed, upon the advice of your attorney. You agreed to plead guilty to one money laundering count and one drug distribution count, with no more than three years in prison. That, as you well know, depends on your complete cooperation and truthful testimony. After the trial, we'll recommend to the sentencing judge what we think your appropriate sentence should be within the three year parameter. I can be both a very grateful guy and a very vengeful guy."

"Got it Mr. Drummond. Molokai sounds great."

"We'll meet one more time before Opening Day when we know more about our targets' movements. See you then Lester."

"What have you got for me Mario? Time is a wasting. Opening Day is next Thursday."

"We're in good shape Nick. I spoke to Lester yesterday. The cartel's head of enforcement is coming as well. He'll be taking a separate car with a third bodyguard. He's leery about having the three of them traveling together. He'll meet them after the races start at the Turf Club. The head of track security is retired FBI. A lot of security for special events are off duty cops. He got a bit hinky when I told him about taking down the top three jefes of the Familia at the track. He relaxed a bit when I told him our plan is to arrest them inside the stall assigned to Puma Sorpresa in the paddocks. He'll supply our agents with track mucking coveralls. We'll have three agents cleaning up horse shit. There will be additional back-ups in track uniforms nearby."

"What about coverage at the Turf Club?"

"That was tougher. We had no problems finding agents who qualified for mucking shit, but being a waiter is another thing entirely. We screened the agents to see if any of them had made an honest living as a food server. It turns out that our very own Pepe worked his way through college as a waiter. Four other agents will be either waiters or busboys."

"What about surveillance of the limos and drop off point?"

"We have agents at the VIP drop off entrance, with cameras. Also, there are agents in maintenance carts to follow the limo drivers to their parking spaces. We'll have search warrants ready to search the limos. We just have to get a supplemental telephonic warrant at the time which will specify the identification information for the limos. A federal judge will be on standby to give the final verbal authorization."

"I know Ana is slotted to be enforcer Sanchez' escort. What about the other two?"

"I rather enjoyed that part of the process. We looked through the personnel files of the female agents between 25 and 35 years old. We found two great candidates. Knockouts and both very proficient in hand to hand combat skills. We threw in the perk of a gratuitous dress of their choice that met both weapon concealment and non-concealment needs."

"What sort of contingent plans do we have if any of this goes south?"

"There's a small private room off of the Turf Club. We could take one or more of them down inside that room. The hitch is—we'll have to get one or more of them in there. All the female agents have toured the premises and will have earplug inserts and hidden microphones. All the rest of the agents will have the same communication devices."

"How are we going to coordinate taking down the rest of the suspects before they get wind of the track arrests?"

"Puma Sorpresa is scheduled to run the fifth race—five furlongs on turf. The post time is at 4:10. We plan the arrests at about 3:45 when the drug bosses are viewing Puma in the paddock area. The horses for each successive race are kept in the stall number corresponding to the number the horse is wearing for the race. Sometime around 3:55, all the horses are brought out of their individual stalls and paraded around a small oval runway in front of the paddocks so the fans can see them up close before the actual race. The horses are then led out through a tunnel under the grandstands to the track. Three levels above, overlooking the area, is the Turf Club. Members of the Turf Club and our agents can view the paddocks from the Club's balcony."

"Okay, enough about the horse parade, what about the other arrest sites?"

"Sorry, I digressed. I can't help it—I love this track. We have eight other arrest locations. The warehouses in Otay Mesa, Salt Lake City, Missoula, Chicago, and Vancouver, as well as the offices of the two money laundering operations along the border, and college boy's residence in Missoula. Agents at each location will be ready for a call around 3:45 p.m. that verifies the arrests have been made at the track."

"What about arrangements for booking our three jefes? You know I want them booked and housed at separate jails. That'll keep them guessing and protect Sendow for awhile."

"This took some doing. Nobody likes the extra work of housing them at three separate jails nor does anyone like the transportation issues of the two who aren't housed at the downtown San Diego MCC jail. One will be at MCC, one will be in Orange County, and one will be in L.A. They will be housed in single man cells, in isolation. They'll be allowed one hour a day outside their cells for exercise and they'll have no contact with other inmates."

"That's great. We'll see how long that lasts after their defense attorneys start weighing in. You're going to be coordinating the take down from an office by the Turf Club. I'll be listening in, but I have to be offsite. I don't want to look like I'm too personally involved in the arrests. I'll let you agents do your thing."

CHAPTER TWENTY-FOUR

Mario got to the track right after the morning briefing—they had had a video hook up with all the agents at the eight off-sites. The gates open at 12:30 and the first race starts at 1:40. Mario went straight to the office of the head of security in the bowels of the track's grandstands. He strolled through the large video bank room where several security guards were checking monitors. At the far end of the room, former FBI agent Sam Fuller's door was ajar. Mario knocked and went in. Sam looked up from his computer. "What have you gotten me into Mario? You know how many things could go wrong with your plan? I have 40,000 fans, many are VIPS. Many don't know a horse race from a rodeo. They just want to be seen. I can just see one of them taking a bullet. The headlines would read, *Opening Day at Del Mar Turns into Wild West Day, Patron Shot.*"

"Feel better Sam. You vented. There's nothing to worry about. We're going to arrest them in a controlled environment, away from people. If, at any time, it looks dangerous, we'll call it off."

"Puma Sorpresa is No. 7 in the fifth race. I'm assigning the normal muckers, who handle stalls 7, 8, and 9 for that race, to other duties so your agents can step in. We have a table set aside for the cartel's entourage in the corner of the Turf Club. Your agents will be the waiters and busboys for that area."

"Perfect. Thank you. Here's a listening device so you can be tuned in to our communications. I'll be coordinating the operation in the room you provided me, right next to the Turf Club. We really appreciate all you've done for us."

"No problem. I just hope I have a job when this is all over."

Mario looked snazzy in his tailored dark suit, multi-colored Jerry Garcia tie, and his contrasting white Panama hat. He could even be mistaken for one of those El Ricos except for the lack of a beautiful young señorita in a tight-fitting dress on his arm. He leaned against the iron railing of the Spanish tiled balcony of the Turf Club, watching all the beautiful people stream through the gates below him. Most of the women wore hats. Some were so extravagant as to be ludicrous. One hat was topped by a two foot tall swan and there were several Carmen Miranda imitations—a plethora of fruit adorning their hats. Here and there were elderly gentlemen in linen suits and hand carved walking sticks, with a woman less than half their age on their arm. Mario knew from his time in vice that high-priced prostitutes did quite well on Opening Day.

Opening Day had come a long way since Bing Crosby first greeted his Hollywood friends when the track opened in 1937. In those years, many of the fans arrived by train from Los Angeles. There was just a two lane road to San Diego then, no interstate.

The Turf Club was beginning to fill up. The men all wore jackets as required for entry into the club. The dress code for women was quite a bit more relaxed and scanty. At least the ladies wouldn't be cold in their revealing dresses in the 75 degree weather. The sun always seems to shine for big events in San Diego.

Just after 1:00, an agent, monitoring the VIP drop off location, reported that Luis and Familia Chief Encinas were getting out of their limo with two bodyguards. Mario whispered into his hidden mike under his suit collar, "Showtime Ana for you and the other ladies. Luis and Encinas are walking in. You three and Lester should come into the club and be ready for the greet."

"We're ready. We ladies all showered with disinfectant this morning." Mario saw the agents and Lester walk through the club's entrance. The agents were stunning. They captured the high-priced call girl look with a strong dose of extra class, perfectly. Mario couldn't help thinking they never looked this good at work. Male eyes turned towards them as they took over the room. More than one man thought, *What in the hell are they doing with that loser?* Lester didn't look like he belonged on the same planet as the ladies. He was wearing an ill-fitted, nondescript suit, with his paunch covering his belt. At least for the time, Lester was the envy of every man in the room. The men's lady friends, wives, and such, tugged at their sleeves, and the moment receded away.

The three agents left seats between them at the table. Lester stood up and walked over to Luis and Encinas as they entered the room. He ushered them over to the table. Ana thought, *the photos of Encinas didn't capture his essence. He exuded an aura of confidence, and his steel grey eyes penetrated right through you. His wavy white hair offset his olive complexion. He had the look of a Spanish aristocrat.* Señor Gomez-Encinas smiled and bent over to lightly kiss the back of Ana's hand. "What a pleasure to meet you. Such a strong, attractive lady. Do I note some eastern European Jewry in your ancestry?'

Ana responded with a demure smile, "You're absolutely right. Romanian. I trust your expertise in lineage is matched by your expertise in horses today."

Encinas' booming laugh preceded his light-hearted response, "A woman after my own heart, the business of horse racing is at hand." He then leaned over to whisper into Ana's hair over her ear. "At this moment I regret my infatuation with rubios. Maybe I'll have the honor of encountering you again."

Encinas then turned and greeted the long haired blonde knock-out, his lips again just grazing her hand. Ana breathed a sigh of relief, he had whispered into the ear that had the inserted communication device. She thanked her ancestors for her thick hair.

There were no such subtleties with Luis and the Hispanic agent. He was already sitting next to her with his hand on her upper thigh.

Champagne flowed, gourmet tidbits were nibbled on, and small talk flourished. Every so often, one of the bodyguards would leave his post to make bets for the table. Mario was getting worried about whether Sanchez would show up. He was supposed to have been there by the second race. After the third race, an agent reported that Sanchez and his bodyguard had just arrived at the VIP entrance. Mario let all the agents know. The three female agents showed no signs that they had heard.

Expecting Sanchez, Ana was looking at the door when he entered. He was dark, with a brooding face, held up by the thickest neck Ana had ever seen. His facial scar, lighter than the rest of his skin, stood out more in person than in his photographs. His eyes had a wild look—constantly flashing around the room. Ana could see how he earned his nickname, *El Toro*. Fortunately, Sanchez was more of the Spanish aristocratic school in his treatment of women than Luis. He took Ana's proffered hand in both his hands, slightly bowed and said, "Encantado, Señorita".

Lester steered the conversation to the fifth race and Puma Sorpresa. Luis and Encinas talked of their dear friend, the owner, and how they expected to make enough cash on the race for them all to have an unforgettable evening. Both Luis and Encinas already had more than enough cash in their wallets for everyone to have an unforgettable evening. But that was besides the point. Encinas and Luis were looking forward to going to the paddocks to personally check on Puma before the race. Sanchez said, "I'm not much for horse racing." Glancing at Ana, "I much prefer beautiful women and vintage wine. We'll stay here while you inspect the horse."

Ana felt her heart dropping. *We can't have them split up. We need to take them all down at the paddocks.* She looked at Sanchez with bedroom eyes and murmured, "I think horseflesh can be sexy. Think of all that power and thrust of a finely tuned animal. Why don't we join them?'

"I don't need the feel of horseflesh to perform." He moved closer to Ana so his legs were pressed up against hers. "We will stay."

Ana placed her hand on Sanchez' shoulder as she stood up. "Fine, I need to freshen up, have a vintage Cab for me when I come back." She headed for the restroom. She spoke into her microphone, "Did you hear that Mario?"

"Yeah. We can still take down the two at the paddocks. Any ideas?" "Sanchez is feeling amorous. You know that private room off of the Turf Club? When the rest go to check out the horse, I will suggest a quick fuck in the private room. I've never known a man who could refuse that." "You may be right but that could be dangerous.

You'd be on your own for a short time. We'd have to first take down the bodyguard outside the private door, and then bust inside."

"I can handle myself. You have Pepe and the rest of waiters take down the guard."

"I don't like it, but all right."

A bottle of 1988 Cabernet Sauvignon awaited Ana as she returned to the table. Sanchez met her eyes, "A waiter was good enough to aerate the Cab so we don't have to wait to taste one of Napa Valley's finest offerings. It's said to be profound, velvety, with long legs. Not unlike yourself."

Ana smiled and swirled the wine in her glass to bring out the bouquet. She put her nose close to the top of the glass and breathed in deeply. "Excellent, Mi Carido, I know I'll enjoy this."

Encinas said, "We will leave you two wine connoisseurs alone to enjoy the fruits of the land. We're going to visit Puma." All the rest of the party except Sanchez' personal bodyguard left the table.

Ana took her time sipping and savoring the vintage Cab. "I like a wine with age. The maturity and richness of the wine is fully released." She placed her hand on Sanchez' inner thigh, rubbing it gently back and forth. Sanchez' stoic look began to crack. A soft glint came to his dark brown eyes and a hint of a contented smile came to his lips. His body was coming alive. In a low, sultry voice, Ana whispered in his ear, "I hope you don't think I'm too forward, but I want you to take me. Powerful, sophisticated men act as an aphrodisiac to me. There's a private room that can be locked along the far wall." She lightly caressed his ear with her tongue before leaning back and locking her eyes with his.

Sanchez, short of breath, breathed in deeply. He murmured, "I'm always at your service. There's nothing I'd enjoy more." Ana stood up, took Sanchez' hand and led him towards the private room door. The room was small, with a couple of chairs and a computer on a desk. Sanchez turned to his bodyguard. "Stay outside, we won't be long." Sanchez locked the door from the inside. "Not that voyeurism wouldn't add to the excitement, but I don't think the stuffy Turf Club could get over it."

"Señor, did you ever see the Godfather movie where Sonny took her right against the wall. I have always wanted to reenact that scene." Ana moved into him, kissing his neck and pulling both of them back towards the door. Her back was against the door as she unfastened his belt. Sanchez' eyes were glazed, his hands fondling her breasts. She arched her back and moaned, using a hand to unlock the door. She gasped, "I can't wait any longer."

"I can't wait any longer was the cue for the other agents. Pepe and three other waiters moved towards the bodyguard. One had a tray with glasses. The first waiter, with the glasses, distracted the bodyguard as he tried to push around him, saying, "Sorry sir, it's so crowded in here." A DEA agent, known as "Iron" for his weight lifting fetish, was behind the bodyguard. He put his bulging fore-arm around the bodyguard's neck, clamping down on the guard's carotid artery, cutting off the blood flow to his brain. In seconds the guard would be unconscious. In an involuntary reaction to the carotid hold, the guard's hands came up to his neck to try to release the hold. One of his arms knocked the tray over, glasses shattering on the floor. Sanchez heard the noise and leaped back from the door, pulling up his zipper. He grabbed a 38 from his breast pocket and pointed it towards the door. He yelled, "Falcone," the guard's name.

Falcone didn't hear his boss call his name. His three or four seconds of consciousness were over. He slid to the ground. Two of the agents tended the guard while Pepe led another agent through the door, guns drawn. Ana stepped to the side and yelled, "Federal agent, you're under arrest" as she chopped down with all the strength of her right arm and upper body on Sanchez' gun hand. The gun was knocked from his hand, bouncing on the floor. Sanchez leaned to pick it up when Ana gave him a vicious kick to the outside of his right knee, tearing cartilage. Sanchez slumped to the ground as Pepe kicked his gun out of reach and the other agent cuffed him. Mario ran into the room and looked around. Ana was standing over Sanchez. "ICE agent Ana Schwartz. You're under arrest for drug trafficking,

Continuing Criminal Enterprise and conspiracy to murder. By the way you disgust me. You're definitely not my type. I'm a beer drinker."

Mario immediately reported to Jerry and the rest of the agents at the paddocks that Sanchez and his bodyguard had been neutralized and to proceed with the other two arrests. The agents and the track security force took Sanchez and his bodyguard from the Turf Club to a service elevator. At the service bay below, two police cars were waiting to transport Sanchez and his bodyguard to Los Angeles.

In the back of stall seven, Luis was running his hand down the flank of Puma Sorpresa. Luis and Encinas had spent the last couple of minutes admiring the two year old filly. A track official had taken the owner out front to the parade ground to talk to him. Besides the muckers, only Sendow, the two Familia heads and their bodyguards remained inside the stall. The three muckers, who were cleaning the stall, were invisible to them, with their grimy coveralls and horseshit on their shoes. The muckers pulled their Glocks out of their overalls in unison. Three more agents rushed in from the front of the paddocks with guns drawn. Multiple voices said, "Federal agents, you're under arrest, hands on top of your heads." The two bodyguards made movements towards their coat pockets. The agent facing them yelled, "Gun!" Two of the muckers brought their guns down on the backs of the heads of the bodyguards. They slumped to the ground and the gun wielding muckers cuffed them.

Encinas slowly raised his hands above his head. "No need to get excited gentlemen. I will cooperate. I'm sure there has been some mistake."

Luis, who was blocked by Puma from the agents who had burst in from the front, turned and clamored towards the rear door of the stall. The third mucker, HSI Agent Jerry Slater, grabbed a shovel he'd been shoveling shit with and threw it towards Luis' lower legs. Luis tripped, went to the right, tried to regain his balance and fell headlong into the muck pile in the right corner of the stall. The green-brown ooze did nothing for his white silk shirt and tailored European suit. As one of the other agents went over to cuff him, Jerry pulled out his iPhone. To no one in particular, Jerry said, "Nick and Ana have got to see photos of this."

The bodyguards and the drug lords were hustled out the back into waiting police cars. Encinas was slotted for Orange County and

Luis for San Diego MCC. Sendow was also cuffed and taken away in a separate police car in full view of Luis and Encinas. Except Sendow was taken directly to the airport for his flight to Maui where he'd board a commuter plane to Molokai.

The "track official", an agent of the arrest team, came back into the stall with the owner after he got the all clear sign. One of the "muckers" explained to the owner that they had left to make bets on the race. "A Mr. Gomez-Encinas said to thank you for your hospitality and he'll be in touch."

Puma Sopresa seemed to take it all in stride—like it was an everyday occurrence for humans to hit each other over the head and throw a shovel. Jerry reported to Mario that all was fine, even the horse. Mario thought, *What the hell. I have a spare $100. If Luis and Encinas couldn't bet that day, I can.* Puma was betting at 8 to 1 odds when he put money down on the filly to place. Mario hoped that Puma would come in first or second. He wasn't going to be greedy. Getting $400 or $500 back on a hundred would do.

Nick swore to himself that he would never place himself in this situation again. To hear what was going on, but not be hooked up to communicate to the agents, was hell. He'd never have let Ana be in a room alone with Sanchez. What was she thinking? Nick entered the security office as the fifth race was running. He saw Mario looking at the video screen of the live race with the head of track security, Sam Fuller. Ana was talking with Pepe by the security office. Nick grabbed her arm and said to her and Pepe that he had to talk to her in private. He dragged her into Fuller's office and closed the door.

"What in the hell do you think you were doing? You scared the living daylights out of me. How could you endanger yourself like that?" Nick was livid and crazed.

"This is getting old Nick—big hulks dragging me into private rooms and closing the door. I've had enough of that for one day. Calm down. I'm safe. You've said that we always need to be ready to improvise. This was needed. We took them down. Now just give me a hug." Nick lost himself in their embrace, several tears making their way down his cheeks. A shout from the other room separated them.

Mario was yelling, "C'mon Puma! C'mon!" With twenty lengths on the turf track to go, Puma was edging up on the outside, a half a length behind the second place horse. With a final burst, Puma nosed out the horse to come in second. "Five hundred bucks! Five hundred bucks! Drinks are on me!"

CHAPTER TWENTY-FIVE

Nick rolled into the office late on Friday. He still had the taste of scotch and cigars in his mouth from last night's impromptu celebration at Days End. The entire team went there after completing the paperwork on the arrests. The arrests at the other locations went down with no problems. The Sakias and Hector Morales were at their offices. Various, lower level cartel members were arrested for their drug distribution activities connected to the warehouses in Otay Mesa, Missoula, Salt Lake City, Chicago, and Vancouver. A total of 18 suspects had been arrested on Thursday for prosecution in federal court in San Diego. Nick felt tired just thinking about the 18 defendants and their attorneys that he and Josh would be facing at the arraignment on the indictment the following Monday morning.

The Canadians would prosecute the Vancouver suspects in their federal court in British Columbia.

Abbie greeted Nick with a broad smile as he tried to sneak by her to get to his office. "Looks like someone had too much to drink last night. Hope it was worth it. I've some fresh coffee brewing for you. Do you want the bad news now Nick, or after your coffee?"

"How about laying it on me when you bring the coffee? I may be hung over, but I'm still in a good mood. You have to see the photos of Luis that Jerry took. In one of them he's face down in a pile of horse shit, and in another he has rolled over to face Jerry's iPhone with a look of utter disgust, manure balls rolling off his clothes. In a third, he's trying to brush himself off with an ivory hairbrush. Nothing you tell me could erase that."

To clear his head, Nick took a few shots with his nerf ball on his wastebasket hoop. After missing a few, he found his range. Feeling a little more like Steph Curry, he was ready for Abbie to bring it. Abbie came in with the steaming coffee and a pile of telephone messages.

"Your phone has been ringing off the hook. Multiple calls from the AG's press secretary, Ed Tellar, two calls from the head of the criminal division and lo and behold, one call from the esteemed one, the AG himself. The press secretary and the AG were heated. Your buddy, the head of the criminal division, was more relaxed. She knows you never carry a cellphone and can be out of contact for long periods of time. Nick you have to join the 21st century. The days of you deleting 500 emails, sight unseen when you're in trial, or not being reachable on a cellphone, need to be over." "Yeah, yeah, I know. I'm getting better. I now check my emails almost once a day, and occasionally I carry my cellphone. Give me the gist of their conversations."

"You asked for it. 'Who in the hell does he think he is! He takes down the three leading cartel members of the Familia at Opening Day in Del Mar, and doesn't even bother to tell the AG, and the Chief of the Criminal Division what's going on.' They were less than pleased to hear about it first from news reporters asking about what happened."

"What are they griping about? They knew about the sealed indictments and that we were going to arrest them at some point. I told the U.S. Attorney about the planned track arrests. I'm prosecuting the case as a Special Assistant U.S. Attorney, not as a state AG. Give me a break."

"Nick. This is the modern media age. It's all about spin and publicity. They want to be in the loop. They don't want to look like they don't even know what's happening in their own office. They want to set up a press conference, with all the bells and whistles."

"Shit. That's one of the reasons I didn't tell them. I just want them to let me do my job with a minimum of distractions. The Chief of Criminal Division knows what it's like to handle a high profile, complex case, but the AG certainly doesn't and nor does he care unless he can get some favorable publicity out of it."

"Stop whining. I suggest you act nice and call AG Hamilton first. He's at the top of the pecking order."

"You're right Abbie. I may need you to translate into 'making nice' what I really think."

"I'll get him on the line for you." Abbie dialed, talked to a secretary and handed the phone to Nick. "He'll be on the line in a few seconds."

"General, good to talk to you. I apologize for not letting you know before the arrests that they were going down. It was pretty crazy around here. We didn't know for sure that we'd be able to arrest them at the track. I want to assure you..."

"Stop your bullshit right now Drummond. You should be fired for insubordination. How dare you not tell me that the arrests were imminent on the biggest transnational drug cartel case our office has ever handled."

"I don't know how well it would play in the press if you fire me, the head of the task force that was able to indict and arrest, on this side of the border, the three top jefes of Baja Norte Familia. Might not look real good come your re-election."

"You insubordinate son-of-a-bitch."

"General, you're repeating yourself. I'll make sure I keep you and the press office informed in the future. I'll even write up a sample press release this morning, extolling your virtues and contribution to our effort to thwart transnational criminal organizations. Lastly, I'll arrange with the U.S. Attorney to have the press conference you want in San Diego after the defendants are arraigned on Monday. We'll even bring out packages of black tar heroin and some of the automatic weapons seized. We can blow up photographs of the bundles of cash seized. And, we'll even mention the joint operation with the Royal Canadian Mounties. The press is going to love it. You can do all the talking. I don't like to talk to the press anyway. They just get in the way."

General Hamilton paused for a long moment. "Are you still on the phone General?"

"You should be thankful I'm still here. Okay, send the draft press release to me and Tellar at the press office." Nick heard Hamilton slam down the receiver.

Nick turned to Abbie and grimaced. "What I say to that phony to keep my job and to keep him off my back. I'm disgusted with myself. I feel like I need a shower."

"Josh, have you got those cases on bail to cite to the judge? We did pretty well on judicial roulette. Larry Orsini was a good draw. Been on the bench a long time, a good Catholic and family man. He'll want to keep the major scumbags in jail."

"You're right, he's a good pick for us on the law and values. But he can be an ornery old cuss to the attorneys. Patience and judicial temperament aren't his strong points."

"His bark is worse than his bite. You just need to bone up on the Detroit Lions. He's a diehard Lions fan. He grew up in Detroit and went to Michigan law school in Ann Arbor."

They were in the presiding judge's courtroom. It was the only courtroom that could hold 18 defendants and their attorneys. Nothing like full employment for defense attorneys. The "Big Six" defendants, being the three jefes and the three money launderers, had hired top flight attorneys. The other twelve had court appointed attorneys, one being a deputy public defender. A deputy public defender can be the best of all defense attorneys. Public defenders often get bad raps. Many are excellent attorneys and are well-experienced. Being around the courts a lot, the good public defenders, like the good prosecutors, know and cultivate the court staff. Having a court clerk, bailiff or court reporter sympathetic to you never hurts. Nick remembered a story he heard from a former prosecutor in Alameda County, a real gregarious, people loving guy. The deputy DA wanted a particular member of the jury to be the foreperson. He maneuvered the bailiff to bet a six pack of beer on the juror the DDA really wanted. When the jury got the case after the closing arguments, the bailiff brought the case file to the jury room and plopped it right in front of the juror the DDA wanted. The DDA had never been happier to pay off a bet.

There was a loud anticipatory buzz in the courtroom. A pool television camera had been let in with a direct feed to the other stations. Two rows of the courtroom were roped off for the print media.

A few family members were allowed seats as were other prosecutors and defense attorneys. It was the toughest ticket to get in town.

Judge Orsini rapped his gavel resoundingly on the wooden "bench" in front of him. "Order! Pipe down! Anyone who talks out of line will be excluded from the courtroom. My clerk has set out name placards for each attorney and defendant. Attorneys find your places. The prosecutors and their investigating officer, Special Agent Cantana, will be sitting at the normal prosecution table. We'll bring in the defendants and I'll give you a few minutes to go over the indictment with them. My understanding is that the indictment has just been unsealed and you all have a copy." He looked around for acknowledgement. He saw 18 heads nod in the affirmative in return. "Let the record show all defense attorneys have acknowledged receipt of the indictment."

Six bailiffs and 18 defendants filed in from a back door of the courtroom that opened up to a hall that led to the court holding tank. The defendants came in according to their pecking order in La Familia. The three jefes first, then the three money launderers, followed by the lower level 12. Nick thought, *You can't get away from priority treatment. Even Southwest Airlines, the people's airline, allow you to board first if you pay a few extra bucks. And Qualcomm stadium was not good enough for the NFL and the Chargers because it didn't have enough luxury boxes for the corporate elite. Enough, no more rumination about class and wealth.*

Several minutes passed as the attorneys and their clients conferred. The gavel shook the room one more time. "I'm going to read the indictment in full. By the way Mr. Drummond, you were quite wordy. Five pages would have done just fine. We didn't need a treatise."

"I apologize, Your Honor."

"Very well." The judge read the indictment and then asked each defendant in turn if he understood the charges against him. Each said, "Yes." The judge then asked each attorney, "How does your client plead to the charges?"

Each attorney responded, "Not guilty." The judge then turned his glare to the prosecutor's table. "Mr. Drummond or Mr. Sterling, please address the bail issue."

Nick stood. He had actually combed his hair that morning and had a brand new suit from Nordstrom's Rack. He didn't look all that bad.

"Your Honor, we're making recommendations on bail amounts on the basis of three levels of culpability and flight risk. "For Mateo Gomez-Encinas, the head of Baja Norte Familia, and his two chief lieutenants, Luis Hernandez-Lopez and Rael Trujillo-Sanchez, no bail. The Familia is a violent, transnational criminal organization. Its tentacles in this case alone have been shown to reach Canada, Chicago, Montana, and Salt Lake City. The cartel deals in death—black tar heroin. Heroin is responsible for dramatic increases in overdoses and deaths of our youth throughout the country, across all economic and racial lines. Not only have we seized hundreds of kilos of black tar heroin, along with thousands of pounds of marijuana, the cartel is laundering millions of dollars each month in complete mockery of our banking laws and legitimate commerce. In this case, these three have gone beyond drug smuggling and money laundering—they are also indicted for conspiracy to murder. Luis Hernandez-Lopez' estranged girlfriend, and prospective material witness in this case, was sprayed with machine gun bullets in broad daylight on a residential street for daring to leave this man, and by extension, the cartel. She was saved from death by task force agents who, in turn, returned fire and shielded the estranged girlfriend from bullets. Agent Schwartz was hit twice and almost died from loss of blood. These three men are all Mexican nationals. Only Mr. Lopez has a residence here which he rarely uses, a condo in Coronado Cays. If any of the three were released, they'd be in Mexico the very same day. Never again to cross the border into the United States where we can arrest them."

"The next category are the three money launderers. They are all foreign nationals, but have had domiciles along the border in California for a number of years. All three have businesses on both sides of the border, which for over a year have been used to launder millions of dollars per month for the cartel. We are asking for two million dollars in bail for each of these defendants."

"Finally, the other 12 defendants were important cogs in the drug distribution and money collection operations over the past year. Nine were either transporting or storing drugs all over the country. For months, the defendants tied to the Missoula warehouse were smuggling drugs into Canada for cash dollars. The last three defendants are long-term, personal bodyguards for the three jefes of the cartel. Eleven out of the twelve defendants are foreign nationals. The exception is Jim Mitchell, a college student at the University of Montana, Missoula. As to these 12 defendants, we are recommending $500,000 apiece. They are all flight risks and are part of the same nefarious, far-reaching criminal organization. If I may approach the bench, this is a one page legal memorandum on the law as to bail prepared by AUSA Sterling. I've already given copies to defense counsel. It sets forth the uncontroverted law that supports our bail and no bail requests. I apologize for not being able to file it earlier."

"You may approach. I understand you've been rather busy the last few court days." The judge read through it. "You're right. It contains nothing I don't already know. I'll allow it to be filed."

The judge looked at each defense team for a moment. "I'll call on each of you in turn, starting right to left, to make your bail arguments." The attorneys for the three jefes argued that no bail was unprecedented in a case of this nature—no one died. Further, the prosecution couldn't tie the shooting to the three of them. They asked for a reasonable, equitable ball of $200,000 apiece.

Judge Orsini replied, "The murder conspiracy is thin, but the master affidavit appears to set forth sufficient facts to support the charge. I order that Encinas, Lopez and Sanchez be held with no bail because of the nature of the crimes, their roles as leaders of a transnational criminal organization, and the very real threat of flight risk if they were to make bail."

The other defendants made their arguments in turn. The judge split the baby as to them. One million apiece for the launderers and $250,000 apiece for the other twelve.

Judge Orsini directed his attention to Drummond again. "When will you have discovery ready for the defendants?"

"It'll be bates stamped and scanned into digital form for transfer onto CDs for delivery to all defense counsel in thirty days. There are approximately 60,000 pages of documents."

"Very ambitious Mr. Drummond. You must have an excellent staff." "We do, Your Honor. The very best."

"Okay. We'll set a status conference in 60 days for setting of motions and a trial date. Do I have a waiver of your constitutional right to a speedy trial to four months from this date or would you rather spend every waking hour over the next two months going over 60,000 pages of discovery?"

The defense, one by one, waived their constitutional right to a speedy trial. Judge Orsini looked around and smiled, "Now that wasn't too bad. I trust we'll get along just fine over the ensuing months. You're excused." Nick spoke to Josh quietly as they walked out of the courtroom. "I was getting claustrophobic in there with all those defense attorneys and defendants. The first thing we have to do is to separate the wheat from the chaff. Work up offers for the lower twelve, from five to ten years apiece. Once those attorneys start pouring through all that discovery and realize how long a trial could take, they'll want out. Although they'll be making money on this case, a long, drawn out proceeding will destroy their client base for their solo practitioner offices."

After a sandwich, Josh and Nick went to the U.S. Attorney conference room in the federal building. The press conference was to start in ten minutes. Nick went over to the U.S. Attorney for the Southern Region of California, Bea Kowalski, and gave her a hug. "Bea, thank you again for what you did for Agent Cantana."

"I would do it for any agent in trouble."

Bea was raised in a small town in Iowa, before going to Stanford undergrad and Duke Law School. Her first job was with the San Diego Office of the U.S. Attorney and she has stayed there ever since. She was a hard-nosed, fair and extremely competent career prosecutor.

Nick turned to look across the room at State Attorney General Ken Hamilton and his entourage. General Hamilton beckoned Nick over. They didn't even pretend to smile or bother to shake hands. "Nick, this better go off without a hitch. The press conference is very important to me. Many people, some in Washington D.C., will be following this case."

"Oh, trying to get appointed *the* U.S. Attorney? You'll miss the weather here. It sucks in D.C. except for two weeks in the spring and a month in the fall."

"No more of your smart-ass remarks Nick. Is everything set? The power point and the seized drugs and guns?"

"Yes, Rona took care of it. Everything will go smoothly. But you better remove that piece of lettuce stuck between your front teeth." Nick turned away and walked back to Josh, leaving the General to pick at a non existent piece of lettuce.

The office holder politicians wanted to be on the podium. Bea Kowalski and Ken Hamilton stood side by side, behind the microphone. They were flanked on either side by the San Diego department heads of DEA, ICE, Homeland Security, California Bureau of Investigation, and the San Diego County Sheriff's Office. Nick and Josh took spots at the respective far ends of the celebrity line. AG Hamilton started out, thanking the various agencies that participated in the investigation and emphasizing that the attorney heading up the task force was from his office. He didn't bother to name Nick. Ken went on to extoll the efforts that his office had undergone to combat transnational organized crime. He was so gratified that these efforts had come to fruition with the indictment of the three top leaders of the Baja Norte Familia.

U.S. Attorney Kowalski made her opening remarks. Much more concise and heartfelt as to efforts of the individual task force members, whom she named. She made the salient point that it wasn't possible to bring these cartel members to justice without the cooperative efforts of several agencies. "We are a team—local, state and federal. We're in this together."

Rona operated the power point projector as Hamilton and Kowalski took turns explaining the photographs of the investigation shown on the large screen. U.S. Attorney Kowalski, tired of the dog and pony show, left to go back upstairs to get some real work done. General Hamilton, flashing his megawatt smile at the reporters, ushered them into a side room to see the seized packages of heroin and firearms. By this time, Nick and Josh had skipped out.

CHAPTER TWENTY-SIX

L uis Hernandez-Lopez sat on the metal bunk in his six-foot by eight-foot cell, getting more and more pissed off. He had been in isolation for over two months at San Diego's Metropolitan Corrections Center. He was going stir crazy. For twenty-three hours each day he sat in his cell. A trustee brought him meals three times a day, sliding a tray through a slot in the cell door. He had a toilet and a small sink in the cell, no chair and no windows. He read by the corridor light that was turned off at 9:00 each night. For the last three weeks, he was reading the grand jury transcripts of the witnesses' testimony over and over, looking for any little thing he could use to his advantage. He kept coming back to an agent's testimony about what Felicia had said about him. *That whoring Bitch. Puta! She was nothing. Nothing but big tits and a good lay. After all that he had done for her. Anything she wanted he had bought for her. He set her up in his estancia outside of Rosarito Beach. That ungrateful Bitch! Always whining about wanting to go back and visit her family in San Diego. She deserved to be slapped around. There was only one way to treat an ungrateful Bitch. She wouldn't be around by the time of trial. Luis promised she wouldn't die easily.*

Jaime Hernandez-Salgado opened the letter from his third cousin, Luis. He hadn't seen Luis for a few years. Jaime had been avoiding him. He wanted nothing to do with Luis and the Baja Norte Familia. Jaime was working hard to make a go of his Mexican restaurant, the Purple Flamingo, under the San Diego side of the Coronado Bridge. He remembered it was at the restaurant that he had last seen Luis. Luis had come in like a big shot, with a beautiful woman on his arm and two bodyguards. He acted like they were the best of friends. Jaime had to comp Luis for the meals and the dozen or so Cadillac margaritas they sucked up. Jaime wanted to keep Luis happy, but at a safe distance. Jaime knew that Luis was being held in MCC. It was in all the newspapers and the talk of the family. Jaime's stomach felt queasy as he unfolded the letter.

The letter was brief and foreboding. *Dear Cousin, I miss seeing you. I look forward to you visiting me this Sunday during visiting hours, 2 to 4. You need to make an appointment online. My prison number is 9743201. See you then. With great sincerity, Luis.*

Jaime thought, *That son-of-a-bitch. He wants me to do something for him. "With great sincerity." What was that supposed to mean? A threat if he didn't show. Of course, I will go. You don't say no to family or the Familia.*

Sunday, at 2:30, a guard escorted Jaime down a long hallway, through a series of secure doors and up two flights of stairs, to a small room with a counter, situated below steel mesh glass. The guard motioned Jaime to sit in the plastic chair next to the counter and the telephone. The guard, in a clipped voice, told Jaime, "The prisoner will sit down on the other side of the glass partition in a few minutes. He'll initiate the telephone contact. When you hear a beep, pick up the phone and follow the instructions. You have 15 minutes of telephone time." The guard left Jaime alone in the room. Five to ten minutes later, Jaime saw Luis shuffle in, his legs cuffed. The connecting chain only allowed him to step a foot at a time. It was completely different to see Luis in an orange jumpsuit, no jewelry, and with bags under his eyes. Even his meticulously kept hair had a few strands out of place. Jaime couldn't help thinking, *It was an improvement.* The guard uncuffed one of Luis hands, leaving the other one connected by a chain to his leg shackles. Jaime thought, *He is smart not to take any chances with Luis.*

Jaime watched Luis fumble with the telephone, putting the receiver in the crook of his neck while he dialed several numbers.

Luis pressed a few more numbers after listening to the prompts. Jaime heard a beep and picked up his receiver. A robotic voice told him that all telephone conversations are taped. If he wanted to talk to the inmate, to press one. Jaime pressed one and Luis started the conversation. "Jaime, good to see you. As you can tell we don't have much privacy in here. All telephone calls are taped and all incoming or outgoing correspondence is read and copied. The prison guards are a bunch of voyeurs."

"Luis, this is the first time I've been in a prison. It's all new to me. How are they treating you?"

"I'm in isolation. I get one hour a day to exercise by myself in a courtyard. The meals suck and are fattening. I've gained five pounds. I'm bored and I feel like firing my attorney who hasn't gotten me out on bail yet. Other than that, everything is fine. I have a quaint studio cell, with just enough room to sleep and use the toilet. I'm not in danger of getting skin cancer—no natural light graces my features."

"Sorry to hear that Luis. But I really don't want anything to do with all of this."

"You're family. You always were the good one. Working hard at your restaurant. I hope nothing happens to it. I hear grease fires are rather common. Could burn the whole building down. You need to be careful. You know I'd help you if anything like that were to happen? We're family. We help each other out. Right?"

Jaime felt the blood leave his head. He began to feel faint. He started to take deep breaths. He stared at Luis. Luis' dark eyes were unforgiving. "Right Luis. We're family."

"Good. Jaime, you don't look so good. If you need to splash some water on your face when you leave, there's a bathroom just off of the public visitor waiting area. You really need to take care of yourself. I know what's best for you."

"Okay Luis. It probably is a good idea to splash some water on my face."

"I'll be seeing you soon Jaime. *Vaya con Dios.*"

Jaime buzzed the guard to be let out. The guard escorted him through the secure doors and said, "Just down the hallway and to the right is the reception area. They'll let you out."

Halfway down the hallway, a trustee, carrying a mop approached Jaime from the opposite direction. As the trustee went by, he whispered out of the side of his mouth with eyes straight ahead, "Under the sink, a note." Jaime battled with himself as he continued down the hall. *Should I pretend I didn't hear and just leave without using the bathroom? Luis is drawing me into his net. Nothing good would come out of this. But something horrific would happen if I don't do what Luis says. Luis wouldn't think twice about having someone torch my restaurant. That would be five years of hard work—gone. I have no choice.*

Jaime went into the bathroom. No one else was there. He reached underneath the sink and felt around. Towards the back of the sink there was a small baggie containing something. He pulled at the baggie. It was stuck to the underside of the sink. With more effort, the baggie pulled away from the sink but was still connected. Jaime felt a sticky substance between the sink and baggie. He broke it off with his fingers. He brought the baggie out and saw freshly chewed gum sticking to the underneath portion of the baggie. Inside the baggie was a piece of paper, folded several times. Jaime wrapped the baggie with a small piece of paper towel and placed it in his front pocket.

Jaime walked to the receptionist window. "I just want to compliment MCC for such a clean and tidy bathroom. I wasn't expecting a public bathroom to be so clean. I'm in the restaurant business. Do you use a particular service?"

"No, the prison trustees do it. They take their time and do an excellent job. It gets them out of their cells and gives them something to do."

Jaime was on his second bourbon and water back at his restaurant before he got the courage to open up the note. Unfolded, the note consisted of a quarter of a letter size page. The note was concise. *Every Sunday visit me at 2:30. When you leave, check under the sink. Green light on Felicia. Probably attending a dental hygienist school out of state under a different name. Top priority. Do not spare resources. Take*

this note to bartender Jesus at the La Frontera Bar in San Ysidro. Put Pato on it." Jaime thought, *What the hell does "green light" mean?*

He checked online and found that La Frontera was on San Ysidro Boulevard, a few blocks east of Interstate 5. Late Sunday afternoon seemed like a good time to drop off a message to Jesus at the bar. Twenty minutes later, Jaime parked his Jetta next to several motorcycles in front of the bar. No curb appeal. A one story, stucco building that needed paint. A flashing neon light, missing several lights, announced you were at La Frontera. A couple of worn Corona posters were hanging in the windows. Jaime ventured in. He could barely make out the long wooden bar through the smoke and low lights. The jarring sound of pool balls hitting each other directed Jaime's attention to the rear of the bar. A middle-aged woman, in leathers with a cigarette hanging out of her mouth, was half sitting on the side of the pool table, lining up a shot. A behemoth, with a ZZ Top beard, was drinking out of a pitcher across from her. Jaime reverted his eyes to the bar. A half dozen people were spread out along the bar. The nearest was grunting as he took a bite out of a double hamburger. Grease dripped down his chin. A grimy sleeve of his work shirt doubled as a napkin. Jaime took a stool as far away from the other customers as he could. Behind the bar, a wide man with long black hair in a ponytail had his back to Jaime. The man was rinsing off some pint glasses and putting them back on the shelves. Jaime didn't see any soap. The man turned, and took a couple of steps towards Jaime. "What are you having?"

"A Coors Light would be fine."

The big man guffawed. "We don't have any of that light beer piss around here. You've got a choice, Corona, Tecate, Budweiser or Pabst?"

"A Tecate is fine. I'm here to find Jesus, the bartender. I'm a cousin of Luis Hernandez-Lopez. I'm Jaime Hernandez-Salgado."

"Make up your mind. Are you looking for a bartender or trying to find your savior?

"I-I-I-I was just told by, by LLLuis…"

"I'm just foolin' with you. You're really wet behind the ears. Are you sure you're related to Luis?"

Yeah, I own a Mexican restaurant in Diego."

"Oh, I know who you are. You're the goody-goody of the family and own that swish restaurant, the Purple Flamingo. Luis has talked about you." The bartender walked right up to Jaime. Jaime could see his bulging arms in his sleeveless T-shirt. On his right bicep was a tat that outlined Baja Norte California and had the word *Familia* in red inside the outline. On his left bicep was a skull and cross bones with the number *187* written in red along the skull. There were several tatted tear drops down his cheek, below his left eye. "I'm Jesus, the bartender."

Jesus put a draft Tecate down in front of Jaime. "On the house. What does Luis want?"

Jaime pulled the note from his pocket and gave it to Jesus. Jesus read it to himself. He said out loud to himself, "I haven't seen a kite in a while."

"What's a kite?"

"You're looking at it. It's the way inmates communicate with each other about things they don't want the guards to know about. Often a trustee will help deliver a kite to the intended recipient."

"What's a green light?"

"You don't want to know *joven*. Let's just say it's not good. You can tell Luis—message delivered."

Jamie downed his beer, dropped a couple of ones on the bar, and left. The jukebox was serenading him with *Jalisco* as he stepped through the door. Jamie went straight home and got on his computer. He looked up the meaning of tattoos. He found that in gang culture, 187 over a skull and crossbones signified the person was an assassin or hit man for the gang. 187 is the Penal Code section in California for murder. Jamie began to shake uncontrollably.

The next morning, Jesus got on his Harley and headed for Luis' compound in the hills above Rosarito Beach. Jesus told front gate security, "I have to see Pato." Jesus was taken to the upstairs study where Pato was looking at three large screen televisions. One was tuned to CNN, one to a stock market channel, and one to Sports Center. Pato's real name was Javier Esquel Ranchez. He was Luis'

protege—just turned thirty, sophisticated, had a degree in economics, and has a way with the ladies.

Pato looked at the note Jesus handed him. "That's Luis' handwriting. I don't think Felicia has long for this earth. It's too bad they missed her awhile back. Would have saved me a lot of trouble. This dental hygiene school sounds like a decent lead. All she could talk about was going back to school to become a dental hygienist. When you have a snitch and Luis is scorned, no rock shall remain unturned in our search. I'll begin a Google search of schools. Knowing the government, they probably placed her as far away from us as possible, like in the middle of the country or with a moose in Maine. Thanks, Jesus. I may need you later on this."

Before retiring that evening, Pato went to Felicia's bedroom that hadn't been touched since she left. Luis used to believe she'd come back to him. Luis had thought, *What woman would not?* On top of her dresser was a framed photo of her with co-workers at a restaurant. Pato recalled that she had worked as a waitress at a steak and seafood restaurant off J Street in Chula Vista. Inside a desk drawer, he found correspondence from her aunt. Felicia used to bore Luis and Pato at meal times with stories of her childhood and her aunt raising her. It might be worth a friendly visit to the aunt to see if Pato could charm some information out of her about Felicia's whereabouts. Pato didn't believe in using a stick unless absolutely necessary. Carrots and sugar always worked well for Pato.

Late afternoon the next day, Pato drove across the border and went to Terry's Steakhouse at the end of J street. He was wearing his casual professional outfit—silk polo shirt, pressed chinos, and loafers. He walked straight up to the bartender, with a big smile.

"Hello, I'm Lorenzo. I'm a lawyer for Felicia Esperanza-Salas. Here's my bar card. She hired me to handle a small slip and fall case at a grocery store. They finally agreed to settle. Problem is, I can't find her. She left her old apartment about a year ago with no forwarding address. Her cellphone number has been disconnected. I remembered her talking about this restaurant. Do you have any idea where she is?'

"No. It seems like Felicia dropped off the face of the earth. She was pretty tight with a couple of waitresses here. One, was Roxanne Drexler, a good looking brunette, who comes on duty for dinner, about six."

"Thanks, if I can come back later, I will."

Next stop for Pato was the aunt's house. He might as well still go with the attorney identity. Getting a forged California State Bar card was easy. Cost only $100 and people never seemed to question it. Felicia's aunt, Rosa Salas-Huerta, answered the door. "You must be Señora Huerta. Felicia has told me about you. I'm a friend of hers. I used to work with her at Terry's Steakhouse while I was going to law school. My name is Lorenzo. Here's my California State Bar card. It's a pleasure to meet you."

"The pleasure is mine. I don't often have attractive young men knocking on my door."

"Ah, Señora. You're too modest. I bet there were many young men knocking on your door not so long ago. One of our old co-workers, Roxanne Drexler, who is a good friend of Felicia's, is having a baby shower. No one seems able to find Felicia. Because I'm an attorney, I got the pleasant assignment to try to find her and invite her to the shower."

"I remember Felicia talking about Roxanne. She came over once for a home-cooked meal. She raved about my homemade tamales. I liked that *muchacha*. Pregnant already?"

"She met a great guy. A marine. They got married a few months ago. Roxanne was upset that she couldn't track down Felicia for the wedding. Roxanne promised that Felicia would come to her baby shower."

"I don't know where she is exactly. She's involved with something. She can't tell anyone where she is. She was shot at by an evil man on a motorcycle a few months ago when she came to see me."

"Oh no! Is she all right?"

"Thank God she wasn't hit. A state agent covered her up and his female partner was shot. I was so afraid."

"I can't imagine anyone wanting to hurt Felicia. She's such a kind, compassionate person."

"She is. I received a call from her, saying how much she missed me. She was coming home by bus. Two days later, she was walking up to my house and was shot at." Rosa put her head in her hands and began to cry. "Now, now Señora. I'm sure Felicia is going to be all right. Let me know if she comes home. Here's my cellphone number. When things are okay again, maybe you can invite me over for your famous tamales. I love home-cooking."

"I'll do that. Good-bye Lorenzo."

Pato hummed a little tune to himself as he walked away. That went well. Two day bus trip. He'd concentrate on the Midwest.

CHAPTER TWENTY-SEVEN

*I*t was only fitting to receive the defense motions right before Halloween, thought Nick as he looked at the three foot pile in front of his desk. The hearings on the motions were scheduled for the Tuesday after Thanksgiving.

In all complex cases the defense files motions based on statutes and case law in an attempt to get the trial court to dismiss part, or all of the case and, at the very least, to limit the evidence the prosecution is allowed to present to the jury.

Nick and Josh had to file their responses two weeks before Thanksgiving which allowed the defense to file any rebuttal briefs the Monday before Thanksgiving. Nick divided up the 22 motions between Josh and himself. Only four of the motions seemed to have real substance. The most compelling was the sufficiency of the evidence to support the conspiracy to murder Felicia and the aggravated assault counts against the three drug chiefs, Lopez, Encinas, and Sanchez. Nick kept that motion for himself. Another was the alleged Fourth Amendment violation concerning the Otay Mesa warehouse property by reason of the satellite photographs taken by the Department of Defense. Nick gave that to Josh because he could better handle high tech arguments. A third motion concerned the use of a drug-sniffing dog to search the vehicle containing black tar heroin and marijuana driven by the college boy outside of Missoula. Nick gave Josh that one—he was there overseeing the operation. The cardinal rule in case responsibility—once your fingerprints are on a part of a case, it's yours. The last motion was better suited for a motion in limine—a motion brought the day of, or the day before trial regarding the inclusion or exclusion of certain evidence. The defense was contending that Felicia's testimony about getting beat up by Luis should be excluded because it would unduly inflame the jurors that Luis had engaged in domestic violence, which they alleged had no bearing on whether the defendants conspired to have her murdered in the motorcycle drive-by. The defense also claimed it constituted improper character evidence—bad acts to show bad character. Nick decided to keep this motion. It was closely tied to the murder conspiracy count in that Luis' prior beatings showed a pattern of violence towards Felicia. Also, although Nick tried to keep his emotions out of the case, it was personal between him and Luis. He firmly believed that Luis ordered the shooting of Felicia that had almost killed Ana.

Nick went over to his family home around six o'clock on Halloween night. He didn't want to miss the family tradition of trailing after his kids while they trick-or-treated around the neighborhood. He knew his daughter Gabriella, in junior high, was too old to have her parents hanging around on Halloween night. She was off with friends. He also knew it would probably be the last year of doing this with his son Jake. He was now an upperclassman in grammar school, fourth grade. Jake dressed up as Roger Federer. Nick admired the choice. Not much effort for the costume, a world class athlete, and a good guy. Jake had on tennis shorts, a multi-colored tennis shirt, the stylized Federer *RF* ball cap and a knock off watch that Nick loaned him that was supposed to represent the fancy brand hawked by Roger. For neighbors who couldn't pick up on the subtleties of Jake's costume, he also carried a Wilson tennis racket. Jake had initially balked at that, wanting to have both hands free for all the candy.

Nick and Judy walked around with a group of parents. They stayed in the middle of the street and talked about their kids while Jake and his mob went door to door. Nick thought how much he enjoyed the family time. He ached when he thought how many family events he had missed over the last year, in fact, how many over all the years because of his work.

They went back to the house where Jake laid his candy out in a row, separated by type. Hundreds of pieces of candy wound around the living room floor like a multi-colored snake. Jake counted all the pieces, category by category. Gabriella rushed in, glowing, with a small bag of candy at her side. She had barely bothered to dress up. She wore black, had a liberal painting of black eyeliner, and had found a witch's cap. She looked great. Nick asked her what she'd had done and if she had a good time. She brushed him off with, "Fine," and "Nothing special, just with friends." Nick didn't relish the future years of cryptic teenage responses.

Jake began to nod off. It was clear that it was time for Nick to go. He was reluctant to leave. Nick wanted to soak up as much of his family as he could before going home to his tropical fish. Judy gently pushed him towards the door with, "I have an early shift tomorrow. I enjoyed spending the evening with you. It was like old times."

"It was. I can't tell you how much I enjoyed it. I miss these family times so much." He gave Judy a peck on the cheek. She smiled with sad eyes. Nick read her face to say, *It's too bad it's all over with us.* Nick wasn't so sure.

The next morning, Ana walked into Nick's Office. He was staring blankly into space. She noticed there were a few more photos of his kids on the bookshelf. "Wake up Nick! Time to come back to earth. There are earthlings that need instruction. Do you still want me to fly to Kansas and make sure Felicia is willing to come out for the trial?"

"Sorry, just thinking. Yeah, I do want you to fly there. But not until it's a lot closer to when we need her to testify. I don't want you to go there, convince her, and then give her time to change her mind."

"Okay. Did you do anything for Halloween other than give away your tropical fish as tricks?"

"Not a bad idea. Wish I'd thought of it. They're taking up too much of my time. I have to feed them pinches of flakes twice a day and clean their tank every three months, whether it needs it or not. Such responsibility."

"Missing the responsibility of your kids? I see a couple of new pictures on the book case."

"Nothing gets by you. Yeah, I'm missing my kids. I saw them last night and trailed Jake around as he trick-or-treated. It was nice."

"Did you go back to Judy's house after going around the neighborhood? "Yes. Jake counted his candy and spread them out in a long line on the living room floor."

"How wonderful Nick. And you didn't even bring me a Snickers bar, my favorite. By the way, I had a so-so Halloween. My neighbor dragged me to a party and I pretended to have a good time while wanting to be with you. Thanks for asking." Ana turned and headed for the door.

"Wait Ana. I've been preoccupied. I...."

The door slammed. Nick thought, *In the doghouse without even trying.*

Thanksgiving didn't go as well for Nick as Halloween. He took his kids out for brunch. There was an outdoor restaurant in Del Mar that Nick liked. It allowed dogs—Gabriella and Jake got to pat a couple. They then walked along the beach. They hunted for sand dollars and sea glass. They scooped up a few, perfectly intact sand dollars. Nick took one home to put in his fish tank. Nick found two pieces of rubbed smooth, green sea glass, which he promised to make into earrings for Gabriella when she was old enough to pierce her ears. She thought it was now, but her mother and Nick had other ideas. Nick had wanted to go over to their home so they could all have Thanksgiving dinner together. Judy's Mom was coming and her brother. Judy nixed the idea. She had said, "We need to see what it's like really being apart, even on traditional family occasions." Nick hadn't fought it. He dropped the kids off at home in the early afternoon and went to the office. There was work to do with the motions hearing the following Tuesday.

Nick got back to his apartment about nine. He went straight to the liquor cabinet, above the broom closet. He brought a bottle of Jack to the table with a six ounce glass. He settled into his lounge chair and drank to the mournful blues song, *St. James Infirmary*, and songs by Duke Ellington. Nick drifted off to his favorite song by Duke, *I ain't got Nothing but the Blues*.

On Monday afternoon, Judge Orsini emailed his tentative rulings on all the motions to the attorneys, with the instruction to carefully consider which motions the parties wanted to argue the next day. A judge will issue a tentative ruling before a motion hearing to assist the attorneys in focusing on the issues the trial court deems important. Nick and Josh had prevailed on most of the insignificant motions. The ones they lost were no big deal and not worth arguing over the next day. They also did well on the four key motions. Only part of one key ruling went against them. Judge Orsini found there wasn't sufficient evidence to proceed to trial on the murder conspiracy count against the cartel's head, Encinas. That left Sanchez, the cartel enforcement lieutenant, and Luis, the lieutenant for drug distribution, still in as named co-conspirators. Nick knew that motion would be contested by both sides and the defense would contest the three other significant motions.

The next morning, Josh and Nick parked their car a block from the federal courthouse. Each had a luggage roller with a box full of files secured with bungee cord straps. They flashed their prosecutor ID cards and were waved through the metal detector. They entered Judge Orsini's courtroom to set up 15 minutes before the hearing was scheduled. The files of the 22 motions were labeled and set out in order on their counsel table. Nick wanted to schmooze with the head bailiff, the court clerk and the court reporter before the hearing. He talked to each in turn, asked how they were doing, and what

Nick and Josh could do to make the hearing easier for them. Over the years Nick had learned how important it was to keep in good graces with the key personnel of a courtroom—on several cases he had received helpful tips.

The platoon of defense attorneys strolled in with their matching boxes of materials. Fortunately, Josh had thinned the ranks of defendants with accepted plea offers by the less culpable defendants. The case was down to a much more manageable six defendants which included the three cartel leaders. Nick was hopeful that they could cull a couple of more defendants prior to trial. A trial with three or four defendants is manageable.

Judge Orsini took the bench at the second the court clock went to 9:30. It served as a reminder to Nick to never be late in Judge Orsini's courtroom. "Good morning gentlemen. If you don't mind me calling you that."

Nick said, "It's a pleasure to be addressed as such. We don't hear that often enough in the practice of law.'

Judge Orsini replied, "That's because counsels don't often deserve that reference. In my courtroom, you will all act as gentlemen. Now, a few house cleaning matters before we bring in the defendants. I'm going to hear each motion as it's listed in my tentative ruling—in my humble estimation, from the least significant to the most significant. First, I want to know from both sides which motions you choose to argue. Mr. Drummond, we'll start with you."

"Just the last, number 22, the motion to set aside the murder conspiracy count. We reserve argument as to any other motions the defense chooses to argue in court. AUSA Sterling and I have each prepared 11 of the motions, and will split the oral advocacy along those lines."

"Thank you Mr. Drummond. Defense?"

"Good morning Your Honor. Lars Flanigan for defendant Mateo Gomez-Encinas. Marc Lipman, counsel for Luis Hernandez-Lopez, and I'll be arguing in turn for all six defendants, depending on which motion is being argued. The defendants would like to be heard on motion numbers 6, 9, 11, 15, and the last four motions, 19 through 22."

"To all counsel, I appreciate you narrowing down the number of motions to be argued. I was afraid we might be here all morning, and into the afternoon. It looks like we can be out of here in time for an early lunch. They're your motions Mr. Flanigan and Mr. Lipman. You may start as soon as the defendants are brought in."

The six defendants shuffled into the courtroom from the private back hallway. Everyone was chained together, with both ankle chains and handcuffs. Encinas managed to keep his patrician air like he was strolling through a slightly distasteful alley. Luis had a smirk on his face; sending the message that these circumstances wouldn't last long. Sanchez had an impenetrable scowl. His scar, down the length of the right side of his face, seemed more pronounced. Armed bailiffs led them and the three others into the courtroom. The six defendants were unhooked from each other and had their handcuffs removed. Their ankle shackles remained. They sat by their respective counsel. A couple of extra tables had been set up near the jury box to accommodate all the defendants and their counsel. The extra bailiffs spaced themselves nearby.

Nick leaned over to Josh and whispered, "Don't you think they look good in jailhouse orange, sandals, and ankle cuffs. The height of fashion."

Flanigan and Lipman argued motions 6, 9, 11, and 15, two apiece. By the luck of the draw, all four responses had been prepared by Josh. After hearing the first defense argument, which presented nothing that wasn't already in their moving papers, Nick whispered to Josh, "Keep it brief, Orsini isn't coming off of his tentative ruling in our favor. I've been watching him tap his pencil during the argument. It means he's heard enough."

Josh followed Nick's advice. He kept it brief for each of the initial four arguments and essentially submitted on the People's filed responses.

For each of the four motions, in turn, Judge Orsini said, "I have read the pleadings filed by all the parties and stand by my tentative ruling. Motion denied."

The first significant motion, number 19, was the defense motion to exclude all the drugs and other evidence seized at the Otay

Mesa ranch. The defense argument was that the DoD satellite photos of the ranch violated the Fourth Amendment right against unreasonable government searches.

Lars Flanigan began the argument with an angry tone. "The satellite photos of the Otay Mesa ranch by the Department of Defense were an unwarranted and outrageous violation of the defendants' constitutional rights to be protected against unreasonable and invasive government actions. No person is safe from the intrusive eyes of the government. Whether it's NSA collecting random data against all our citizens or the Department of Defense spying on our homes from satellites, miles above, undetectable by the naked eye. By a phone call, without cause, Prosecutor Drummond summoned the unlimited resources behind the Department of Defense satellite system to focus on one small farmhouse in Otay Mesa. There's nothing the defendants or any homeowner can do to protect their privacy from such intrusion. In these high tech times, with innovations in technology changing on a day to day basis, the courts need to step in and apply the brakes to the government's runaway technology train that is crushing all of our privacy rights. The legislature can't or won't keep up. Without the satellite photos, there wouldn't have been sufficient cause to support the search warrant of the Otay Ranch property. Under the Constitution, this court must exclude the evidence!"

"Thank you Mr. Flanigan. Prosecution?"

Josh stood up immediately, and looked Judge Orsini directly in the eye. "Thank you, Your Honor. Mr. Flanigan's anger is misplaced. Technology has grown at a rapid pace, mainly for the good. The capabilities and benefits of our satellites aren't in dispute—communication, national security, and assistance with weather and disaster analysis. The fact that we have flying objects in our airspace that are capable of looking earthward, whether from miles above the ground or from 200 feet above the ground, is well-known. Google Earth takes pictures from above of all our properties to help others locate them and provide directions. There isn't a protected cone of privacy above land or any building. Only when technology is used by the government to detect items or persons within a building, that aren't detectable from outside the premises, does the Fourth Amendment come into play. The applicable marijuana grow cases find a Fourth Amendment violation where police direct overflights of property, using heat-seeking, infrared devices to ferret out marijuana grows inside buildings that otherwise couldn't be detected. That isn't the situation here. The satellite photos show individuals outside a building, unloading duffle bags from an oil tanker truck. This could have been detected by a helicopter flying over the property. No special devices were used to detect anything inside the buildings. No Fourth Amendment rights are implicated here. The defense motion must be denied."

"I thank both counsel. The rapid increase in technology is a concern as to how it interfaces with some of our basic rights, including the Fourth Amendment right against unreasonable government searches. There are many things the courts and the legislatures will have to come to grips with. However, this isn't the time or place for this court to extend the penumbras of Fourth Amendment rights to include aerial photos of a property where no special devices were used to seek out information from within the buildings. The fact the photos were the product of a billion dollar satellite program is irrelevant. Motion denied. The evidence seized at the Otay Ranch property can be presented by the prosecution at trial. Next on the agenda is motion number 20. We're going from satellites to drug-sniffing dogs. Defense?"

"I'm up again Your Honor," replied Mr. Flanigan. "The stop of the truck driven by a University of Montana college student, outside of Missoula, was an orchestrated attack on the Fourth Amendment by the government. It was a pretense stop. Find some minor traffic violation, pull the truck over, and bring in the canine unit that is waiting for the stop so it can arrive at the scene for an invasive sniff. The Montana Highway Patrol Officers were just going through the motions of getting the student's driver's license and car registration to stall for time for the canine unit to pull up. Without the positive alert by the dog for drugs, there was no probable cause to search the truck. Bringing in the drug sniffing dog delayed the traffic stop. Without the dog, a normal traffic stop for a rear brake light violation would have taken a few minutes. Here, they were roadside for thirty minutes while the dog sniffed its way around the truck and the drugs were seized and inventoried. This constitutes an unreasonable delay in the detention of the driver of the vehicle. The drugs later found in the truck must be excluded under the Fourth Amendment."

Josh stood up again. "If I may respond, Your Honor?"

"Go ahead."

"As set forth in the multiple declarations attached to the People's response, there was no unreasonable delay at all from the time the truck was initially pulled over, to the time Klink, the highly qualified, drug-sniffing German Shepard, commenced the sniff."

Judge Orsini interjected, "I don't believe that the defense is contesting the qualifications of the dog. Is that right Mr. Flanigan?"

"Correct, Your Honor. We don't question the qualifications of man's best friend."

"Okay. Mr. Sterling, you may proceed."

"As the declarations indicate, it took only two minutes from the time of the stop for Klink to commence the exterior vehicle sniff. Mr. Flanigan, in his argument has already acknowledged that a normal traffic stop for a brake light infraction takes a few minutes. So, while the Montana Highway Patrolmen were dutifully adhering to the protocol for the traffic stop, the canine unit had already commenced the exterior sniff. The commencement of the sniff terminates any further unreasonable detention delay analysis. In any event, the declarations indicate that Klink made a positive alert for drugs within one minute of commencing the sniff. Thus, no more than three minutes transpired between the initial stop and the positive alert. Three minutes is well within the acceptable time parameters under the Fourth Amendment for a traffic stop. The fact that it took another 25 minutes for the canine unit to seize the drugs from the truck and inventory them isn't attributable to the initial traffic infraction, but to the positive alert for drugs. The positive alert gave the officers cause to search the truck for drugs and inventory what was seized. The cases that disallow a canine search of a vehicle stopped for a traffic violation on the basis of an unreasonably long detention of the driver occur when there's a significant time span between the initial traffic stop and the arrival of the canine unit to commence the sniff, like 30 minutes. That's not the case here."

"Further, Mr. Flanigan's conjecture that it was an 'orchestrated pretense stop' by law enforcement has no bearing. As this Court is well aware, the United States Supreme Court, in *Whren v. United States*, held that as long as a traffic stop is objectively reasonable, it doesn't violate the Fourth Amendment, irrespective of the subjective intent of the officer making the stop. Here, it's not in dispute that the rear right brake light on the truck wasn't working, a violation of Montana's Vehicle Code. This stop and positive alert are controlled by the 2005 United States Supreme Court case, *Illinois v. Caballos*, which upheld a vehicle search based on a positive canine drug alert that occurred almost simultaneously with the traffic stop. The defense motion must be denied."

"Thank you again counsel for your concise arguments. The cases in the various circuit courts are whittling down the time between the initial traffic stop and the commencement of the exterior canine sniff for drugs. There has never been a bright line as to how much time is allowed under the Fourth Amendment to commence the sniff once the traffic violation protocol is completed. Here, we don't have an unreasonable detention delay between writing a traffic ticket and the commencement of the canine sniff. The sniff began before a reasonable time for the traffic ticket protocol was completed. The motion is denied and the evidence remains in the case."

"Marc Lipman for the defense on motion number 21. My client's former girlfriend, Felicia Salas, told police when she was stopped at the border that my client beat her up the evening before and had knocked her around previously. The prosecution wants to use this unverified claim to prejudice the jury against my client as to extremely serious charges. Domestic violence is a hot button issue. It's in the public eye and alleged abusers are portrayed as monsters by the press. The allegations of abuse have nothing to do with the charges in the indictment—drug trafficking, money laundering and conspiracy to murder. The jury could very well convict Mr. Lopez on these unrelated, serious crimes because of these trumped up domestic violence allegations. The extreme prejudice of the flimsy evidence greatly outweighs any potential relevancy and should be excluded under rule 403 of the Federal Rules of Evidence. In addition, the admission of the abuse evidence would lead to a mini-trial within a trial, proving or disproving the domestic violence allegations; thereby distracting the jury from the true issues in this case. It'd constitute an undue consumption of time. Finally, it's improper character evidence. All evidence of domestic violence must be excluded at trial."

"Thank you counsel. Prosecution?"

Nick's knees creaked as he stood up—loud enough for the Court and defense counsel to hear. "I apologize for the creaky knees. The miles on my knees are well over warranty."

"That's quite all right counsel. This courtroom doesn't depend on finely tuned knees, hips, or shoulders. Go ahead."

"Thank you, Your Honor. Defendant Lopez's various acts of physical abuse towards Felicia are highly relevant to establish a scheme of violence against Felicia that culminated in the motorcycle drive-by shooting directed at Felicia as she was walking up to her aunt's house. This is the same shooting where Agent Schwartz took two bullets protecting Felicia. It also shows defendant's continued intent to harm and control Felicia. He demanded complete obedience, even forcing her to tattoo his name on her breast. While this conduct may be reflective of Defendant Lopez' character, it's not improper character evidence because of its relevance to a common scheme or plan, and intent. Further, the beatings go to Felicia's credibility as a witness. Defense has attacked her credibility extensively in their various moving papers. The beatings, and in particular, the last beating, gives the jury an accurate picture of what Felicia was going through. How difficult it was for her to tell law enforcement about Mr. Lopez at the border and how difficult it will be for her to testify about her former boyfriend and the cartel at trial. She has been living under utter fear of Mr. Lopez and the cartel. This evidence is absolutely necessary to give the jury the true picture of a key prosecution witness."

Judge Orsini reflected a few moments before saying, "These acts do raise competing interests under the law. The idea that the jury should hear all relevant evidence versus the need to protect a defendant's right to a fair trial and not have a jury unduly influenced by overly inflammatory evidence. In listening to all the arguments, and weighing all the considerations, I rule that the beating the night before Felicia was stopped at the border, comes in, while the earlier beatings do not. And, Mr. Lopez' name tattooed on her breast is also excluded. However, because some of the issues can be influenced by the course of evidence presented at trial, the ruling is without prejudice. Both sides are free to bring up the issue upon a change of circumstances at trial. That leaves us with the defense motion as to sufficiency of the evidence to support the conspiracy to murder and aggravated assault counts of the indictment."

Mr. Lipman immediately stood. "I've been waiting for this argument, Your Honor. Your tentative ruling found insufficient evidence to support the conspiracy to murder and assault charges against Mr. Encinas, but sufficient evidence as to Mr. Lopez and Mr. Sanchez. This court was absolutely correct in ruling insufficient evidence as to Mr. Encinas, but there's also clearly insufficient evidence tying Mr. Sanchez and Mr. Lopez to the motorcycle shooting. Unfortunately, there's widespread violence in Chula Vista. Drive-by shootings aren't uncommon. Many are without apparent rhyme or reason. Some gang-banger shootings are motivated by revenge over perceived slights. Innocent family members of a person targeted by a gang can also be the victims of this crazed street culture. The three defendants were all in Mexico at the time, attending to legitimate concerns. The prosecution certainly isn't contesting that any of the three were either the driver of the motorcycle or the shooter. There's no direct evidence that any of the three were involved, or in any way conspired to have the shooting occur. The murder conspiracy taints the entire case. Having this count puts the defendants in a different, highly negative light before the jury. It's one thing to be an alleged drug dealer or money launderer, but a murder conspirator? It will irrevocably prejudice these three defendants in the eyes of the jury."

"Thank you Mr. Lipman. Prosecution?"

Nick believed his best approach was to first attack the defense argument that there was no evidence to support the conspiracy and assault charges and to end with a reminder to the judge of how little evidence it takes to support a count in an indictment.

"There was more than sufficient evidence presented to the grand jury to support the conspiracy to murder and assault charges against the three lead co-defendants. Alan, Felicia's cousin, told a couple of older gang-bangers, who have ties with the Familia, that Felicia was coming home the next day. It just so happens, the next afternoon, when Felicia was walking up to her aunt's house, two young Hispanics, on a red Ducati Streetfighter, opened fire with an automatic rifle. Felicia was saved from being shot by Agent Schwartz' and Agent Cantana's heroic actions. The grand jury heard that defendant Lopez owns a red Ducati Streetfighter, an expensive motorcycle, way out of the financial reach of a couple of local thugs. Defendant Lopez wanted absolute control over Felicia, not allowing her to leave the compound without a bodyguard escort. He beat her just before she managed to escape his clutches. Mr. Lopez can't stand for anyone to leave him. Also, the cartel has only one solution for members or associates who turn on them and go to the police. A cartel expert explained to the grand jury that the consequence for snitching is death. There is a strong inference from the evidence that when Felicia dropped completely out of sight, the cartel believed she went to the police and was in witness protection. That same cartel expert told the grand jury that before a hit on a snitch is approved, the hierarchy of the cartel must approve—the approval must come from as high up as the lieutenant in charge of enforcement. In this case that is defendant Rael Trujillo-Sanchez."

"Additionally, defendant Lopez all but admitted to accountant Lester Sendow that the cartel had taken out a hit on Felicia. A few weeks after the shooting, Sendow visited Lopez at his compound in Mexico. He asked Defendant Lopez where Felicia was. He replied, 'We won't be seeing that bitch anymore. She's being taken care of.' Finally, Felicia's cousin, Alan, saw the two Familia wannabes a couple of weeks after he told them that Felicia was coming home. They threatened him and told him that the Familia never misses twice. Your Honor, when you look at all of this evidence, together with the reasonable inferences derived from the evidence, there is sufficient evidence to support the murder conspiracy charge in the indictment against all three lead defendants. At the very least, there was an implicit agreement to terminate Felicia for snitching on the cartel. Plus, the case law is clear. There doesn't need to be substantial evidence to support each count of the indictment, just some evidence in support of each count. The People have met that burden as to Encinas, Sanchez and Lopez on the conspiracy to murder and the aggravated assault counts."

"Anything more gentlemen? Seeing no response, I'll proceed with my ruling on motion number 22. My tentative holds. There's clearly enough evidence as to Felicia's ex-boyfriend, Mr. Lopez. It's a closer question as to the other two defendants. The cartel expert, a highly qualified law enforcement agent from the Drug Enforcement Agency, testified at the grand jury, 'That the head of enforcement for the cartel had to approve a hit on a snitch.' That is enough to keep Rael Trujillo-Sanchez in as a defendant on the murder conspiracy and assault. However, the expert didn't testify that the head of the cartel had to know or to approve. I'm dismissing the conspiracy to murder and assault counts against Defendant Mateo Gomez-Encinas."

"Remember, we're scheduled to start the trial on January six. I won't look favorably upon any last minute continuances. Happy Holidays. This court is adjourned."

The attorneys said in unison, "Thank you, Your Honor."

Nick whispered to Josh on the way out, "I wish he had kept Encinas in on the murder conspiracy. But it was real thin. I thought Orsini showed some smarts in his ruling about what to keep in and what to keep out on the domestic violence and the titty tat. He was very general in his reasoning. No appellate court can attack his ruling for relying on something specific. Just a legitimate exercise of broad judicial discretion. He's a cunning old man."

CHAPTER TWENTY-EIGHT

Pato sat in Luis' office and thought about his next step in tracking down Felicia. He had various Familia distributors check out the main dental hygienist schools in the Midwest. They all had a recent photo of her and were told not to make any contact. It helped that Felicia was Hispanic because mainly Caucasian females attend hygienist schools in the Midwest. There were two promising leads. A woman who looked like Felicia, but with a different hair color, was attending a school in St. Louis, and another woman with shorter hair than Felicia, who wore dark glasses, was attending a school in Topeka. Pato figured if he wanted to be sure, he would have to fly out to these America's garden spots in the winter and see for himself. He booked a flight to St. Louis under his attorney persona, Lorenzo. He hated commercial flights, the crowds, the security checks. It'd only be worse during the holiday season. He would arrive the week before Christmas.

On arrival, Pato carried his small valise to the car rental office near the airport. He was tempted to rent a Range Rover, but this trip called for him to be discreet. He got unlimited mileage on a white Ford Taurus and drove over to the St. Louis school. Online research indicated there were only 40 students. He parked under a tree across from the school and spent the early afternoon alternately glancing down at a newspaper and over to the school's entrance. It wasn't until just after 3:00 that he saw the young lady who'd been identified as possibly being Felicia. Her facial features and skin coloring closely resembled Felicia's. Her hair was quite a bit darker than Felicia's. This could easily be explained by an attempt to dye her hair to help conceal her identity. Pato studied her closely as she walked across the street in front of his car. She was talking to another student and not paying any attention to her surroundings. She had Pato's undivided attention when she walked away from him down the sidewalk. Pato was a connoisseur of the way women walked. He loved the nuances when shapely women swayed side to side. This woman wasn't Felicia.

Pato set the GPS and headed towards Interstate 70. He figured the 300 miles across Missouri to Topeka would have him arriving around nine o'clock.

The next morning, Pato was camped outside the Topeka dental hygienist school by 8:30. He wasn't disappointed. He knew Felicia immediately from her walk. He saw her get out of her Tercel in the adjacent parking lot and walk into the building. She had this sexy, athletic walk that was hard to duplicate. He had seen it many times at Luis' compound. Pato flashed back to the times he saw her walk around the pool. Above her shoulders, her hair was quite a bit shorter now. She looked more sophisticated and business-like with the shorter hair. Pato liked it. Too bad she wouldn't be around for long. Pato knew from the class schedule that Felicia would get out at two. He had time to kill. He had read about the Combat Air Museum which was located at Forbes Field.

The F-14 Tomcat Flight simulator was ever so sweet. Pato felt like he was flying the real plane. He dreamed about the Familia picking up an old jet fighter. Luis, being such an adrenaline junky, would love it once his legal entanglements were resolved.

After the museum, Pato had time for some barbecue. Hard to imagine how a dark, run down restaurant could come up with such great barbecue. He had six, meat-laden beef ribs, with tangy sauce dripping all over. Add some barbecue beans and slaw, and Pato was ready to renounce enchiladas and tamales as his favorite dishes. He engaged in flirtatious banter with the college age waitress. Pato assumed a slight Castilian accent of a traveling Spanish businessman, who didn't understand American football, but deeply appreciated the fairer sex. By the end of the meal, he had her number and promised to call her the next time he was in town on business. Her short cut-off jeans, and gingham blouse tied in a knot below her breasts, had spoken to him. Leaving a 40 per cent tip, Pato grazed the waitress' hand with his lips in farewell, and glided out of the restaurant.

When he got back to the school, Pato parked farther away. On schedule, Felicia headed towards her car, climbed in and drove away down the street. Pato followed a half block behind. Felicia didn't seem to be in a rush and there was very little traffic. She travelled several blocks and took a right down a tree-lined residential street. Five blocks later, she turned into a driveway of a well-kept, smaller house with a front porch. Pato watched as she used her key to open the front door and walk inside. He took a few pictures of the house and her car and left.

Jaime found himself drinking more and more. He couldn't think about anything except how he had gotten into this nightmare—being a note courier for his cartel cousin, Luis. In a standard routine over the last month, Jaime would get a note from Jesus at the Frontera Bar, and stick it under the sink of the public restroom off the jail's reception area before he visited Luis each Sunday. After each visit, Jaime would go back to the bathroom, and dislodge a new note that was left for him while he was visiting Luis. He would dutifully deliver the new note to Jesus. The latest note, delivered to Luis on the Sunday before Christmas, said, *Dorothy has been found in Kansas.* The note ended with, *Let me know what type of tornado you prefer. P.*

The Sunday after Christmas, Jaime delivered a note to Jesus from Luis. *I enjoy dramatic weather fronts. They leave a lasting impression on all that see it. They remind me of Fourth of July celebrations, rockets and high caliber detonations. It would be a shame if Dorothy's house was consumed by a tornado.*

Pato read the note on Sunday evening. He needed to get moving on the logistics of taking out Dorothy and her house. He figured a 50 caliber machine gun and a rocket launcher from a Humvee would make an adequate statement.

That same Sunday evening, Nick was fighting an urge to call Ana. His holidays hadn't gone so well. His school of Dalmatian Mollies tropical fish were thinning out. He was down to 15 from 25 just a few weeks earlier. He wondered if the holiday malaise had gotten to them as well. He'd have to start playing more upbeat music. Too much of the mournful blues could get anyone down.

Nick had spent Christmas morning with his kids, opening presents at the family home. It had been wonderful to be with them. Jake still had an all-encompassing exuberance when he opened his presents. The new bike Nick got for him went over big. At the same time, he was unbearably sad that his former family life seemed to be over. Judy wasn't making any effort to reconcile. To the contrary, it seemed that she had mentally moved on. Nick didn't feel like a part of her life anymore.

Now, a few days after Christmas, Nick wondered if Ana would take his call. He had forgotten to get her a Chanukah card or even wish her a Happy Chanukah. Enough obsessing, he dialed her number.

"Hello Nick. I was wondering if you'd get up the nerve to call."

"Ana, I've been thinking about this call for weeks. I know I was the one who said we can't have a relationship outside work until this trial is over, but I need to see you, touch you."

"Nick, just because you're getting horny, it doesn't mean you can expect me to fall into your arms at your every whim. Your stay away order made sense no matter how much I disliked it. It's easier for me not to see you until the trial is over."

"How about a compromise. I see you for just an hour. I grovel for 10 or 15 minutes. We can talk a little shop about the case. Then, I get to kiss you good night. That's it. I promise."

"You drive a hard bargain. You know how much I like to see a grown man grovel. Just an hour. See you in twenty minutes."

In record time, Nick was ringing Ana's doorbell. She was wearing a black dress, with white pearls encircling her neck. The pearls glistened against the backdrop of her olive skin. "You haven't assumed the appropriate groveling posture. I believe it's on your knees."

Nick dropped to his knees. "I have no shame. For the countless miseries I have put you through, I deserve to be lashed and wear a hair shirt over the open welts. You can have my kingdom if you will forgive me. To be completely honest and in the interest of full disclosure, that consists of only a dwindling population of tropical fish, a beat up old vehicle, and a top flight stereo system. Can that possibly be enough to regain your favor, my princess?"

"No, but it's a good start. If you had a hot motorcycle to throw in, that might have been enough. Rise my tarnished knight. I don't want to take you to the emergency room for putting too much weight on your knees."

"Your compassion overwhelms me." Nick rose and gave her a kiss on the cheek.

"Be careful Nick, you're going to use up your one kiss. I'm holding you to that. I'll get you a glass of port. That seems like a safe aperitif and shouldn't lead us to any trouble." They sipped port and watched the fire Ana had lit. She used real logs in her living room's fireplace. Nick tried to turn the conversation to their personal lives, but Ana would have none of it. "There's plenty of time for that when the trial is over. I'll be waiting."

So, Nick told her about his game plan for the trial. He was going to start with the Yaak, Montana guys and then move on to Felicia. He was worried that Felicia would get skittish again, like at the grand jury, and refuse to testify. "Ana, are you still able to go to Topeka a couple of days before we need her to testify and make sure she comes? You have the best rapport with her. She owes you and Pepe her life."

"Sure, I've always wanted to see Topeka in early January. I know how important she is. I'll go. However, your hour is up. Thank you for coming over."

Nick bent over her. He put his right arm around her shoulder in an enveloping embrace. He stared into her eyes. A hint of a smile crossed his face. He lifted Ana's chin slightly with his left hand, and gave her a light, but lingering kiss on her lips. "Goodnight Ana. I adore you." Ana tried to murmur a response. He put a finger to her lips. "Shush. I know there's nothing to say now. I'll let myself out."

CHAPTER TWENTY-NINE

"Nothing like sitting around on a Sunday, talking about prospective jurors," said Nick.

Josh responded, "No other place I'd rather be. I know a secretary at defense attorney Lipman's firm. She just happened to mention that they've hired a juror consultant to help with picking a jury. The defense team will put on a mock defense before the 12 'average' citizens they brought in."

"Good for them. Let them waste their time going through a mock trial and listening to some academic expound on who'd be the perfect juror. There are some rules of thumb, but nothing is etched in stone. When it's time to go with a juror or to kick him or her, an attorney's gut controls. I don't go out of my way to pick accountants or engineers. They have a tendency to want every "t" crossed and "i" dotted in the prosecutor's case. I also shy away from teachers. They often have too much empathy for the underdog. But also, I've had good jurors from all those professions. What do you think about age and gender for this trial?"

"Well, Nick, I haven't done nearly as many trials as you have, but I do have some thoughts on it. I'd stay away from youth. Some of the young women may be swayed by Luis' good looks. And who knows what younger males think about drug dealing. I'd be concerned about jurors discounting a drug case if this was solely about marijuana, but with the black tar heroin and violent assault thrown in, I'm not worried."

"I agree. But I expect you to charm any young women on the panel we may end up with. I'll take care of the middle-aged women.

I'd like to have a couple of intellectually sharp people on the panel who can help ferret out the money laundering counts. What about race Josh?"

"We're going to have to be careful with that."

The Supreme Court made it clear in *Batson v. Kentucky* and *Miller-el v. Dretke*, as well as other cases, that a prosecutor who excuses a juror on the basis of race violates the defendant's right to be tried by an impartial jury and the right to equal protection of the law under the Fourteenth Amendment.

Josh continued, "I'm thinking Asians as a whole would be good. Law abiding, family values. I have no problems with whites or blacks. We should pay closer attention to Hispanics considering the ethnicity of the defendants."

"I'm expecting most of the panel to be white. But if we end up with minorities on the panel, I'd prefer there not be just one of any group. That person could feel isolated. It'd be best to have at least two of each group. The bottom line Josh—we want at least one, strong, pro-prosecution juror, who can sway others. An attempt to get a favorable jury is part of trial advocacy, dirty tricks aren't."

"So no old school tricks. Too bad, I loved your story about the prosecutor in Oakland who tied a fishing line to the bowler that a flashy San Francisco attorney used to wear in court and gently pulled on the bowler during the defense attorney's final argument. I can just picture the jury paying more attention to the bowler moving across counsel's table than to the defense argument."

"That happened way back in the early fifties, even before *Miranda* warnings were required. By the way, good job getting those last minute pleas from the three money laundering defendants. Eight years apiece in prison is enough for them. Having only the top three dogs in the cartel as defendants is so much more manageable. Rona and I thank you."

"My pleasure Nick. I'll see you tomorrow."

"You'll be sick and tired of me Josh by the end of tomorrow. Orsini's clerk should have copies of the prospective jurors' written responses to questionnaires to us by three in the afternoon. Monday will be a late night—going though 100 questionnaires, twenty pages a piece, and rating each juror one through five."

"I know. Rona is going to make an extra copy as soon as they come in so we can each go through them, make notes, and rate the jurors. Then we can squabble and come up with a joint rating and any follow up questions we need to ask."

"We'll be ready for the crap shoot jury selection process on Tuesday. Get a good night's sleep. May be the last one for a while."

On Tuesday morning, Nick wound his way through the press in the hallway outside the courtroom, pulling his case boxes behind him in a luggage carrier. He ignored questions. He just waved and said, "I have to be in court." Pepe and Josh were already inside the courtroom. They were setting up their materials on the counsel table closest to the jury box. The defense attorneys came in together a few minutes later and arranged their materials on counsel tables to the left of the prosecution's table.

"At exactly 9:00 a.m., Judge Orsini entered the courtroom through a door to the private hallway that led to various judges' chambers. The attorneys started to stand. "No need to get up. Remain seated. We have some housekeeping matters to take up before the defendants come in and I allow the press vultures to enter. I have entertained a joint petition from our "friends" in the television media for these proceedings to be televised. I don't see any way around it. I won't allow them to film jury selection, but once the jury is sworn in, they get their one representative camera. The one television station can share the live video feed with their brethren. Any thoughts?"

The attorneys shook their heads, no. It was a foregone conclusion, in a high profile case, that the media would get their camera.

Judge Orsini continued, "Seeing no objection, I'll let them have a camera and the print media can also attend after the jury is sworn in. Next, moving on to jury selection. In thirty minutes there will be 100 prospective jurors crammed into the courtroom. Some of you are aware that I prefer to question 24 jurors initially. The first 12 will be seated in the box, and as you go through your challenges of the 12 in the box, the second 12 will fill in as needed. Once 12 of the original 24 prospective jurors are excused, 12 more will be selected for questioning. We will keep up that process until we have our final 12 jurors and three alternates. The defense will get a total of 12 peremptory challenges, and the prosecution will get their standard six. Of course, in theory, you have unlimited challenges to excuse a juror for good cause. We'll discuss each cause challenge in chambers, out of the presence of the jury. I warn you, I don't want to go back to chambers on unsubstantiated cause challenges. If it's evident from the questioning that there is good cause to excuse a juror, I'll ask, is there a motion? One of you will just say, 'motion', and hearing no objection from an opposing party, I'll order that juror excused for cause. You already have a twenty-page jury questionnaire that all the prospective jurors filled out yesterday. I'll allow each defense attorney and one prosecutor to follow up on a juror's questionnaire. Don't strain my patience—make the questions brief and don't use the questions to argue your case. Do I make myself clear?"

All counsel replied, "Yes, Your Honor."

"Finally, defense. If you think there are grounds for a *Batson* racial bias motion as to the prosecution using a peremptory challenge to excuse a minority juror, just say *Batson* to me and we'll go to my chambers to discuss it. I won't tolerate any outburst in open court about discrimination. We're in recess until they bring the panel in."

The jury selection process was wearing on Nick and Josh. The second full day of it was mercifully coming to a close. There were yellow stickies all over Josh's and Nick's jury charts of 24. Each prospective juror had a stickie that had the key facts about the juror from the questionnaire and how they rated them. They added cryptic comments to the stickies based on the in-court questioning. Occasionally, their initial rating of a juror changed due to a juror's answers to questioning and his or her demeanor.

The prosecution had two peremptory challenges left and the defense had three. Nick believed there were at least eight current jurors in the box that all parties would accept— none had strong personalities nor seemed to favor either side. Each side was kicking any prospective juror who had a strong personality and hinted at leaning towards the opposition. Of the eight jurors expected to remain, four were men and four were women. No one was under 30. Four were in their sixties. There were one black, one Hispanic and six whites. No elementary teachers, but there was one male high school political science teacher, who also helped coach the school's baseball team—he seemed down to earth. One of the eight worried Nick some. She was an accountant. But she worked out of her house, appeared practical and no nonsense. She would definitely help with the money laundering counts. Nick hoped she wouldn't hold him to a higher standard than guilt beyond a reasonable doubt.

Judge Orsini talked to the attorneys after the prospective jurors were excused for the day. "I think we're close. I want a jury and the alternates by the end of tomorrow's session. That leaves Friday for opening statements and some introductory instructions about their general duties as jurors. On Monday, the prosecution will start calling witnesses in their case-in-chief. We already have the People's witness list, but I want you Mr. Drummond, on Friday, to give the court and defense the chronological list of witnesses you plan to call on Monday, Tuesday, and Wednesday. Any problem with that?"

"No, Your Honor. However, we haven't received a witness list from the defense yet. I realize the defense can reserve their right to call their respective clients as witnesses until the last minute, but we're still entitled to a witness list."

"That seems fair. Counsel, with the exception of your individual clients, I want a prospective defense witness list from each of you by Friday. You're excused for the day."

Back in the office that evening, Nick met with Ana. "Things are moving along rather quickly in court. We should have a jury by tomorrow and start with witnesses on Monday. I'm starting with the Montana witnesses and then will have Felicia testify on Tuesday. I need you to fly to Topeka on Sunday and fly her back on Monday. I'll go over her testimony on Monday evening. By the way, you look great and I miss you. I have some knee pads in my desk drawer in case you want me to grovel again."

"That won't be necessary. I have a picture of you on your knees etched in my mind, beseeching me. That will sustain me at least until I return from Kansas. You wouldn't happen to have any ruby slippers in my size? I hate flying commercial."

Nick laughed. "If I had a stock of ruby slippers, I would pop into Kansas with you. Have a safe trip Dorothy. Give my best regards to Toto."

The court day on Thursday started with selecting and questioning another 12 prospective jurors from the audience. The opening peremptory challenge went to the defense, and they chose to excuse a retired military man sitting next to the sole black juror. The next juror to be placed in the box was black. Nick scanned his notes on the juror and didn't like what he saw. They had rated him only a two out of five. His questionnaire indicated that a couple of relatives had served time for drug dealing. He worked as a social worker for the county. Nick knew that he'd have to set a good foundation in his questioning to bounce this juror. He also didn't like the fact that two black jurors were seated next together. It was better to split up minority jurors to avoid a clique and to encourage all the jurors to interact with each other. Nick also noticed that the second juror left in the audience to fill an open juror seat was also black. Nick quickly scanned his notes on her and liked her. She worked as an office manager in a medical practice.

"Mr. Drummond, do you have any questions of the juror just called to sit in the box?"

"Yes, I do, Your Honor. Just a few."

"Proceed."

"Sir, I see that two of your relatives were convicted of drug dealing. What are your familial ties and are you close to them?"

"It was my father and my older brother. I don't see much of my father but I'm very close to my brother."

"Do you think they were fairly treated by the criminal justice system?"

"My father was, but they came down too hard on my brother."

"Wouldn't the unfair treatment of your brother make it difficult for you to be fair and impartial in this case?"

"No, I can be fair. It happened awhile back."

"How far back?"

"He was released from state prison a year ago."

"I see you are a social worker. Do you work with any people making the adjustment back to civilian life after being in jail? Do you sympathize with how difficult it often is to make that adjustment?"

"I do work with some former inmates making the adjustment to life on the outside. It's extremely difficult for some of them and I sympathize with their plight."

"Thank you, no further questions."

"Defense, any questions of this juror?"

Mr. Lipman responded, "Yes, just a couple."

"Go ahead."

"Sir, does the fact that you're performing this admirable job, helping people reintegrate back into society, have any effect on how you will view this case?"

"Not at all."

"Can you follow the court's instructions to put aside any feelings pro or con that would impact your ability to be a fair and impartial juror?"

"I can. I pride myself in being fair."

"Thank you sir. No further questions."

"Your challenge, Mr. Drummond."

"Thank you, Your Honor. I'd like to thank and excuse juror number eight, the man we just questioned."

Mr. Lipman jumped out of his seat. In a strong, disgusted voice, he said, "*Batson*, Your Honor, can we approach?"

"Yes, the attorneys to my chambers. Madam court reporter, please come with us."

Once they were all seated in chambers, Lipman couldn't wait to start in. "Your Honor, I move for a mistrial based on the defendants' right to a fair and impartial jury under the Sixth Amendment as well as their rights under the Equal Protection Clause of the Fourteenth Amendment. Mr. Drummond excused that last juror solely on the basis of race. He didn't like the fact that there would have been not just one, but two black jurors in the box. The juror is a credit to our community, has a spotless record, and toils away as a social worker. My client and the other defendants are entitled to a mistrial for prosecution misconduct. Excusing the juror on the basis of race is abhorrent."

"Okay Mr. Lipman. I get it. Try to keep the theatrics down a bit. Mr. Drummond?"

"I didn't excuse the juror on the basis of race. It was clear from his questionnaire and my questioning that two family members, his father and older brother, were convicted of drug dealing. As to his brother, in answer to my question if he believed the criminal justice system had treated him fairly, he responded, and I quote, 'They came down too hard on my brother.' His brother was only released from state prison a year ago—it's still fresh on the juror's mind. He also said that he sympathizes with some of his clients that he tries to reintegrate back into society from jail. Here, we have a drug case, with three leading cartel members, who everyone knows will go to prison if they are convicted. The people don't have to rely on a prospective juror's statement, 'I can be fair and put aside any feelings of sympathy or prejudice.' The People are also entitled to a fair trial with unbiased jurors. Excusing the juror was entirely proper."

"Thank you Mr. Drummond. You've made your record for appeal Mr. Lipman. Your *Batson* motion is denied. There were justifiable, non race-based reasons for the prosecution to excuse the juror. We'll go back in and take a 15 minute recess."

By mid-afternoon, it had worked out as Nick had planned. A Hispanic woman, in her forties, was seated next to the then one remaining black juror, and the next juror to be seated was a black woman, who sat at the other end of the panel. Josh and Nick had the Hispanic woman ranked at a four—a solid juror, hardworking, with two sons who were good students and active in school activities. Nick, in an attempt to throw the defense off, made a show of not being too happy with the Hispanic women, hoping they would take the bait and keep her on the panel.

There were only three peremptory challenges left, two for the defense, one for the prosecution. All the attorneys were frantically looking back at the next several jurors in the audience who would be called to fill the excused jurors' seats. The peremptory challenges were used. The last three to be selected as jurors didn't pose a threat to either side. They seemed like they would go along with the majority. One was a 26-year old male. He had obtained a masters in library science and was working at a university library. He seemed well-rounded—he surfed, ran, and liked to travel. The final composition of the jury was seven women and five men, of which two were black and two were Hispanic. The remaining jurors were white.

By late afternoon, after three days of picking a jury, all the attorneys were mentally exhausted. Judge Orsini was indefatigable. He was going to make sure they picked the three alternate jurors by the end of the day. The prosecution and the defense each got two additional peremptory challenges for the alternates. Twelve prospective alternates were questioned. Each side knew what juror came next if they challenged an alternate. Judge Orsini had successfully beaten the attorneys down. The prosecution and the defense used just one challenge apiece. They had their three alternates by 5:30 p.m., an hour over the normal court day. Judge Orsini excused the jurors until 10:00 the next morning, telling them that the attorneys and he had to go over some instructions before the jury would hear opening statements.

The next morning, everyone was in place when Judge Orsini directed Nick to give his opening statement. Nick was glad that Rona was so accomplished in preparing power point demonstrations. In Nick's opening, he projected maps of Yaak, Montana, the various warehouse locations, and north coast San Diego, along with key photographs of the drugs seized and the motorcycle shooting scene. This helped the jurors visualize the case and better appreciate what the prosecution intended to prove. Nick went over the charges and the expected evidence to prove the charges. He managed to keep his opening statement to around an hour. Nick kept constant eye contact with the jurors. He walked around some and changed his voice inflection occasionally to keep the jurors' interest. When he came up to an hour, he noticed a few of the jurors drifting. He summarized the rest of his opening statement and had the jurors' complete attention at the end. "The evidence will show that the defendants are guilty of all the counts in the indictment!"

The three defense attorneys gave credible statements. For the most part sticking to what they expected the evidence to be. Infrequently, one of them would cross the line into improper argument. Nick chose not to object because the instances weren't that blatant. There's nothing worse than objecting to opposing counsel's opening statement or closing argument and having the judge side with the opposing party. It makes it look like the prosecutor is trying to unfairly impede what opposing counsel is saying. The prosecutor has to remain the good guy in the jury's eyes—the presenter of truth.

After the opening statements, the judge read some instructions about jurors' basic duties and how to assess witness credibility. Orsini excused everyone for the weekend at 4:00 p.m.

Nick and Pepe drove back to the office, talking about the witness prep interviews scheduled for the Montana witnesses over the weekend. Nick was looking forward to seeing Drury again and meeting his sidekick Zack. Also, Biker Sue should be a treat. However, what Nick really anticipated the most was to bring Luis' former battered girlfriend, Felicia, from her safe house in Topeka to face Luis at trial. Her suffering and her fear of Luis and the cartel would demonize the defendants in the eyes of the jurors.

CHAPTER THIRTY

Topeka P.D. Lieutenant Tom Jasco arrived at the destroyed home five minutes after the first responder. Fire trucks were already using high velocity nozzles to pour water on the flames. It looked like one side wall and the back wall of the single story house were still standing. Nothing else. He could feel the heat a hundred feet from the front of the house. Neighbors were cordoned off one hundred yards away. A local television station was filming. A reporter began to interview neighbors.

Many of the neighbors were wide-eyed, with tormented faces. A few were sobbing. It reminded the Lieutenant of scenes he had seen during Desert Storm. The devastation was on a much smaller scale. But the terror and grief of the civilian population was the same. A sedan had crashed into a pole down the street. Firemen and medics had surrounded the car.

Firemen and police began to move around the back of the house as the flames died down. Sgt Hillis was leading the police team. A minute later, Hillis came running from the backyard, yelling, "Medics! We have a woman down in the backyard. Still breathing. Looks like multiple broken bones." An emergency team, with a stretcher and portable oxygen, rushed around back. Lieutenant Jasco followed them.

He wasn't prepared for what he saw. A young black woman was face up, 20 feet from the back wall of the house. She looked like a rag doll. Limbs flung out in every direction. Her hair and face were singed. Blood was coming from wounds on her face, leg and arm. She wasn't moving. Jasco watched as the medics placed a neck

Jim Dutton

brace on her, and slipped the stretcher underneath her, with minimal movement of her body. An oxygen mask was over her face. As the medics carried her to the emergency medical vehicle, Jasco was told she'd be taken to Municipal Hospital. As they were hooking up an IV, Jasco gently searched for ID. He pulled out a law enforcement flasher, identifying the victim as *Deputy U.S. Marshal Lily Perkins*. He called dispatch to have the U.S. Marshall's 24-hour line called. That's when the dispatcher told Jasco about Deputy Attorney General Nick Drummond's call. Jasco told dispatch he'd get back to Drummond when he had more information to report.

From what dispatch relayed to him, Jasco thought he'd better check out the crashed car as it might involve the San Diego agent. The airbag hadn't deployed. A medic was checking a woman's vitals while another was bandaging her head, stemming the bleeding. There was a Glock by her feet on the floorboard. She was unconscious. Jasco asked the medic if he could check for identification. "Carefully," he replied. Jasco went through her purse and found his second law enforcement flasher of the evening. *Ana Schwartz, Special Agent, Immigration and Customs Enforcement.*

The medics were tenderly removing her from the car onto a stretcher. "What can you tell me about her condition?" asked Jasco.

"She's breathing fine. She has quite a bump on her forehead where she hit the steering wheel. She hasn't lost a lot of blood. Probably has a concussion. We need to get her to Muni right away. There may be brain swelling." Jasco watched as they hooked her up to an IV in the emergency vehicle and sped away.

His radio blared. "Lieutenant, this is Officer Belden, you need to come straight down Elm two blocks and take a right on Third Street. There's a burned-out army Humvee in a vacant lot."

"Be right there." Instead of getting into his unmarked car, and attempting to weave his way through all the police cars and emergency vehicles, Jasco took off in a jog down Elm. When he turned onto Third Street, he saw a fire engine and two police cars at the end of the block. He picked up his pace, thankful that he worked out on a treadmill three times a week. The husk of an army Humvee was in the middle of the lot, still smoldering, but no visible flames. A machine gun was

258

mounted onto the middle of the Humvee and a rocket launcher was charred by its side. Jasco spoke into the radio transmitter hooked to his shoulder. "We need a vacant lot at Third and Fern cordoned off and a forensics team here immediately. We have the vehicle and the armaments used in the attack of the residence."

Jasco walked around the street adjacent to the vacant lot. He saw fresh red drops coming from the sidewalk, closest to the Humvee, going across the street to the opposite curb. He immediately spoke to Officer Belden, "It looks like blood, probably coming from someone who was in the Humvee. Cordon this off. Point it out to forensics. They're on their way."

Jasco walked back to the primary scene. Mentally trying to take it all in. What could possibly have brought on this devastation? He needed to talk to prosecutor Drummond. He dialed Drummond's number. Nick answered immediately. "Hello, this is Drummond. Is this Topeka P.D.?"

"Yes, this is Lieutenant Jasco, and I'm at the scene of 131 Elm. I saw your Agent Schwartz. She crashed into a pole. High velocity rounds, probably 50 caliber, went through the back of her sedan...."

Nick interrupted. "Tell me she's alive! Is she okay?"

"She's alive. She's unconscious." He told Drummond exactly what the medic told him. Jasco also told Drummond about the demolished house, and the burned-out Humvee, with the 50 caliber machine gun and the rocket launcher. "Someone wanted to take down that home real bad. What do you know about this?"

"A lot. We just started a federal trial against the top three heads of the Baja Norte Familia cartel. They have taken ruthlessness to a whole new level. They run their drug and money laundering organization through fear and deadly efficiency. 131 Elm Street was a safe house for our protected lead witness in the case, a former girlfriend of one of the chiefs of the cartel. Deputy U.S. Marshal Perkins was the witness' handler. Agent Schwartz was going to fly back with the witness tomorrow morning. Is there any sign of the witness, a female Hispanic in her early twenties?"

"No. Hopefully, she wasn't in the house. No one could have survived the explosions and fire."

"Have the fire fighters gone through the house yet?"

"Not yet. It's still too hot. A team is forming. They'll go through the ruin and ashes shortly."

"I'm flying there on the first flight out of San Diego tomorrow morning. I want to meet with you."

"Can do. I'll be working this case tomorrow and many days after."

"Thank you for getting back to me. If anything breaks before tomorrow, please call me."

Nick dialed Josh. He started to fill Josh in. Josh cut him off. "Turn to CNN. There's a live feed of the burned-out house." Nick did. The horror of what happened to Felicia, Deputy Perkins and Ana was brought into his living room.

"Josh, I'm going to Topeka tomorrow morning, first flight out. Call the defense attorneys, tell them we're asking for a two day continuance, that I'll be in Topeka. Keep the Montana witnesses here. I still want the trial to go on. We're not going to let these bastards off the hook. Research if we can get any of Felicia's statements into trial, now that she's dead. We have to think she's dead if she was in that home. If anything breaks, I'll let you know. Have Pepe fill you in as soon as possible about Luis sending messages out of the prison through a trustee. We need a connection between Luis and the residence attack if we're going to get it into evidence at trial."

Nick hung up. He just sat in his lounge chair, staring into the fish tank. Worry and thoughts were swirling around in his head. *Was Ana going to be all right? Was it possible that Felicia was somehow alive? How were they going to get this into evidence? How inflammatory would it be? Would they be risking a mistrial if there was insufficient evidence to tie the attack to the three cartel members? If Nick could only prove the connection to Luis, how would they handle the other two defendants? Separate trials?* Nick only wanted to do this trial once. There was nothing worse than having to retry a case. It was always more stale the second time, and a thousand-fold more tedious.

Nick eventually dozed off in his chair.

Fireman Percival was going through the house in the area where the backdoor had been. He removed charred wood and ashes from the tile floor. He saw a metal latch, charcoal black from the fire. He noticed a square indentation in the tile around the latch. He yelled out to his fire captain, "We may have something here!"

Percival and another lifted up the latch and peered into the depths. Percival's flashlight illuminated a ladder descending six feet down to a concrete room. Cowering in the far corner of the room was a Hispanic woman. When the light lit up her face, she said, over and over, "No, please no." Percival said in soft, tender voice, "We're not going to hurt you Madam. We're firemen. The blaze is out. You're safe." He pointed the flashlight to his face and fireman's uniform.

"My God. My God," sobbed Felicia.

"We'll take you to the hospital. Just hold tight. I'll get medics here to check you out."

"Stay, don't leave me!" responded Felicia between sobs.

"I won't. I'll go with you to the hospital."

Jasco had been at the scene for an hour when he saw medics bring Felicia out. They told Jasco that she seemed to be in fairly good shape. Some smoke inhalation, a sprained ankle from the fall into the storm cellar, and a few bruises. She was still in shock. She kept asking about Lily. No one was going to tell her about Deputy U.S. Marshall Lily Perkins yet.

The Saints Go Marching In was pounding in Nick's ear. He dreamingly thought, *Was he in New Orleans?* Nick woke up enough to realize it was his ringtone on the cellphone in his lap. Groggily, Nick answered in a hoarse, low voice, "Hello."

"This is Jasco. Sorry to bother you, but I know you'll want to hear this. Your witness has been found alive in a cement-lined storm cellar under the floorboards of the pantry. She's in extreme shock, but seems to be in pretty good shape physically. A sprained ankle, some small cuts and bruises. She'll be taken to the same hospital as Agent Schwartz for observation."

"Yes! Thank God! Any update on Agent Schwartz' condition?"

"Yes, she has regained consciousness. She has a concussion. They're keeping her up."

"Fantastic news!" yelled Nick into the phone. "Thank you. Thank you."

"Easy on the ear drums. I'm glad that things are looking a lot better than they first seemed. I'll see you tomorrow."

Nick immediately called Josh and filled him in. "If Felicia can make it, I'll try to fly her out to testify on Thursday." Nick then called Pepe to tell him the good news.

CHAPTER THIRTY-ONE

J osh was in Orsini's courtroom with the defense attorneys before the jury was scheduled to come in. He had just spoken to Pepe about the jail investigation into Luis smuggling notes to the outside. He had a copy of the note found under the bathroom sink and a hastily handwritten report by the jail watch commander who had headed the investigation. Josh had already turned copies of the material over to the defense attorneys.

Judge Orsini took the bench. "Gentlemen, what is this all about? My clerk told me something about a bombing of a safe house for a key protected witness of the prosecution."

Josh immediately began speaking, "Defendant Luis Hernandez-Lopez' former girlfriend's safe house in Topeka, Kansas was destroyed early last night by three rockets and 50 caliber, armor piercing bullets shot from a machine gun mounted on an army surplus Humvee. The Humvee was left, burned-out, in a vacant lot a couple of blocks away. The ex-girlfriend, a protected witness, managed to get into a cement storm cellar at the beginning of the attack. She's injured and is in shock. As the court is well aware, she is a key prosecution witness and was scheduled to testify tomorrow. Special Agent Ana Schwartz, who helped investigate this case, was also injured in the attack. Fifty caliber bullets slammed into her car as she approached the residence. Agent Schwartz is also scheduled to testify in this case. The protected witness' handler, Deputy U.S. Marshall Lily Perkins, was blown out of the house by one of the rockets and is in critical condition. Her doctor doesn't know if she'll survive. Since last night, there has been an intensive investigation into the link between defendant Lopez and the Topeka attack. I've a copy of a note which was placed under a sink in the restroom off the jail's reception area by a trustee. This note was apparently written by defendant Lopez and was seized yesterday afternoon. It reads, *I can't wait for this evening's Kansas weather report. L.* Visitor records show that Defendant Lopez' cousin, Jaime Hernandez-Salgado, visited Lopez every Sunday afternoon. DOJ Special Agent Cantana interviewed Jaime last night. He admitted visiting the defendant but refused to say anything else. He was quaking with fear and sweat was pouring down his face. He kept saying, 'There's nothing you can do to me that'll be worse than being dead.' Combining this with the evidence that supports defendant Lopez ordering the earlier motorcycle hit against the protected witness, one can only conclude that Lopez and the cartel ordered a second hit on the eve of our key witness' testimony."

"We're requesting that the trial be trailed for two days until Wednesday. Mr. Drummond is in the air right now on his way to assess the situation in Topeka. We anticipate introducing the evidence of the Topeka attack in this trial."

Defense attorney Lipman interjected, "Can I be heard, Your Honor?"

Judge Orsini looked toward Josh, "Anything else at this time Mr. Sterling?" Seeing Josh shake his head side to side, Judge Orsini said, "Go ahead Mr. Lipman."

"The defense deeply sympathizes with the tragic events in Topeka, but..."

"Your Honor, what total bullshit! The defendants caused these unspeakable, heinous acts."

"Mr. Sterling, sit back down. I won't tolerate any outbursts in my courtroom. I'm prepared to excuse you this one time considering the trying circumstances, but not again."

"I apologize, Your Honor."

"Continue Mr. Lipman."

"Thank you, Your Honor. There's nothing to tie the defendants to this horrific act. We have a right to a speedy trial. The jury has been picked. Any continuance will inconvenience them which they may hold against the defendants. If Your Honor is unwilling to proceed with the trial today, the court should order a mistrial. The prosecution can start over, if it chooses, once all this is sorted out."

"Mr. Sterling, any additional comments?"

"Yes, Your Honor. Mr. Lipman is suggesting that the defendants be rewarded with a mistrial for an action that appears they were responsible for. The People have been investigating and preparing this case for over a year. Dozens of witnesses are lined up. This atrocious act came out of the blue. Two law enforcement agents connected to this case are down and a key witness is in shock and injured. We hope that the protected witness can testify shortly. We'll know by Tuesday afternoon. There's ample cause to briefly trail this matter until Wednesday. The People want to proceed."

Judge Orsini looked at the attorneys in turn. He was silent for what seemed like minutes, but was probably only 30 seconds. "All the possible ramifications of these horrific acts are difficult to assimilate. I'm going to trail this matter until tomorrow afternoon at 4:00. I'll entertain argument at that time as to the appropriateness of the Topeka attack coming into evidence. The prosecution will call their first witness on Wednesday morning. Mr. Bailiff, bring in the jury and keep the press out."

"Ladies and Gentlemen of the jury, thank you for your patience. I know you've been in the hall for 15 minutes beyond our scheduled start time. I've some news. The attorneys and I were speaking about an unforeseen event which causes me to send you home for the next couple of days while the situation is worked out. You aren't to speculate about what the event is, or how it was caused. I want to reiterate my previous admonitions to you. This is very important and you all must strictly adhere to this. You're not to talk about this case with anyone, that includes your spouses, significant others, and friends. You're absolutely not to watch or read any news, no matter what the source is. You're not to discuss any topics in the news with anyone. If I find this is a problem, I'll have to seriously consider sequestering the entire jury in a hotel throughout the entire trial to ensure compliance. Does everyone understand how important this is? Seeing affirmative nods from you, I'll excuse you until 9:00 a.m. Wednesday."

Nick's jet touched down at noon, Topeka time. Before he unfastened his seat belt he was on the phone with Josh. "Orsini trailed the matter until tomorrow at four for a hearing on the admissibility of the evidence of the Topeka attack."

"I'll try to be back for that. Do a page or two pocket brief to file at the hearing in support of admissibility. I'd start with the attack showing consciousness of guilt and to explain Felicia's demeanor as a witness if we can still get her to testify. We're deplaning right now. I'm going straight to the hospital to check on Ana. I'll call you later." Nick hung up, without saying good-bye or waiting for a response from Josh.

Municipal Hospital was an old six-story building, painted army barracks grey. Nick hoped that the quality of the medical services far exceeded the looks of the building. From the outside of the building, Nick expected the doctors were still using leeches for bloodletting. Nick showed his Attorney General flasher at the reception desk and was sent to the fifth floor, rehabilitation. Nick thought it was a great sign Ana was not in intensive care. He brushed by a nurse leaving Ana's room and saw Ana in an agitated sleep, eyelids fluttering.

Ana was dreaming about the New Jersey shore when she was eight. It was the first family vacation she could remember. She asked her father, "What are the numbers on your forearm?" Her father always wore long-sleeved shirts.

He responded, "A group of people, the Nazis, put it on me to dehumanize me. They put me, my family, and millions of other Jews in concentration camps. We worked for them as slaves. They killed a great number of our people, my entire family."

"Don't you hate them?" murmured eight-year-old Ana.

Her father, with sad eyes, replied, "Not anymore. The hate and bitterness were eating me up inside—I learned to let it go and concentrate on positive thoughts. We must persevere."

Little Ana looked up at her tall, gaunt father, and said, "I love you Abba, but I don't like them. I wouldn't have let them do that to you if I'd been there."

Nick pressed Ana's hand. She slowly opened her eyes and focused on the room. Then, they just looked into each other's eyes for an unknown time. Ana eventually smiled, "Well, big guy, you didn't waste any time getting here. I like that."

Nick gently hugged her, pressing the side of his face to her cheek that wasn't swollen and bruised. "Remind me to never assign you to work outside of the office without a SWAT team along. You attract trouble like a garbage can attracts bears."

"I love being compared to a garbage can—so romantic."

"When I heard it was just a concussion and a few character-enhancing stitches above the eye, I promised to go back to church every Sunday. I don't think God will recognize me—I haven't been to his house in a few decades."

"If this is what it takes to have you see the spiritual side of things, it's worth it. Who knows, maybe you'll convert someday to the chosen people. You'd look cute in a yarmulke."

"Yeah," said Nick, "I'd look great in a Jewish beanie. I don't even look good in a ball cap."

"Thank you for being here. I was up all night because of the concussion, thinking of you."

"Every thought I had from when I first heard you were unconscious, wrapped around a pole, was of you and how I was going to get the bastards responsible."

"They told me Felicia miraculously survived, but nothing about Lily.

Did she survive?"

Nick's voice softened, "Last I heard she's in a coma and is in real bad shape. I'm going to check on her condition now, then check on Felicia, and I'll be back to see you later this evening. I love you."

"I think that's only the second time I have heard you say that—both times in a hospital bed. We'll have to work on you mustering up those beautiful words in a different environment."

"Those words are kind of tough for a good old boy WASP to get out. To make amends, I will sneak some rugalach in for you tonight if I can find a Jewish deli in Topeka."

Nick had to wait 20 minutes before Dr. Light, the neurosurgeon treating Deputy Perkins, could see him. "Mr. Drummond. Ms. Perkins is very lucky to be alive. She was on the operating table for six hours last night. I had to drill a hole in her skull to relieve the pressure of her swollen brain. She has a broken pelvis, shoulder, and ribs. She also had multiple fractures of her right tibia and femur. Not to mention various broken bones in her hands. Finally, she has third degree burns to her right arm. We believe she used it to shield her face. The outer layer of her skin and the entire under layer, the dermis, of her arm were destroyed, leaving blackened and charred residue. She'll need extensive skin grafts from her legs and other arm if she survives. Her face received second degree burns, injuring the outer and lower layer of her skin. Thankfully, she won't need skin grafts on her face. Ms. Perkins is still in a coma, which is probably a good thing. It'll give her the best chance to heal. Give me your card and I'll have my staff contact you about any significant updates."

Next stop for Nick was the psychiatric ward where Felicia was speaking to a black-haired woman in a finely tailored suit. Felicia turned her head towards Nick as he came into the room and burst into tears. The well-dressed woman turned to Nick, with a frown. "I'm Dr. Lepinsky, the patient's psychiatrist. What in the hell are you doing in this room?"

"Can we speak outside? I'm the prosecutor in a federal trial in San Diego that your patient is scheduled to testify at."

They walked outside Felicia's room. Nick gave the doctor the background about the case. He asked her about Felicia's mental state. "I can't give you any confidential details. She's doing as well as can be expected after undergoing such a traumatic event. She was in severe shock last night. She's been under medication. She's no longer in shock and had calmed down until she saw you."

"It's vitally important that I talk to her. Can you please go inside and tell her that."

"I'll let her know. But I won't let you talk to her unless she agrees and calms down." Ten minutes later, Dr. Lepinsky came out and told Nick that Felicia was willing to talk to him. "But you can only have a few minutes with her and I'll be by her side."

Nick slowly walked through the door. He smiled, "I apologize for rushing in on you without any warning. I'm so glad you're doing better. I just want you to think about this. We've continued the trial for a couple of days for you to testify on Thursday, if you can. You have every reason to be scared out of your wits. I just saw Agent Ana, they shot at her car as she was coming up to your house and she crashed into a pole. She was unconscious and suffered a concussion. She's much better. She's two floors below you and asked about you. She told me her prayers are for both of you to be strong. You've gone through so much together. Lily is in very serious condition and still in a coma. The doctors are doing everything they can for her. A task force is working full time on the attack. The best way to ensure that you'll be safe is to convict Luis and the other two bosses of the cartel. All the other, more low-level defendants have plead guilty and are serving prison sentences. They are no threat to you. Please, please just think about it. I'll come back tomorrow morning and we can talk some more."

Tears welled up in her eyes. She smiled slightly. "I'll think about it. Tell Ana that my prayers are with her as well. I'll never forget what she did for me."

Nick got on the phone with Rona. "I need the direct line to the U.S. Marshal's Special-Agent-In-Charge, Topeka, ASAP. I also need the address of any downtown Topeka Jewish bakery or deli. Don't ask why."

"Just a minute. I'm on my computer. I'm going through the passwords to access the federal law enforcement consolidated data-base. Here, it is. SAC Roger Poon. I'll text you the number so you'll have it. As for the deli—I can send you a link. Oh, I forgot, you don't have internet access on your phone. You still haven't gotten a smart phone. Do you realize the Department would get you one for free?"

"Yeah, I know, but I'd probably lose it. I lost my only iPhone within two months. Anyway, I don't have the patience to look up this stuff. Also, what would you do with your free time?"

"Careful there. I could have a normal life if I wasn't working overtime babysitting you."

"For that I'm eternally grateful."

"You should be. You're in luck. There's a deli three blocks from the hospital. From the hospital, go two blocks and take a left. It's in the middle of the block on the right, *Zeb's.*"

"Thank you. Remind me to double your holiday bonus."

"Thank you so much my esteemed, gracious boss. I won't know what to do with $10. Ciao."

Nick called SAC Poon as he walked to the car. He explained the situation and Poon was happy to meet him at the crime scene in a hour. Nick drove straight to Zeb's. Who'd ever think it? A New York style deli in the heart of Topeka. A middle-aged bearded man, with deep creases along his forehead, was behind the counter. He greeted Nick with a taciturn smile, "What can I get for you?"

"Some of those," pointing to the raspberry and chocolate, mini-size rolls of dough under the counter. Nick was afraid to try to pronounce the name of the treats. He had enough trouble with English.

"You mean the rugalach," stressing the "a" in the last syllable and letting it roll off his tongue.

"Yes. Four of the raspberry and three of the chocolate." He might as well eat one of the raspberry ones immediately.

Nick went to the home on Elm Street. He hoped that Lieutenant Jasco would still be there, overseeing the processing of the three scenes. A four-block area was cordoned off. Police cars and fire trucks competed for space. Some were parked on lawns. Nick showed his ID and asked for Lieutenant Jasco. A uniformed police officer said, in a respectful voice, "I believe he's at the command post, sir. See that large trailer across from the burned-out home?"

Nick must be getting grey. Young officers he didn't know never used to treat him with such deference. Then again, maybe it was a Midwest cultural thing. After showing his ID a couple more times, he entered the command trailer. Three men and a woman were huddled over a large composite drawing of a four block area. Nick introduced himself. Besides Lieutenant Jasco, there was the Assistant Special Agent in Charge(ASAC) from the local FBI office, the ASAC from DEA, and a woman who was the SAC for the Narcotic Division of the State AG's Office. They went over the diagram together.

Jasco told the others, "This is to scale. My forensics team spent all night collecting evidence and measuring distances. This morning the computer geeks used their software magic to enter all the information and spit out the diagram." The left of the diagram showed where eight bullet casings had been found from Agent Schwartz' Glock, ejecting from the back left of her gun as she was firing outside the driver's window. An accident reconstructionist made a preliminary finding that Ana was traveling at about 40 miles an hour when she hit the pole. The speed estimation was based on there being no skid marks, the car lost some speed when it jumped the curb, and the extent of the damage to the car when it hit the immovable object, the pole.

They moved on to the center of the diagram. Fresh oil stains, and ejection patterns of the 200 or so casings from the 50 caliber machine gun, showed that the Humvee was located in the center of the street, approximately 70 feet from the front wall of the residence. Twenty casings were found on the other side of the Humvee, suggesting the machine gun had rotated 180 degrees to fire at Agent Schwartz' oncoming vehicle. The FBI ASAC looked at Drummond. "Your agent sure has a huge set of balls to drive straight into 50 caliber fire."

Nick responded, "Do I ever know that. I'm just trying to keep her balls and the rest of her intact." Nick knew that the FBI ASAC had given Ana the highest form of compliment. "What about the rockets?"

Jasco answered, "The forensics techs from Fire and PD confirmed that three high velocity rocket grenades were fired into the house from the Humvee. From grenade residue in the house, they've been identified as 93mm heat warheads. They leave anything they hit demolished and in flames."

The far lower right of the diagram set out the torched Humvee in the vacant lot. Jasco, exasperated, said, "They did a good job torching it. No trace evidence, no title documentation, not even a chewing gum wrapper. However, with chemical assistance, we were able to bring forth the VIN number. We traced the VIN to an army surplus sale two years ago in Kansas City. We're still checking on the sale transaction records. We're also making some progress on the trail of red drops from the Humvee to the curb across the street. A random sample of the drops tested positive for human blood. The FBI lab is testing the blood for DNA. They can get it out faster than our lab."

Nick asked, "Did anyone see the vehicle they must have left in after they torched the Humvee?"

Jasco said, "We have canvassed the entire neighborhood. A few people remember seeing a late model, dark-colored sedan driving slowly away from the area of the burning Humvee. No consensus on the make or model and no license plate number. Most of the neighbors say there were two or three, darker skinned men in the car. Which means darker than white in this community. No further descriptions at this point. But speaking of vehicles. It may be nothing, but a neighbor, close to where Agent Schwartz crashed into the pole, looked out from drawn curtains of her window and saw a sedan slowly drive by her smashed car in the opposite direction of the Humvee assault."

SAC Poon came into the command center. After introductions and condolences about Deputy Perkins' critical condition, the others filled Poon in. Afterwards, Nick took him aside. Poon said, "I've been briefed on the San Diego case. Our agency is at your disposal to get the sons-of-bitches who did this and help with your case."

"Being your poor state cousins, we often hear how our federal cousins are awash in money. Does your agency have a private jet that could fly Felicia directly to San Diego?"

"We do and we can. I've already spoken to the Director of our agency and he's given me carte blanche in this case."

"Montgomery Field is a small public airport, just minutes north of downtown San Diego. I believe it can handle a small private jet. If not, hopefully landing rights will be granted at Miramar Naval Air Station, also minutes north of San Diego. For security reasons, I want to avoid having Felicia fly by commercial airline into the main San Diego International Airport. If you would, please coordinate with my team member, HSI Special Agent Jerry Slater, for the airport pick-up and secure transport to the courtroom. We want her to testify at 9:00 a.m. on Thursday morning and fly out of San Diego at the end of that same day to a new location of your agency's and her choosing."

"We can do this."

"Thank you." Nick gave Agent Slater's number to SAC Poon. "The only thing I need to do now is to sell it to Felicia. I'm seeing her tomorrow morning. Please set up the flight and I'll either confirm it or call it off after I meet with her."

Nick went back inside to talk to Lieutenant Jasco. He agreed to email copies of all photos and reports on the attack to Rona. For the next 30 minutes they walked around the crime scenes. Nick didn't think he could be shocked anymore by human behavior. He was wrong. The leveling of Felicia's home by military grade weapons shook him to his core. The unimaginable in the United States had happened—a different world from the one he grew up in.

Nick checked into a hotel near the hospital, took a quick shower, and went down to the cafe on the ground floor to grab dinner. Salisbury steak, mashed potatoes, and green beans seemed Midwestern enough. He gobbled it down and went back to the hospital.

Nick politely knocked on Ana's closed door. "Ana, it's me, I have something for you."

"Come in. I love gifts."

"Three chocolate and three raspberry rugalach. I admit, I ate a seventh before I even left the deli."

"You wouldn't be the man I've come to love if you didn't. Let's not waste any time. We need to eat them all right now."

"Ana before I forget, did you see anybody in a vehicle parked in the vicinity of your crash?"

Ana closed her eyes. She grimaced and shook slightly. "The last second, before the machine gun opened fire on me, is etched in my mind. I looked up the street to my left to take an evasive maneuver. I was aiming for a lawn just beyond the pole. I remember a car parked on the curb at the far side of the lawn. I believe it was a Volvo. I'll never forget, the male driver had a smile on his face. I swerved left at the same time that machine gun bullets slammed into the back of my car, which directed me into the pole."

"Is there anything else you can remember about this man?"

"Not really. He seemed to have dark hair and was youngish, but, not a teenager or anything."

"Sorry to put you through the flashback. Let's change the subject. When are they letting you out of here?"

"I'm negotiating with the doctors. So far they're winning. They're saying, at the earliest, the end of the week. I'm not supposed to fly until they completely clear me on my concussion."

They spent the rest of the evening talking quietly and holding hands. Ana dozed off. Nick left a note at her bedside and slipped out of the room.

The next morning Nick was at Felicia's bedside. Color was back in her cheeks. "How are you feeling today?"

"Much better. I took a few laps around the hospital floor and didn't need a cane. My sprained ankle is on the mend. Just a limp. They told me I can be discharged tomorrow, or Thursday morning at the latest. Dr. Lepinsky even signed off on it."

"Great! I'm so glad you're feeling better. On a different note, have you given much thought about flying out to San Diego on Thursday?" Nick noticed the fear spread across her face and her eyes dilate. "Before you say anything, the Marshal's Office will do absolutely everything to insure your safety. A private jet with a security detail will fly you out on Thursday morning in time for court in San Diego at 9:00. You won't even be landing at Lindbergh Field, the international airport, but instead at Montgomery Field, a smaller airport in north county. You can testify on Thursday and fly out the same day to a new location that you and the Marshal's Office agree on. I won't even know for now. Until at least the convictions come in, an agent will be with you full time."

"Nick. Can I call you Nick now?

"You can, we're way past Mr. Drummond after all you've gone through."

"You can stop the hard sell. I'll go. Ana left just before you came in. She's the one who walked me around the corridors. We're in it together. There'll be no peace for either of us until they're put away for good."

"You have my word that I'll do my very best to see that come about."

"I know you will Nick."

Nick took the stairs down two floors to Ana's room. He felt like leaping in the air and screaming for joy. He didn't believe Felicia could be convinced so quickly. Leave it to Ana. The trial was saved. Nick burst into Ana's room. "I don't know what to call you—Iron Lady Margaret Thatcher or Mother Teresa. Somehow you got Felicia to go."

"We had a sisterhood bonding. We're in this together. She knows she has to testify and we have to do everything we can to support her and convict these assholes."

"As you wish. It will be done. I'll see you this weekend."

"Thank you for the note. It put a smile on my face when I woke up."

Nick made calls to SAC Poon, Pepe, Josh, and Rona from the taxi to the airport. Poon confirmed that a private jet would be ready to fly Felicia to San Diego on Thursday morning. They were cleared to land at Montgomery Field. Pepe would pick Nick up today at the airport at 3:30 p.m. to rush him to the 4:00 court appearance. Nick told Josh he'd be in court at four. If he was a little late, to stall. Josh filled Nick in on the law to admit the assault evidence.

"Mr. Sterling, it's 4:02. Where is your colleague, Mr. Drummond?"

"Well, well, Your Honor. aaaah."

"Speak up Mr. Sterling. Has a cat got your tongue?"

"No, Your Honor. Mr. Drummond just called in. He was just left off in front of the courthouse."

"I hope so for your sake. The prosecution will start argument at 4:05."

Judge Orsini retired to his chambers. Josh paced behind counsel table. The three defense attorneys were smirking. Josh muttered under his breath, "Run you son-of-a-bitch. It's my ass on the line." Judge Orsini stormed back into the courtroom. He was about to live up to his nickname, "Fire and Brimstone".

Simultaneously, with a pound of the gavel, the courtroom door slammed open. In strode Drummond, with a smile on his face. "I'm here, Your Honor, straight from Topeka, Kansas. I apologize for being late. I didn't even wait for the elevator. I came up the stairs as fast as my knees could carry me."

"I can see you're here counsel. Start your argument!"

"To summarize, the safe house in Topeka, Kansas, where our protected witness was staying, is a blackened rabble. Three high velocity rocket grenades were fired into the house from an army surplus Humvee after the front of the house was strafed and penetrated by armor piercing, 50 caliber bullets. Against all odds, the witness managed to survive, in shock, with minor physical injuries. Deputy United States Marshal Lily Perkins, who was inside the home at the time of the Sunday evening attack, was not so lucky. She's still in a coma, with a swollen brain and numerous broken bones.

It's unknown whether she will survive. Special Agent Ana Schwartz, also a witness in this case, and victim of the drive-by that attempted to kill the same protected witness, was fired upon by the Humvee machine gun as she drove towards the house. She has a concussion and is still hospitalized in Topeka."

Nick continued, "My co-counsel has already provided to defense counsel a two page memorandum on the admissibility of the assault into evidence in trial. If I may approach Madam Clerk, I would like to have this filed with the Court."

"We object to the filing of the memorandum. We only received it 10 minutes ago, without prior notice."

"Mr. Flanigan, considering that this hearing was only ordered yesterday, about an incident that happened less than two days ago, no additional notice can reasonably be expected. I'll consider the memorandum. Do you have a memorandum for me?"

"No, Your Honor. I ask that we be allowed to file points and authorities."

"Mr. Flanigan, after I make my ruling today, if you choose, you can file your authorities as part of a motion for reconsideration tomorrow at 8:30, before the jury is brought in. I trust that won't interfere with any dinner plans."

"No, Your Honor. I enjoy eating fast food at my desk.

"Proceed Mr. Drummond."

"As set forth in our memorandum, only the three defendants could be responsible for ordering the horrendous attack. The intended victim, defendant Lopez' former live-in girlfriend, was already the subject of one attack. That incident is the basis of two counts in this case, one being conspiracy to commit murder. After their unsuccessful motorcycle drive-by, defendant Lopez told the cartel accountant that we'd not be seeing the bitch anymore, referring to Felicia, and that she was being taken care of. Every Sunday, for the last several months, Mr. Lopez has been visited by his cousin, Jaime Hernandez-Salgado. Last Sunday afternoon, jail authorities uncovered a note courier scheme between Lopez and his cousin, using a trustee who hid notes from Lopez under a sink in the bathroom, off the jail reception area. Last Sunday's note, which has been authenticated as being in defendant

Lopez' handwriting, said, *I can't wait for this evening's Kansas weather report. L.* It is clear the defendants orchestrated this attack.

Three different legal bases support the attack coming into evidence. One, the attack shows a continuing course of conduct of violence by the cartel towards the protected witness—showing the common intent with the motorcycle drive-by to silence her forever. Two, we're planning to have the witness testify by the end the week. She's been in shock and, understandably, is expected to be in great distress when she testifies. The jury is entitled to know the reason for her distress to help evaluate her demeanor as it relates to her credibility. Third, the attack shows the defendants' consciousness of guilt. They want to take out a key prosecution witness. They know they'll be convicted if she testifies and is believed by the jury."

"Mr. Flanigan."

"Thank you, Your Honor. First, only two of the three defendants are charged with the counts involving the motorcycle drive-by. Those counts against my client, Mr. Encinas, were dismissed by Your Honor for lack of evidence. There is also a lack of evidence tying the Topeka attack to any of the three defendants. So a family member visits Mr. Lopez each Sunday. Jail authorities found one note, which the prosecution says has been authenticated as Mr. Lopez' handwriting. The note makes some obscure reference to the weather in Kansas. That doesn't prove anything."

"Finally, if this Court deems that the evidence is relevant to just one of the defendants, how can the evidence possibly come in without prejudicing the other two defendants the evidence doesn't pertain to? This evidence shouldn't come in. If it's allowed in any fashion, I expect this case will eventually end in a mistrial. The evidence is that volatile and prejudicial."

"Thank you Mr. Flanigan. Counsel can relax for a few minutes while I read the People's memorandum." As Judge Orsini was reading, the opposing groups of counsel were quietly huddling.

Nick whispered, "Josh, if this only comes in against Luis, we may have to pick another jury for the defendants that the evidence doesn't pertain to. That could be a nightmare and a huge pain in the ass."

Judge Orsini swung his gavel. The attorneys immediately shut up and looked towards the judge. "There's enough evidence to tie Mr. Lopez to the attack, not the others. They're being housed in separate facilities. If it comes in against defendant Lopez, we may need a separate jury for the other two defendants so the second jury won't hear this evidence. I agree with Mr. Flanigan that this evidence is highly volatile. Alternately, I could allow the evidence in only to explain the witness' demeanor as it relates to her credibility, with an admonition to our current jury to not consider who engaged in the attack or who was in any way connected to it. Any thoughts Mr. Drummond? It's your evidence."

"Can I have a minute to confer with Mr. Sterling?" Judge Orsini nodded. Nick and Josh turned away from the defense and the court. Nick whispered, "Josh, we're screwed. If we push for it coming into evidence against Luis, we're looking at a second jury panel. That could delay the case quite a bit, and the judge might decide to start over with two new panels. And I like our panel. If it comes in for demeanor only, with an admonition, we have a built in appellate issue because the attack is so inflammatory. Also, it doesn't add much to explain Felicia's demeanor. We already have ample evidence to show why she will be distressed on the stand, with the drive-by and Luis punching her out."

"Nick, I agree. I don't see a way out of this."

"Your Honor, upon further consideration, and with the benefit of your analysis, we withdraw our motion to present evidence of the Topeka attack."

"That settles it. We'll see you tomorrow morning."

Nick knew he shouldn't look over at the defense when he was helping pack the prosecution materials. But he couldn't resist. Luis' lips were upturned slightly, in a cold, penetrating smirk. The anger in Nick continued to build.

Nick, in a barely controlled voice, rasped, "Josh, let's get the hell out of here. I can't stand the sight of the defendants any longer."

CHAPTER THIRTY-TWO

Nick closed his eyes and tried to relax at counsel table, waiting for the jury to be called in. He hadn't slept well the night before. He had prepped Biker Sue and Wildfire Drury during the evening at the office. Josh was going to handle Drury's sidekick, Zack Reynolds, the former Bakersfield Detective. Biker Sue should entertain the jurors. She was next to impossible to keep on message. A plain yes or no to a question wasn't in her repertoire.

Judge Orsini took the bench. "Anything from counsel before the prosecution calls its first witness?"

Counsel Lipman responded, "Yes, Your Honor. Defense moves to exclude all prospective witnesses from the courtroom for the duration of the trial."

Nick rose quickly to his feet, "No objection except that my case agent, Pepe Cantana, to my right, should be allowed to remain."

"With that caveat, the defense motion is granted. Call your first witness Mr. Drummond."

"The people call Sue Von Zandt to the stand." Pepe was already up, moving to the courtroom doors to get Biker Sue from the hallway. Nick watched the jury as she entered. A few of the men smiled. Two of the middle-aged women grimaced. Biker Sue wouldn't ditch her trademark blue bandana tied across her forehead. A checkered shirt, blue jeans and black, mid-calf boots completed her outfit. She was shown the witness chair and sat down with a resounding thump. The clerk swore her in.

Nick went to the lectern with Ms. Von Zandt's witness binder. The binder included Nick's witness question pages, which only contained subject categories and expected answers underneath. Nick never wrote out the questions. It was the expected answers that were important. He could craft the questions to pull out the answers he wanted. After each expected answer, the police report and page number were listed, or the prior grand jury transcript page where the witness had previously stated the expected answer. If the witness had difficultly remembering a portion of her expected testimony, Nick could easily refresh the witness' memory with the specified report or transcript in the witness binder. Copies of the exhibits that Nick expected to show Ms. Von Zandt were also part of the binder. Rona prepared all of the witness books in this manner.

"Ms. Von Zandt, please state your full name for the record."

"Nick, you can just call me Biker Sue, everyone else does." A titter went through the jury. Judge Orsini favored Nick with a stern look as if to say, *Control your witness.*

"Ms. Von Zandt, this is a formal proceeding. I, and everyone else, will be calling you by your last name. Please, state your full name."

"Yes, Mr. Drummond. It's Betty Sue Von Zandt." Nick proceeded to take her through some background questions, establishing that she was from Orange County and moved up to Yaak, Montana, ten years ago. He elicited that she was in the real estate business and had an office in Libby, some 35 miles south of Yaak. She was the primary agent handling real estate in Yaak and the surrounding area up to the Canadian border. Nick established that most of her clients were people who lived in Montana, either moving or looking for a vacation home.

"Ms. Von Zandt, I want to direct your attention to a year ago last September, 16 months ago. Did anyone stand out who came to your office about real estate? Didn't fit your normal client profile?

"Sure did. A couple of city folk, driving a Cadillac, a Black Escalade, with dark tinted windows and fancy wheels. I thought I was watching a *gangsta* TV show."

Lipman jumped to his feet, "I object to the witness' last statement, move to strike it and request that the witness be admonished."

Judge Orsini looked right at the witness, like it was just her and him in the cavernous room. "Motion to strike the reference to the

TV show is granted. The jury is instructed to disregard that statement. Ms. Von Zandt, just answer the question posed. It's improper for you to give off-the-cuff comments. Understood?"

"Yes, Your Honor."

"Why did the Cadillac stand out to you?"

"First of all, you hardly ever see a Cadillac in Montana. It's mostly pickup trucks and standard American sedans. There are a few of those foreign cars, mainly the tourists 'drivin' em'. Also, no one has dark tinted windows. Be way too dangerous for driving at night. No street lamps in Montana to light up the various wildlife on the road. Trust me you don't want to slam into a deer—it might end up through your windshield and into your lap."

Judge Orsini interjected, "Remember just stick to answering the question."

"Tell me about the person or persons who were in the Cadillac?"

"A plump white guy, in his thirties, with glasses. Looked like he hadn't been outdoors for a while. The other guy was a slender Mexican, also in his thirties, dressed like he was going out to a fancy dinner in Missoula. Hair slicked back, not a hair out of place."

"Here's a photo board with a number of pictures on it. Do you recognize if any of the photos show the white guy? Biker Sue took a close look at the board and pointed to photo C.

"That's the guy, in photo C."

"May the record reflect that Ms. Von Zandt identified photo C, who is one of the named defendants in this case, Lester Sendow, but isn't on trial.

Judge Orsini responded, "The record will so reflect."

"Do you see the Hispanic gentlemen in court today?"

Ms. Von Zandt stared around the room, at the audience, the jury, and the men at the counsel table. She was squinting. Nick was thinking, *Oh shit, she can't identify him. Nothing like looking like an asshole in front of the jury on the very first witness.*" Nick went into crisis mode. "Your Honor, I see that the witness is squinting. Can I ask her some foundation questions about her eyesight?"

"Go ahead."

"How's your vision for seeing far away objects?"

"Not very good. I can see up close really well. But after 10 feet things get blurry. I have prescription motorcycle goggles for riding."

"Does the DMV require you to wear glasses when you drive?'

"Sure does. But I don't want to look like some old lady wearing glasses. That's why I got the special goggles."

"Your Honor, can I escort the witness around the courtroom so she can see the people from a distance at which she can recognize someone?"

"I allowed you to start down this path. Go ahead."

Nick approached her and took her by the arm. He was aware how unusual this procedure was and wanted to make as good a record as possible for appeal. He wasn't going to directly take her to Defendant Lopez' chair, and say, "Is this the guy?" Nick gave a running commentary for the record as he strode slowly up and down the middle of the aisle of the audience, having Ms. Von Zandt look in both directions. He then took her by his own counsel table where he held his breath. Pepe was Hispanic and looked like he could be in his late thirties. Nick took a mental gasp of relief as she went by Pepe without identifying him. Next Nick took her by the counsel tables of the two other defendants, both older than in their thirties. She passed that test. As Nick strode towards Luis Lopez' table, Ms. Von Zandt stopped Nick.

"That's him. I would know him anywhere. I never forget a face."

Nick let a quick smile escape from his lips before going back to his demeanor that this was no big deal, pretending things like this happen every day in the courtroom; when in fact, this was the first time Nick had ever done this or seen it done. Nick was ecstatic that it didn't turn into an O.J. moment where the prosecutor asked O.J. to try the bloody gloves left at the murder scene, and O.J. captivated the jury for what seemed like an eternity, struggling to get the gloves on. It gave rise to Cochran's memorable line in final argument, "If it don't fit, you must acquit." It was an incident that stuck a dagger in every prosecutor's heart.

"Ms. Von Zandt, what did they want?"

"They asked about rental property for a corporate retreat around Yaak. They asked about off-roading and how far Yaak was from the Canadian border. They talked about team bonding exercises."

"Are there any convention centers in Yaak? Places for corporate team building?"

"Are you kidding me? The largest home you can rent would be 2,200 square feet and three bedrooms. Yaak has two bars, a gas station, a volunteer fire department, and a one room schoolhouse. Who ever heard of a corporate retreat where the only food you can order in town is burgers and fries?"

"Did either of them say what business they were in or where they were from?"

"Yeah, the white guy said he was an accountant from San Diego."

"Did the other man say anything about his work or where he lived?'

"No, but he gave a dirty look to the white guy when he said he was an accountant from San Diego."

Nick asked a few more questions of Biker Sue. Then, the defense worked on her—trying to portray her as a flaky transplant from Orange County who couldn't possibly remember an event 16 months ago. Unfortunately for the defense, the more they questioned her, the more certain Biker Sue was in her responses. She wasn't dumb by any stretch of the imagination, and she saw what she saw. She wasn't afraid to be herself. The words "back down" weren't in Sue's vocabulary. She had a steel spine.

Judge Orsini called for a recess after Biker Sue stepped down from the witness stand. Josh whispered to Nick, "You dodged the bullet on Sue's witness identification promenade around the courtroom. What happened to the attorney's adage, don't ask a question unless you know the answer? Or don't stick your neck out to be chopped off unless there's no other alternative. Or you only make a Hail Mary pass when there's two seconds left, not on the first play."

"Okay. Okay, I get it. Once in a while you have to trust your gut. I rolled the dice. We won this time."

After the recess, Nick called his next witness, Drury Betts. Nick played up his background as a wildfire fighter, jumping out of planes. Nick figured if he was impressed, the jury would be impressed. He used Drury to describe Yaak and the surrounding region. Drury was comfortable with maps and aerial views. He was able to point out, on various exhibits, the roads leading into and out of Yaak, as well as the old logging road that went to the Canadian border. Nick touched on his photography background, but didn't spend much time on the technical aspects of photography. He didn't want the jurors' eyes to glaze over. Nick went through the various times Drury was in the vicinity of the border logging road when he saw off-road vehicles hauling duffel bags. Nick had Drury identify Luis in court as being the driver of one of the off-road vehicles he first saw in October. He also identified Lester Sendow as being Luis' passenger from photograph C on the photo board. The jury was eating up the elements of Drury's country living—from his Pabst Blue Ribbon beer to his behemoth four wheel truck called "Mammy", short for Mammoth. At this point, Nick shifted the focus to the incident when one of the drug smugglers pulled a gun on Drury.

"After you set up on the U.S. side of the border and Zack set up on the Canadian side, waiting for off-roaders to come down the logging road, what did you see?"

"A Ranger off-road vehicle came down the logging road on the U.S. side the same time as an old model, long bed truck, rolled down the logging road on the Canadian side. We saw the duffle bag exchange between a pair of Hispanics, on either side. Zack and I snapped photos of the exchange."

"What happened after the exchange?"

"When the two were walking back to the Ranger, I coughed, I couldn't help it. It's those damn lungs of mine, scorched too many times by hot smoke inhalation. My cough was like a rifle shot in the stillness of the early evening. The older of the two Hispanics came through the trees towards me. I got out of the crook of the tree I was set up in, and walked towards the noises he was making in the brush. For me, as a photographer, I had to make one of the toughest decisions in my life—delete the photos I had just taken in case he forced me to show him my recent photos or just pray it never came to that. Surprisingly, I did the smart thing. I deleted the dozen or so photos as I walked towards him."

"What happened next?"

"He yelled at me to come out. I told him to shut up, he was scaring away the animals. When we met, the Hispanic had his hand on the handle of a gun stuck in his waist band. I told him in so many words to relax, I was just trying to take some photos of bear and elk. He didn't buy it since it was almost dark. I tried to play nice. I asked him, 'How do you like my camera?'"

"He pulled out his gun and placed the end of the barrel on my forehead, saying, 'How do you like my gun?' All these thoughts were going through my head. *This is it. Zack is too far away to help and doesn't have a gun. I always thought I'd die in a wildfire.*"

Lipman leaped up, "Object, irrelevant and prejudicial!"

Nick responded, "Goes to his state of mind."

Judge Orsini ruled, "I'll allow it. Proceed."

Nick followed up with the classic prosecutor "tell us more" question, "What happened next?"

"The gunman insisted on seeing my recent photos. He took my camera after I pushed the playback button. He took a few steps back, still training the gun on me, while he flicked his eyes back and forth between me and my most recent photos. All he saw were recent wild-life photos from Yellowstone National Park. He handed me back my camera, put the gun back in his waistband, and said, 'It's dangerous out in the woods at night. You never know what type of predator is roaming around.'"

"Do you remember what the gun looked like?"

"I can see it like it happened moments ago. It was a black, long barrel revolver, a 44 caliber magnum. A showy gun with real stopping power. Not a gun someone would carry if they wanted to be discreet."

"The kind Clint Eastwood carried in Dirty Harry?" Nick waited for an objection. None came.

"Yeah, that's right." Nick stole a glance at the defense tables—they were engrossed in notes that they had been passing back and forth.

Nick ended his examination with Drury identifying the gun wielder as the person shown on photo F on the board. A stipulation was read into the record. *The parties stipulate that the photo F on the board was Samuel Suarez, and DEA agent Lon Ruggers would testify that Suarez was a member of the Baja Norte Familia Cartel at the time of the events testified to by Drury Betts."*

Defense counsel Flanigan added, "It's understood by the parties that the stipulation isn't stating that the man in the woods was Mr. Suarez, just that photo F. depicts Mr. Suarez."

Nick said, "That's correct, Your Honor."

The defense worked on Drury for some time. They referred to the police reports where he never said anything about the type of gun. Drury responded, "They never asked me what type of gun it was."

Defense attorney Flanigan followed up with, "Weren't you so scared looking at that big black barrel, that you couldn't tell what gun it was, or identify who was holding it?"

"I've been fighting wildfires for twenty years. Several times a summer, I'm put in life and death situations where I have to keep my cool to survive. In those situations, as in this one, my senses sharpen, my acuity goes into overdrive, and I remember everything about the situation."

Flanigan knew when to quit and had no further questions.

The trial court took the afternoon break and then it was Zack Reynolds' turn. Josh smoothly directed Zack through several background questions, focusing on the fact that Zack had been a Detective with the Bakersfield Police Department. Zack made it clear that his pal Drury was the risk taker, that Zack didn't think it was the greatest idea to set up photography blinds on people traveling along old logging roads at dusk, in off-road vehicles with duffle bags. Zack explained, "Drury can talk me into drinking warm beer and liking it."

Josh focused on the incident where Suarez pulled a gun on Drury. "Once you saw the four men meet at the border, what did you do?"

"A little bit of Drury rubbed off on me. I was getting good photos of the faces of the Hispanics on the U.S. side, but because I was on the Canadian side, I just saw the back sides of the Canadian Hispanics. I decided to brush the rust off of my old Barn Owl hoot from when I was a teenager, and make a call. It came out pretty good, and when the Canadians turned in my direction, I got some clear shots of their faces. Drury gave me a ration of shit, excuse me, crap, later about the call. He said, 'Any outdoorsman or naturalist knows that the Montana-Canadian border isn't a habitat of the Barn Owl.' It seems that the smugglers didn't major in wildlife biology at college."

"Objection, speculation."

Judge Orsini responded, "Which part Mr. Lipman, that they are smugglers, that they went to college or they didn't major in wild-life biology?"

"All three, Your Honor."

"Granted, Mr. Reynolds' last statement about smugglers, college and majors is stricken. You're not to consider it."

"Please describe Mr. Betts' demeanor when you first met up with him after the persons at the border drove off."

"He was ashen, and in a very emotional state for him. He usually speaks slow, draws out his words. As soon as he saw me, he was rapid fire and loud."

"About how long was this after each of the parties at the border turned to walk back to their respective vehicles?"

"Only a few minutes."

"What did the ashen-looking Mr. Betts say to you in this loud, rapid fire voice?"

Mr. Lipman leaped up, "Objection, Your Honor, may we approach the bench for a sidebar?"

Judge Orsini responded, "Yes," and motioned the court reporter to come over. Once the parties were huddled around the court reporter, Judge Orsini asked Josh, "What do you expect Reynolds to say?"

"I expect Reynolds to testify that Drury told him, 'That Mexican son-of-a-bitch thrust a gun in my face.' It's an excited utterance, a rule 803(2) of the Federal Rule of Evidence exception to the hearsay rule. The credibility of the statement is assured because it was made to describe a traumatic event while the victim of the event was still in the throes of the excitement and anxiety caused by the event. We've set that foundation, Your Honor."

Judge Orsini turned to Mr. Lipman, "Defense?"

"The prosecution can't have it both ways. Before they portray Mr. Betts as being so cool under pressure that he remembers every little detail, being used to life and death situations fighting fires. Now they want to portray him as a traumatized, excited victim, minutes after the event. Further, this is duplicative of Mr. Betts own testimony and wastes the jury's time."

Judge Orsini pondered the matter for a few seconds. "I'm inclined to go along with the defense on this one."

Judge Orsini sustained the defense objection in front of the jury and had Josh proceed with the questioning. Josh carried on like the objection was of no matter and the rest of Zack's testimony came in without further objection. The defense worked on Reynolds, but with a singular lack of success. Reynolds had spent too many days being examined by defense attorneys when he was a detective to get tripped up.

After the jury was excused for the day, Flanigan asked the judge to order the prosecution to provide the chronological order of the witnesses for the next day.

Nick responded, "They have the names of the witnesses we plan to call over the next two days, including the protected witness. Because of serious security concerns, we don't want to inform the defense of the exact time the protected witness is expected to testify."

Judge Orsini responded, "Under the circumstances with the multiple deadly attacks directed towards the protected witness, Mr. Drummond you have fulfilled your obligation of notice. Adjourned for the day."

CHAPTER THIRTY-THREE

Nick sat in a bullet-proof town car. Four armed U.S. Marshal deputies were outside. Two other town cars were parked beside his. They were all waiting on the tarmac at Montgomery Field for the jet carrying Felicia to arrive. It was landing in a few minutes. Nick thought how best to handle Felicia as a witness. He'd be gentle, treating her like a sexual assault victim. He would ask Judge Orsini to allow him to stand near her while he questioned her. He could block her vision of Luis until he asked her to identify him. This day was a long time coming, many sacrifices by many people had been made. Deputy U.S. Marshal Perkins was still in a coma.

The sleek, 12-passenger jet taxied right up to a deputy marshal who was speaking into a radio. A staircase descended from the front of the plane. Nick got out of the car and walked to the plane. He could barely see Felicia coming down the stairs behind a burly deputy. As the deputy passed Nick, he saw Felicia's eyes, brown and large, like a doe's eyes, afraid that a predator was nearby. When she saw Nick, she gave him a nervous smile. Nick walked over and gave her a hug. He held her for several seconds until Felicia relaxed and gave him a hug back. He whispered to her, "Being of English descent, hugging hasn't always been my cup of tea. But I'm so glad to see you. You'll get through this. I'll be with you at all times."

Nick then went to greet the U.S. Marshal SAC, Roger Poon, who was the last to descend from the plane. "Thank you Roger for arranging this."

"You have our total support—we've a deputy fighting for her life back in Topeka. The plane will be on standby until Felicia finishes her testimony. We'll fly her out to the new safe house location." They briefly discussed the security measures for Felicia's arrival at the courthouse and getting her into the courtroom. Nick went back to his town car and sat next to Felicia in the back seat. A deputy was on her other side and a second deputy was in the front passenger seat. SAC Poon and other armed deputies took their seats in the other two cars. The motorcade pulled out, with Nick's and Felicia's car in the middle.

Nick spent most of the ride to the courthouse going over Felicia's expected testimony. He wanted to just hit the highlights and not keep her on the stand too long. He knew the defense attorneys would go after her, trying to make a bloodless kill on the stand. Nick wanted her on and off the stand in one day. Nick cautioned her to take her time in answering the questions and to just answer the questions asked. And if she didn't remember or didn't know something, it was fine to say, "I don't remember or I don't know." On cross-examination, he emphasized the importance of listening to the defense questions carefully. He explained that sometimes a part of their question may call for a "no" response, while the other part a "yes" response. If there is an objection to a question, she must wait until Judge Orsini rules. The bottom line he told her was to tell the truth, and not embellish or understate. Finally, Nick told her that a jury senses when someone is telling the truth and will support that witness.

They drove to the back of the federal courthouse, down a steep driveway leading from a street-level iron gate. Deputy marshals were waiting for them at the loading dock at the bottom of the ramp. Nick and Felicia were ushered into a freight elevator with three deputies. The elevator took them up to the courtroom floor where they were whisked into a private, back hallway. Felicia was placed with her escorts in a small waiting room near Orsini's courtroom while Nick entered the courtroom.

The jury, the defendants and the attorneys were all accounted for when Judge Orsini took the bench. He looked towards Nick, "Call your first witness."

"Your Honor, the People call Felicia Esperanza-Salas to the stand." There was an audible gasp in the courtroom. The "professional" court watchers in attendance, who had been following the case in the news, were aware of Felicia's importance. Nick continued, "Based on the circumstances, may I be allowed to question the witness from in front of the witness stand, instead of from the lectern?"

"You may," responded Judge Orsini. Judge Orsini looked toward the audience. "There will be no more outbursts from anyone viewing these proceedings. The person or persons making any further outbursts will be removed by a bailiff."

Felicia was led from the back hallway by a bailiff. Nick strode toward her, smiling. Her eyes were downcast and she seemed to have shrunken into herself. Felicia was sworn in and gave her full name, at all times her eyes never left Nick. Nick, in his most soothing voice, established that Felicia was from San Diego, and had attended a local community college. The background questions calmed Felicia. She straightened up in the witness chair and spoke more forcefully.

Nick asked her whether she knew a Luis Hernandez-Lopez. She described how they met at the races in Del Mar a year and a half ago. Felicia related her first impressions of Luis—so handsome, smooth, and sophisticated. He'd talk to her about his travels in Europe and South America as if they were everyday occurrences. It was a whirlwind romance. She felt like Cinderella, discovered by a man of the world. The fine dining, the fancy nightclubs, and the new clothes he bought her were irresistible. She didn't hesitate when, a month after they met, he asked her to move into his palatial grounds in the foothills above Rosarito Beach. It was exciting at first. He took her out on his Donzi ocean speedboat and she rode on the back of his red Ducati motorcycle.

Felicia became homesick. Luis controlled her life. He wouldn't let her call her aunt. She could only write her letters.

At first, Felicia admitted she was excited by the armed guards patrolling Luis' compound. Luis told her not to think anything about them. There were a lot of kidnappers in Mexico. They were there to keep them safe. Felicia noticed that when a couple of older Mexican gentlemen would visit Luis, that they had armed guards with them, and Luis had more guards posted. She described one of the men as a distinguished, silver haired, aristocrat-looking man. The only man that she ever saw Luis defer to. Asked if the older man was in court, she identified defendant Mateo Gomez-Encinas.

Felicia described the other older man as being solidly built, with a bull neck and a pronounced scar down the right side of his face. He was always scowling. Felicia identified him as defendant Rael Trujillo-Sanchez.

Felicia spoke of sumptuous dinners with the men. Fresh lobsters, from a nearby fishing village, Puerto Nuevo, were brought in. At a few of these dinners, a paunchy gringo with glasses attended. She identified him from the People's photo board as Lester Sendow. She remembered that he lived in San Diego and was an accountant. After each dinner, Luis sent her to her room while the men smoked cigars, drank brandy and talked in the den. Before going to her bedroom, Felicia caught a few words about poppies in the Mexican state of Sinaloa, and warehouses throughout the United States.

She remembered, towards the end of her stay at the compound, that Luis, Señor Encinas and Señor Sanchez had been drinking a lot of wine. There was tension around the table. She tried to make polite conversation, but the men ignored her. She hung outside the den more than usual that night before going upstairs. Heated words were exchanged between Señors Encinas and Sanchez. "Señor Encinas said in a loud voice, in Spanish, 'Tell me before you decide to take somebody out!'"

"Sanchez responded, 'I'm in charge of enforcement, it was my call.'"

Felicia testified, "Luis interjected, 'We need to quiet down. No one will miss that *culebra*.' Sorry, *culebra* means snake in English."

Nick asked her, "What did you think they were talking about?" Counsel Lipman jumped up immediately.

"Objection, speculation!"

Nick responded, "Goes to her state of mind to explain her future actions."

"I'll let it in for that purpose."

"Go ahead Ms. Salas," Nick urged.

"The last bit of conversation I thought was about killing someone. It fit with prior conversations I had overheard, and observations

I had made. Luis kept telling me that he was partners with the other two in an agricultural, import-export business. It made me question if they were really involved in a legitimate business. All the armed guards, the huge compound, the fancy toys. I began thinking of it as a drug dealing organization."

"Did that cause you to do something the next day."

"Yes, I went to explore the garage when no one was in the area, under the pretense I was looking for a missing cat. Luis had told me several times not to go into the garage."

"What did you find, if anything?"

"At the far end of the garage, there were several crates stacked up. On the floor, next to the bottom crate, was the largest bullet I had ever seen."

"Describe it for us."

"It was about six inches long, mostly gold in color, with the top third being copper with a black tip. It was clean and shiny. It looked brand new."

"How do you remember it so well?"

"I picked it up and looked at it carefully. I never knew that a bullet could be so big."

"On the overhead screen, to your rear, is a photo of a bullet, with a tape measure by its side, showing the bullet to be six inches long. Did it look like this bullet?'

"Yes, exactly."

"Your Honor, it is stipulated by the parties, that the photo is of a 50 caliber, armor piercing bullet."

"What did you do, after you found the bullet?"

"I told Luis about it that night. He said it was just probably some old bullet lying around from the previous owner. He told me that I wasn't supposed to be in the garage and for me never to go in there, for my own safety. I ignored what he told me and I snuck into the garage the next day. The crates and the bullet were gone."

Nick took Felicia through more questioning that strengthened their case against the defendants. He elicited that she saw oil tanker trucks outside of the compound garage on several occasions. Nick would later argue that they were being used to transport large amounts of marijuana into the U.S. as was shown by satellite photos of the oil tanker truck at the cartel's Otay Mesa warehouse. He also brought out details that supported Luis and the cartel using Luis' Donzi as part of their north coast San Diego smuggling operation. She spoke about speeding along the crest of the ocean waves at speeds of up to 70 miles per hour and Luis' obsession in keeping his Donzi spotless. There were no marks on it. Felicia also described Luis asking her about north San Diego County beaches and if anybody was on them late at night. Lastly, she described seeing Luis checking out tide patterns for the beaches on his computer.

Nick then breached the sensitive area of Luis' domestic violence towards her. "Do you recognize this photograph?"

Felicia squirmed in the witness chair. She looked sad, frightened and embarrassed, all at the same time. "It's me, taken at the U.S. Border Patrol office after I escaped from Luis."

Nick smiled to himself, he liked the tone of anger in Felicia's voice. Nick asked to have the photo passed among the jurors. It'd have more impact that way—be more personal than looking at a photo projected on a screen. Nick looked at the jurors as they passed around the photo. Most had a look of disgust on their faces. A couple of the women had sympathetic, sad looks. "Ms. Salas, how did you get a swollen, black eye, and multiple bruises on your face?"

Felicia's response burst out of her, "The evening before, Luis beat me. He hit my right eye with his closed fist, and slapped me several times, hard, in the face, with the back of his hand. He also kicked my legs a number of times, but the photo doesn't show those bruises."

Felicia begin to quietly sob. Nick asked, "Do you need some time?"

"No, no, I need to get through this."

"Okay, what happened just before defendant Lopez beat you?"

"We were arguing. I told him I felt like a prisoner. I could never leave the compound without his armed guards. He wouldn't allow me to go back to San Diego to visit my aunt and friends. He called me an 'ungrateful bitch' and that he had given me everything I wanted. When I told him I wanted to leave him and go see my aunt, that's when he started to beat me. He kept saying over and over, 'You're not

295

going anywhere, bitch. You're mine. No bitch leaves me unless I kick her out on her ass."

Nick stepped aside so that he was no longer blocking Felicia's view of Luis. Do you see Luis Hernandez-Lopez in the courtroom today?"

Felicia stared right at Luis. Her lips dropped, her eyes closed, anguish registered on her face. She began to tremble. The jurors' eyes were transfixed on her. "Yes, that's him, sitting at the far left table, with the blue tie," as she pointed her finger directly at Luis. "I had never wanted to see him again," shielding her eyes from his view.

Lipman's voice rang out, "Object, last statement, unresponsive!"

Judge Orsini responded, "Sustained. Strike, 'I had never wanted to see him again,' and you're not to consider it." That was fine with Nick. The judge had repeated Felicia's words—her testimony, her anguish, and revulsion in hiding her eyes from Luis would remain with the jury. Nick stepped back, again blocking Felicia's direct view of Luis.

"How were you able to leave the next day?"

"Later that evening I pretended to make up with him. He apologized to me and said he never wanted to see me go. I lied to him. I told him I was really happy there, but I just got homesick once in a while. That seemed to appease him, and the next day the guards weren't paying attention to me. At the side of the main house, there was an old Toyota that servants use to go to town to buy groceries and household items. I grabbed the keys off the pantry hook and waited for the gates to open for an incoming vehicle. I had a shawl wrapped around my head and shoulders like I was one of the servant girls who worked there. My heart was racing. I was almost too afraid to try it. I made myself drive normally through the gate, not looking at the one guard that was nearby. I waved my hand. I headed straight for the border."

"Did you have anything in the Toyota's glove compartment?"

"Yes, some cocaine."

"What happened to you after you were stopped at the border?"

"You and other people interviewed me. I showed Pepe there, pointing to agent Cantana, sitting next to Nick at counsel table, and Agent Ana where Luis's condo was located in the Coronado

Keys. I also showed them where his ranch-warehouse was located in Otay Mesa. You had me speak to an attorney and I was placed in witness protection."

Nick had instructed Felicia that they couldn't talk about what happened in Kansas, but could talk about the motorcycle shooting.

"At some point, when you were in witness protection, out of state, did you come back to San Diego?" Nick wasn't worried about establishing exact dates with Felicia. Other witnesses could establish when she came across the border, and when she came back to San Diego.

"Yes, I got so homesick. I wasn't supposed to communicate with anyone back home for my safety. I bought a cheap phone at a convenience store and called my aunt. I said I was taking the bus and I would see her in two days. I took a Greyhound bus to Vegas and then on to the downtown terminal in San Diego. From there I took a local bus that stopped a block from my aunt's house in Chula Vista."

"What happened next?'

"I was so excited to see my Tia. I got out of the bus and hurried towards her home. I was thinking about the big, warm hug she was going to give me. I stepped on her driveway when I heard a roar of a motorcycle down the street. The next thing I remember, Agent Pepe slammed into me, knocking me down. Gunfire was all around me. I couldn't breathe, Pepe was on top me. Gunshots were going off in my ear. I heard Ana yell out. The motorcycle noise passed and the gunfire stopped."

"Were you hit by gunfire?"

"No. Pepe protected me by shielding my body from the bullets. I screamed when I saw Ana down on the sidewalk, with blood pouring out of her. Pepe yelled for me to go into my aunt's house and call 9-1-1 and say there was an officer shot. I ran into my aunt's house and called."

"What were you thinking?"

"I was so scared, I couldn't think. I was numb. I just cried into my aunt's shoulder."

Nick waited a few moments to let it sink in with the jury. "No further questions at this time."

During the lunch recess, Rona brought in fish tacos for Felicia, Pepe, Nick and Josh. They stayed in the small room off of the courtroom. The defense had started questioning Felicia before the recess, but so far hadn't made any significant inroads. Nick was a little surprised that Sanchez' counsel had handled her with kid gloves. He expected that to change.

Encinas' attorney, Flanigan, started his cross-examination after lunch. He spent some time establishing that his client had always treated her well. Never a coarse or angry word towards her. He got Felicia to say that Encinas reminded her of her grandfather. A dignified, civil man. After softening Felicia up, Flanigan started on the cocaine found in the Toyota's glove compartment at the border.

"Ms. Salas, it was quite a lot of cocaine, three ounces?"

"I don't know how much cocaine there was. There was some."

"Here is a lab report, it shows 3.2 ounces of a white powdery substance, containing cocaine. Does that refresh your memory?"

"Whatever it says, I'm sure it's right."

"Do you know how many people in California are prosecuted for possession of cocaine for sale for having three ounces of cocaine?

Nick stood up, "Objection, Your Honor, irrelevant, argumentative and assumes facts not in evidence."

Judge Orsini said in a slightly annoyed voice, "Sustained, move on counsel".

"Ms. Salas, you intended to sell all that cocaine when you crossed the border into our community." Nick knew "in our community" was argumentative, but decided to let it pass. He couldn't be seen by the jurors as objecting too much.

"No Mr. Flanigan, I intended to use it myself."

In a disbelieving tone, "All that cocaine for yourself?"

Nick objected again, "Argumentative, asked and answered."

"Sustained."

Flanigan continued to emphasize the points that supported his case. Felicia acknowledged that she never heard anyone talk about distributing heroin or marijuana. She didn't see any marijuana or heroin at Luis' compound. She was also aware of the spate of kidnappings in Mexico and the armed guards at the compound could certainly be there for that reason.

Flanigan completed a few more areas of inquiry before he turned over the cross-examination to the final defense attorney, Marc Lipman, attorney for Luis.

Lipman wasted no time in attacking Felicia. "Isn't it true that my client gave you thousands of dollars in gifts out of his love for you?"

Nick objected right away. He had to keep Lipman honest and set the tone. "Object to, 'Out of his love for her', calls for speculation."

Judge Orsini said, "Strike 'out of his love for you'. Ms. Salas, you can answer the question that Mr. Lopez gave you thousands of dollars in gifts."

"Yes. He gave me clothes and jewelry."

"You became bored in Mexico when Mr. Lopez wasn't able to spend as much time with you?"

"Yes. Over time he spent less and less time with me."

"You kept bugging him about spending more time with you?"

"We talked about it."

"You didn't just talk about it. You yelled and screamed at him?"

"A few times."

"Didn't you also hit him and scratch his face in one of those arguments?"

"I was sobbing one time and beat him on his chest. He grabbed me hard by my upper arms. I screamed that he was hurting me. He wouldn't let me go. That's when I scratched his face."

Nick interjected, "Can we approach the bench for a sidebar conference?" Judge Orsini nodded for the attorneys to come forward. "Your Honor, Mr. Lipman has opened the door to evidence about all of the domestic violence inflicted upon Felicia by his client before the night she left. He raised the issue of arguments and a prior physical confrontation."

Judge Orsini, looking directly at Mr. Lipman, said, "Mr. Drummond has an excellent point—any more questioning along those lines Mr. Lipman and it all comes in, including the breast tattoo." Lipman, ashen, nodded his assent, and the attorneys went back to their seats.

Lipman continued his questioning, "The evening before you were caught with cocaine at the border, it was you who started the fight?"

"No. I told him I wanted to leave. He started hitting me."

"Didn't you start beating him first, and hit your right eye on the side of a dresser when he protected himself by pushing you away?"

"No, it didn't happen that way."

Lipman gave Felicia a look of disbelief. "Well, let's move on. You were caught at the border with three ounces of cocaine. Right?"

"Yes,"

You knew you were in big trouble. You didn't want to go to jail?"

"I didn't know how much trouble I was in. I didn't want to go to jail."

"Didn't law enforcement tell you that you could go to jail for the cocaine."

"Yes, someone mentioned it."

"You would do anything to stay out of jail. You would tell law enforcement anything they wanted to hear about Mr. Lopez so you could avoid going to jail?"

"No, I told them the truth."

You knew that law enforcement was after suspected members of the Baja Norte Familia?"

"I knew they were concerned about the Familia."

"You're no dummy. You've been around the block. You knew how to spice up your story to try to put Mr. Lopez and the other defendants in a bad light?" Nick could have objected to, "around the block" as being argumentative, but Felicia was on a roll—handling the questions well.

"I didn't spice up my story."

"You have a deal with the prosecution that if you cooperate and testify, no charges will be brought against you for the cocaine?"

"Yes".

"What do you think the prosecution gets out of this deal? They want to stick it to the defendants!"

Nick leaped up, "Object, Your Honor, highly improper, speculation, argumentative."

Before, Judge Orsini could respond, Lipman said, "I withdraw the question." With a disgusted look on his face, he added, "No further questions."

Judge Orsini looked at Nick. "Would you like a few minutes before redirect?"

"Yes, Your Honor, thank you."

Nick and Josh conferred. It was decided that Nick would just ask questions on the subjects where the defense had scored a few points and leave the rest alone. They wanted Felicia back on the airplane.

"Ms. Salas, you told the defense that the cocaine in your purse was for personal use. How much cocaine were you using when you were at Mr. Lopez' compound?"

"Luis and I would snort about a half an ounce a day."

Lipman almost screamed, "Object, unresponsive, move to strike, improper character evidence!"

Judge Orsini said, "I will allow it. Mr. Flanigan opened the door to this line of questioning when he asked the witness about the cocaine being possessed for sale."

Nick continued, "So for you alone, the three ounces would be less than a two week supply?"

"Yeah, I guess so. My math isn't that good."

"Here is your photo at the border." Nick stepped aside, put the photo on the big screen. "Did these bruises and black eye come from hitting the side of a dresser?"

"No." Felicia looked directly at Luis, anger emanating from her face. "I didn't hit a dresser; Luis did that to me with his closed fist and the back of his hand."

"Did you make up your testimony about the six inch bullet and the crates in the garage?"

"No."

"Did you make up testimony about the defendants' after dinner conversations that you overheard when they were in the den?"

"No."

"Did you make up the heated conversation where Defendant Encinas said, 'Tell me before you decide to take someone out'" and defendant Sanchez' response, 'I'm in charge of enforcement, it's my call,' and finally Defendant Lopez' comment, 'No one will miss that snake.'"

"No. They said those exact words."

"The agreement you signed with law enforcement that if you cooperated, no charges for the cocaine would be filed, wasn't that dependent on you telling the truth?"

"Yes."

"Do you want to be here?"

"No. I want my life back. I'm scared to death."

"No further questions, Your Honor. Can this witness be excused?"

Judge Orsini looked at the attorneys for the defense. "Any further questions gentlemen?" Seeing negative head shakes, Orsini excused the witness, telling Felicia she could exit the courtroom after the jury leaves.

As soon as the jury left, Nick rushed over to Felicia and ushered her out the back hallway. He had a fear that somehow a defense counsel would call her back to the stand. Nick and Felicia felt a huge sense of relief on the way back to the airport. Felicia had done well and she didn't have to face Luis anymore. Testifying at trial significantly reduced the risk that Luis would orchestrate another attack. However, Nick couldn't be absolutely sure of Felicia's safety even if Luis was convicted and locked away for decades. He was a vengeful son-of-a-bitch.

Nick ended the day the same way he started it. He gave Felicia a big hug on the tarmac before she climbed the stairs to the jet. With both hands, Nick gripped SAC Poon's hand and said, "Thank you. Felicia came through for all of us today, including Deputy Perkins."

CHAPTER THIRTY-FOUR

Nick woke up Sunday morning, actually feeling refreshed. He felt like he hadn't had a full eight hours sleep in years. He hadn't realized how worried he'd been about Felicia's testimony. It was a huge relief that it was over and that she had done so well. The evidence on Friday also came in well. Josh and Nick had shared the law enforcement witnesses who had monitored additional duffle bag exchanges at the Canadian border. Homeland Security Investigator Slater enthralled the jury with the harrowing mountain pass detour to pick up the surveillance on the college kid's pickup after a duffle bag delivery. He told the jury where the Missoula drug warehouse was located and described Agent Pepe Cantana's muddy, ice water bath while crawling under the pickup to place a GPS tracking device.

Nick felt so good that he decided to treat himself to an early morning run along Pacific Beach. At 7:00, he didn't have to navigate around any sunbathers, tag football games, or kids building sand castles. Other than dodging a couple of overly energetic youth running to the water with their surfboards, he had the beach to himself. He got into a rhythm and let his mind wander. His thoughts turned to Ana and her flying in from Topeka this evening at six. The thought of her coming home and being cleared by the doctors were the real reasons why he felt so alive this morning. He was going to cook her a dinner she'd never forget. Time to pull out all the stops and channel his Italian mother. She loved to cook and had imprinted that love in her son. Nick had put it on the back shelf for a long time. It was time to dust it off.

Nick picked up the pace on the way back to his apartment, planning the dinner. Mushroom risotto, his mother's favorite. No store bought chicken stock for the risotto—it had to be homemade—the secret to Mama's risotto. Nick knew that Ana was not much of a beef eater. But a duck salad should work, and sautéed spinach. He'd top it all off with chocolate mousse. Ana had a sweet tooth for chocolate.

Without showering, Nick got into his car and rushed to an Italian deli in Little Italy. He bought morel mushrooms, Italian arborio rice, and chicken backs, feet, and necks, as well as onions, carrots, celery, and a leek.

Back at his apartment, he diced two parts onion, one part carrots and one part celery for the *mirepoix*. He wrapped peppercorns and a clove of garlic in a cheese cloth for the sachet. Parsley stems, thyme, and bay leaves were wrapped in a leek leaf for the bouquet garni. Nick put the *mirepoix*, sachet, and garni with the chicken bones in a pot and added water. He brought it to a boil and then lowered the gas flame to a simmer. After six to eight hours of simmering, he'd then strain the chicken stock. Nick would end up with a clear quart of chicken stock, just perfect for a couple of healthy portions of risotto.

While the chicken stock was simmering, Nick went to the expensive organic market nearby. He hadn't been in the market before, not wanting to spend the money. But, today was an exception. He bought two duck breasts, goat cheese, a basket of raspberries, and an orange for the duck salad. He also bought a hefty bunch of organic spinach and luscious dried cranberries for sautéed spinach. For the mousse, he bought semi-sweet chocolate, whole milk, vanilla, whipping cream, and strawberries.

Back at the apartment, the aroma of the chicken stock lured Nick into the kitchen. He lifted the lid to the pot and and breathed in the wafting smells. He pictured his plump mother, bending over the family stove, in her faded blue apron. She had been gone for ten years. Today was the first day he had thought of her in a while.

Nick started working on the chocolate mousse. He placed the chocolate, a bit more than called for, in a sauce pan at low heat, stirring in milk and sugar. Once the mixture had blended, he poured it over fluffy egg whites that he had beaten in a separate bowl. He continued to stir this mixture under a low heat until it thickened some. Nick was careful not to overcook it, and placed the small saucepan in a large pot of cold water to slowly cool it. He then put the saucepan in the refrigerator.

In a separate bowl, he whipped a half cup of whipping cream until it was stiff and added a teaspoon of pure vanilla extract, the special ingredient for delectable chocolate mousse. Nick then blended the whipped cream with the cooled chocolate custard. Next, Nick macerated half the basket of ever so sweet raspberries. He placed the macerated raspberries into two small dessert bowls and covered the raspberries with the chocolate mousse. Both of the mousse bowls went back into the fridge.

Nick wanted everything ready to go when he took the makings of the dinner to Ana's condo to cook it. He sliced the morel mushrooms into thick slices, realizing they would be significantly reduced in size when he later sautéed them before mixing them in with the risotto. He sliced the strawberries for the topping on the mousse. Nick planned to bring the refrigerated items with him in a cooler to the airport to pick up Ana. He would also bag up and bring along the rest of the dinner. His Mama always said, "The path to a woman's heart is through the kitchen by a lovingly crafted, home-cooked meal." He would see.

Nick, anxious to see Ana, arrived at the cellphone lot near the arrival terminal a half hour before Ana's plane was scheduled to land. Forty-five dreadfully boring minutes later, the text came through, "I have my luggage, I'll be under the overhead pedestrian bridge." In two minutes Nick was there, out of his truck and hugging Ana.

"I guess you missed me big guy."

"You don't know how much." Nick caught her up on the case during the drive to Solana Beach.

As they were nearing her condo, Ana asked, "How about some take-out? I'm hungry."

"Don't worry about take-out, I have a home-cooked meal for you. Just unpack your things, take a shower, and leave it to me."

"That's a very kind offer Nick. But I don't feel like macaroni and cheese and micro-waved chicken wings."

"Ahhh, how the lady disparages me. There are a few things you don't know about me. Just wait and taste." When Ana went to her bedroom to unpack, Nick went back to his truck and carried up the food.

Nick was using all four burners on her stove when Ana walked in. She was wearing a silk robe, and her damp hair hung straight down. Nick couldn't help but notice that Ana wasn't wearing a bra under the thin sheen of silk. "What in the hell have you done to my kitchen?!"

"Let me explain princess. Pine nuts are roasting on the back, right burner for the sautéed spinach. Olive oil lightly covers the large frying pan on the left rear burner, ready for me to sauté the spinach. I'm scoring the duck breasts in the frying pan on the front right burner to render out fat and make it crispy. The *piece de resistance*, that I have been stirring while you unpacked and cleaned up, is mushroom risotto, on the left front burner. About half the quart of my homemade chicken stock has been absorbed into the special arborio rice from Italy, known for its absorption properties. See that plastic container to my left, that is the remaining stock that I have to stir in."

"I can't believe this. Why do you preside over an uncouth, barebones bachelor pad, when you can cook like this?"

"Priorities my dear, priorities, and I wanted to hold something back from you. It's always nice to surprise."

"True. I'll see if I'm really surprised after I taste your meal."

"Always the cynic."

"Being Jewish, I come by it honestly."

"Remember, you said that, not me. Stir the risotto while I flip the duck breasts for a minute before putting them in the oven. Also, give the pine nuts a shake so they get browned on the other side."

The meal was coming together. Ana did most of the risotto stirring while Nick put together the composed, duck salad. He sliced the duck breasts into eight oval pieces and laid four a piece, over a small bed of mixed greens on two plates. Nick placed a half dozen raspberries to one side of each plate and a couple of orange slices on the other side. Small chunks of goat cheese adorned another side of each plate and chopped organic tomatoes on the fourth side. A balsamic vinaigrette dressing was lightly applied over the greens.

"Nick, why don't you toss the salad?"

"Each ingredient is a separate flavor to be savored and contrasted to the other tastes."

Ana lightly rapped Nick on the head. "Is the real Nick in there?"

"No, Ana, it's really my Italian mother. You don't see much of her in me, day to day. My grumpy work demeanor comes from my British father. I also blame him for my drinking. He was part Irish."

"That's more than you've told me about them in the two years I've known you."

"I told you I could change. At least I think I did. Maybe it was Judy I kept saying that to."

"Finally, back to the real you. The spoiler of intimate moments."

"Let me make amends by my dinner. It's almost ready." Nick tasted the risotto and it was at a perfect consistency, very moist, with each rice kernel bulging with liquid. However, it needed salt. Nick mixed in pinches of salt until he was satisfied. Over the next two minutes, Nick sautéed handfuls of spinach in olive oil, adding the roasted pine nuts. The spinach reduced down from an overflowing frying pan to two portions. He turned off the heat, and placed some dried cranberries and crumbles of goat cheese on the sautéed spinach. He served ample, but not overwhelming, portions of the risotto and the sautéed spinach on each of their plates. Nick had to balance his predilection for heaping portions with his mother's admonition that smaller portions presented much better. The duck salads were served on separate plates at the same time.

Nick already had a chilled bottle of chardonnay on the dining room table. "This wine befits you—it is described as having *an intense mix of flavors with a long finish*. Parker has given it a rating in the upper nineties. It should be an excellent pairing with the duck."

"A wine connoisseur too. If I'd only known, I'd have been attracted to you sooner."

"You mean my always mussed hair, and growing pot belly weren't enough?"

"Don't destroy my newly discovered mental image of you. Let's eat."

Ana started with a taste of the risotto. She chewed it slowly, then swallowed. Her eyes closed and a smile blossomed on her face. "Heavenly and rich, but not heavy, and so moist."

"I'm glad you like it. Try the salad. Spend a moment with each part. Ana took her time tasting the various parts—the crispy outer skin of the duck, the mild goat cheese, the sugary taste of the raspberries, and the pungent, but sweet orange slices. She finished her tasting adventure with a mouthful of greens, lightly coated with a citrus-infused balsamic vinegar.

"Your mother was right. The taste treats of the individual parts of the salad far exceed the taste of everything jumbled up in a mixed salad. 'To your mother,'" raising a glass of the chardonnay. Ana smelled the bouquet before taking a generous first sip. "And the chardonnay, I can't believe the complexities of the flavors."

They didn't talk much during the main course. It would've interrupted their eating and sipping of wine. Ana brought up the case at one point. Nick said, "Let's not talk anymore about it tonight. Pretend it's far away. We'll just enjoy each other and the evening. Can you say now that you're surprised? If not yet, I have one more gastronomical treat for you, dessert."

"Does that mean I have to say I'm not yet surprised so I can get dessert? I definitely want dessert."

"I know you do and it's chocolate mousse."

"You know all my weaknesses." Nick brought out the two bowls of mousse from the refrigerator and placed the sliced strawberries on top. Ana grabbed one of them out of Nick's hands, "I can't wait. Give me a spoon."

Nick complied and Ana had her first bite before she sat down. "This is so, soooo good! I'm utterly surprised and pleased and thankful for your cooking, master chef."

After an Amaretto aperitif while looking over the ocean, Ana and Nick ended up in her bed. "I thought we weren't supposed to do this Nick."

"We aren't, but sometimes good things happen. We just have to let it flow." Nick spent endless moments in time, caressing and kissing her scars, on her leg, her arm, and the newest one, the stitches over her eye. "I can't put into words how much I feel for you."

"You don't have to. You let your cooking do the talking."

CHAPTER THIRTY-FIVE

Nick looked over the Sunday New York Times at his breakfast table—his one indulgence on Sunday morning. The multigrain cheerios with dried strawberries, bathed in non-fat milk, was a far cry from the gastronomical delight he had prepared for Ana two weeks earlier. It seemed like months ago. The trial had gone pretty well over the last two weeks. Josh and Nick had split the witnesses. They introduced evidence of drug seizures—the college boy's vehicle stop in Missoula and all the warehouse seizures. The evidence got tedious after awhile. But the jury perked up when Nick showed them the Department of Defense satellite photos of the oil tanker truck being unloaded at the Otay Mesa ranch.

The jury seemed to understand the extensive reach of the Familia cartel and the high volume of heroin and marijuana being distributed. Agents testified about the seizures at Vancouver, Missoula, Chicago, and Salt Lake City warehouses, demonstrating the national and international nature of the cartel's distribution. Nick and Josh, through surveillance testimony at the various locations, were painting a picture that the thousands of pounds of marijuana and the hundreds of kilos of black tar heroin that were seized were just the tip of the iceberg as to the actual quantity of drugs distributed by the cartel.

The emphasis on the amount of drugs supported the investigation's evidence of the millions of cash dollars being deposited into U.S. border banks for transfer to a Mexican financial account. The money laundering side of the cartel's operation would be explored later in the week after testimony the next day about boats smuggling drugs to north county San Diego beaches.

Nick started the testimony on Monday morning with the gun battle between the Coast Guard and the drug runners' Donzi speed boat. Nick was trying to establish by the end of the trial that not only was it Luis' Donzi, but he was driving it the night of the shoot out. Commander Ritter wowed the jury with his description of the 87-foot Marine Protector, with the two, fifty caliber Browning machine guns mounted on either side of the foredeck. The jury was enthralled by his riveting description of the smaller rigid hull inflatable boat (RHIB). The Marine Protector had launched the RHIB to intercept the smugglers' outboard-powered, inflatable boat at South Ponto Beach, Carlsbad. As the RHIB approached the surf, it took automatic fire from the second smuggler's boat, the high speed Donzi ocean racer. Commander Ritter told how he sped towards the gunfire at full throttle and within seconds had engaged the Donzi with his twin 50 caliber machine guns. Bullets flew over the low lying boat. The Donzi immediately swerved away from the RHIB and headed down the coast towards Mexico. The Protector couldn't keep up. Its radar tracked the Donzi traveling at 70 miles per hour. Ritter contacted the trailing Coast Guard Defender Response Boat to intercept the smuggler's boat.

Coast Guard Lieutenant Ron Selby, who commanded the Defender Response boat, testified about the intercept.

Nick asked, "After you received the order from Commander Ritter to intercept the smuggler, what did you do?"

"I headed north at top speed, just under 50 m.p.h., in wind-caused chop. Our mobile surface radar system picked up a speeding boat approaching us on our right side. My radar operator estimated contact in 20 seconds."

"What order did you give, if any?"

"I ordered my crew to prepare for incoming fire and to retaliate on my command. I heard the loud whine of a rapidly approaching boat along the shoreline. In just seconds I heard automatic fire. As we closed, I saw a man, standing, braced on the front passenger seat of an ocean racer, firing a machine gun. Its bullets raked the front right of my boat. I ordered my crew to return fire. Three of my crew-men opened fire with automatic weapons. The boat passed within 15 feet of us. It was like a high speed, high tech, medieval joust, using machine guns instead of lances. Our fire struck the man standing in the passenger seat. He fell into the water as we passed."

"Could you see the driver of the smuggler's boat?"

"He was crunched over, only exposing the upper, right side of his body. He continued to drive past."

"What happened next?"

"I radioed Commander Ritter for instructions as to following the ocean racer south, or picking up the body in the water. He told me we wouldn't be able to keep up with the smuggler's boat and ordered me to rescue the man in the water."

"Did you do that?"

"I drove directly over to him and two of my crew donned life jackets, jumped into the water and hoisted him into our boat by the rear, water level, platform. We had a medic on board. He checked his vital signs. He was already dead. He had multiple gunshot wounds to his upper torso and a couple to his upper thighs."

"Were any of your men injured in the encounter?"

"One man sustained minor cuts to his face from shards of fiber-glass being kicked up from one or more of the smuggler's bullets. He was taken to the Naval Hospital, treated and released."

"Are you familiar with ocean racers?"

"Yes I am. I attend ocean races and occasionally act as one of a two-member crew on a racing boat. Sometimes I drive, other times I'm the navigator."

"Can you describe the smuggler's boat that you exchanged gun fire with."

"Yes. It was a 20 to 23 foot ocean racer, with a deep hull, no windshield. Its engine was on board, powering an outboard shaft and propeller. By its lines, speed, and engine configuration, it was a Donzi. The photos from the Defender's foredeck night camera con-firmed my visual observation. It was a 22-foot Donzi Classic."

"Is this a photo of the Donzi taken that night?

"Yes, it is. The photo shows the passenger still standing. The view of the driver is blocked by the passenger. The photo shows the entire right side profile of the Donzi."

"Your Honor, may I publish this photo to the jury by showing it on the overhead?"

"You may counsel." Agent Cantana projected the photo. Nick looked at the jury for their reaction. It seemed to make an impact on them—the menacing, dark clothed man, facing towards the Defender, firing a machine gun.

Nick's final witness was a member of the interdiction team at South Ponto Beach. He identified the tar heroin and the marijuana seized from the duffle bags brought to the beach by the smuggler's inflatable boat. He identified Sergio Bustamante, also known as *Chacal,* as the dead smuggler transported to the RHIB by the Defender and brought to the beach. Bustamante was the same person who had accompanied Luis and Sendow on the first drug delivery across the Canadian border.

Friday night, Nick rewound the prior week in his mind. The coastal drug smuggling perked the jury up, giving them a much needed mid-trial shot of adrenalin. The testimony about the cartel's money laundering operations was a bit dry. It's difficult to make testimony about Hector Morales, and his L&M Freight company, sexy. The same with the testimony about the Sakias' import-export front company, Latin American Productos. However, even in our jaded, celebrity, big money culture, the jury was impressed by 65 million dollars laundered by the two money laundering operations over a year's time.

The Marshal's Office was flying protected witness Sendow in from Molokai tomorrow. They arranged a safe house with a four-man team to provide around-the-clock security. Nick was looking forward to a meeting with him on Sunday evening to go over his testimony. A Marshal's Office contact told Nick a few weeks ago that Sendow had changed. Nick was curious, but his contact hadn't elaborated on the change.

CHAPTER THIRTY-SIX

On late Sunday afternoon, Nick drove north to Cardiff-by-the-Sea, a sleepy beach town known for its donut shop. Nick loaded up on a baker's dozen, and ate the thirteenth donut on his way to the safe house. It was located a few blocks inland, at the end of a cul-de-sac. DEA had seized the house a few years back from a biker gang who had used it to cook meth. The hazmat team had scrubbed the house clean. After the property was forfeited to law enforcement, it was kept as a safe house. It was out of the way, no homes backed up to it, and the side neighbors had no direct view of the house.

It was a small three bedroom house with one bath. Its wood floors were in pretty good shape but the kitchen needed remodeling. DEA could probably sell it, "as is", for close to a million dollars. Nick couldn't help comparing it to his sparse apartment that he rented for two grand a month. Maybe it was time to move to Yaak, Montana, and hang out with Drury and Biker Sue.

Pepe was already there when Nick arrived. All four deputy marshals were on the premises. Sitting in the living room was a man Nick almost didn't recognize. Lester Sendow, past accountant for the Baja Norte Familia cartel, now government witness, had lost 40 pounds over the six months he had been living on Molokai. His face was gaunt. He had a weather-beaten tan and his eyes were arresting. Nick had never noticed Lester's eyes before. He couldn't have told you their color. Nick saw they were deep blue, and sparkled. He thought, *What in the hell happened to this guy?*

314

When Lester stood up to shake his hand, Nick noticed the plain crucifix hanging around his neck. That was new. "You're looking great. What's with the new look?—slender, tanned, and an aura of calmness."

"I've changed, I've been accepted as a candidate for priesthood by the Catholic diocese. At the leper colony at Kalaupapa Peninsula, I was only needed a few hours a day to help with the bookkeeping. Elaine's Bar, the gift shop, and the Honolulu diocese were my only 'clients'. It gave me time to hike around the peninsula, and explore the rivers and creeks cascading down from the towering cliffs. The beauty overwhelmed me. I knew God had played a role in such beauty.

"The awe-inspiring surroundings conceal the harsh conditions of eking out a life. One would think that all plants would flourish in the ten square mile wonderland, but they don't because of the volcanic soil. The early Hawaiians living there had to depend on sweet potatoes and taro.

"In 1866, the first victims of the Hawaiian king's policy to isolate lepers were thrown into this harsh paradise, with nothing. Many of the people with Hansen's disease, then called leprosy, died in the early years. People suffered and sacrificed so much until Hawaii finally abolished the isolation policy in 1969, twenty-three long years after Hansen's disease was arrested in the peninsula's residents from a cure found in the early forties. My faith was inspired by many, including Father Damien, now Saint Damien, a Belgian village priest, who came to live on the peninsula in 1873, and built shelters and a church for society's castaways. He died of Hansen's disease in 1889 in the arms of now, Saint Marianne of the Franciscan order, who arrived in 1888. She tended the outcasts until she died in 1918. The sisterhood still cares for the last few residents. Father Damien and Sister Marianne knew that once they stepped upon the peninsula, they could never leave."

"You do seem at peace with yourself. Your nervousness and fidgeting are gone."

"I've placed myself in the hands of God. Once I released myself fully to him, my everyday concerns went away, even the upcoming trial, which used to torment me daily."

"I'm glad you've found relief. However, placing myself in the hands of another, even God's, doesn't come easy to me. I believe one is responsible for one's own actions and people must act to combat the ill behavior of others. I can't just leave it in God's hands."

"We're not that different. I also believe in taking positive, affirmative action. My actions will speak for themselves and hopefully give others some solace. The consequences of everyone's actions are in God's hands. I can't, nor do I want to, control that."

"I could spend the rest of the evening talking religion and philosophy with you, but we need to go over your testimony. We'll disclose your criminal past and your cooperation agreement to the jury upfront. You need to listen to the questions—mine and the defense attorneys', carefully, and answer truthfully."

"That won't be a problem." They spent the next several hours discussing his testimony.

While Nick waited for Judge Orsini to take the bench, he thought about his session with Lester the previous evening. *What a dramatic change. He wondered if it was for real.* Nick had seen a lot of defendants who had conveniently found God before they were to be sentenced for crimes. Nick chastised himself for being so cynical. Lester seemed sincere. He was the prosecution's clean-up hitter—nailing down the three defendants as leaders of the Familia and tying them to the money laundering operations. Nick needed him to do well.

The jury were in their seats, Judge Orsini came to the bench, and the media pool camera was poised when Nick called Lester Sendow to the stand. He had insisted on coming through the public entrance to the courtroom, discounting Nick's entreaties about security concerns.

Lester had to walk between Nick's counsel table and the counsel table where Luis and attorney Lipman sat. As Lester went by, Luis leaned towards him and whispered, "You are *muerto*." Nick always had acute hearing. He was taken aback by Luis' statement of death in open court. Lester glanced at Luis when he made the statement and kept walking towards the witness chair, no expression on his face. Nick waited while Lester took a seat and was sworn in. Nick then asked to approach the bench, with defense counsel, for a sidebar discussion.

Judge Orsini nodded his consent and motioned for the court reporter to come over. "Your Honor, I just heard Defendant Lopez say to Lester Sendow when he passed by, 'You are *muerto*,' meaning, 'You are dead.' I plan to ask Mr. Sendow about it. It's highly relevant, showing an effort by Defendant Lopez to intimidate a witness, and is also relevant to Mr. Sendow's demeanor as a witness."

Luis' attorney, Marc Lipman, immediately responded, "I object to Mr. Drummond's proposed inquiry. If Mr. Drummond is allowed to go into this, I'll call Mr. Drummond as a witness on the purported intimidation. Mr. Drummond, being a witness, must be recused from the rest of the case. Mr. Sterling will have to finish the case on his own."

"This isn't a basis for my recusal from the case. If Mr. Sendow testifies he didn't hear anything when he passed by, that will be the end of it. I won't separately testify to hearing it. If he testifies to what I heard, my testimony will be collateral, and I'll only have become a witness because the defense called me. That's not a basis for my recusal as a prosecutor. As this Court is well aware, prosecutors occasionally accompany law enforcement on search warrants and technically can be witnesses to the execution of those warrants. That doesn't preclude them from later prosecuting the case."

Judge Orsini replied, looking directly at attorney Lipman, "Mr. Drummond will be allowed to make his inquiry. If Mr. Sendow testifies as Mr. Drummond relates, you're free to call Mr. Drummond as your witness for any possible clarification or elaboration. Frankly, I don't see why you'd do that because it'd likely reinforce Mr. Sendow's testimony on the subject matter. If you choose to call Mr. Drummond, that won't be a basis for removing him from the case. Mr. Drummond, you may proceed with your questioning."

"Mr. Sendow, when you walked between counsel tables on the way to the witness stand, did you see or hear anything out of the ordinary?"

Mr. Sendow looked at Luis. "Yes, I did. Mr. Lopez said in a quiet voice to me, 'You are *muerto*.'"

"What do you understand that to mean?"

"*Muerto* is Spanish for 'dead.' I understood it to mean, 'You are dead.'" Nick looked over at the jury. Several were aghast. Nick let it sink in for a moment before moving on to Lester's criminal background and how he met Mr. Lopez and the other defendants. Lester told the jury about his receiving stolen property conviction for embezzling client funds. Lester then described how he ran up a large debt, betting on the ponies. He was referred by his bookie to Mr. Lopez as a person who needed an accountant and could help out with his debt. Lester met Mr. Lopez, and they hit it off, talking about horse racing. Mr. Lopez offered him a $50,000 retainer, the amount of his gambling debt. Mr. Lopez told Lester that he was a wholesaler of agricultural products grown in Mexico. Over the next several months, Lester met the other two defendants, described as business partners, at dinners at Mr. Lopez' compound above Rosarito Beach. They never got into any detail about the type of agricultural products they were selling. They spoke of moving the product throughout the United States and into British Columbia, Canada.

In response to another question, Sendow replied, "We also discussed the movement of cash dollars across the border."

Nick asked, "Did you think the business was above board when you started to work for them?"

"I tried not to think about it. I didn't ask many questions. I liked the money."

"Did you help them with moving U.S. dollars across the border?"

"Yes. Luis told me they had a big cash problem—their buyers were paying for the products in dollars because dollars were a more stable currency than pesos. The defendants' business couldn't deposit the cash dollars into Mexican banks because of Mexico's drastic limits on the amount of cash dollars one could deposit. Mr. Lopez told me that they were delivering the cash dollars to a chain of Mexican exchange houses, called Numero Uno, that for a three percent fee Numero Uno would courier the money across the border, deposit it in U.S. border banks, and then wire the money to a Mexican financial account.

The Mexican regulations don't restrict the wire transfer of dollars to Mexican accounts or even the deposit of checks in dollars—only the deposit of cash dollars. The defendants were concerned about a couple of the exchange house couriers being busted by the feds for transporting over $10,000 in cash across the border without declaring it."

"Did you help them out with this process?"

"Yes, I told them to use legitimate business partners to transport the cash across the border and have those people declare the currency on the U.S. Treasury form, which is called the Currency Monetary Instrument Report. If the cash is declared at the border, it is perfectly legal to bring it across. Once the cash is across, I told them to deposit the full amount into a U.S. bank. I told the defendants not to worry about the filing of a Currency Transaction Report(CTR) by the banks for cash deposits in excess of $10,000. I explained to them that the banks were trained about criminal enterprises structuring cash deposits under $10,000 to avoid the filing of a CTR. The structured cash deposits trigger banks to file Suspicious Activity Reports(SARs). Law enforcement has access to SARs and reads these reports. Law enforcement doesn't look at CTRs unless an investigation has already commenced."

"So, did they change their business model for bringing the cash over and depositing it in U.S. banks?"

"Yes, they followed my suggestions. Further, they used two businesses that they had worked with, L&M Freight, operated by Hector Morales, a trucking business, and Latin America Productos, an import-export food business, owned by the Sakias. The businesses took the money across and deposited it in their U.S. accounts. Then the money was either wired to the Mexican account under the defendants' control, or cashier's checks were written to the Mexican account."

"Did you ever meet with Mr. Morales and the Sakias?"

"Yes. I met with them several times. They had business offices on both sides of the border. They appeared to be running legitimate businesses. One of the Sakias' businesses, World Food Imports, had numerous warehouses in the United States and Canada."

"Where exactly?"

"In Otay Mesa, Salt Lake City, Missoula, Chicago, Vancouver, and New Orleans. There may have been others." Nick thought, *Shit!, we missed the New Orleans warehouse.*

Nick continued with the questioning about the movement of cash. Lester corroborated the agents' testimony about the U.S.-based accounts, and confirmed that the two front companies, combined, were moving about a $5.5 million in cash, per month, across the border into various U.S. border banks and then immediately transferring the money to a Mexican account.

Nick then directed Lester through his adventures in Yaak, Montana. Lester described Biker Sue down to the blue bandana wrapped around her head. He told the jury how he and Mr. Lopez had stood out in the brand new Escalade in a wilderness of cowboys and pickups. He described Biker Sue's quizzical look when they asked about property for a corporate retreat by the Canadian border. She told them about Yaak and various logging roads on either side of the border that could be used for corporate bonding through off-road, four-wheeling. She suggested they get some jeans and cowboy boots, or at least tennis shoes, to fit in better. He and Mr. Lopez later drove around Yaak and found a logging road which led to the Canadian border.

Lester explained he was surprised, when about a month later, Mr. Lopez told him to meet him at Lindbergh Field—they were flying to Spokane, Washington, in a private jet where they would rent a car and go over to Yaak for some R&R. At the turnout to the logging road, they met up with two Hispanics, driving a flatbed truck with two Ranger four-wheelers. Lester described how he watched them unload the off-road vehicles and throw duffel bags in the back of each one. Lester could smell the odor of marijuana.

Nick asked, "Did you say anything to Defendant Lopez at the time?"

"Yes. I asked him what was going on. He looked at me and smiled. He said, '200 pounds of marijuana and 50 kilos of black tar heroin are in those bags. The penalty for federal drug distribution is 20 years. You're one of us now. No going back.' He took me by my shoulders and had a callous glint in his eye. He asked, 'You understand what I mean by no going back?'"

"I stuttered a response, 'I did.'"

"What happened next?"

Mr. Lopez and I got in one of the off-road vehicles, he was driving, and the two Hispanics got into the other. We drove close to five miles along the logging road until we saw two posts and a chain with a sign that said, *Canadian Border Ahead, Do not Cross.* We got out and lugged the duffle bags to a small clearing at the actual border. Within a few minutes, a pickup truck drove up from the Canadian side. We exchanged duffle bags. We brought the bags back to the flatbed truck at which time the bags and the off-road vehicles were loaded onto the truck."

"Did anyone say anything when you were back at the flatbed?"

"Mr. Lopez said, 'Mr. Money Man Accountant, have you ever seen two duffel bags full of 100 dollar bills?' Before I could answer, he unzipped the bags. Stacks and stacks of $100 bills were banded together."

"Did you think there was any way out for you after defendant Lopez brought you along on the drug exchange?"

"No, I thought my life was finished until you and your agent approached me about turning state's evidence and being placed in a protective witness program."

"Did you have an attorney who went over a cooperation agreement with you?"

"Yes. It depended on my complete cooperation and truthful testimony. I would plead guilty to one money laundering count and one drug distribution count, and would serve no more than three years in prison. It'd be up to the judge to sentence me within the three year parameter."

"Did you have an occasion to wear a wire as part of the investigation?"

"Yes. I wore a wire when I met Mr. Sakia at his business office and when I met Hector Morales at his business office. We discussed their money laundering operations for the cartel."

"Your Honor, I won't be asking any questions about the taped conversations with this witness because the tapes have already been played for the jury through the agent monitoring the conversations."

"Thank you Mr. Drummond. I'm glad you're conscious of not wasting the jury's time."

Nick moved on to a highlight of Lester's testimony. "A couple of weeks before we initially approached you about cooperation, did you go to Defendant Lopez' compound?"

"Yes."

"When you had been at the compound before, had you seen a young lady in defendant Lopez' company?"

"Yes, Felicia."

"Was she there on your last visit before we contacted you?"

"No, I asked Mr. Lopez where she was. He said, 'We wouldn't be seeing that Bitch anymore. She was being taken care of.'"

"What did you understand that to mean?"

Mr. Lipman immediately rose and said, "Objection, calls for speculation and it's irrelevant what Mr. Sendow thought the statement meant."

Judge Orsini sustained the objection, "The jury is capable of giving whatever weight and meaning to the statement it chooses." Nick gave the jury a puzzled look, trying to convey that an answer to his question should have been allowed. Judge Orsini gave Nick a hard look and Nick moved on.

"Please describe defendant Lopez' appearance at that time."

"His right arm was in a sling. I saw blood seeping through. I asked him what had happened. He replied, 'Nothing, just twisted my shoulder a bit.'" "Did you ask him how he had blood seeping through when he had just twisted his shoulder a bit?"

"No, I knew when to keep quiet."

A prosecution timeline showed that Lester saw Luis' bloody arm shortly after the Donzi ocean racer engaged in a shoot out with the Coast Guard during the early morning smuggling operation. Nick had no further questions.

The defense poked around quite a bit. They tried to portray Lester as an untrustworthy criminal, who'd say anything for law enforcement to save his own skin. It didn't seem to stick with the jury. Lester answered each of their questions calmly and fully. He never got defensive. The defense wasn't able to rattle him. They wisely gave up after attorney Flanigan asked, "You seem awfully calm up there, are you on any drugs or medication?"

Lester smiled, "I'm not on any drugs or medication. I feel better than I have ever felt in my life. I'm in God's hands, I'm a candidate for the Catholic priesthood."

Nick couldn't help but notice that one of the last jurors impaneled, a Hispanic woman, in her forties, who was active in community affairs, was wearing a crucifix much like the one Lester was wearing.

Nick called Pepe as his last witness for the day. Pepe described how, a week after the Coast Guard interdiction of the drug smuggling, he was an observer with the Baja Norte State Police in their safety inspection of the Rosarito Beach harbor. They inspected defendant Lopez' enclosed boat dock and took photos of his 22-foot Donzi Classic ocean racer. Nick displayed the photos to the jury which showed multiple bullet holes along the right side and top of the boat.

The defense knew better than to question Pepe at length. Nick thought, *All things considered, a very good day.*

CHAPTER THIRTY-SEVEN

Nick only had two witnesses left to call in his case-in-chief. A forensic scientist, who could trace the tar heroin seized in the investigation to a 10-mile strip of land in the coastal mountains of the state of Sinaloa, and a DEA agent who took samples of soil along the 10-mile strip and other regions of Mexico. Nick was holding back Felicia's cousin Alan for rebuttal. He was gambling on Luis, and the other defendants, putting on alibi evidence to try to demonstrate they had nothing to do with the motorcycle drive-by shooting. Alan's testimony would remind the jury at the end of the case about the shooting in Aunt Rosa's front yard that almost killed Ana.

The morning evidence went in smoothly. The DEA agent explained that he was part of a joint project with Mexico to take soil samples at various agricultural regions of Mexico known to produce marijuana or poppies. Two years ago, the agent and his Mexican counterparts took several soil samples from a 10-mile stretch of coastal land in the state of Sinaloa, known for the production of poppies for the Baja Norte Familia cartel. The project resulted in hundreds of soil samples throughout Mexico's illicit grow regions. The agent described the protocol for withdrawing the samples from the ground—packaging each sample in a vacuum sealed container and personally delivering the samples to the DEA lab for analysis.

Dr. Len Trotter, employed by the DEA lab in Washington D.C., related his curriculum vitae to the jury. He had doctorate degrees in microbiology, as well as pedology, the study of soil. The first ten years of his professional career consisted of working with major vintners in California and France, studying the soils in wine producing regions and quantifying the soil profiles that were most effective in producing high quality grapes. For the last 15 years, Dr. Trotter had been working for the main DEA lab in Washington D.C., analyzing the mineral components of illicit drugs, derived from plants. He spoke of a five-year project that consisted of analyzing the mineral components of heroin seized by law enforcement, and tracing them to specific geographic regions in the world by matching a drug sample with a soil sample taken from the particular poppy grow region.

Dr. Trotter testified that the various amounts of Mexican black tar heroin, seized in the Baja Norte Familia investigation, were analyzed for their exact mineral components. The profiles of each batch of heroin seized, which included exact percentages of calcium, iron, magnesium, nitrates, phosphates, and potassium, were remarkably similar. The profiles were then compared to the soil samples taken from the 10-mile coastal region of the state of Sinaloa, as well as other poppy growing regions in Mexico. Dr. Trotter opined that the tar heroin seized in this case came from the tested coastal area in Sinaloa.

Nick didn't want to go into too much detail with Dr. Trotter. He wanted to keep the jurors interested. He believed he had accomplished this with the assistance of several color graphs depicting the soil and heroin mineral compositions. Let the defense bore the jurors on cross-examination. The defense took the bait and had Dr. Trotter on the stand for hours with questions about the lab's scientific protocols.

Nick only had one question on redirect. "Dr. Trotter, considering all the questions by defense counsel over the last few hours, has your opinion as to the origin of the black tar heroin changed?

"No. The black tar heroin seized in this case came from a 10-mile mountainous region along the coast of the state of Sinaloa, Mexico."

"Thank you Doctor. No further questions. The People rest."

Judge Orsini informed the jury, "The People have completed their presentation of evidence in their case-in-chief. The defense now has the opportunity to present evidence. They'll start tomorrow, as it is almost 4:30. Have a good evening. Remember don't discuss the case with anyone, or watch or listen to anything about this case. You're excused. See you tomorrow at 9:00."

Nick had a strong feeling of relief as he packed up his briefcases. Lester's testimony the day before had gone well and although today's testimony lacked the *wow* factor Nick would have preferred to leave the jury with, it was still interesting and solid. Any boredom today was attributed to the exhaustive defense questioning. The prosecution's evidence over the entirety of the case went in well.

Nick liked to evaluate his performance and the case at every important milestone of a trial. Nick believed that his performance, and how well a case went in, weren't entirely predicated by a jury's verdict of guilty or not guilty. Sometimes, he wasn't at his best and the jury still came back with a guilty verdict. Others times he felt he had performed like Clarence Darrow and the jury came back with a not guilty verdict. One case like that still bothered Nick. It was an assault with a deadly weapon case where the victim lost vision in one eye. The jury came back with a not guilty verdict, buying the defendant's self-defense claim. The real problem with the case was that the victim looked and spoke like a stereotype dirt-ball defendant, while the defendant was a school teacher, tall, handsome, and well-spoken. The jury believed that the defendant, who could have lived next door to them or taught their kids, had been reasonably provoked by the victim's angry words into swinging a baseball bat to the victim's head. Nick learned a long time ago to never take a jury for granted.

It had been two weeks of defense witnesses. A seemingly endless parade of businessmen from both sides of the border, espousing that the three defendants were legitimate businessmen. This was interspersed with alibi witnesses and the wonderful things the defendants had done for the community.

Nick and Josh made their points where they could on cross-examination. Contrary to the defense contention that Mexican businesses were paid in cash dollars, the Mexican businessmen acknowledged, on cross-examination, that they were often paid by check, credit card or pesos. Additionally, Nick and Josh knocked out most of their community "enhancement" witnesses on relevancy grounds.

The defense made a tactical blunder when they called the Chief Finance Officer for Numero Uno, a chain of Mexican casas de cambio, or exchange houses, as a witness. The CFO testified that his chain of casas had engaged in legitimate business with the defendants for the transport of cash dollars to the U.S. from the defendants' sale of Mexican grown food. He spoke of his and the defendants' mutual friend, Armando Ruiz Castillo, a high level official in Mexico's Secretaria de Hacienda y Credito—Mexico's Department of Treasury. The name registered in Nick's mind. Nick leaned over to Pepe and told him to call the office and check the name out. Pepe came back a few minutes later, and passed a note to Nick. Nick glanced down and smiled.

Nick's cross-examination focused on the mutual friend, Señor Castillo, and how often the defendants and the CFO met with him. The CFO described many dinners, as well as all of them attending Señor Castillo's daughter's wedding. Nick confirmed that Señor Castillo's office was located on the Plaza Reforma, on the fringe of the Zona Rosa in Mexico City. He also confirmed that Señor Castillo, because of his high rank in the government, was afforded diplomatic immunity when he visited the United States. Nick, by his questioning, appeared to be duly impressed, leading the CFO to elaborate about the closeness of their relationships. Nick asked a final question of the CFO, "By the way, do you know a San Diego-based accountant named Lester Sendow?"

This question paid off for Nick when the CFO replied, "I don't know any Lester Sendow." This destroyed the defense contention that any money laundering was set up by Lester and wasn't known by the defendants. Nick couldn't wait to put on rebuttal evidence that the one Mexican bank account, which millions of dollars flowed into from U.S. banks, was in the name of Armando Ruiz Castillo.

Nick paid close attention to defense witness Javier Esquel-Ranchez. Javier testified he graduated from the University of Mexico in economics and went to law school for a year before moving on to business endeavors. He was rather vague about what business or businesses he was involved in. It appeared that he had family money and had traveled quite a bit. He professed to be a family friend of defendants Luis Hernandez-Lopez and Mateo Gomez-Encinas. He was well-spoken, sophisticated, and a bit too slick. He reminded Nick of a younger version of defendant Lopez. Javier provided Luis with an alibi for when Ana was gunned down by the rider on the Ducati Streetfighter motorcycle. But he acknowledged that Luis had a motorcycle that was the same model and color as the shooter's. Javier testified that he and Luis had taken a three day motorcycle camping trip around Guadalupe Valley, Baja Norte's wine country. He remembered that the third day of the trip corresponded to the date of the shooting. He waxed on about the fine wines they tasted. Javier particularly liked the red organic wines of La Casa de Dona Lupe and the Cab and Merlot at Monte Tanic. Nick had Pepe go into the hallway and google the wineries. They checked out.

On cross-examination, Nick tried to show that Javier didn't know anything about camping. Javier fended that off well. He testified they just had a tent, air mattresses and sleeping bags. They ate out at all of the fine restaurants nearby.

Nick bit his tongue and asked the risky question, "How do you remember the exact dates of your camping trip?"

Nick paid for the answer, "The third night was my grandfather's birthday and I called to wish him a happy birthday." Javier was sorry, but he didn't have his grandfather's phone number or address with him. "He lives in Guadalajara."

Nick knew that greater Guadalajara was the second largest urban area in Mexico, with over four million people. The grandfather wouldn't be easy to track down. Nick had to hand it to Javier. He was well-prepared and smart with his answers. The Mexican authorities couldn't realistically track down whether or not Javier and Luis camped for three nights because campers usually paid in cash, and there was no documentation. If Javier had testified he stayed at a hotel in Guadalupe Valley, that could be checked out. Nick chalked the witness up. One win for the bad guys.

Back at the office, after Javier testified, Nick had Jerry run all the criminal databases on Javier Esquel-Ranchez. He came back clean. The next day Jerry told Nick that he checked with a Mexican contact working in Mexico City. His contact confirmed that Javier was an alumni from the University of Mexico, with a Bachelor of Science degree in economics.

After another day of defense witnesses, the trial was turned over to Nick and Josh for their rebuttal witnesses. They only had a few. The judge, the jury, the attorneys, and probably even the defendants were getting tired of the trial. It was time to wrap it up.

Nick's first witness was a business professor at a local community college, who specialized in U.S. and Mexico businesses along the border. He had been born in Mexico and had owned businesses on both sides of the border before becoming a professor. In addition to his academic pursuits, he was a consultant, advising businesses on both sides of the border about import duties, trade paperwork, and border business practices. Professor Ramirez came across very well. He even wore the standard college professor attire—a corduroy sport coat with elbow patches, no tie, and loafers. Professor Ramirez explained to the jury that although some businesses in Mexico paid in U.S. dollars, the vast majority paid in pesos. The small businesses who bought legitimate, Mexican grown agricultural products had pesos. Their customers paid pesos for the food at their retail stores. Professor Ramirez further explained that large corporate clients of a wholesale agricultural products business would normally pay by check or credit card. Those were the most effective methods to keep track of their corporate business transactions. The defense worked hard on finding chinks in Professor Ramirez' armor. They managed to get him to say that it was possible that some businesses would pay their wholesalers in cash dollars.

Nick eagerly looked forward to his next witness. He was the Vice-President in charge of Mexico-U.S. operations of the U.S. correspondent bank for the Mexican bank, Banco Real. A Mexican bank has to have a U.S. correspondent bank to facilitate and oversee fund transfers to its bank from all U.S. banks. Banco Real held the account into which the cartel's money laundering operatives transmitted funds after the cash dollars were transported and deposited in U.S. border banks. The U.S. correspondent bank had access to Banco Real's account information in order to facilitate the transfers. Nick projected the various summary charts which summarized all the wire transfers and cashier's checks written to the Banco Real account. For a year, over five million dollars a month went from the U.S.-based border accounts, held by L&M Freight, owned by Hector Morales, and Latin America Productos, owned by Mr. and Mrs. Sakia, to the one Mexican account with Banco Real.

Nick asked the witness, "Who is the account holder of the Banco Real account?"

The Vice-President answered, "Armando Ruiz Castillo, address, 3798-1 Plaza Reforma, Mexico City, Mexico."

"Do the account documents list his occupation?

"Yes. He lists his occupation as Asistente Secretaria De Hacienda."

"Are you familiar with that title?"

"Yes. It's the Assistant Secretary of Mexico's Department of Treasury.

"Quite high up?'

"You can only go one step higher."

The defense didn't have any questions, futilely trying to convey to the jury that the evidence had no bearing on the case.

Nick had saved Felicia's cousin, Alan, for his last witness. He wanted to bring the violence of the motorcycle shooting back to the jury's attention and show how the cartel's influence permeated San Diego communities. The most important part of the trial for Nick was to see Luis go down on the conspiracy to murder count.

Alan described his horror when he was told by Detective Mario Cipriani of the shooting earlier in the day, how his cousin Felicia was almost killed, and how Agent Schwartz had taken a couple of bullets to protect her. He told the jury he was unable to breathe and almost fainted onto the high school gym floor.

Alan related that the day before the shooting, he had run into a couple of older guys from the neighborhood, who were Baja Norte

Familia "wannabees". They asked him about his hot cousin, Felicia, and made jokes about getting into her pants. Alan told them she was coming home the next day, "But there wasn't a chance in hell that they could get into her pants."

Alan teared up on the stand and told the jury how he blamed himself. His statement was stricken, but it still made an impact on the jury. Nick only had a few more questions for Alan.

"Alan, did you ever see the two guys again?"

"Yes, a couple of weeks after the shooting at the same mall."

"What did they say to you, if anything?"

"They told me, 'Felicia got lucky. The Familia never misses twice. You tell us the next time she comes into town or you'll be the one dodging bullets.'"

"Are you afraid today, that someone will put bullets into you?"

Attorney Lipman bounced up, "Objection, irrelevant, and violates rule 403!"

Nick responded, "It's highly relevant, goes to his demeanor and willingness to testify." Nick knew it was relevant but was worried that Judge Orsini might sustain the objection under rule 403 of the Federal Rules of Evidence, which prohibits unduly prejudicial evidence.

Judge Orsini thought for a few moments, looking at the witness and the defendants, and then ruled, "You can answer the question young man."

Alan shrunk down in the witness chair. He averted his eyes from the defendants and looked at the judge. In a soft voice, he murmured, "I've been so afraid since they threatened me. I've hardly been able to sleep. But I felt I had to testify for Felicia's sake."

The defense crossed Alan and presented a couple of short, unimportant rebuttal witnesses. Nick and Josh didn't put on any sur-rebuttal witnesses. All the evidence was before the jury. In mid-afternoon, Judge Orsini recessed the trial until the next morning for closing arguments.

CHAPTER THIRTY-EIGHT

Nick was at his desk working on his closing arguments. The prosecutor has the first closing argument, or opening argument, and after the defense argues, the prosecutor has the final, or rebuttal, closing argument. The prosecutor gets two arguments to one for each defense attorney because a prosecutor must prove his case beyond a reasonable doubt.

Nick and Josh had jotted down notes during the trial about what Nick could use in his closing arguments. The weekend before, Nick had made a list of the exhibits he wanted to show the jury during the opening argument. He also pulled his file marked, *closing arguments*, which contained their trial notes as well as argument themes that Nick wrote down while preparing the case for trial. Now he had to integrate the material into cogent opening and rebuttal arguments.

Nick had four hours before his moot or practice opening argument for Josh, Pepe, Ana, and Rona. Nick had always pooh-poohed giving a practice argument before the real thing until he was talked into it in a complex fraud case that he had tried in federal court in Los Angeles a number of years back. The typical draconian federal judge had only given him three hours to argue three months of testimony and 800 exhibits. On the eve of that argument, Nick was in his fourth hour of stumbling through a disjointed, passionless practice argument when he realized he really needed to get his act together. The young federal co-prosecutor had a look of, *Oh shit, we're in trouble*, but the lead agent, a Vietnam Vet that had been through hell, assured everyone that Nick would do fine. As it turned out, the agent was right, but it took another four hours for Nick to clean it up.

At six o'clock, Nick was surprised to hear his phone ring. Everyone on his team knew that he was working furiously on his opening argument and not to bother him. Attorney General Ken Hammond was on the phone, the last person Nick wanted to talk to. The General wasted Nick's valuable time offering his unsolicited advice on what to emphasize in his arguments. Nick finally couldn't take it anymore.

"I've been listening to you General for twenty minutes on the eve of my opening argument. You're wasting my time. I have to get back to work."

"How dare you talk to me like that. I've heard about you. The scuttlebutt from the San Diego office is that you're a washed up drunk."

"Excuse me General. You're telling me I'm washed up. You, whose most significant trial was a misdemeanor domestic violence case. Why don't you go back to being a politician. Don't interfere with someone who's working on substance."

"That's it. You're fired!"

"Am I? I know you aren't used to someone standing up to you. Probably hasn't happened in a decade. Instead of worrying about firing me, worry about actually doing the job the people elected you to do. How about doing what is in the best interest of the people of California instead of your interest in getting elected to the next office? How about timely reviewing the important legal papers that cross your desk, instead of waiting until the last minute because you're too busy fundraising, making political hay or just plain indecisive? How about appointing competent people to top spots in your administration, instead of political hacks who don't know what they're doing? Who are you going to get to fire me? Donald Trump? Or maybe, your second in command, who we not-so-fondly refer to as 'Hot Dog' Barrett. She doesn't even know how to find her way to San Diego. She only knows how to smell out the next press conference for you."

"You, you, you, ingrate!"

"Is that the best you've got General? Go ahead and fire me the evening before my opening argument when I'm going to hand our office convictions in the highest profile case we've had in decades. How would that look when you make your run for Governor or Senator next year? Goodnight General."

Nick actually felt good when he hung up the phone. It invigorated him. Maybe the 20 minute delay was worth it.

Nick's dry run later that evening went fairly well. He received valuable input—what to tighten up, and a few things to add. After putting the finishing touches on his argument, Nick was able to get six hours of sleep. Nick never was one of those who could work all night and function well the next day, either on a college exam or in an important trial. He needed his sleep. Nick looked at a trial as being an ultra marathon. He had to be in good physical shape, he needed daily exercise and sufficient sleep each night. The only way you could avoid long nights during trial was by thorough trial preparation. A steady diet of 60 to 70 hour weeks in trial prep and in trial was far superior to inadequate trial prep, and 90 to 100 hour weeks in trial.

Nick's opening argument lasted the entire morning. He kept the jury's attention, walking around some and modulating his voice to emphasize important points. The exhibits and various projected power points helped educate the jury and kept their interest. Nick emphasized the evidence supporting the counts of the indictment concerning the drive-by motorcycle shooting. Cartel head Encinas had already avoided liability for those counts when they were dismissed for lack of evidence against him prior to trial. Defendants Lopez and Sanchez were still facing those charges. The conspiracy to murder Felicia count would add another 20 years to their sentences, and the assault with a deadly weapon, with serious bodily injury as to Ana, would add quite a few more. Nick knew these were the weakest counts in the indictment because of the lack of strong proof tying Lopez and Sanchez directly to the shooting. But Nick was heartened when he saw a few of the jurors affirmatively nodding their heads when he went through the evidence on the counts.

Nick covered all the drug distribution counts and the money laundering counts. He was fairly confident the jury would come back with guilty verdicts on these counts. Nick also focused on the Continuing Criminal Enterprise count because it packed such a big punch—20 years to life. The jury had to be persuaded that the three defendants had supervisory roles in the drug distribution organization, a series of drug sales occurred, and the defendants each obtained substantial income from the enterprise. The evidence clearly supported the count.

The three defense attorneys spent the entire afternoon and the next day giving their respective arguments. Nick took notes of the defense arguments while Josh was in charge of objecting. As Nick's fingers started cramping from taking notes, he wished they had ordered "dailies" from the court reporter. For a substantial additional expense, the court reporter would type up transcripts of each day's testimony or argument and present it to the paying attorney the next day. The government didn't want to pony up the extra money. What was that saying? *Penny wise, pound foolish.*

The defense didn't have much evidence to work with except for the lack of compelling evidence tying defendants Lopez and Sanchez to the motorcycle shooting. In particular, Lopez' attorney spent a lot of time on the shooting-related counts and Lopez' motorcycle camping trip alibi.

All three defense attorneys spent significant time attacking the credibility of the prosecution's two key witnesses, Felicia and Lester, knowing that if they were discredited, much of the prosecution's case would fall apart. They portrayed Felicia as a gold digger and spurned girlfriend, who made up stories about the defendants to please law enforcement and save her backside from a cocaine possession for sale charge. They portrayed Lester as a convicted criminal that couldn't be trusted to tell the truth. They railed against the sweet deal given Lester by the prosecution—up to only three years in prison. They argued this was just another example of the government misplacing its resources, spending all this money on witness relocation for Lester when he was the architect of any money laundering that may have occurred. The defense claimed their clients didn't know what Lester was doing with the money. They hired him as a professional accountant to take care of it. They argued that Lester lied about the defendants' knowledge for the same reason that Felicia lied, to save his own bacon.

Nick studied the jury to see if they were receptive to the defense's character assassination of his two key witnesses. Most of them weren't buying it. With a few, however, he couldn't tell. Nick needed to prop up Felicia and Lester in his rebuttal argument.

Nick started his rebuttal argument by refuting various purported facts that the defense argued. He told the jury that a legitimate business, the size of defendants' purported wholesale agricultural business, which brought in revenues of at least five and a half million dollars per month, didn't get paid in cash dollars. He reminded the jurors that even the defendants' business witnesses testified, on cross-examination, that a business would be paid in a combination of cash dollars, pesos, checks and credit cards.

Nick also hammered home the fact, based on the defense's own witness, the CFO of Numero Uno, that the defendants were the close friends of Mexico's Assistant Treasury Secretary, Armando Castillo—even going to his daughter's wedding. Castillo being the same man who held the account with Banco Real which was the payee of all the wire transfers and cashier's checks from the money laundering operations. He was the same man who had diplomatic immunity if he traveled to the United States. There was no reason to transmit the money to Castillo's account if the defendants were operating a legitimate business. Also, the CFO of Numero Uno didn't know accountant Sendow. Thus, Nick emphasized, it was clear the defendants were the ones who set up the framework for the cartel's money laundering operations, not Sendow.

Nick passionately argued how brave Felicia and Sendow were to testify in light of the Familia's violence. How they had given up their normal lives to be whisked away into a witness protection program.

"You saw them testify—their demeanor and how they fully answered each of the defense questions, with nothing to hide. They were straightforward in an emotionally charged atmosphere. You're the sole judges of witness credibility. All the circumstances of this case fit together and demonstrate that they told you the truth."

Nick continued to make his points, leading up to his summation that defendants Lopez and Sanchez knew about and approved the motorcycle assassination attempt on Felicia. Rona had prepared an eye-catching power point presentation which brought up, in different bright colors, the key facts that supported the conspiracy murder count against the two defendants.

The next to last power point slides showed a matronly looking woman putting ingredients in a tin for apple pie. The final slide showed a delicious looking pie being removed from the oven, the crust slightly browned and hot apple cinnamon syrup bubbling up from holes in the crust.

Nick told the jury, "It takes a number of special ingredients to make Mom's apple pie. One or two ingredients aren't enough. But when you put them all together, you know it's Mom's apple pie. Like Mom's apple pie, you've heard all of the evidentiary ingredients that lead to only one conclusion, that beyond a reasonable doubt, defendants Lopez and Sanchez are guilty of the conspiracy to murder and the assault with a deadly weapon charges."

Nick concluded, in an impassioned voice, looking directly in each juror's eyes in turn, "I request that you return guilty verdicts on all counts against all defendants because the evidence compels guilty verdicts. Felicia's middle name, Esperanza, means *hope* in Spanish. Our society has one compelling hope, that there'll be justice. The return of guilty verdicts is justice in this case. Thank you for your attention and service."

Nick was mentally exhausted during the time Judge Orsini read the jury instructions. He had Josh pay close attention to the instructions to ensure the judge properly delivered them to the jury. Nick just looked blankly at the judge, pretending to listen. He thought about how much he had been through in this case. How much the entire team had been through, especially Ana. After the instructions were read, the jury was sequestered in the jury room to pick a foreperson. Because it was so late in the day, Judge Orsini told the jury that once they picked a foreperson, they could go home for the weekend and start their deliberations on Monday morning.

This was the first weekend in months that Nick didn't have trial prep or trial work hanging over his head. A full weekend for anything he wanted to do. Friday night he just went home and slept for 14 hours. On Saturday, he went to his son's Little League game. Judy had called him on Saturday morning to congratulate him on finishing the case. She had followed it on the news. She knew how much he had put into it and how relieved he must feel now that the trial was over. They fell back into a nearly forgotten pattern of conversation. Nick shared case insights with Judy. Judy caught Nick up on what the kids had been doing the last couple of months. Judy ended the conversation by saying, "Come to Jake's baseball game, I'll pack us a picnic lunch."

Nick watched the game, sitting between Judy and Gabriella. Gabriella snuggled up next to him, sitting on grass above the field. Judy even held his hand for a short time. It reminded Nick of how wonderful the good times were with his family before Judy and he had grown apart. Jake played well—he had two hits and pitched a couple of innings. The game went down to the bottom of the sixth where the opposing team's eighth batter, who had struck out two times, was up with the bases loaded and two outs. Jake's team was ahead by one run. On a two-strike count, the closer threw an inside fastball. The hitter turned away and brought up his bat in self-defense. The ball hit the handle and looped over the first baseman's outstretched glove. The opposing team was screaming for the stunned batter to run to first base. He finally got going and raced down the line. Two runs were going to score. Jake's team had to get the batter out at first base. The throw came in. Nick thought it was in time. The umpire behind home plate yelled, "Safe! Tie base goes to the runner!" It was over, Jake's team had lost at the last possible moment by a fluke. Nick hoped it wasn't a bad omen for his case.

Nick got another surprise call during the weekend. On Saturday evening, the Commissioner of the Attorney General's Basketball Association, better known as the AGBA, called. The Commissioner, Tommy Daly, had the thankless task of trying to rouse his out-of-shape attorney colleagues to play basketball. Anywhere from six to eight weekend warriors played, all dreaming of better days when they could jump high and finish a drive to the basket. Most didn't bother to dream that they could make a three-point basket. A game was set at the Coronado High School gym at seven, Sunday morning. One of the other AGBA ballers had a key to the gym. Nick told Tommy he'd be there. Nick called his good buddy from the office, Cam Anthony, to get a ride to the gym. It was kind of on the way for Cam. Cam reluctantly agreed, "It's only because I haven't seen your ugly mug in person in a few months while you've been off cavorting with the media."

Nick replied, "Yeah, its been a relaxing few months, just messing around. Don't you think my best profile is from the left side?"

"Only if you want people to turn off the news."

Commissioner Tommy went over the AGBA ground rules for the two graduate law students who were interning at the office. "Only two things you young guys have to remember, no jumping, and you don't call steps on the old guys if you ever want a job at the AG's office." By AGBA standards, it was a good game. No one pulled a muscle or sprained an ankle. The Commish even sank a three, Nick had a pull-up basket that reminded him of the old days, and Cam threw a few well-placed elbows in Nick's gut. The only attorney who had kept a decent portion of his skills, probably because he was quite a bit younger than the senior statesmen of the AGBA, was Cleve Ryder. He could still shoot and jump. Needless to say, he dominated. The two young interns guarded each other. They didn't want to show skills in case Tommy was being serious about getting a job.

On the way back, Nick opened up to his old buddy. Cam had a way with people where they felt comfortable confiding in him. For a lot of the younger deputies, he was "Uncle Cam". Nick was very private. He could count the people he confided in on one hand. Nick told Cam about Ana. Cam feigned disbelief, "There's no way she would go for you. She's too hot. Did you get overheated at the gym? You must be hallucinating."

Nick responded in kind, "Some of us still have it Cam. I'm sorry that your days of attracting the ladies are over. That doesn't mean you can't be happy for me. Jealousy doesn't become you. On second thought, drop a few lbs., buy a sports car, keep dying your hair, and there's a chance even you can make a comeback with the ladies."

"Hey asshole. Just because you have grey hair, doesn't mean I do. You're looking at the unvarnished me—full head of jet black hair, virile, engaging, a catch for any attractive lady, even decades younger."

"Okay. Enough with the B.S. What do you think I should do about Ana and Judy? You know Judy and I have been separated for over a year. Yesterday, on the phone, and at Jake's ballgame, she finally showed some interest and affection."

"Up until the last six months, you kept telling me you wanted to get back with her, but she wasn't interested. What has changed?"

"My feelings for Ana have changed. We've been through a lot in this case. I think about her all the time. I had put Judy out of my mind. She hadn't shown any interest in getting back together until yesterday."

"Your call Nick. Don't rush into anything. Things will work themselves out. Bottom line, follow your heart. But know it's your heart, not your dick."

"Thanks Dr. Phil. Enough of the touchy feely."

"What about the case? How does it look?"

"I feel good about the case—it went in well. I think we'll get guilty verdicts on most of the counts. The ones I'm worried about and really want, are the murder conspiracy count and assault with a deadly weapon count where Ana took a couple of bullets and almost bled out. I know that bastard Lopez was behind it. He's a sociopath. He beat up his girlfriend Felicia and tried to have her killed twice, once by the motorcycle drive-by where Ana was shot and once when a few crazies leveled the safe house in Topeka where Felicia was staying as a protected witness."

"I remember seeing that on the news. The house was completely destroyed. Didn't they use a rocket propelled grenade launcher and a 50 caliber machine gun?"

"Yes. Felicia survived by hiding in a storm cellar and Ana almost died again, crashing into a pole to avoid machine gun fire as she approached the house. I know Lopez was behind it, but I can't prove it. This is hush-hush, nobody outside the case knows about the connection."

"Your secret is safe with me."

The rest of the ride was standard guy talk—Chargers football, Aztec basketball being the only team that didn't suck, movies Nick hadn't seen, and a good looking new hire at work that Nick hadn't met yet. Nick's and Cam's immediate boss, Arch Waterford, had a penchant for hiring tall, comely blonds, while at the same time writing persuasive, sometimes caustic appellate briefs. Nick liked that. Occasionally, defendants and their appellate attorneys deserved to be tweaked.

Nick enjoyed talking to Cam about everyday things. He was sorry to say good-bye when Cam dropped him off at his apartment.

CHAPTER THIRTY-NINE

On Monday morning, Judge Orsini had a few more instructions for the jury about the process of deliberations. He told them to consider all the evidence and the points of view of the other jurors, who each have unique life experiences. However, ultimately each juror's vote reflects his or her own belief, based on the evidence.

Nick was pleased that the foreperson was the Hispanic woman with strong family values and active ties to the community.

After the jury was excused, Judge Orsini told the attorneys they could go back to their offices and be on twenty-minute call for any jury questions or verdicts. The defense attorneys agreed their clients didn't have to be brought over from the holding facility for jury questions or requests for testimony to be read back.

In mid-afternoon, the jury requested the court reporter to read back Felicia's direct examination—an excellent sign for the prosecution. Nick studied the jury while the court reporter read. They all listened intently. They exhibited very few facial expressions. Nick couldn't get a feel for what they were thinking. The jury still seemed to be getting along well as a group. Throughout the trial, Nick noticed that the jurors were talking together in the hallway during the recesses. It wasn't always the same few who talked to each other; the jurors mixed it up socially which was also a very good sign. Nick wanted a jury that got along, respected each other, and hopefully felt the need to reach a consensus, a guilty verdict on each count.

The next morning, Nick was sitting in his office, waiting for the phone to ring. It rang, but it wasn't the court clerk whom he had expected, but SAC Roger Poon from the Topeka's Marshal's office.

"Nick, I have some bad news. Deputy Perkins didn't make it. She never regained consciousness. The doctors told her family and her fiancé that she was brain dead. They decided last night to take her off life support."

"Those bastards. I wish I had enough evidence to bring murder charges against them. After this case, anything I can do to build a case against those murderers, I will."

"Thank you Nick. You're probably one of the few people who can appreciate how badly the Marshal's Office wants to get whoever is responsible. We have a new lead. Remember when you told me that Agent Schwartz saw a man in a Volvo parked near the destroyed house just before she crashed into a pole. We took your advice and checked the car rentals at nearby airports for a rented Volvo around that time by a man flying in from San Diego or Los Angeles."

"Great, what did you find?"

"International Car Rentals rented a Volvo to Lorenzo Boleti, an attorney living in Chula Vista, California, the day before the house attack. He brought the car back the morning after the attack. His flight originated from San Diego. He had a California Driver's License in that name. We checked out his address. It doesn't exist and the California Department of Motor Vehicles doesn't have a Lorenzo Boleti on file. It looks like he used forged ID."

Nick interjected, "Damn it! Nothing concrete."

"Wait a second. You didn't let me get to the good part. The car rental office has a surveillance camera. Maybe you can run his picture by your local law enforcement contacts and come up with a hit. I'll send you an email with the video clip from the car rental."

"Thanks. I'll be sitting at my desk, staring at my computer, waiting for the email."

A minute later, Nick's computer gave its annoying ding, signaling that a message had arrived. He opened up the clip and was stunned. Javier Esquel-Ramirez, the defense witness, who had provided Luis with the motorcycle camping alibi, stared at him from the computer screen. Nick forwarded Poon's email to Rona, asking her to isolate the best frontal shot from the video, and to print out several color photos.

Nick got back on the phone with SAC Poon and told him Boleti's true identity and what he testified to at trial. "Roger, the case went to the jury. It's next to impossible to reopen a case for additional evidence once a jury starts deliberations. I wish we'd known about this earlier. I would have loved to ask him what he was doing in Topeka, parked a block from the safe house, at the time of the attack."

"Nick, we just got the surveillance video yesterday."

"I'm not faulting you. I was just thinking and wishing out loud. No offense intended. We can work it on this end, after the verdicts. Thanks for filling me in."

"Let me know what you find out and tell me the verdicts when they come in."

Over the next few days, the jury had a couple of questions about jury instructions. One was about the definition of conspiracy. Instead of risking instructional error by further clarifying certain terms in the instructions, Judge Orsini just reread the pertinent part of the instructions and told them to do the best they could.

Nick was too preoccupied with the case to enjoy himself over the weekend. With such a long case, it was expected that the jury would deliberate at least a week before they returned verdicts. He wouldn't start worrying about a hung jury until a few more days of deliberation had transpired. Nick firmly believed that all the counts, except those relating to the motorcycle drive-by, were solid.

Nick spent most of the weekend exercising or sipping Jack Daniels while listening to jazz. He thought about calling Ana, but felt it would be better to leave it alone until after the verdicts. He was keeping Cam's sage advice in mind, *Follow your heart, not your dick.*

Monday, Tuesday and Wednesday were more of the same. A couple of jury questions were easily handled, and defense witness Javier's testimony was read back on Wednesday. Nick didn't like that at all. It didn't bode well for his murder conspiracy and aggravated assault counts for the jury to request the testimony of Lopez' alibi witness.

On Thursday afternoon, the foreperson sent Judge Orsini a note. *We have verdicts on all the counts except two. What should we do?*

The attorneys and Judge Orsini discussed the note. It was agreed that they'd bring the jury in and discuss the status of the two counts they couldn't reach a verdict on. The Judge informed the attorneys that after they discussed the two counts, he would receive the verdicts on the remaining counts.

The jury was brought in. They looked tired. Some smiled, a couple frowned, and a few more avoided eye contact. Nick thought, *They aren't looking like the "get-along" jury of past days.*

Judge Orsini asked, "What are the two counts you can't agree on?"

The foreperson responded, "The murder conspiracy count and the assault with a deadly weapon count against Defendant Luis Hernandez-Lopez."

"Please listen carefully, Madame Foreperson. Please tell me how the jury split on the last vote on the two counts. Don't tell me which of the two numbers went for guilty, or which of the two numbers went for not guilty. Just tell me the numbers."

"Eight to four on both counts."

"Do you think, with additional deliberations, there's a reasonable chance you can reach verdicts on the two counts?"

Madame Foreperson looked around to gauge her fellow jurors. Most nodded their heads in the affirmative. The rest were nonresponsive. "I believe so, Your Honor."

"Okay, we'll send you back for further deliberations. But before we do, we'll hear your verdicts on the other counts." The bailiff had already collected the verdict forms and had given them to the court clerk. The court clerk gave them to Judge Orsini. He spent a few minutes going over the verdicts. "They are all signed and look in order." He gave them back to the clerk. "Please read the verdicts."

Nick felt his stomach knot up. Two years of work comes down to this. Most of the jurors smiled when they looked in his and Josh's direction. Several of the jurors avoided looking at the defendants. That was positive.

The first verdicts read by the clerk concerned the Continuing Criminal Enterprise count, the drug conspiracy count and the money laundering conspiracy count. All of these counts came back guilty as to each of the three defendants. Nick relaxed. He didn't feel joy, or even vindication, just relief. That meant that the jury would come back with guilty verdicts against each defendant on all of the individual drug distribution and money laundering counts.

The only two counts that Nick had to worry about were the murder conspiracy count and the assault with a deadly weapon count against defendant Rael Trujillo-Sanchez. It didn't look good. If the jury was hung up on those counts against Lopez where there was more evidence than against Sanchez, they'd probably acquit Sanchez of the counts. Nick was right. The clerk read not guilty verdicts for Sanchez on the counts. Even though Nick expected it, he felt a deep anger rise within him. Those counts were personal. Ana almost died. It was one thing to sell heroin and marijuana, and launder the proceeds, but when the cartel tried to take out a protected witness and almost killed Ana, it was an entirely different matter.

After the verdicts were read, and each juror was polled about the verdicts being their true verdicts, they were excused for further deliberations. Judge Orsini informed the prosecutors and attorney Lipman that if verdicts on the two counts weren't reached by 11:30 tomorrow, they were all to come back at 11:45, including defendant Lopez, to discuss whether Judge Orsini should declare a hung jury and grant a mistrial on the two counts.

Nick didn't want a mistrial. It would mean that the two counts against Luis would probably be retried. Although it would likely be just a one month trial, instead of two, both Felicia and Lester would have to be brought back to testify. Nick didn't know if Felicia could hold up for another trial. The evidence certainly wouldn't go in as well a second time.

At 11:45 the next morning, they were back in Judge Orsini's courtroom. Judge Orsini told them, "Still no verdicts. What do you want to do?"

Lipman said, "Can I have a few moments to discuss this with my client?"

"Go ahead."

A couple of minutes later, Lipman spoke in a surprised tone, "My client insists that we give the jury more time. He says he had nothing to do with the shooting."

Judge Orsini looked at the prosecutors, "What are your thoughts?"

"Fine by us to give the jury some more time," responded Nick. Nick was pleasantly surprised by the defendant's insistence to give the jury more time. He knew that Lipman personally wanted a hung jury and a declaration of a mistrial. This would constitute a "victory" for the defense. Lipman knew that many problems can arise for the prosecution before a retrial. It might never happen. Also, if the jury split ran strongly in favor of the defense, like ten to two, or eleven to one for acquittal, Judge Orsini may not let the prosecution try the case again. It'd be an enormous drain on public resources, especially when the defendant had already been convicted on multiple counts, one being the CCE count that carries a sentence of 20 years to life.

"Okay gentlemen, I expect you back at 2:30. I'll allow them to deliberate some after lunch, but I want to hear from the jury how deliberations are going at that time." Judge Orsini then addressed the bailiff, "Will it cause any trouble for the jail staff to bring defendant Lopez back and forth?"

"No, Your Honor. We had the jail pack defendant a bag lunch. We'll keep him under guard on this floor."

Nick and Pepe decided to have lunch at the courthouse food court. No sense going back to the office for a couple of hours, only to return. However, Josh had to go back and clean up something on another case.

Pepe and Nick were just finishing up their leisurely lunch of fish tacos and fries, when Pepe noticed several deputy marshals rush out the front door of the courthouse. They were yelling into radios attached to their chests, but Pepe and Nick couldn't make out what they were saying. Moments later, Nick's cellphone rang. It was the court clerk. Her voice was trembling, "Judge Orsini needs you here right now." Nick thought, *What in the hell is going on? Did someone have a heart attack?*

Nick and Pepe rushed to the elevator and entered the court-room a couple of minutes later. Judge Orsini looked like all the blood had been drained from his face. Nick asked, "Are you all right, Your Honor?"

"I'm fine, but defendant Lopez has escaped!"

"What? How could that happen?!" yelled Nick.

"That's what I want to know. Lipman is on his way. He was down the street having lunch. My bailiff will be here shortly to give us a preliminary report."

Lipman and the bailiff came into the court at the same time. Nick told him that his client had escaped and the bailiff was going to fill them in. Lipman look shocked. He muttered, "That dumb, arrogant son-of-a-bitch."

Nick replied, "Finally, we agree on something."

The bailiff told them that Lopez had been kept in the court-room next door because it was convenient and wasn't being used. They took off one of his handcuffs so he could eat lunch and cuffed it to a wooded strut. He was eating his baloney sandwich when his guard stepped out of the courtroom to take a phone call. Five min-utes later, he stepped back in and Lopez was gone. One cuff was still attached to the wooded strut, the other was empty. The inside of the empty cuff had some sort of lubricant on it. It looked like mayon-naise. An all points bulletin had already been issued. Marshals were interviewing all personnel at the various exits. A marshal at the rear exit of the courthouse remembered a guy wearing a dark suit, fitting Lopez' description, walking past him and out the back, courthouse door. Lopez was wearing a dark suit to be presentable to the jury. The marshal thought he was another attorney. Attorneys and law enforcement were the only people who were supposed to know about the rear exit.

Judge Orsini in a controlled, commanding voice told his bailiff, "I want Lopez found. Use whatever resources are needed to bring him in." He then turned to Nick and Lipman. "We'll allow the jury to continue their deliberations. Maybe this can be salvaged. If Defendant Lopez is captured by the end of the afternoon, the jury doesn't need to know it ever happened. Be within 20 minutes reach."

Pepe and Nick went to Pepe's car. Pepe had driven Nick to the courthouse. Nick called Rona to tell her what was happening and to fill everyone else in. Nick turned to Pepe, "Let's see if we can track this baloney sandwich loving asshole down."

"I'm with you, Boss Man. Where to?"

"Where would I go if I were him? He hasn't any money. I think he'd go the one place close where he has someone he can trust, someone with money. That one person and place is his cousin Jaime at the Purple Flamingo restaurant under the Coronado Bridge. It's only a couple miles from here. He has about a 15 to 20 minute head start on us. Let's go check it out."

"Sounds good. But this could get dicey. You're an old man with bad knees. Are you sure you're ready to chase him down."

"Shut up, you upstart. I got my Glock in my overcoat in the back seat."

"That's great. But do you remember how to use it?"

"I may have creaky knees, but I go to the range every month, except for the last few."

In ten minutes, they were parked down the street from the restaurant. Pepe said, "I'll go through the front of the restaurant, you go around to the alley and cover the back door. If you see him, try to get him to stop and yell for me."

Nick headed for the alley. It was just wide enough for a small delivery truck to get through. There were a number of garbage cans.

The back sides of three-story buildings rose up on either side. The sun was blocked, it was dark and the garbage stank. Nick could feel adrenalin kick in. Nick thought, *Just my luck, with my heightened sense of smell, the stench is overwhelming.* There was nobody around. Nick stood behind a large garbage can by the restaurant's back door. A few moments later, he saw a slender man, wearing dark clothes, turn into the far end of the alley. The man was walking rapidly towards where Nick was crouched behind the can. As the man got within ten feet of the back door, Nick stepped out, raised his arm and pointed his Glock. "Hello, Luis. Stopping in for some Mexican food on the house?"

"Well, if it isn't Mr. Prosecutor. What a surprise." Luis saw the angry glare in Nick's eyes as Nick pointed the gun at the center mass of his body. Luis stopped and raised his arms over his head. "You got me. You wouldn't care to have lunch before you take me in. Jaime has great homemade tamales and serves savory Cadillac margaritas. Of course, on the rocks, not blended."

While Lopez was spouting off, acting cool, Nick thought about what he had done in the case. *The ultimate scum, a sociopath. Not caring what he took, who he abused or who he killed. He was as responsible for shooting Ana as if he had pulled the trigger. It might as well have been him who launched the rockets into the Topeka safe house, murdering Deputy Marshal Perkins, and again exposing Ana to deadly force. He also probably had something to do with Nacho's murder and Pepe's kidnapping. This scum was going to walk on the counts that mattered the most, the assault and the murder conspiracy.*

Lopez' face took on a worried expression. "Hey, what gives? What's with the brooding silence? Take me in, you're the good guy."

Nick's focus narrowed. He felt hot and sweaty. Nick snapped, "That's where you're wrong. I'm not a good guy today." Nick saw red. He fired two bullets, a double tap, that entered Luis' heart. Luis crumpled to the ground, in the stench. Hearing gunfire, Pepe yelled for everybody to stay inside the restaurant before he burst out the back door. With a glance, Pepe took it all in. He shouted for Nick to put down his gun as Pepe knelt at Lopez' side. Pepe put on the Teflon evidence gloves he had in his pocket and removed a second gun he had strapped to his inner right leg, just above his ankle. It was a snub nosed, 38 caliber pistol, loaded. He wiped the gun down with his handkerchief. He put the 38 in Lopez' right hand. Pepe then stood up and went over to Nick.

"Calm down Nick. I know you've never shot anyone before. I'll get you through this. Just listen to me. I put my throw down gun in Lopez' hand. It'll only have his prints. You saw him walk down the alley. You told him to stop. He went for his gun. You had no choice. You had to shoot him. It was self-defense."

"No, no, Pepe. That isn't what happened. I had to kill the bastard. He had to be stopped. He had gotten away with so much, Ana almost died. And Felicia and Lester would never be safe until he was dead."

"You're too good of a person to go down for shooting scum. Look at it as a mercy killing for society. Remember! You had to shoot him. He had a gun. It was self-defense."

Something clicked in Nick's mind. He came back to being a clear-thinking attorney. "He better not be left handed."

"Boss, you know me better than that. I never take a chance. I watched him at trial writing notes with his right hand. I'm going to call this in. We'll wait right here for the police. Touch nothing, do nothing."

Five minutes later, San Diego police were on the scene. Everything was cordoned off. They wanted Nick and Pepe to come down to the central station on Broadway for questioning. They allowed Pepe to drive his car. He ditched his ankle holster in the trunk. Nick was politely escorted to the station in a police car.

Nick held up well under the questioning at the station. Nick told them that he and Pepe decided to check out the Purple Flamingo, knowing that Lopez's cousin owned the place. Lopez came down the alley. Nick raised his gun and told him to stop. Lopez continued to walk towards him and pulled a gun. Nick had to shoot. It was self-defense.

Pepe waited until they had finished questioning Nick. Nick got into Pepe's car. As they were driving away, Pepe looked at Nick with compassion, and said, in a soft voice, "I don't know if you want to hear this right now. I just spoke to Josh."

"Tell me. What did he say?"

"The bailiff told Josh that in the early afternoon the jury reached verdicts on the two counts and the foreperson signed the forms. Because of the escape, the verdicts were never presented to the court. The jury came back guilty on both counts against Lopez, the murder conspiracy and the assault, with the great bodily injury enhancement."

"Oh shit! He wasn't going to walk on those counts."

"Are you okay Nick? How do you feel?"

"When I pulled the trigger, I was sure Lopez was going to get off on those counts." With a weak smile, Nick said, "I guess you never know what a jury is going to do. I'm going to call Ana. I just want to see her. Can you drop me off at her condo?"

"Sure."

Nick dialed Ana's number. "You're home. I need you." Nick closed his cellphone and turned to Pepe. "She's home."

EPILOGUE

Nick was reveling in the blueberry pancakes that Ana had prepared for him. He couldn't remember when he had ever had breakfast in bed. A steaming cup of piñon nut coffee from New Mexico and freshly squeezed orange juice topped off the decadent eating experience. Ana dropped the front pages of the Union Tribune and the Los Angeles Times on his lap. "Don't get used to this service. It may never happen again. But you had a big day yesterday. It's not often a person gets to do everyone a big favor and in self-defense."

Nick hadn't told Ana the true story of the shooting. He didn't want to burden Ana, or anyone else over it. Also, for Pepe's sake he couldn't speak about it. And to be honest, for his sake. Nick didn't want to be prosecuted. He didn't know the exact impact his shooting of Lopez would have on his psyche, but he did know, one way or another, he'd pay a steep price. It was a secret he and Pepe would keep to their deaths. To forestall further introspection, Nick asked, "So what's in the news?"

"What do you think is in the news? You are. Front page stories. They're calling you a hero. One headline, *Prosecutor Pursues Justice Inside and Outside the Courtroom*. Another, *Modern Day Wyatt Earp Gets His Man*. The article compares what happened in the alley to the shoot out at the O.K. Corral. There's an editorial column about how few heroes we have. It ends, *Finally, a person stands up for our safety.*"

"I don't feel like a hero. The only aspect comparable to the O.K. Corral was the stench. I imagine there was a lot of horse shit at the corral."

"Stench or no stench, you better get used to being a hero."

Ana's cellphone rang in the kitchen. "I better get that Nick."

"Go ahead, mine has been turned off since I called you after leaving the police station. I didn't want to speak to anyone except you."

"Nick, it's Pepe. He needs to talk to you." Ana handed Nick the phone. "What's up Pepe?"

"Sorry to bother you, but things are crazy around here. The Attorney General has been calling everyone since last evening trying to find you. I played dumb as long as I could. But the pressure is really on. Will you call him?"

"Yeah. Even though it may ruin the rest of my breakfast."

Nick got his cellphone out of his jacket and dialed the General. "Hello General. I heard you're looking for me. It's Nick Drummond."

"Nick, where have you been? I've been worried about you."

"I had my cellphone turned off. I had a pretty traumatic day. Wait a minute. You're worried about me? Is this the same Attorney General who fired me a couple of weeks back?"

"That's all water under the bridge. I've moved on. In fact, I want to have a press conference with you. Everyone is calling you a hero. The public deserves to hear from you. It'll be great for our office."

"General, I am sure it'd be great for you. But, as I said, it was quite traumatic. I'm so tired. I need bed rest. I'll have to get back to you. Good-bye General."

MY THANKS
AND GRATITUDE TO

My wife, Heidi Weisbaum, for her assistance and support; and
My colleagues and friends, Bill Salisbury, Barry Klein,
Bonnie Friedman, Gary Mitchell, Dan Voge, Dan Aposhian,
Brett Weiss and Anita DuPratt, for their valuable input; and
My colleague and friend, Nona Seaman, and my sons,
Nick and Josh, for their technical assistance.

Printed in the USA
CPSIA information can be obtained
at www.ICGtesting.com
LVHW021202161223
766529LV00003B/118